Love Lies Dying

by

Steve Gerlach

Probable Cause Publishing

Published in Australia by Probable Cause Publishing
steve@stevegerlach.com
stevegerlach.com
Copyright © Steve Gerlach 2016
The moral right of this author has been asserted
Art copyright © Matthew Revert

Typeset in Dustismo Roman Copyright © 2002 Dustin Norlander
http://www.cheapskatefonts.com

ISBN: 978-0-9578641-1-5

To Richard Laymon for all your help and support. I can never thank you enough. You left us too soon. I hope "the Dick is pleased."

And Zoe Y for the inspiration. Even though you never knew.

Steve Gerlach novels
coming soon to
Probable Cause Publishing

Hunting Zoe and other Tales

Lake Mountain

The Nocturne

Rage

Autopsy I: Flesh of the Dead

Autopsy II: Darkness Burning

Autopsy III: All That Remains

PART

I

<u>One</u>

She lay on the sofa, reading a book. She was naked. John Murdock closed the front door and placed the keys in his trouser pocket.

"Hello?" he said.

No answer.

Slowly walking down the hallway, he placed the bunch of flowers he was carrying on the hall stand.

"Helen?" he called as he walked closer towards the lounge room and to her. His footsteps echoed in the quiet of the house.

But he knew it wasn't Helen. He could tell. There was no doubt about it.

The girl lying naked on the sofa was not his wife.

She was stretched out on her side, her back towards him. She was reading a book and ignoring his calls.

John didn't know what to do, or where to look. Her brown-blonde hair was shoulder length. Tied back in a ponytail, it hung to one side of her right shoulder. The way she was laying, propped up with one arm with the other holding the book, accentuated her shoulder blades and her spine.

His eyes followed her spine down her thin and muscular back. The girl was fit and strong, there was no doubt. Her buttocks hung slightly over the edge of the sofa, sticking out, pointing in his direction. The round tanned cheeks looked soft and tiny as he walked closer.

It was almost as if she had positioned herself that way. So that when he entered the lounge room he would be drawn to her buttocks and then, just a little further down, he would catch a small glimpse of the folds of her vagina.

Her legs, bent to fit on the sofa, were long and tanned. He could see her muscles under the smoothness of the skin. Even her feet looked athletic in the lamplight that shone from the corner table.

And then she turned a page.

Taking one last look along her body, his eyes resting on her most secret parts once more, John's mind regained control and he focussed on the question of why some stranger, some girl, some *naked* girl was in his lounge room.

"Er...excuse me, Miss?" It sounded so stupid, but what else could he say?

She turned to look over her shoulder at him, and smiled.

He couldn't help it; he had to smile back. Her face was small but almost perfect in every way. Her eyes were dark brown and her stare enveloped him. Her nose was slightly bent, as if it had once been broken, but her smile was lively and infectious. Her hair fell around her ears, some of it escaping the ponytail as she turned over.

Her whole body moved in one fluid movement and suddenly she was facing him, stretching her arms over her head and laying the book on the table by the sofa.

Her breasts were small and round, perfect, and delightful to look at. Her stomach was muscled and tight, even tighter than his own, and her tan seemed to shine in the light, to make her glow. The top of her belly button was pierced with a gold ring and hanging from the ring was a small diamond, sitting neatly and comfortably in her belly button hole, as if it was a perfectly natural place for a diamond to reside.

Further down, John couldn't help but see what was only hinted at when she had her back to him. With her legs apart as she stretched to place the book on the table, he could see it all. She was completely shaved between her legs, leaving nothing to the imagination. Even her tan spread between her dark folds. John's eyes darted back to her face and he noticed she was watching him. Her smile had turned into a sly grin.

"Hi, Johnny," she said in a soft and lulling voice.

John leaned against the doorway and looked around the lounge room. They were alone. The rest of the house was dark.

Where's Helen? he thought.

The sight of the girl still laying there, naked and on display and enjoying it, made it hard for him to get his thoughts in line. He didn't know what to say; he didn't know what to do. All he knew was that there was a strange girl in his lounge room and he felt like he was swimming, and possibly drowning, in her beauty.

He grabbed one of the dining chairs and sat down. At least now he could get his thoughts together and hide the erection that was beginning to grow.

She moved again then, sat up and looked him over.

John stared back. She wasn't as tall as she had looked when she was lying down. Now she seemed quite small, certainly smaller than him.

The light caught on the tiny diamond dangling in her belly button, the reflection caught his eye from across the room. His eyes were drawn there again, and then once more, lower to the other regions she was making no attempt to cover.

"You're not very talkative," she said.

John shook his head, trying to clear the mist.

"Do…I'm sorry, but…do I know you?" he stammered.

Her grin grew bigger as she leaned forward and stared across the room at him.

"I'm Zoe," she said.

There was a pause, as if she was waiting for some reaction.

"Yes, and…?" was all he could come up with.

"Zoe. Zoe Barber?" she continued.

John shook his head.

"You mean Helen didn't tell you about me?" she spread her arms in surprise. As she did so, her breasts jiggled in the air, her nipples hard.

"Er, no, actually." John replied. "No, she didn't."

"Hmmmm, weird," Zoe said. "That's not like her at all."

The conversation stopped. Zoe stared back at John, the smile still on her face like a schoolgirl with a secret. John's mind whirled with question after question, but seeing her sitting in front of him made his mouth go numb and he couldn't get the words together.

As they sat there, Zoe pulled her hair out of the ponytail and ran her fingers through it. It bounced in the lamplight and fell around her ears and head, finally resting into position, framing her face with a brown-blonde border.

"She didn't say anything," John managed after a minute.

"Well, that sure is strange." Zoe leaned back into the sofa, her hands on her hips. She grabbed her left foot and tucked it up on the sofa in front of her. Then she grabbed her right and tucked that in front too. Suddenly, she was sitting in a yoga-like position, her elbows resting on her knees, which were spread wide in front of her, exposing her most secret folds to his view again.

"I mean, I know I dropped by unexpectedly, but you think she would have mentioned it."

"Yeah, you would." John replied. And then he saw his opportunity. "Where *is* Helen?"

"Oh, sorry," Zoe giggled to herself. "I should have said! You must have been worried."

"Well, I was –"

"You know how she said she'd be late tonight?"

"Yes."

"Well, she'll be even later now."

John wasn't surprised. It happened all the time. Late nights, working overtime – they'd argued about it in the past. And there was the time Helen's sister suddenly appeared one night and said she'd be staying for a month. They'd argued about that too – and that had been a bad one. Helen had said she'd forgotten to tell him, she'd been too busy. But he wondered if it was planned that way. John didn't like Helen's sister and she didn't like him that much either. They'd argued about her staying for a long time. Another argument – one of many.

But they got over it – as usual.

But now it had happened again. Another one of Helen's plans she'd forgotten to tell him about? John knew only time would tell.

Still, at least Zoe *wasn't* Helen's sister.

She sure isn't! he thought.

John sighed deeply. Why was he so surprised?

"Something wrong?" Zoe asked.

"Hmm?"

"Anything wrong?" she repeated.

"No, no. Just thinking, that's all…"

"I'll be in town for a few days and I dropped by to surprise her," Zoe continued. "We haven't seen each other for years and I got a kick out of knocking on the door and giving her the surprise of her life. I like to surprise people." She smiled.

John smiled back. Finally, all the pieces were coming together.

"Anyway, we had a good long chat and I sort of asked if I could stay with you guys while I'm here. I don't have a lot of money and I don't want to stay in some seedy hotel." Her face fell into a look of uncertainty and vulnerability. All signs of the smile were gone as her eyes left John's face and fell to the floor.

"I hope you don't mind," she said, glancing up at him, worried. "Helen said it was okay."

John smiled at her, wanting to make her feel comfortable.

What the hell, he thought. *They could argue about it afterwards. He knew they would.*

"It's okay if Helen said it is. You can stay as long as you want."

Zoe's face broke back into a huge smile. She sprang from the sofa and was over the other side of the room before John had a chance to move. She grabbed his hands and pulled him to his feet and placed both arms around him, hugging him tightly.

John didn't know what to do. He didn't want to pull her away, but he couldn't just hug her back. This girl was *naked* after all. He patted the back of her head, which came up only to his chest, and he looked down at her shiny hair. It smelled fresh and fruity; a wonderful fragrance he'd never smelt before.

"Thanks Johnny," she said as she took a step back to look up into his eyes. Her smile was beaming.

John hoped she hadn't felt his erection. "And Helen?" he asked.

"Ah, duh!" Zoe slapped her forehead. "Sorry. She's gone out to get some extra food and champagne to celebrate my glorious arrival!" She broke into a giggle once more as she turned and headed back to the sofa.

John's eyes followed her small, wiggling buttocks. The backs of her shapely legs were finely toned.

That's what I call a hard body, he thought.

Then he tore his eyes away and looked at his watch: 11:34pm.

"At this time of night?" he said. The streets could be dangerous and he didn't want Helen getting into any trouble.

"She said she'd only be a few minutes. She'd only just got home herself, you know, from working late. It was mighty cold sitting on your front doorstep for hours, I'll tell you." Zoe giggled. "She was going to go down to some all-night food place a few minutes away by car."

"Which one?"

"Oh, I don't know. I don't know Parkhurst too well. As I said, I've only just blown in." Zoe repositioned herself on the sofa, on display for John to see all. She was still smiling. "She only just left when you arrived. She won't be long."

"Okay." John sat down again but he still felt uncomfortable. "Er…aren't you cold?" he finally said.

"Me?" Zoe pointed at herself. "No, why?"

"Well, ah, you're sort of naked," was all John could manage.

Zoe burst into laughter and rocked back and forth on the sofa. "You're funny, you know that?" she said. "Helen told me to make myself comfortable. And, well, this is me comfortable."

John stared at her. He couldn't believe how out of control of the situation he felt. In his own home, a naked stranger could leave him stumbling like an old man for his glasses.

"Why? Does it make you uncomfortable?" she asked.

"Slightly, yes," John said.

"Oh, okay. Sorry. I don't want you feeling on edge in your own home. I'll go and put on some clothes. Why don't you make us some coffee while I get changed?"

Lacking any better plan, John agreed. He stood and walked to the kitchen, and as he did so, he watched out of the corner of his eye as Zoe disappeared into the main bedroom.

Maybe having unexpected guests isn't so bad, he thought.

John got the coffee started and tried desperately to get the images of Zoe out of his mind.

She was just sitting there naked, he thought. *Like it was a perfectly natural thing to do!*

The last thing he needed was Helen walking in with a sack of groceries in her hands only to find him with an erection and Zoe sitting naked in the lounge room.

Even flowers wouldn't help that situation!

Flowers!

John remembered putting them on the hallstand as he entered the house. Sidetracked by Zoe, he'd forgotten about them. He left the coffee brewing and headed back down the hall.

He may not be able to hand them to Helen, but he could at least make them look presentable when she came in. All he needed was a vase.

Grabbing them from the hall stand, he turned to walk back up the hall. Stopping for a moment, he decided to check the front door. He'd been distracted when he had entered, and who wouldn't be if they found a naked stranger on their sofa?

He checked the door.

It was unlocked.

Typical, he thought. *Anyone could've got in.*

He threw the bolt to lock the front door. Then he placed a hand in his pocket. He dragged out the front door keys and placed them on the key rack on the wall by the door.

He put them on his hook, right next to Helen's car keys.

Helen's car keys?

John stared at the key holder for what seemed like a long time. Both sets of keys now resided there.

"Johnny?"

He turned to see Zoe leaning against the wall at the other end of the hall.

"Is the coffee ready?"

John took one more look at the keys and then turned to face her.

"Ah, almost, yeah," he said.

He turned and walked back up the hall.

Zoe was wearing black button-up jeans now. Each of the silver buttons glinted in the light and reminded John of the diamond positioned snugly in her belly button. She wore a black top too, tight and figure hugging. It had no arms, so her muscled forearms and biceps were still on display. Her neckline and left shoulder visible through the L-shape neck cut into the top.

Her hair was back in a ponytail again, with only a few strands escaping to the side of her face. She wore nothing on her feet and for the first time John noticed her toenails were painted bright red.

"Great! It will be our first coffee together," she said. She smiled at him as she turned and headed back to the sofa.

As John walked into the kitchen, Zoe said over her shoulder, "You know I've heard all about you. It's like I know you already."

John glanced at his watch: 11:47.

But the keys!

He put the flowers to one side.

"Did Helen say she was driving?" he asked.

She looked up from the book now back in her lap and stared at him through the archway dividing the kitchen and lounge. Her face smiled but he was sure there was something different about it.

"What do you mean?"

"Well, you said she'd gone to get some food." John poured the coffee into two mugs.

"Yeah, so?"

"But her car keys are still in the hall."

"Ahuh?" Zoe looked at the book again, and then met his gaze as he brought the coffee around to her. "Don't worry too much," she said. "Helen took my Jeep. It was parked out the front anyway."

"It seems like a strange thing to do."

"Nah, not really," Zoe took the coffee. "It's literally a brand new Jeep, only a few weeks old. It's red and very, very cool. Helen was staggered when she saw it. I just threw her the keys and said, 'Knock yourself out'! She couldn't resist taking it for a spin. But she shouldn't be long now. Maybe she's driving around, having a free spin, getting the feel of the Jeep! You know, she's probably lost track of time. You know how she can be sometimes."

John nodded. He knew alright.

"She should've called me before I left work, I could have picked up something on the walk home from the train station."

"She probably didn't want to bother you. Sugar?"

"Huh?" John said.

"Do you have any sugar?"

"Oh, okay, sorry." John walked back into the kitchen. "Milk?"

"No thanks."

Something didn't feel right. Something, something…

He grabbed the sugar bowl and brought it to the table by the sofa.

"Hope you didn't mind me grabbing one of your books." Zoe said, pointing at the hardback with one hand while she scooped sugar into her coffee with the other. "But when Helen went out there wasn't much to do."

"No problem. I'm surprised you didn't go with her."

Zoe shook her head and yawned. "Nope, I'm too tired. It was a long trip, you know. I've been driving since Wednesday. Non-stop. I wasn't even sure I'd make it here for the weekend."

"So," John said as he settled into an armchair by the sofa, "you and Helen have been friends for a long time?"

"Yep, ages!" Zoe smiled.

"She's never mentioned you…"

Zoe put the coffee down on the table and placed the book next to her. She pulled her legs up onto the sofa and crawled to the end where she rested her elbows on the side-arms and stared directly at John.

"Did I make you feel uncomfortable before, Johnny?"

"Er…look I –"

"I didn't mean to. Helen said get comfortable and that's how I am when I'm comfortable. I'm sorry if I made you on edge or nervous. I really didn't mean to."

John watched as a range of emotions swept across her face. Her smile broke into a worried frown and then into a look of sadness. She almost looked as if she was about to cry.

He had only known her for a few minutes, but he already felt as if they had been friends for a long, long time. His suspicions and worries were slipping from his mind. And he was letting them.

She sat back in the sofa, "I'm sorry," she said.

"No, no, no," John felt the need to let her know everything was fine. "Don't be like that. It was just a shock, you know. I come home and I think I'm going to see Helen and then I find you…"

Zoe smiled again as if everything was solved. "Good, I'm glad."

She sat back, reached for the coffee and took another sip.

"You make great coffee."

"Thanks."

"I like your coffee."

"Thanks again."

John looked at his watch: 11:53.

"Helen should be back by now," he said as he frowned.

"Well, she only just left here before you got home."

"Still, if she's driven down to the closest store and got some food, she should've been back about ten minutes ago. They're never too busy on a Friday night."

"Well, you know Helen can get a little crazy sometimes," Zoe leaned forward and patted his arm. Her smell wafted over him again; that fresh, fruity fragrance.

"I've never known Helen to go crazy," John said. "She's never like that. Quite the opposite, in fact."

"We all go a little crazy sometimes." Zoe giggled once more, and spilled some coffee onto her jeans, "Oops," she said as she wiped away the spill. "You'll learn I giggle too much."

"So, how long are you in town?" John asked, hoping to fill in the time and make it pass quicker – bringing Helen home sooner. An easy conversation could make them both feel more comfortable.

"I don't know yet. I've got some matters to take care of. It shouldn't be long though. It depends how difficult it all becomes. At least by arriving here tonight I can rest over the weekend and then get down to business on Monday. Don't worry, though, I won't stay too long."

"No, I didn't mean it like that."

She smiled, "It's okay, Johnny. I won't outstay my welcome."

He smiled back.

How could you *ever outstay a welcome?* he wondered.

"What do you do for a living?"

"I'm a researcher!" Zoe replied eagerly. "You want things found out – I find 'em! For a price, of course. I do freelance stuff mostly."

"Sounds exciting."

"Yeah, it can be. But mostly it isn't. And when it's slow, it's really slow. Usually I spend my time serving coffee in a shopping centre somewhere just to make ends meet."

She giggled again. John couldn't help it and he joined in too.

Then there was a pause.

"You haven't asked me what I do?" John said.

Zoe waved a hand at him, "No need. Helen has told me everything! You're the Engineering Manager for American Eagle Electronics, right here in Parkhurst."

"Wow, you know your stuff. So, how do you know Helen?"

"We met years ago – best buddies in school."

"Funny," John scratched his head as he thought back. "I'm sure she's never mentioned you."

Zoe shrugged her shoulders, drained the last of the coffee from her cup and stared deep into his eyes. John found himself mesmerised by the deep brown pools.

"I'm probably a secret, Johnny," she said. "We all have secrets, you know."

John sunk backwards and broke her stare. He took a gulp of coffee and looked at her again, at her smile, and at her perfectly formed straight white teeth. Her smell wafted over him again. He noticed for the first time that she had a small scar running across her left eyebrow.

"It all depends who we tell about them," she said as she sat back and picked up the book.

John looked at his watch: 12:04.

After midnight? This has gone on too long.

"Okay, I better go and find Helen," John said as he stood and placed the coffee mug to one side. "She's been gone way too long."

"Don't have a fit, she'll be back soon."

"No, I better –"

"Now *you're* going a bit crazy."

John turned and headed down the hallway, grabbing a coat off the hall stand as he went.

"Johnny, I wouldn't," Zoe called after him.

"Don't worry, I won't be long. I'll take my car and be back in a few minutes."

"She's probably got caught up somewhere. Or taken that drive I told you about! The moment you leave she'll arrive and we'll have to search for you!"

John grabbed his keys from the key rack by the door and turned to face her, "I'll be back soon."

Zoe was standing at the other end of the hall, "Don't go crazy on me, Johnny."

"I'm not going crazy. I'm just going to find Helen and then we'll both be back," he said.

"Don't do it!"

"Just relax and I'll be back in a few minutes."

"I don't think so..."

John stopped and stared at her. Her face was a mix of emotions again, making it hard for him to read her. The silence between them was heavy.

"You can't stop me," he said.

Zoe's hands went to the back of her jeans and then swung around quickly. The blur of movement solidified before his eyes.

He stared at the revolver pointed at him.
"Yes I can."

<u>Two</u>

"You can't leave me, Johnny," Zoe whispered.

John stared back at the revolver, his mind whirling.

"What are you doing?" he asked.

"I told you, you've got to stay here with me."

John ran a hand through his hair.

Is she serious? he wondered.

"Look, I have to go and try to find Helen," he began, nice and slowly. "She shouldn't have been gone this long. The store's only down the road and if she drove she should have been back by now. She could be in trouble and I have to go find her."

Zoe leaned against the hallway door. The gun was still aimed at his chest. She stared at him but didn't say a word.

"You understand, don't you? I mean, Helen's your friend too. You'd want to help her if she's in trouble, right?"

She stared at him, but he could tell what she was thinking. Her forehead furrowed and her face changed from anger to uncertainty.

And then she began to cry.

John stood at the other end of the hallway, car keys in hand, watching as Zoe lowered the revolver and dropped it to the ground. The gun clattered onto the wooden floor by her bare feet. Her hands went to her face and she buried her tears in them. Her chest heaved as she pulled in gulps of air and strands of hair escaped from her ponytail as she shook her head from side to side.

The muffled sobs carried down the hallway to John. He continued to stare at her and occasionally down at the gun now lying on the floor.

"I'm sorry, Johnny," she said between sobs. "So sorry."

Her voice sounded so afraid, so childlike. Suddenly the woman before him had turned into a scared, sad child. How quickly she could change.

John placed the keys back on the key holder and draped his coat on the hall stand as he walked towards her.

"Hey, now," he whispered as he neared her. "There's no reason to get all upset."

When he was in reaching distance, Zoe looked up through her hands at him. Her face was red and tear-streaked, her eyes were puffy and her nose was running. She tried to smile, but couldn't. She broke into another long sob and buried her face in her hands once more.

"Sshh," John whispered as he stood in front of her. "You're tired. You need some rest."

Zoe shook her head.

He reached out with one hand and rubbed her left arm, trying to give her some comfort. Her arm was nicely tanned, with hundreds of little blonde hairs shining in the light, and he could feel her tense muscles. The top she was wearing, with the L shaped neck, allowed him to view her neck and left shoulder, and his eyes wandered across her skin as her smell surrounded him once more.

He continued to rub her arm. He didn't know what else to do.

She looked up at him and tried to say something, her mouth attempting to form words, but she couldn't do it. All that came out was a pitiful half-cry and she threw herself at him with her arms open.

Before John had time to react, she was hugging him hard, pulling him closer to her and wrapping her arms tightly around his body. Her face was pushed into his chest and he could feel the tears soak into his shirt as she continued to cry, harder now.

He rubbed her back and held her tight.

They stood in the hallway, holding each other, until she stopped crying.

When John was sure that her crying had subsided for good, he walked her towards the sofa. She continued to hold onto him, but she let herself be guided from the hallway and across the lounge room.

"Here," he said as they reached the sofa. "Sit down and you'll feel better."

Zoe shook her head, he could feel its movement across his chest, but as he pulled her away, she let go of him and flopped into the sofa.

"Can I get you anything? Another coffee or something?" he asked.

"A glass of water, maybe?" Zoe whispered. Her bottom lip was curled over and pouting and her large eyes looked up at him. She wiped the tears from her face with the back of her hands.

"No problem," he said.

John turned away and headed to the kitchen. On his way there, his eyes focussed on the gun still lying in the hallway.

Why would she have that? he wondered. *And why threaten me with it?*

He filled a glass with water and brought it back to her.

Zoe was sitting cross-legged on the sofa once more, and she was placing the escaped strands of her hair back in her ponytail. She had regained some composure in the short time he had been gone and her face was no longer so red or tear-marked.

She smiled as she took the glass of water from him. "Thanks."

"No trouble. I just wanted to make sure you're okay."

She took two huge gulps of water and then placed the glass on the table by the sofa.

"You must think I'm an idiot," she said. Her eyes fell to her hands. She was fumbling with the cuffs of her jeans.

He sat down in the chair next to the sofa.

"Why do you say that?"

She looked at him and tried to smile, but she looked sad. Different emotions broke across her face like waves on a beach. Too many for John to read at once.

He smiled at her and reached out and rubbed her knee.

"I don't think you're an idiot," he said. "I would never think that."

Zoe touched his hand and gave it a squeeze. "Thank you," she whispered. Her face almost broke into tears again, but she restrained herself and took a deep breath. She ran her fingers through her hair once more to check it was all still in the ponytail and then she closed her eyes.

John watched as she sat there, in a yoga-like position, breathing deeply.

After a short while, she opened her eyes and smiled at him.

"I'm better now," she said.

"Good," he replied.

"And I'm sorry."

"Sorry for what?"

"I pulled a gun on you!" she whispered. "What must you think of me?"

John's eyes darted back to the hallway. Just inside the door he could see the gun still resting on the floor.

"Don't worry about it," he said.

"Yeah," Zoe let out a giggle. "I can see who's worried about it. You can't keep your eyes off it!"

"Well, it just came as a bit of a shock, you know." John said. "You shouldn't go around pointing that thing at people. It'll get you into all sorts of trouble."

And that was it. Her face changed in a second, like a storm-cloud had blown over it, and she was crying again. The large, fitful sobs were accompanied by fast flowing tears that streamed from her eyes.

John didn't know what to do or say. He watched as she fell apart in front of him. She rocked back and forth on the sofa, her hands to her face once more, the crying so deep and rhythmic that he thought she was having trouble breathing. Her sobs sounded so pitiful.

He had no choice.

He stood up and moved to the sofa and sat down beside her. He took her in his arms and hugged her tightly, rocking her slowly.

She cried loudly in his ear and the whole of her small body shook with every intake of breath.

He rocked her and hugged her until she cried herself out.

They sat on the sofa in silence for quite a while. He couldn't tell if she was still awake, but he wasn't game to pull away or leave her. He wanted her to regain some control. She continued to hold him tight, but at least the crying had stopped and her breathing had returned to normal.

"I'm sorry," she whispered after a long, long time.

He turned to look at her and found she was already looking up at him.

"Don't be," he said.

"No, I've acted like a fool. None of this is your fault. It's not even your problem, but I've come here and made it your problem."

"I don't understand."

Zoe pulled away from him and sat back on the sofa, turning herself to sit sideways so she was facing him, and John did the same.

She reached out and took hold of his hands and squeezed them gently.

"I shouldn't have come here. But I had nowhere else to go." She tried to smile, but her face wouldn't let her. "And now I've involved you and Helen."

John shook his head, "Hang on, I'm not following you. Start from the beginning and tell me everything. Then I'll know what you're talking about."

Zoe stared at him for a moment, then took another deep breath and nodded. "Okay," she said. "Everything."

<u>Three</u>

"I'm in trouble, Johnny. Big trouble," Zoe whispered. Her hands squeezed his again, as if for reassurance, and her eyes seemed to suddenly stare straight through him.

"Go on," he whispered.

"I didn't want to tell you any of this. I don't want to burden you with it. But when it all happened I had nowhere to go. I just had to get out and run and I had no idea where I was headed. Next thing I knew I was here with Helen and I had to tell her all. I need your help, Johnny. I really do. I didn't want you to know, or to get involved, but I think I owe you some sort of explanation for my actions."

"Okay, okay," he replied. "But start at the beginning."

"I've killed a man," she said.

"What?" John drew back slightly, alarm bells ringing in his mind.

"Well, at least, I think so. Pretty sure, I guess. But I didn't mean to."

"From the start, Zoe," he prompted.

Her eyes focussed back on him then and she smiled.

"I like that," she said.

"Like what?"

"That's the first time you've called me by my name." She reached over and kissed him lightly on the cheek, "I like it."

"The story…" John prompted.

She sat back and composed herself, "Everything?"

"Everything."

"Okay. Here we go."

She paused, as if to get her thoughts in order, and began.

"I think I may have killed my boyfriend."

Worry crossed her face as she paused for his response.

Stay calm, he thought.

"Go on."

"Have you heard of Ricky Fox?"

"No."

"Really?" she seemed surprised.

"Can't say I have."

"Well, he's a businessman on the west coast. I've known him for a long time, quite a few years in fact. We were just sort-of friends and then eventually, you know, we decided to get together."

"Uh-uh."

"Well, you see, I thought he was this big successful businessman and everything. He had lots of money and fancy cars and people who would do whatever he told them to do. But it wasn't until I got in too deep that I realised what he really was."

Zoe looked down at her hands again as they squeezed his even tighter.

"Ricky did things for people and, well...you know, *to* people," she met his eyes once more. "Do you understand?"

John stared back. He thought he understood, but wanted to be sure.

"Tell me," he said.

"He would do things for money. Real *bad* things. Didn't matter who for, as long as the money was right. He could rough up some guy or he could put him into hospital depending on what he was paid for doing the job. And then... sometimes, he'd go even further."

"You mean he'd kill people?"

"Yeah, I think so. I never knew any of this stuff when I first met him. And then, after I got to know him, I started to see and hear weird things and it didn't take me long to put it all together and work out exactly what was happening. But by that time, it was all too late and he wouldn't let me go.

"I tried to get out, I tried to tell him I didn't want to see him any more, but he wouldn't let me go. He'd hit me and lock me in his house and tell his guards not to let me out."

"His *guards*?"

She nodded, "It was horrible. And when I did get out of the house or go to parties with him, he'd take me home and yell at me and beat me because he thought that I was flirting with any guy who happened to pass by or talk to me.

He thought I was cheating on him all the time, but I wasn't, I swear. I could never get any time alone with anyone to even have more than a small conversation! How could I find the time to cheat on him? He was mad, Johnny, mad. He just wouldn't let me live. He didn't understand me, and he didn't want to understand. He wanted what he could get and on his own terms. He was a bastard."

John nodded his head. *It sure sounds like he was,* he thought.

She stared directly into his eyes with pure hate, "Men can be bastards sometimes, and he was the worst bastard there is."

She took a deep breath, "Or was."

"So you *killed* him?"

Zoe glanced over at the gun on the hallway floor.

"Yes," she said. "With that gun."

John turned and followed her glance, "But couldn't you have gone to the police or put a restraining order on him, or something?"

She shook her head, "You don't understand, Johnny. I couldn't go *anywhere* without one of his thugs following me. It got so bad that I even think I was being spied on inside his own house when he wasn't there! Like there were cameras or microphones in the walls or something. There was no way I could make a call without it being logged and there was absolutely no chance that I'd be allowed to just walk into a police station to make a complaint."

"Yeah, I guess so. But what about your work as a researcher?"

"As I said, I was freelance. Freelance usually means 'rarely employed' in my line of work. A bit like 'between jobs'."

"I see," he nodded.

"I mean, I was working in a coffee shop trying to make ends meet when one day this suave guy walks in and orders coffee. Then he starts to come in every day of the week and won't take his eyes off me. For fun, I flirt with him and then, one day, he asks me out. What am I, crazy? He was so good looking and fun to talk to. So I say yes! We have a great dinner at a five-star restaurant and we go back to his place for coffee. Once I see the house I know I'm never going to have to serve coffee or research anything ever again if I play my cards right. But at that stage I didn't know what kind of business Ricky was in. And when I did find out, there was no way I could leave."

"So he had you trapped?"

"Sort of. But last month was the final straw. I couldn't take it any more. We went out to some party somewhere. See? I don't even know where we went! He wouldn't even tell me that much. I was just the girl who had to hang from his arm and smile and be nice and speak when I was spoken to. And that was it. It was a big party. Ricky was getting some citizen's award for outstanding development or civic duties or something, he has so many anyway, and while he was on the stage giving his speech I was talking to a guy who was sitting at our table. He was fun and nice and good looking and so I thought I was doing the right thing by sitting there and talking and laughing and trying to have a good time. But I paid for it when I got home. Paid for it badly."

John shook his head, "He beat you for *that?*"

She nodded, "As soon as we were in the door. It turns out the guy was some kind of competitor or enemy or something. But how was I to know? I thought I was doing the right thing! I tried to tell him but he wouldn't listen."

Zoe stopped talking.

John thought she was going to start crying again.

"Don't go on...unless you want to."

Zoe smiled, "No, it feels good to get this all off my chest." She reached over and patted John on the arm. "It feels good to confide in you, Johnny."

"I'm a good listener," he replied.

She giggled, "Yeah, I can tell. And I'm a good talker, as you're finding out."

"Go on when you're ready."

"I hope you'll confide in me one day," she said.

"Go on."

Zoe sighed once more.

"Okay. So, let's just say that he beat me unconscious that night."

"What?"

Zoe nodded, "He did a lot of things to me that night, if you know what I mean... But the end result was that I was knocked out. It was the first time he had gone that far and it scared the hell out of me. He knew his stuff; he didn't hit anywhere where the bruises would show. He never broke any bones because he didn't want doctors to be involved. That's why he was paid so much by these people he worked for. He knew how to cause the right pain in the right places.

"I woke up bruised and sore – both inside as well as outside. You should have seen me! Luckily, I heal pretty quickly and the bruises have all gone now, but I couldn't walk for a day or two. I just sat in bed and tried not to move."

"Sounds like a real asshole."

"You said it. And I was mad at him, but even madder at myself. Does that make sense?" She stared deeply into his eyes, searching his soul for the truth.

"I guess so."

"Because I'd placed myself in this situation and I hadn't really tried to get out of it."

"So you decided to do something about it?"

"Well, what made me really mad was that the couple of days I spent in bed and in pain stopped me from continuing with a plan I had already started. And, after that beating, I wished I had completed my plan earlier."

"So you had decided to break it off with this guy?"

"Yeah, but I knew it wasn't going to be easy."

She smiled at him, let go of his hands, leaned back and lifted her black top up off her stomach.

John's eyes were drawn to the diamond sitting in her belly button and the tanned and muscled skin surrounding it.

Zoe slapped her stomach with the palm of one hand.

The noise of skin on skin sounded loud in the room.

"See this stomach?"

"Ahh, well, yeah."

"It wasn't always like this, you know. I was a bit more, shall we say, plump when I first met Ricky."

"Really?"

"Not obese or anything, don't get the wrong idea. Just a bit more, well, let's say undefined."

John smiled back, "Okay."

Zoe pushed her top back into place and John found himself trying to burn the memory of her stomach into his mind.

"And, after all, he wouldn't let me out of his house unless someone was with me, so I ended up using his gym equipment. And believe me, he could afford almost a fully functional gym! So, more out of boredom than anything else, I thought to myself, girl, it's time to get in shape.

"When I began, I was still in love with Ricky and thought he was my knight in shining armour. The least I could do was get in shape for him, right?"

"Yeah, I suppose so."

"Well, that's what I thought too. So, with all this time on my hands, I started to get fit."

"It was certainly worth the trouble," he smiled at her.

Zoe giggled once more. "Thanks, that's really nice of you to say that. I can tell you really mean it."

"I do."

"Ricky always lied about things. All the time. He was going to give me this and that and we were going to live happily forever. But then he turned into a bastard and got all jealous even if I just *looked* at someone. Shit, one night he got me home and punched me hard in the stomach because I talked to a girl for too long! He thought I was turning into a lesbian!"

John shook his head, "He sounds crazy."

"He was. Believe me. And then, no matter where we went or who we saw, when we'd get home he would always check me out."

She paused.

"Huh?" John said, unsure of what she meant.

"You know," she whispered, her eyes dropping to the floor. "Internally."

There was silence between them.

She sighed and continued, "He would check me out internally to see if I'd been with anyone."

"No!" John was disgusted. "He treated you like *that*?"

She nodded, "Yep. Even if I'd been with him all night, as soon as we got home, he would make me strip naked and bend over. Then he'd use his fingers to check if I was wet or…you know…different inside."

"That's disgraceful," John muttered.

"I know. She stopped talking and John held her hands, giving her time to compose herself.

She sighed deeply and continued, "So, in the end, I decided I was getting fit and using his gym not just to pass the time of day, but to help me get out of there. There was only one way I could escape his house, his compound, and that was if I could fight my way out. I was going to confront him last month, but he wasn't around too much because of business and then there was this party and I decided to stick by him until after he received his award."

"And then he beats you unconscious."

"Exactly. But not before he checked me out again because he thought I was getting it on with the guy at the table. And then he did more…"

"More?"

"Yeah. He sort of fooled around with me while I was unconscious."

"You mean…?"

She nodded. "Sexually, yes. But worse than the other times. And he used things on me. I'm trying to forget it all, but it's hard."

"Fucking sick bastard."

"I know. Men like that shouldn't be allowed to live."

"I agree."

"So that was it. But I had to wait until I could move again and put up a good fight before I tried to leave."

"And you did that earlier this week?"

Zoe nodded her head, "Yeah, Tuesday night."

She was silent again.

There was a long pause. John wasn't sure how best to handle the situation. He didn't want her breaking down again, he knew this was going to be hard for her, but he needed to know everything if he was to help her.

"So, when did you buy the gun?" he asked, hoping this would make it easier for her.

"What?"

"The gun," he pointed over to it. "When and how did you get away from him and his people long enough to buy a gun?"

"I didn't," she replied in a whisper. "It's Ricky's gun."

"Oh," John replied. "I just assumed –"

Zoe nodded, "That's okay. I would have assumed it too. But that's not the way it happened."

She uncrossed her legs and scooted further up the sofa to be closer to him. They were face to face now, no more than inches apart, and she placed her hands on his thigh. He could smell her once more; the fresh smell that intrigued him so much. Her eyes were big and dark, he felt himself falling into them.

He wished he could.

He stared at the scar cutting across her left eyebrow and wondered if Ricky Fox had inflicted the pain that caused it. All of a sudden, he felt so sorry for Zoe. She was a slight, slender woman, young and full of vitality. She deserved so much more than an asshole like Ricky Fox.

So much more...

"Tell me what happened and I'll do anything I can to help."

She smiled her engaging smile once more. "Thanks Johnny. I knew you would."

Glancing over at the gun again, she continued.

"Tuesday nights are the nights he goes out to bars with some friends. Usually, he takes his best guards with him to keep them happy and loyal. They go to strip clubs and watch girls undress for money and they drink too much and usually come home so drunk they just fall into bed and remain unconscious for hours. I'm often left with some of the younger, less experienced guards and I thought this would be my best chance. I'd never thought much about trying to leave before. I was always going to sit down and try and reason with Ricky to let me go."

"Guys like that usually don't take reason too well."

"Yeah, I'd come to realise that. So, when I finally decided how best to plan my escape from Ricky, I worked out Tuesday nights were the best. He'd be out with his best men, they'd be drunk, and sometime during the night I could bribe one of the younger guys to let me go."

"But how much money would you need to give them? Surely they're paid really well by Fox."

Zoe stared deep into his eyes. "I wasn't going to bribe them with *money*."

"Oh..." John whispered, turning away.

"I'm a pretty girl, Johnny. Aren't I?"

Ain't that the truth, he thought.

John nodded his head. "Yes, you are."

"People would like to have sex with me, right?"

"Ah," John was suddenly finding it hard to speak. "Yes, you're probably right."

"They'd like to run their hands over me and explore me and find my most secret places."

"Yeah, okay, I get the picture." John adjusted his seating position so she wouldn't see his erection starting to grow. "So you were going to have sex with one of Ricky's guards?"

"Exactly. And I knew which one too. There was a young guy, he didn't seem to speak much English, but I'd caught him watching me a few times. And he always seemed nice and willing to help me with anything. So, my plan was to get out of there with his help."

"I see."

"But it all went wrong."

Zoe sat back in the sofa and stared off into the distance. Emotions danced across her face as her thoughts played inside her head. She was reliving the scene and John could tell it was going to be traumatic for her.

"Go on," he squeezed her hand.

"Something went wrong. Ricky came home early. It was as if he expected something was going to happen. He came home without any of the other guards and snuck into the house and caught me in my room throwing my clothes into a suitcase. He must have sent the others on ahead of him and doubled back to check on me. Maybe he really did have cameras in my room after all! I really don't know how he got there or how he knew I was going to do something, but one second I'm packing my case and the next he's screaming at me from the bedroom door."

She paused to compose herself, her hands automatically fixing the hair in her ponytail, even though no hair was out of place.

"He had the gun and he had a handful of cash. He told me he'd tried everything to keep me happy; money and jewels, a fast and happy life. He didn't mention the beatings though. It was as if he never remembered hitting me or doing anything else. None of the bad stuff. Like he had selective amnesia or something."

"Women-beaters can be like that, I hear."

"Well, it's certainly true. He threw the money at me and it spilled onto the floor and bed. He said he'd got it that day when he closed a deal and that he was working his arse off to keep me in this kind of luxury."

"What kind of deal?"

"I didn't ask and I didn't want to know. It was a lot of money though. A real lot. So I assumed he'd killed someone for it."

"You really do think he would *kill* people?" John was astounded.

Zoe nodded. "Yes, of course. He did go that far, and often. Which is why I was scared that if I did something wrong one day he'd go that far with me too."

"That's understandable, I guess."

"Luckily, I was already pumped up because I thought I was going to get away from him and that place. His arrival surprised me, but I was also ready for the unexpected just in case the young guard turned me down or something. So...I can't believe this..."

"Go on."

"So, I...I marched up to him and told him what I thought of him."

Zoe turned to John and smiled. Suddenly she looked radiant.

"Really?" he asked, smiling back.

"Yep, I went right up to his face and screamed at him that he was a no-good slimy little woman-beating fucker with a small mind and even smaller dick."

John couldn't help it, he burst out laughing. He tried to stop himself, but he couldn't. He didn't want to upset Zoe, but one look at her showed him his laugh was the best thing for her right then.

Zoe started to laugh too.

Within moments, they were both laughing hysterically. John watched Zoe as she threw her head back and laughed. All of a sudden her features became even more breathtaking as her face became so vibrant.

They continued to laugh for some time, until John's sides started to ache. He hadn't laughed like that for a long time.

For years...

"Sorry," John said as they began to calm down. "I didn't mean to -"

"That's alright" Zoe replied. "I've been living with this tension for three days. I feel great now that I can laugh it off."

"But there's more to the story, right?"

"Yeah, and this part isn't funny."

"What did he do?"

"He was stunned. He really was. He didn't know what to say or do. He just stood there with his mouth wide open, like he was in mid-scream or something, but he just stood there. I said I'd packed my bags and there was nothing he could do about it. But then he came at me with the gun raised like he was going to hit me with it, you know? I mean, he didn't have it pointed at me by then, he was holding it the other way, by the barrel and it was like he was going to hit me with the handle-part."

"The butt of the gun?"

"Yeah. But I was ready and I was pumped and I wrestled with him."

"Really?"

"Yeah, it's hard to believe, I know. He was a big guy and I didn't know if I was strong enough. But this was the first time I had shown any resistance so I think he was a bit surprised and that's why I managed to throw him off balance and we ended up on the bed."

"Good for you!"

"It was a surprise to me too, though. One moment I'm yelling at his face and the next we're on the bed and I'm on top of him and we're wrestling for the gun."

"So what happened then?"

"Ricky's fighting me with one hand and trying to reach the phone on the bedside table. When you picked up the receiver and didn't dial, it would go straight through to the gatehouse where security was stationed. That's what he was trying to do. He was trying to knock the phone off the hook so the guards could hear there was trouble. So I had to try and keep him away from the phone and fight him for the gun too. The next thing I know, we're both tumbling off the bed, the bedside table is falling on top of us along with the phone, the lamp and vase, and we hit the floor all at once."

Zoe took a deep breath.

"And that's when the gun went off."

John rubbed her arm and nodded his head. "Okay, but it was self defence, right? I mean, he came at you with the gun. They can't hold that against you."

"But that's just the problem," Zoe replied. "Don't you see? I panicked. I didn't stop. I screamed when I noticed he wasn't moving. I jumped off him, grabbed my suitcase, the gun, and as much of the money as I could and ran. The guards were panicking too because of the gunshot and I managed to slip through them while they were looking for Ricky."

"But that's fine. Go and tell the police. I'm sure they'll understand."

"Johnny, don't you get it? I don't even know if Ricky is dead!"

"Huh? But you said the gun went off?"

"It did. But I don't know for sure that I killed Ricky. He could just be hurt or maybe the bullet missed him completely and he was knocked out by the fall to the ground. What if the bedside table knocked him out or the lamp or something?"

"Didn't you check for a wound or anything?"

"No, I didn't have time. I panicked and fled and just left with the money and the suitcase as quickly as possible."

"I see," John nodded his head. "So you can't go to the police because –"

"Because if Ricky is still alive he'll get at me somehow."

John grabbed both of Zoe's hands and stared deeply into her eyes. "Is he *that* powerful? *That* dangerous?" he asked.

Zoe's face fell. "Yes," she whispered. "He is."

"So that's why you've driven clear across the country for three days?"

"Exactly. I didn't know I was coming here to Parkhurst at the time, Johnny, honest I didn't. My first plan was to get away from the house. I did that by jumping in my Jeep and driving off. He'd bought the Jeep for me only a few weeks ago after he came back from Vegas. He said he'd won the money at one of the casinos over there and had decided to buy me the Jeep because I'd been good. But I think he got the money by doing a few extra jobs while he was there. I was speechless when I first saw it. He blindfolded me and led me out to the driveway. It was brand new! I'm sure of it! I couldn't believe it. My very own brand new Jeep! It even had personalised licence plates.

"Anyway, I jumped in the Jeep and just drove as fast as I could. I kept my suitcase so I could change clothes whenever I needed to, and I kept the gun by my side at all times for protection. Then I just drove and drove until I found myself here."

John nodded his head. It was all starting to come together now. He looked at his watch: 1:43am.

Everything was becoming clearer.

"Helen's not coming home, is she?" he asked.

Zoe shook her head.

"And she's not down the street buying food."

"Nope."

John continued to nod. "It all makes sense now."

Zoe leaned over and rubbed his back. "I'm sorry, Johnny, truly I am. I didn't want to get you involved in this mess, and certainly not Helen. But what else can I do? She was the only person I could think of who could help."

"I understand. I just wish you had told me to begin with."

"I'm sorry, Johnny. But I swore Helen to secrecy because the fewer people who know about this the better. I don't want *anyone* to know if I can help it. Ricky has friends everywhere."

"But what were you going to tell me when Helen didn't return?"

"I'm sorry for all that. But you surprised me coming home when you did. Helen said you were going to be late and she gave me the impression you were going to be *really* late. So you arrived before I had a chance to work out what I was going to say."

"Okay," John said.

"I didn't want to lie to you, Johnny. But I thought it was for the best at the time. But it wasn't all lies. She did tell me to make myself comfortable and she did take my Jeep so she could take it for a spin."

"Don't worry about it," John said. "It's all fine now. I understand."

"Good. And I'm sorry about pulling the gun on you."

"That's okay. It was a bit of a shock though."

"But I thought if you left and went to find her before you knew what was going on, you might blow the only chance I have."

"So Helen is at the hospital?"

"Yep, I knew she worked for a hospital, but I couldn't remember what her job was. So I was thrilled to get here and find out she was a hospital administrator. I asked her if it was possible for her to pull some strings, to call around some of the hospitals on the west coast and see if Ricky Fox had been admitted."

"Do you think he would have?"

"I don't know. He liked to steer clear of hospitals if anything went wrong, but if he was close to death, his guards may have taken him to an emergency ward somewhere."

"But they wouldn't admit him under the name Ricky Fox, would they?"

"Don't worry, I gave Helen a full list of all his aliases. He uses about a dozen. She said she'd check them all out. Along with morgues and places like that. It's a long-shot, but I can't work out my next step until I hear one way or another."

"If she finds he's dead?"

"His empire will crumble. He's got no family and no backup. He works for himself and his staff take orders only from him. If he's dead – I'm free."

"And if she can't find anything?"

"Then Ricky is still alive. And I'm a dead girl."

<u>Four</u>

J ohn leaned over, pulled her closer and hugged her tight. "Don't worry. Helen will find out some news and we'll look after you."

She smiled at him and kissed him on the cheek once more.

"Thanks, Johnny," she replied. "I'm glad I can trust you."

"Did Helen say how long it could take her?"

"She said probably all night. She told me you'd be home late and that I should go to bed and try and get some sleep. But I don't know if I can sleep tonight, Johnny. There's too many unknown factors and I keep seeing the fight with Ricky in my head over and over again."

She hugged him tighter.

"Will you stay up with me for a while and talk?"

"Sure," John said. "I can do that."

"It's been a while since I've been able to talk with people. You know, *really* talk, without having to worry that Ricky's watching me and going to beat me when I get home."

"I can imagine." John replied. "But that's all behind you now. You're free of him."

"I hope you're right."

Zoe went quiet for a moment or two before she placed her head on his shoulder.

"You're a good listener, Johnny. I feel I can talk to you."

"I'm happy to help in any way and I'm glad you were able to tell me the whole story. You seem more relaxed now."

"Yeah, I was in such a state when I arrived here and Helen opened the door. I'm sure she didn't recognise me to begin with. I haven't slept well for weeks, and certainly haven't had the chance to catch more than a few hours sleep each night since Tuesday. I must've looked like a mess. I couldn't even formulate my words and thoughts to tell her my whole story. I had to just tell her the main facts and she said I could fill her in on the rest when she gets back. So you're the first person I've really talked to about this."

"I'm glad I could be of help."

John's eyes focussed on the gun lying in the hallway.

Must get that out of Zoe's sight, he thought. *It'll only remind her of the events she wants to forget.*

"Do you need anything? Or want anything?" he asked, hoping to use a trip to the kitchen as an excuse to remove the gun from its present position.

"No," she replied. "I just want to sit here with you."

I won't say no to that, he thought.

"Okay."

"And talk."

"Okay."

"About anything other than Ricky Fox and me."

"Okay."

"I've been living with this whole situation for ages and now all I want to do is forget and move on."

"Yeah, but it's not going to be that easy, is it?"

"It all depends whether the bastard is dead or not," Zoe whispered.

"Well, hopefully we'll know more soon."

Zoe hugged him tighter and burrowed her head into his shoulder. Strands of hair that had escaped her ponytail tickled his chin and her clean, fresh smell enveloped him again.

Poor girl, John thought. *She deserves so much more.*

He moved her hair from around his chin. The strands were soft and smooth.

"So, tell me about you," Zoe whispered.

"Well, there's nothing much to tell. You keep in touch with Helen. I'm sure she's told you everything about me."

"Are you happy?" Zoe's head turned and she looked up at him.

"What?"

"You and Helen, are you both happy?"

"What on earth makes you ask that question?"

Zoe shrugged and placed her head back on his shoulder. "I just want to know. I know what it's like to be unhappy in a relationship and I just want to make sure yours is okay."

"Everything's fine."

"Good. I'm glad."

Now who's lying? he asked himself.

John rubbed her left arm and could feel her muscles tense beneath her skin. He wondered if she was trying to sleep or whether she was staring at the gun still on the hallway floor.

"You should try to relax and get some sleep," he said. "A good night's sleep will do you the world of good."

"I know," Zoe whispered. "But if I go to bed and get any sleep, it will be interrupted by nightmares that I just don't want to have. Ricky's still in my head and I'll dream of him beating me and coming at me with the gun and..."

Her voice trailed off and she shuddered.

"Hey, take it easy." John whispered, "I thought we weren't going to talk about Ricky Fox any more?"

Zoe tried to laugh, but it came out as a strangled cry. "Yeah, you're right. Sorry."

She sat up, pushed away from him and turned to face him once more.

"You're a good man, Johnny," she said as she smiled. "I barge in here unexpected and pull a gun on you and cry and act like a child, but you still listen to me and try to help. You still care. I'm not used to that."

"Don't worry about it, Zoe. Helen and I are both here to help."

She smiled. "You called me Zoe again. That's twice now. I like it when you call me that."

"Well, that *is* your name, after all."

"I know. But it just sounds so right. Ricky called me a lot of things, some horrible things, but he never used my name."

Her face became a swirl of emotions once more. Her bottom lip quivered and John could tell more tears were on the way. He leaned forward and stroked her cheek.

"Ssshh," he said. "That's enough for tonight."

She reached up and touched his hand, held it to her lips and kissed it.

"Thanks, Johnny. Thanks so much."

"Don't worry. I know you've been through a lot, but try and put it behind you as best you can. Don't relive it every few minutes."

She clutched his hand tighter, closed her eyes and kissed his fingers again. Her lips were warm, wet and soft.

Then she opened her mouth and placed it around his index finger. Her tongue danced over it as she sucked his finger slowly, rhythmically, up and down.

"Hey," John tried to pull away, but she held his hand tight.

Her mouth was hot and strong and her teeth pressed lightly on his flesh, as if teasing, threatening to bite if he made the wrong move. Her eyes stayed closed and her toes curled as she continued to suck.

"Zoe, please!" John said.

Her eyes sprang open at the mention of her name. She pulled his finger from her mouth and smiled.

"That's three times now," she said. "I could get used to you calling for me."

She let go of his hand and John pulled it back and placed it on his lap.

"Well, get used to it, Zoe. Because it's your name and that's what I'm going to be calling you from now on. Okay?"

"Great!" she giggled.

"So, let's make a deal," John continued. "I'll call you Zoe, if you stop keeping tally of how many times I call you by your name. Okay?"

"Okay," she smiled. "But you've said it five times now."

"Fine. But I don't need to know the running score, alright?"

"Whatever you say, Johnny," she slid across the sofa and kneeled next to him and hugged him once more. "I'll do whatever you say."

"Good."

He rubbed her bare shoulder once more; it felt cold.

"Are you cold?" he asked. "Do you want a blanket or sweater or something?"

"Nah," Zoe replied by his ear, still hugging him. "Just hold me and I'll feel safe."

They sat that way for a long time. So long that John thought maybe Zoe had fallen asleep.

I should get her into bed for some proper rest, he thought.

But there was no denying that she was a nice girl, a *real* nice girl, and if she wanted to hug him all night long, well, there was nothing wrong with that.

He could live with it.

As long as Helen didn't make a surprise entrance.

Just imagine trying to explain that! he thought.

But Zoe said Helen would be gone all night.

Does it take all night to find out if a patient has been admitted to a hospital on the other side of the country? John didn't know. Helen's job had always been a bit of a mystery to him. Only because he didn't really care what she did.

"A job's a job," he had told her once. "We've all got one. But when I come home I don't want to think about mine and I don't want to hear about yours."

It was a harsh thing to say, and he'd said it in the heat of one of their arguments. Helen always felt he didn't take enough interest in her job, but she didn't take any in his either. He was fine with that, but she obviously wasn't.

Now he wished he had listened to Helen when she told him about what she did. At least now he'd know what she was doing.

John turned his head slightly to look over at the gun once more. Zoe's head was resting on his left shoulder so he was sure she wasn't looking at the gun now. It was a reminder of what she had lived through and he had to move it or hide it so she wouldn't see it. He didn't want those memories resurfacing every five minutes or so. He had to make sure she kept her mind off it all until they found out if Ricky Fox was alive or dead.

Ricky Fox. What a fucking sick bastard, he thought. *Hope you are dead, you pathetic son of a bitch.*

He held Zoe tight. The heat from her body radiated through his left side. She was hard up against him, pinning him to the side of the sofa. He wasn't uncomfortable yet, but he couldn't last all night in that position. He rested his head against the back of the sofa and closed his eyes.

I'll give her a few more minutes, he thought.

And then he fell asleep.

* * *

Running.
Must run.
But what if I'm caught?
Turn around, look.
No one.
Still gotta run.
Gotta run.
Run.
Run, RUN!
I can't.
My legs. I can't.
My legs!
They're after me and I can't.
I can't run.
They'll get me.
Turn around and look again.
There's nothing there. It's too dark.
I can't see anything!
Why is it so dark?
I've gotta run and I've gotta run now!
Where?
I can't see where to run!
It's so dark!
Why?
Why can't I run and why can't I see?
They're gonna find me before I even move!
Run, damn it, just RUN!
RUN RUN RUNRUNRUNRUNRUNRUN!
Too dark.
Where're the lights?
There must be some light somewhere.
Oh my GOD!

It's too dark.
It's too dark because I can't see!
I CAN'T SEE!
My eyes.
I HAVE NO EYES!
I can't see.
My GOD. WHAT HAVE YOU DONE WITH MY EYES?
WHERE ARE MY EYES?
Laughter, I hear laughter.
Where are you? You fuck, where the hell are you?
GIVE ME BACK MY EYES!
Pain.
More Pain.
Shit, you hurt me.
What have you done now?
My stomach? No, lower down.
You fuck, what have you done to me?
Wet.
Sticky.
What have you done to me?
Have you killed me?
My God, you've killed me?
How could you?
GIVE ME BACK MY EYES SO I CAN SEE WHAT YOU
HAVE DONE TO ME!

* * *

John woke with a start.

He was still sitting on the sofa but Zoe had moved. She was beside him now and it felt as if she had curled herself into a ball and was lying down next to him, her head resting on his thighs. He opened his eyes and stared down at her. He rubbed her back once more and placed a hand on her head.

It was then that he felt her hot, wet lips. He could feel her sucking gently on his erection, slowly, rhythmically. Exactly as she was doing to his finger earlier.

"Hey!" he said as he grabbed her shoulder. "Hey! Stop that!"

She continued, stronger now, as if satisfying him might change his mind.

"Zoe, please. Stop it." He pulled at her shoulder. "Don't!"

After one last loud and wet suck, she slowly withdrew her mouth, her tongue playing with the very top of his throbbing cock as she pulled away.

She sat up and looked at him, sadness in her eyes.

"I'm sorry," she pouted.

"What's wrong with you? Jesus!"

"I'm sorry," she repeated.

"It's okay," John struggled to get his fully erect cock back into his pants. "You just, you know, you just don't have to do things like that."

Zoe sat back on her haunches. "I just wanted to say thanks. Thanks for everything. All the help and everything."

"Then just say it," John said as he pulled his zipper up over the bulge. "I know you were in a pretty strange relationship and maybe this is the way that Fox guy got you to say thanks, but you don't have to do that any more and you don't have to do it to me."

"Didn't you like it?" she asked.

"What?"

You're kidding? he thought. *Did I* like *it?*

"Didn't you like it? You know, what I was doing. Isn't it nice to wake up to that warm, lovely feeling?"

John didn't know what to say. "Well, ah, yeah, of course it was *nice*, but you don't have to say thank you that way. Okay?"

"Okay."

Zoe still looked sad.

"Don't be upset, Zoe. It's just not right. We just don't do that sort of thing here, okay?"

"Why?" she asked.

"Huh?"

"Why can't I do that to you if I want to? You enjoyed it. I enjoy it. So where's the harm?"

John sighed. "The harm is, I'm *married*! And Helen is your *friend*. We *can't* do it."

Zoe crawled closer to him and placed her face inches from his. Her dark brown eyes enveloped him as they
searched his whole face. She lifted her right hand to play
with his hair.

"Does that matter?" she asked.

"Does it matter? Of course it matters!"

"But are you *really* happy?"

"Happy?

"Yeah, with Helen. Can she give you everything I can?"

John was speechless.

This girl shoots straight, that's for sure, he thought.

"I mean, is she as good as me?" Zoe continued in a whisper. "Is she?"

Her left hand rubbed across the bulge in his pants. She
squeezed slightly.

John just stared at her.

"Is she?"

John grabbed her hand and pulled it from his pants. He
pushed her aside and bolted from the sofa.

"Look, Zoe," he said over his shoulder as he walked over
to sit on the dining chair on the opposite side of the room.
"I know you've had trouble and everything. But we just can't
do this, okay? I love someone *else*. I'm *with* someone else. Do
you understand that?"

Zoe's face fell, "I'm sorry."

"It's okay. I understand. I really do. Just as long as we
know what the boundaries are. Okay?"

"Okay."

"Good."

They stared at each other across the lounge room for a
while.

"But have you ever thought about it?" Zoe finally asked,
her head tilting slightly.

"Thought about what?"

"You know, having sex with someone else."

John shook his head and sighed. "I don't think we need
to talk about this."

"No, I'm just interested." Zoe rearranged herself on the
sofa into her favourite yoga-like position once more; legs

spread, arms resting on her knees. "When I was with Ricky, towards the end when things were rough, I always had to fantasise that I was with someone else. Like I was doing it with someone else. It was the only thing that kept me going."

"Well, when you're with an asshole like that, I'm not surprised."

"So do you think about it?"

"I don't see what good discussing this will do."

"Have you ever thought about having an affair? I mean, you *must* have, right? Who hasn't thought about it? You know, you're in a stable relationship, but things can get boring. The same old same old. People get boring, the positions get boring, the sex gets boring. You get bored and you start thinking."

"Zoe, this isn't going to help…"

"Haven't you thought what it would be like to do it with someone else? Even for just a minute?"

John sighed. *What's the use?* he thought.

"Okay, you win. Of *course* I have. Everyone does. It's not that unusual."

"I know," Zoe said as she pushed herself up off the sofa and walked towards him. "I agree. It's not unusual."

She stopped when she reached him and kneeled down in front of him.

"So, all I'm saying is," she smiled at him again, "if you get the opportunity, you should go for it."

She reached out towards him once more, her deep eyes and wide smile drawing him closer.

John leaned forward, reached out and took both her hands. He brought them together inside his and pulled her closer.

"I'm sorry, Zoe," he whispered to her. "I *love* someone else."

Her face fell as he let her hands drop. She sat back on her haunches and looked to the ground.

"Now, I think you're tired and a little upset," John continued. "Which is certainly understandable considering what you've been through."

He stood and looked at his watch: 3:19am.

Boy, what a night!

"It's been a long night and I think it's time you got some sleep. You want to be fully recovered when Helen returns with whatever news she has."

Zoe turned her head to stare up at him. "You're right," she said as she began to stand. "I've been a fool and I'm sorry that –"

"Ssshh," John interrupted her. "Say nothing more now. Just go to bed and try and sleep. Okay?"

She smiled once more, "Okay. You're right, Johnny. Thanks."

"Good night," he said.

She stood slowly and walked past him.

"Good night," she said over her shoulder. "Pleasant dreams."

He swung around to watch her leave the room. Her ponytail swung from side to side, mirroring her buttocks. She made a detour to pick up the unfinished glass of water left next to the sofa. She turned to face him and smiled once more.

"Thanks for all your help, Johnny."

"My pleasure," he said. "Now, go to bed."

She nodded and headed for the bedrooms.

John watched as she opened the door to the main bedroom and walked straight through, leaving the door open behind her.

He waited to see if she was moving her clothes to the spare bedroom, but no light came on and she didn't reappear.

Maybe she doesn't know there's a spare bedroom, he thought to himself. *Or maybe she's tempting me.*

John stood there for a minute or two, just in case she did reappear. But she didn't.

She is *tempting me!* he thought. *She's going to be a handful. But you can't say no to a beautiful girl in trouble.*

He smiled and turned out the lounge room light. Shaking his head, he followed Zoe towards the main bedroom.

John stopped in the doorway to the main bedroom. He peered into the darkness but couldn't see any movement. Zoe must have been so tired that she'd fallen asleep straight away, not realizing she was in the main bedroom.

Or *had* she?

He reached out and grabbed the doorknob and slowly closed the door.

He ran his hand through his hair as he walked down the small hallway that housed entrances to the bathroom and spare bedroom.

He hoped Helen was able to find something out to help Zoe; any kind of news that would give her some certainty as to what her next moves should be.

Otherwise she was just going to be a bundle of nerves for days on end.

Then again, no news meant she'd have to stay with them longer, and John began to think he'd enjoy that.

She's going to be a handful, he thought again.

He walked into the bathroom, turned on the light and stared at himself in the mirror.

It had been a long day and he was exhausted. He really couldn't be bothered doing anything other than standing there staring at his reflection in the mirror. His eyes looked tired and his short brown hair was all ruffled from his nap on the sofa.

But what a way to wake up! John thought as he smiled to himself. Her mouth, hot and wet around him, had felt so good.

"You've still got the pulling power," he whispered to himself as he looked at his reflection.

He smirked, *Yeah, right! Who am I fooling?*

He had always thought of himself as quite attractive to the opposite sex, he'd certainly had no trouble in his college days, but he'd never had women just throw themselves at him. He was good looking with sharp defined features, and college football had kept him in good shape. He looked in the mirror now, stared at the few strands of grey hair that had begun to appear on his head and at the slowly forming wrinkles around his eyes. Still, not bad for a guy in his early thirties.

And Zoe proved that he was still attractive to at least some of the female population.

He remembered then the first time he had seen Helen. It was part way through his senior year of college. He'd never seen her before then, because she was a freshman.

He'd spent so much time trying to impress the cheerleaders that any girl not on the squad just wasn't worth his time. And that had been his big mistake.

Sure, he was good looking, but he wasn't the best looking on the team. The cheerleaders were more interested in Donny DuBois and Marty Klavan.

Some guys had it easy.

Meanwhile, guys like John and his best pal Richard Dunbar had to work for their conquests.

And, for John, Helen had been the sweetest of them all. So sweet, because it had been so easy.

John folded his arms on his chest and watched as his reflection did the same.

"Yeah, you've still got it," he said.

Part way through his final year everything was going great, except for his love life. It was a black hole of loneliness and depression. But then out of nowhere Helen appeared.

He'd been dragged into a post-game party that Donny DuBois had thrown at the house he and a few friends were renting just off campus. He really didn't want to be there, but with nothing much to do and the adrenaline still pumping, he had decided to go along.

Richard had told him to blow the guys off and tell them to jam their party where the sun don't shine. But Richard was like that. He was the one who was always going to be the writer and would return to his dorm and type out page after page of one novel or another on an old rickety typewriter.

John had told him he was going to the party and that Richard should come along.

"It'll be fun," John had said to him.

"Jam it," Richard had replied as he fed another blank page into his typewriter.

But when he got there he wished he had listened to Richard in the first place.

It was a boring party full of boring people who were only interested in getting on Donny's good side, or naked side, depending on whether they were male or female.

Most of the guys were from the team and John had nothing too much to say to them – he saw them every day of the week anyhow. And most of the female flesh was better left on the rack.

Girls like Patricia "Pattie the Fattie" Bourke and Maureen O'Reilly were there hoping to get lucky. But the rolls of fat around their stomachs and their truly sad make-up made them only good for teasing and laughing at.

Some girls just didn't get it. Or, more likely, they were hoping someone would get drunk enough to help them get it. But you'd have to be mighty drunk to want to pop their stale and tasteless cherries.

Sad, sad girls, John shook his head as he thought back. *What kind of a life would they lead?*

John remembered standing in a corner for most of the night, checking out from afar the breasts on Christie Baker, Donny's number one squeeze and the team's number one cheerleader. She was also number one wet dream pin-up girl for most of the male population on campus. Now there was a girl with class, tits and ass. How she managed to have her tits defy gravity was of constant amazement to John. They were large and nicely rounded, but Christie never wore a bra and they just stuck out from her body, on display for everyone to see. Her nipples were usually erect and enchanting too. An absolute feast for the eyes, and a true natural wonder of the world.

Finally, after only about an hour or two, John decided to go home. There was no action at the party and the only thing worth waiting around for was another sly glimpse of Christie Baker's breasts. But he knew he was never going to get his hands on them, so there was no reason to hang around. He slipped out of the main lounge room skilfully dodging the hot and clammy hands of "Pattie the Fattie" and Maureen. He was wiping his hands and heading down to the front door when it opened and Helen walked in.

He remembered stopping in his tracks, amazed at her long curly blonde hair that flowed over her shoulders.

And then he saw the angry look on her face.

"What the hell do you think you're looking at?" she'd yelled across the hall at him.

John was stunned. He tried to speak, he even tried to turn and walk away, but he couldn't.

"Well?" she placed her hands on her hips.

"Ah, I was just leaving," he said as he continued towards her and the door. "The party's in the main lounge." He pointed the way.

"I'm not here for some stupid party," she yelled at him.

"Oh, okay, sorry," he pushed past her and walked out the door.

"Hey," she called from behind him. "Where are you going?"

He turned to face her after he walked down the front steps.

"Home," he said.

She still had her hands on her hips but she had a strange look in her eyes.

"You know anything about cars?" she asked.

"Well, yeah, a little," he replied.

"Think you can fix mine?"

"Don't know," he shrugged his shoulders and placed his hands in his pockets. "What's wrong with it?"

She rolled her eyes, "If I knew that, I'd be fixing it."

She smiled and he laughed.

"Okay," he said. "Where is it?"

"Just across the street," she pointed. "It's that old shitheap of a Buick. My dad won't buy me anything new."

"Well, let's go and have a look at it then."

They walked across to the car and he checked under the hood. Helen climbed in the car and turned the key in the ignition. The engine sounded pretty dead to him and he suggested maybe it was the battery.

"Shit," she hit the steering wheel. "How the hell am I supposed to get home now?"

"I could take you," he'd replied. "If you don't mind a bike?"

And so he had taken her home on his bike, and she had invited him inside for coffee.

And that was when they really hit it off. He found out she was at college too, but they were doing different courses and subjects for the most part. She found out he was on the football team, "A game for small-minded people played by athletes with even smaller minds," she had said, and he had discovered that there was something much more interesting in the world than football. And even more interesting than Christie Baker's breasts. Helen was cute, intelligent, great to talk with and fun to be around.

But she had spunk too. She would call it as she saw it and wasn't afraid to speak her mind. He liked that, and he hadn't found it in any of the cheerleaders he knew. Most of them would bend over backwards without a word of complaint – literally. They would lie and cheat to get what they wanted. The girls he knew had no substance at all. But Helen did. Helen was completely different.

After working so hard with so many relationships that had never worked out, John suddenly found himself talking with someone who was just right for him. He didn't have to try hard or pretend. He just had to be himself and everything clicked into place.

And he had fallen in love right there.

Nothing mattered any more. All that did matter was the girl sitting across from him.

Helen...

John sighed as he rubbed at the stubble on his chin. His mirror-image did the same.

How things can change...

The reflection of the light from the chain around his neck caught his eye. He pulled at the chain and the pendant attached to it popped out from his shirt. He held it in his hand and stared down at it. It was a gold half-heart pendant, the other half he had given to Helen when they decided to get engaged. It was cheap, all they could afford at the time, but it had meant so much to both of them.

He had one half of the gold heart-shaped pendant. The other half of the heart still hung around Helen's neck after all these years.

He stared at the pendant now, and smiled. Helen had fallen for him just as quickly as he had fallen for her.

So many years ago, he thought to himself. *But you've still got it, John.*

"Yeah," he said to the man in the mirror.

Some girl who's been treated like shit by her asshole boyfriend goes down on you to say thanks and you think you're the hottest guy ever to walk the earth.

John shook his head. "Dream on."

He turned off the light and walked out of the bathroom. He stopped in the hall to listen for any sounds from the main bedroom, but he could hear nothing.

She's asleep, poor kid. The events have finally caught up with her, he thought.

Opening the spare bedroom door, he walked inside and got undressed in the dark. He closed the door behind him and climbed under the cool sheets of the single bed.

The single bed.

The bed they bought for his son.

The son they had never had.

He remembered the excitement when Helen had told him she was pregnant. He remembered all the champagne corks popping and the celebratory messages from their friends and family.

He could recall how they rushed around town, buying clothes and a cradle, a cot and toys. And the bed for when the baby got older.

And he also remembered the doctors telling him that his son had no heartbeat and was dead. There was nothing they could do.

Nothing.

He remembered walking back into this room after hearing the news, dismantling the cot, packing up the toys. They would never be used.

They hadn't got around to selling the bed. In fact, they hardly ever talked about it any more.

It was something Helen never liked to talk about. It was as if she blamed herself, as if it were her fault the baby had formed the way it had. He'd tried to talk to her about it countless times, but she just wouldn't listen, wouldn't open up. She'd just leave the room.

And now here he was, sleeping in the bed himself, with a strange woman sleeping in his bedroom.

Zoe.

In some ways, Zoe was a child herself. She seemed to look for direction, for guidance, for a nod that everything is okay.

That bastard Fox better be dead, John thought. *He deserves nothing better.*

And then maybe Zoe could start again.

A new life with no strings attached. How nice would that be? he wondered.

He closed his eyes, placed his hands behind his head, and let his mind wander back over the events of the night.

Coming home and finding Zoe naked on the sofa was a complete shock. But a nice one just the same. She had a wonderfully fine body, and he could certainly see that the countless hours she had spent on Fox's gym equipment had done her the world of good.

She's gorgeous, he thought.

He remembered her pierced belly button and the nestled diamond. He couldn't remember seeing anything so wonderfully sexy in his life. And then there was her tanned and muscled stomach, and legs...and vagina.

He felt himself growing hard again. He tried to think of other things. Tried to think about what kind of searches Helen would be doing at the hospital.

She had her mouth around my cock, he thought.

He grew harder still.

She was so hot and wet and so good.

"Didn't you like it? Isn't it nice to wake up to that warm, lovely feeling?" she had asked.

Boy, it sure was, he thought to himself and smiled.

He turned over in the bed and tried to get some sleep. He tried to clear his mind of images of Zoe naked, her legs apart, sitting on his sofa, showing him the shaved folds of her sex.

"Have you ever thought about having an affair?" she had asked him. "I mean, you *must* have right? Who hasn't thought about it?"

He shook his head.

Come on John, he thought to himself. *Get a hold on the situation. You're married! You love someone else! Get her out of your mind.*

John turned over onto his other side and punched at the pillow. He didn't know how he was going to get any sleep with images of Zoe in his mind.

Naked, tanned and willing.

He closed his eyes tighter and wondered if Zoe was having as much trouble falling to sleep as he was.

"Shit," John mumbled to himself. "She's going to kill me."

* * *

Long hallway.
No, not a hallway.
A door.
A door a long way away.
But getting closer.
Running.
No, I can't run.
I'm not running.
Flying?
Am I flying?
Yes, I'm flying towards the door!
It's getting closer.
Bright light on the other side.
Songs.
I hear songs.

No, it's screaming.
Screaming?
Laughter?
They're all around me.
The door is coming closer.
Too close.
Too fast!
I must stop!
Too fast!
The light!
Too bright!
Quiet now, and dark.
No laughter and no light.
Something's behind me.
I can hear it running. It's getting closer.
I can't see it but it's getting closer.
I've got to run, run while I can.
But I'm stuck! My legs won't move! I can't run.
Over there, I see them. I can see the hands over there,
reaching for me.
HELP ME!
I'm trying to get there.
I can hear the footsteps behind me.
There's no one there but I know they're getting closer.
I'm stretching, stretching for the hands. Help me.
Help me move closer, stretch closer.
It's raining now, raining all around.
The rain hurts. The rain goes straight through me.
HELP!
The rain is tearing me apart!
Laughter again, I can hear it all around me.
The rain is eating through my flesh.
Help!
The pain!
Stretch hands, stretch out and help me!
Fingers stretch.
The footsteps are closer.
Help me escape!
Yes, yes!

YES!
I have reached the hands. Hands, pull me to safety!
Pull me to safety now!
Yes.
That's it. I'm moving now. The footsteps won't be able
to catch me.
Hands, pull me to safety.
Pull me into the arms of the one I now love.

<u>Six</u>

John rolled over and reached out for Helen, but he only found the side of the bed.

He opened one eye and squinted into the sunlight.

The spare bedroom. The single bed.

And then he remembered all about last night.

He closed his eye when he stretched and rolled onto his back, letting a yawn escape him. As he moved his legs he heard the jiggling of crockery.

"Careful, you'll spill it all."

He waited a second, unsure if he had really heard the voice. Opening both eyes, he sat, lifted his head and stared down at the end of the bed.

Zoe was sitting there, smiling back at him. She wore his blue bathrobe and, from what he could tell, nothing underneath. The robe was tied loosely around her waist, allowing the sunlight to shine on the top-most part of her chest. She was sitting with one leg folded in front of her on the bed and the other stretched to the floor, holding her steady. He could see her bare thighs and he knew if she moved too far one way or the other he would probably see much more.

Her hair was in two shoulder length braids, one down each side of her face. He'd never seen a grown woman wear her hair that way, it was usually only little girls who did, but it was the most charming thing he had ever seen. She sat on the end of the bed like a little pixie or angel. He'd never woken up to anything so delightful in his life.

"Good morning, sleepy head," she said. "I've brought you some breakfast." She pointed down at the tray resting beside her.

"Thanks," he replied as he cast a glance over the steaming hot coffee, toast and cereal. "But you didn't have to do all this."

"Hey, it's the least I can do. You're letting me stay here after all, so I should be able to make you a meal or two."

John ran a hand through his messed hair and smiled back at her. "I *am* hungry," he said. "What time is it?"

"It's a little after eleven."

"Wow, I slept in, huh?"

"Well, we did have a late night last night," Zoe replied.

"Yeah, we did." John pulled himself up into a sitting position.

Zoe's eyes fell to his chest as he did so. He realised then that this was the first time she had seen him without a shirt. He was glad he'd kept his boxers on last night. She might be able to walk around naked in front of strangers, but John sure as hell couldn't.

"So, did you sleep okay?" he asked.

Her eyes darted back to his and she smiled. "Okay, yeah, I guess. I woke up a few times, you know, because of the dreams I have. They're nightmares really. Sometimes pretty strange and violent ones, but I think I slept better last night than I have in ages."

"Good."

Zoe picked up the tray holding the food and leaned closer towards him. He reached out and took the tray from her and placed it in his lap.

"Thanks."

"As I said, no problem at all," she sat back at the end of the bed. "I hope you enjoy it."

"I'm sure I will!" John said as he took a sip of coffee. "Ahh, nice! I'm not used to this kind of service."

Zoe giggled, "It's no trouble, really."

They sat in silence for a moment while John took a spoonful of cereal and began to eat. Zoe checked her braids to make sure they were still in order and then let her eyes slip back down his chest.

"Have you been up long?" he asked, more to put an end to the silence than anything else.

"An hour or so," she replied. "I hope you don't mind, but I took a shower and this was all I could find to wear." She pointed at his blue bathrobe.

I don't mind at all, he thought. *You look great in it.*

John shook his head while chewing another mouthful of cereal, "That's fine. Use whatever you want."

"It's just that I woke up feeling dirty and horrible, probably because of my dreams, and I just knew if I could have a long hot shower, I'd feel much better."

John thought about Zoe in a long hot shower, the steam all around her, her hair wet and plastered to her head. The hot water coursing down her body, flowing onto her, around her, down her breasts and stomach and over her pierced belly button. Lower…lower…

He was glad the tray was resting across his lap.

"Johnny?" Zoe said.

"Hmm? Sorry, I was a million miles away. What did you say?"

"I asked whether the coffee is okay for you. I don't know how you have it."

"No, no, it's fine." He smiled. "I love it. Thanks."

"Good."

He continued to eat, and she sat on the end of the bed and watched him in silence. Slowly, her smile disappeared and he could tell by the different emotions flowing across her face that she was troubled once again.

When the second piece of toast was almost finished, she said, "I cleaned up around the house for you too."

"You what?"

Oh my God, John thought. *The gun! I forgot to move the gun. No wonder she's depressed again!*

"There was no need to do anything like that," he said.

Zoe shook he head. "No, it was good for me. It kept my mind off things. It's always good to keep busy, you know?"

John nodded.

"And I found your newspaper on the front doorstep."

Zoe went quiet and looked down at her hands.

"And…" John prompted.

"Nothing," she said as she met his eyes once more. "I checked it three times, from cover to cover, Johnny, and there's nothing in the paper about Ricky."

John placed the tray by his side. "But that doesn't mean anything."

"Yes, it means he's still alive!"

She looked like she was about to cry again, so John reached out his arms and she climbed along the bed, came and sat next to him and hugged him hard.

"If there's nothing in the papers," she whispered, "it means he's out there somewhere looking for me."

"Not necessarily." John stroked her hair. "You said yourself that he didn't like doctors and that he used aliases. Maybe he's lying on some morgue slate somewhere under the name of Ghengis Khan or something."

She giggled and looked up at him, "That wasn't one of his aliases."

"Okay, well sure, fine. But you know what I mean. If he's been admitted under a different name, no one's going to know!"

"I've been checking the papers every day, Johnny. Every day since I escaped and started driving! And there's been nothing."

"Well, that's good," John said. "It means that you've probably nailed the sucker and they're keeping it quiet."

"But what if he's alive and only wounded? What if he's just recuperating and will then come after me?"

"That's a lot of 'what ifs', Zoe. Why don't we wait until Helen gets back this morning and we'll look at any information she has managed to dig up, okay?"

Zoe hugged him tighter, then let her left hand slide slowly across his bare chest. "Okay. Whatever you say, I'll do it, Johnny."

John placed the tray on the floor and swung his legs out of the bed. He rested on the side of the bed for a second, waiting for Zoe to leave the room, but she continued to sit on the bed.

"Well, to begin with, I better get up and showered. Helen could be home any minute."

And I don't want her to find us like this, John thought. *That would be all I need.*

Still, Helen had been the one to leave Zoe here with him. She must've known what Zoe was like; they'd been friends for years.

Or so Zoe says...

"She's not coming home," Zoe whispered.

John sat staring out the window, through the sunlight and into the yard. He let her words sink slowly into his brain, making sure he had heard correctly. "What did you say?"

"She's not coming home," Zoe met his eyes as he turned to her. "At least, not yet. That's why she phoned."

"Huh?" John was confused. "Hang on, back up a little and start again. You've gone too fast for me."

"The phone," she said.

"Yeah, what about it?"

"Well, it rang and –"

"When?"

Zoe stared at him with a confused look in her eyes. "Just before. Like, fifteen minutes ago. Didn't you hear it?"

John shook his head.

"But, you must have! That's why I decided to bring your breakfast in here. I thought the phone would've woken you."

It usually does, John thought.

"Well, it didn't," he said.

"Oh, okay. You must have been in a really deep sleep. Anyway, it was Helen."

"Helen called," John said, unsure whether it was a question or whether he was just repeating the fact.

"Yeah, she said she'd been calling around all night and was even checking out computer databases or something. I'm not really big on technical terms and she reeled off plenty, but it seems she was calling people and doing searches for Ricky, but she'd come up with nothing."

Zoe looked like she might start to cry again, so John reached over and rubbed her arm.

"I'm sorry," he said.

Zoe tried to smile. "I don't know what to think," she said. "If there's no news that might mean he's dead and already buried in some quiet ceremony to cover everything up and I'd be free of him. Or, it means he's got some private doctor somewhere to look after him. Or maybe he was just knocked out and now he's following me across the country and is going to find me and grab me and beat me and kill me and..."

She could take it no more, the tears began to roll down her face again and she collapsed into John's arms. The warm tears pattered down his bare chest as she hugged him closer. John found it strange that he was hugging someone in his own bathrobe; its soft cloth brushing against his arms.

She looks better in it than I do, he thought.

"That's enough," he whispered. "Don't get yourself into another state like last night. You need a clear head today to work out your next move."

"I know, I know," she whispered between sobs. "It's just hard, so hard."

"Yeah," he said. "Sometimes it can be better to know at least something rather than nothing, and then you can plan from that."

Zoe pulled herself back into a sitting position and wiped the tears from her face with the back of her hand, "That's right. And right now I know a big fat nothing."

"Did Helen say anything else?"

"Only that there were a couple of places she hadn't tried, you know, small private hospitals or funeral parlours or something. They're not listed on any computer database and don't have staff on the phones in the middle of the night, or something like that. I really wasn't listening after she told me she'd found nothing out. I was kind of stunned and didn't take it all in. I was sure she would have found *something.*"

She checked to make sure her braids were still bound tightly. "She said she wanted to check those places out and a couple of others, and she was waiting for some other people to call her back with results from their searches. It all takes time, she said. Maybe all day. She said she would meet us for an early dinner around five and fill us in from there. She's going to call back about four o'clock and we can arrange to have dinner somewhere."

John signed. "Okay, sounds like the best plan we have."

"She told me to rest and take it easy and if I needed anything to ask you for it."

"Yeah, that's okay with me," he replied. "Did she ask to speak with me?"

Zoe smiled and he smiled back, "No."

Typical, John thought.

"Oops," she leaned forward and wiped the tears from his chest with her warm hands. "Sorry," she said. "I didn't mean to get you all wet."

"That's okay. The shower will fix it."

She sat back and tilted her head to one side.

"So, what do you want to do?" she asked.

"Do?"

"Well, we've got a whole lot of time to kill before four o'clock. What can we do?" she smiled at him.

John moved back into his sitting position on the side of the bed. "Well, I'm going to have a shower."

"And..." Zoe asked, her right eyebrow rising.

"And what?"

"What will we do after that?"

Careful, John thought. *You're both nearly naked.*

"What would you like to do?" he asked.

"Oh, I don't know," Zoe let herself fall back onto the bed, his blue bathrobe falling open slightly, exposing her left breast. "Anything that comes to mind."

John stood up and walked towards the doorway.

"Give it some thought," he said over his shoulder.

"Don't worry, I will," she replied and giggled quietly.

"Yeah," John muttered to himself as he walked into the bathroom. "That's what worries me."

Seven

John spent longer in the shower than usual. The water was hot and steamy and felt great on his body, but he also wanted to use the time alone to think about Zoe and the situation she was in.

It was such an amazing story. Almost unbelievable. But why would Zoe invent something so fantastic? Anyway, Helen believed her and Helen wasn't one to be suckered! Still, he needed to give the whole situation more thought.

He wanted to, but all he could see was Zoe lying naked or sitting naked on the couch, Zoe sitting at the end of the bed in his blue dressing gown, Zoe's breasts, Zoe's hair, Zoe, Zoe, ZOE!

And no matter how he tried to stop it, he soon found himself erect and throbbing.

He tried to move his mind onto other things, to help his erection subside, but as soon as it looked like he was succeeding, she would pop back into his mind and blood would automatically flow back into his cock.

She's young and so different from what I'm used to, he thought to himself.

"Have you ever thought about having an affair?" she had asked him. "I mean, you *must* have, right? Who hasn't thought about it?"

"Oh, Zoe," he said to himself. "Things just aren't that easy."

"What isn't that easy?" she replied.

He turned to find her standing by the shower screen, his blue dressing gown still draping her shoulders and a towel in her hands.

"What are you *doing*?" he asked, placing his hands on his hips.

She ran her eyes up and down his body, stopping at his erect cock.

"I just came in here to help you out," she said.

John realised standing with hands on hips wasn't helping his situation. He swung around so his back was to her and cupped his hands over his groin as a second line of defence.

"Seems like you need some help," she nodded her head towards his hands. "Naughty thoughts?"

"No," he said. "Nothing like that."

"So you usually get all hard in the shower?" she teased. "My, you are a naughty boy. You'll go blind, Johnny, unless you let a good woman take care of you."

Keeping one hand over his erection, he used the other to turn off the water and then he reached back towards her"I believe you have a towel for me?"

She handed him the one she had been holding.

Quickly, John wrapped it around his hips and knotted it in front. Luckily, the knot seemed to hide most of the bulge from between his legs.

Zoe giggled, "So, spill the beans."

"Beans? What beans?"

"You said that things aren't that easy. What were you talking about?"

"Nothing," he walked from the shower and headed back to the main bedroom. "It doesn't matter now."

"Tell me," she asked as she followed.

"No, I was just talking to myself."

"That's the first sign of madness, you know."

"Very funny."

He walked into the main bedroom and headed straight for his underwear drawer by the bed. He noticed that the double bed had been made and that Zoe's suitcase was pushed into the far corner in front of Helen's wardrobe, along with one of Helen's bedroom chairs. She *had* been busy with the housework.

"So, why were you talking to yourself?" She jumped onto the bed and crawled across towards him.

He turned to watch her as she came closer. His bathrobe was fully open now and her breasts jiggled as she approached. They were the perfect shape and so lovely and tanned.

Turning back to the underwear drawer, he searched for an old pair of boxers. There was plenty of Helen's underwear in the drawer, but only a couple of pairs of his pushed to the back. He could smell Helen in the drawer and in the room. It was a different smell from Zoe; not as fresh or as exciting.

He continued digging around, needing time to focus on something mundane to ease his pulsing erection.

"Obviously," he continued as he inspected the contents of the drawer closer than ever before. "I wasn't talking to myself if you were in there with me."

"Exactly! But you didn't know I was there!"

"That's right," John said. "Which leads me to ask, *why* were you there?"

There was silence from behind him. He wasn't going to turn around, he wanted to make sure he got an answer.

"Well?" he picked a pair of boxers, bent over and pulled them up his legs and under the towel, making sure they were positioned correctly before turning around.

"I just wanted to help you, Johnny. Honestly."

"You don't have to help me *that* much," he said as he turned to face her.

She was lying on the bed, her legs and arms apart, the bathrobe flung open. She lay there like an angel with blue wings. Her body shone in the sunlight and she looked more tanned than before, as if the sun's rays were gently caressing her body and warming her, ready for him.

He couldn't help it, his eyes moved from her painted red toenails up along her muscled and perfect legs, and rested on the bare, hairless folds between them. With her legs spread wide, John could see more of her vagina than he had last night. The underside of her perfectly round buttocks and the crack between them drew his eyes up higher to the pink flaps sitting bare and moist and waiting for him. He tried hard to pull his eyes away, but he found it almost impossible. His erection thudded inside his boxers as if it were going to break out.

Oh, God! he thought.

Then she moved.

She brought her knees up and spread her legs even further, widening the gap between them, and opening herself to him even more.

"I just want to help you, Johnny," she whispered.

He tore his eyes from her lovely mound and looked at her face. She smiled back at him once more.

Such an angel, he thought. *Such a beautiful angel.*

His eyes worked their way from her face down along her breasts. They were sitting perfectly still and her nipples were hard and standing on end, like dollops of dark chocolate.

Her stomach rose rhythmically and he could see her ribs through the skin. He was drawn again to her tight muscles and the diamond sitting in her belly button and then lower, once more, to the inviting cleft between her legs.

Such a body, he thought.

"Have you ever thought about having an affair?" she had said to him last night.

Who hasn't? he thought.

His erection was pushing against the boxers and the towel now. If he didn't do something soon the towel would unwind and he'd be in a worse situation.

"You asked me to think about what I would like to do today," she whispered. "I've decided."

John ran a hand through his hair.

"Zoe, look −" he began.

"The only question is whether it's what *you* want to do today too."

"I'm flattered, really I am. But you have to understand, okay? You've got to see that I *love* someone else. I'm spoken for. I'm *with* someone *else!*"

Zoe nodded her head. "I do understand that, Johnny. You told me that last night."

"But you don't seem to understand!"

"I do!" she replied. "That's okay, you love Helen, I'm fine with that. But she's not here *now. I am.* What we do doesn't have anything to do with Helen. Sex has got nothing to do with love."

John sat down next to her and sighed, "Of course it does, Zoe. I don't know what strange ideas Fox put into your head, but I only have sex with the person I love, I don't go around having sex with just anyone."

Zoe's face fell. She grabbed the sides of the bathrobe and wrapped them around her body, cutting off his view.

"So that's all I am?" she whispered. "I'm just *anyone*."

John sighed deeply, "That's not what I meant."

"I'm repulsive, aren't I?" she whispered.

"What?" John stared at her.

"You don't want to have sex with me because I'm repulsive."

"Come on, Zoe. You know you're not."

"You don't want my body. You don't want me. I'm no good to anyone except Ricky Fox."

"Don't talk like that."

"I shouldn't have left him," she mumbled as she crossed her arms over her chest.

"Okay, now you really *are* being stupid," he stood and walked over to his wardrobe. He couldn't take much more of this. "You know that's not true. You know you did the best thing. You had to get out of there."

"Fat lot of good it did me, I'm no use to anyone else now I've been with him. I'm ugly, dirty and tarnished."

He slid open the wardrobe door to look for something to wear. It stuck on the tracks and he had to push harder. Helen's overstocked wardrobe was always too full, making it difficult for him to slide open his door.

I'll have to talk to her about that, he thought. *Again!*

"Don't be silly."

"You hate me."

He turned to face her, his arms spread wide. "Look, Zoe, stop all this. I don't hate you. I like you, I really do. I just won't have *sex* with you, do you understand?"

"But why?" She rolled onto one side to face him and spread the dressing gown open once more so he could look at her again. "Why wouldn't you? What's so repulsive about this?"

He glanced at her body and slowly made his way over to the bed. He kneeled on the ground and looked deep into her brown haunting eyes.

"There's nothing wrong with you, Zoe. Believe me, please? You are the most beautiful girl I have ever met. You caught me with an erection in the shower because I was thinking about *you*, okay? I can't get you out of my head! I'll admit it. Since I found you naked on the sofa last night I haven't been able to get you out of my mind. You're a picture of beauty and I'll probably fantasise about you until the day I die, but I'm in *love. Love!* Do you understand? And even though I'd dearly love to give you what you want, and what I want for that matter, it's not going to happen. Okay?"

He continued to stare at her and he watched as the emotions whipped across her face. Her lip trembled and she half-smiled.

"That's the nicest thing anyone's ever said to me, Johnny," she whispered.

"Well, it's all true," he said.

She took one hand and wrapped the bathrobe around her body.

"Helen's a lucky girl," she said as she leaned forward and kissed him on the forehead. "I'm sorry for all this. So sorry."

"It's okay," he replied as he stood and walked back to his wardrobe. "Just as long as you now understand exactly what I'm talking about."

She giggled, "Yeah, I do. Sorry. I can be so pig-headed sometimes. I always like to get what I want."

John nodded as he picked out a shirt for the day. "That's okay," he said over his shoulder. "As long as you realise you're not going to get *me!*"

She giggled again from behind him. He heard the sounds of the sheets rustling and footsteps on the floor.

"I'm sorry," she said as she came up behind him and hugged him once again.

"Zoe..." he warned.

She stepped back and he turned around to face her. Her arms were stretched out and she had an innocent look on her face.

"Hey, I was just hugging a good friend, that's all. Nothing else!"

She smiled and giggled again.

"Just as well," he gave her a half-hearted stern look.

"Well," she turned around and headed to her suitcase. "I better get dressed so you can show me the town."

"Huh?"

"We've got to fill in some time before Helen comes to meet us at five. You told me to think about something to do today."

"Yes, but I thought –"

"And number two on my list was a guided tour around wonderful Parkhurst," she smiled.

"But shouldn't we stay here? I mean, can you risk being seen outside if Fox is trying to hunt you down?"

She shook her head as she pulled the suitcase up onto the bed and opened it.

"I thought about that, Johnny. But we can sit around here all day doing nothing, with me thinking about Ricky and worrying about what he could do to me if he ever finds me, or you can take my mind off it all by showing me a good time in town somewhere. It's your choice, but I think we both need to get out of this house and to keep our minds occupied, otherwise this bed could be too much of a temptation for *both* of us."

John nodded his head.

Ain't that the truth! he thought.

She turned to face him with her hands on her hips.

"Well?" she said.

"Yeah, I see your point," he agreed. "Maybe we do need to get away from here for a while. It can't hurt, right?"

"Exactly!"

"And we can meet Helen at five and worry about things then."

"That's right."

"Shouldn't you rest up or something? I mean, you've had a pretty hard week."

She shook her head, "Don't worry about me. I feel fine. I bounce back pretty quickly. I just think I need to get my mind off things."

John nodded and smiled. "Okay, you've got a deal."

He cupped his hands around his mouth and shouted, "Murdock's Tours departing in half an hour!"

Zoe giggled, "John, you're such a ham!"

He laughed and turned back around to the wardrobe to reach in and pull out an old pair of jeans.

Helen called this old ratty pair his "weekend jeans."

"You never wear anything else on the weekend," she had said once.

"Hey, it's the *weekend!*" he had replied. "I'll wear anything other than a suit if I can help it. And I *don't* wear them *every* weekend, just *most* weekends!"

They'd laughed about that, right here in this bedroom. They used to laugh about a lot of things before Helen got pregnant and the troubles began. If only she didn't blame herself for losing the baby.

If only...

He hoped she'd be able to find out some news for Zoe. Anything. Even the slightest piece of information might be able to help her decide what to do next.

Then their lives could return to normal.

John smiled as he thought about a normal life. With Helen working long hours and his own late nights at work, he wondered what was *normal* anyway. He thought there must be couples out there who spend the weekend together, trying to cram everything into every minute before it was over and their jobs divided them again. He thought about calling Helen to check how everything was going, but she'd only bark down the phone at him for dragging her away from her work. Just like usual.

She didn't even ask to speak to me when she called, he thought.

He knew she was playing another one of her games. Games were all they played these days.

Five o'clock will get here fast enough, he thought.

He turned around having picked his shirt and jeans and faced Zoe once more.

She was still standing there looking at him, with her hands on her hips, a strange expression on her face – part fear and part anger.

He raised his shoulders. "Did I miss something?"

She giggled and her stern look was broken.

"What?" he asked.

"Ah, I'd like to get dressed," she smiled across the room at him. "You know, in private. But you're kinda, well, in the room with me."

John threw back his head and laughed. "Okay," he said. "Sorry. Don't know what I was thinking."

He turned and headed for the door.

"Thanks," she said as he went.

"No problem. I'll be in the spare bedroom finishing getting dressed, if you need anything."

"Okay."

He walked out into the hallway and closed the door behind him. He smiled. His talk had finally made it through to her, by the looks of things.

Finally, he thought.

"Johnny!" he heard her call through the wall.

"Maybe not," he muttered.

He turned around and walked to the doorway. He knocked on the door before opening it, and then stuck his head through into the bedroom.

"Yes?"

She was sitting on the bed with the bathrobe still around her. Clothes were strewn all over the bed and she was picking through them, as if trying to find something in particular.

She turned to face him with her perfect smile.

"I'm sorry," she said.

"Sorry?" A frown crossed his face, "Sorry for what?"

"For causing you to fantasise about me until the day you die."

He laughed again and then she joined in.

"Believe me," he said between laughs. "You're never going to be someone I forget!"

She giggled again and her eyes fell to the floor. She fiddled with the hem of one of her dresses spread out before her.

"Thanks, Johnny," she said. "I don't know what I'd do or where I'd be without you."

"You'd be going into town alone, that's what you'd be doing. And if you don't hurry up and get dressed, you'll miss the tour!"

Her eyes met his again and she smiled.

"Come on," he said. "Twenty-five minutes is all you've got!"

He closed the door to the sounds of her giggling and headed back down the hallway with his clothes.

He had no idea where he would take her, but he agreed that getting out of the house and getting her mind off everything was probably the best thing for her.

Anything that reminded her of that Fox asshole was probably the last thing she needed right now. And to be perfectly honest, he didn't know how he'd handle it either.

He didn't want to get involved in a potentially violent situation, but what could he do? He couldn't turn his back on one of Helen's friends.

If Helen were here we could all discuss it.

He entered the spare bedroom, sat on the bed, and climbed into his jeans.

Zoe was a hard girl to read; so full of emotions that could change from one moment to the next. One second she's happy and the next she's sad. She wasn't going to be someone he'd be able to handle if she got out of control.

And then he remembered her lying on the bed with his robe around her. Her legs open and inviting, her body so tanned and muscled and tight. He had wanted to, there was no doubt about it.

What man wouldn't? he thought.

But that didn't change anything. Sure, maybe nine out of ten men would have jumped right on that bed and fucked her brains out (after all, she wanted it), but if he did that it would only make things even more complicated for all of them.

He put his arms into his shirt-sleeves and began to button up.

He had to keep control of Zoe, and himself.

For *both* their sakes.

The last thing he needed was Helen walking in and finding them going at it like animals.

But she has such a fine body.

Or worse still, Ricky Fox kicking down the door with a gun in each hand.

The gun!

Shit, John thought. *I didn't move the gun!*

He walked quickly out of the spare bedroom and up the hall, trying hard not to make too much noise and alarm Zoe. He had to hide the gun, just in case it gave her any more flashback memories like last night.

As he left the hall and entered the lounge room, he checked the door to the main bedroom.

It was still shut.

She wasn't ready yet.

Quickly, he turned around to face the kitchen and looked at the hallway entrance.

The gun was gone.

<u>Eight</u>

Ten minutes later, Zoe opened the bedroom door and walked out into the lounge room.

She was wearing blue cut-off jeans that ended just above her knees, an old pair of sneakers and a tight pink top that accentuated her breasts and covered very little else, leaving her arms and stomach bare.

John's eyes looked her over and checked to see if her diamond was still nestled in her belly button. It was.

"Ready," she said as she walked into the room.

"Are you sure you'll be warm enough?" he asked.

Zoe giggled, "Don't worry about me. If you've got it, flaunt it."

John nodded, "That's a flaunt alright."

"Don't be embarrassed, Johnny," she walked closer to him. "It's just skin."

He smiled at her and crossed his arms.

"So, where do you want to go?" he asked.

"Hey, you're the tour guide," Zoe punched him on the shoulder. "I'm in your hands."

"Is there anything in particular you want to do or see?"

Her forehead furrowed as she gave it some thought, and then her eyes lit up and she smiled.

"Can we do some shopping?" she asked.

"*Shopping?*"

"Yeah! I mean, only if you want to, Johnny. But I've only got a small suitcase of stuff and I don't have too many clothes."

"But the bed in there was covered with clothes," he said, remembering the clothes spread around her in the main bedroom.

"That's hardly enough," she said. "Besides, Ricky bought me those clothes and he knows what I wear. I'd like to buy some new stuff. Clothes that have nothing to do with him." Her eyes fell to the floor and she pulled at one of her braids.

"And clothes that make me look different. You understand? Just in case."

John nodded, "Okay, that makes sense."

"And don't worry about the money," Zoe looked into his eyes, took a step forward and grabbed his hands. "I still have the money I took from Ricky. Not much, but enough. I don't expect you to pay for any of it, you know."

"You don't have to convince me any more," John smiled. "A shopping tour it is!"

I can't believe I'm letting myself do this! he thought. *Only for Zoe...*

"Great!" Zoe jumped on the spot. "Let's get going. We've got to be back in time for Helen's phone call at four."

"I know, I know," John turned and headed down the hall towards the front door. "I'm sure we'll have enough time."

He heard Zoe following behind him.

"Don't bet on it, Johnny," she said. "I'm crazy when it comes to shopping."

"Now why doesn't that surprise me?" he said over his shoulder as he grabbed the car keys from the key holder and unlocked the door.

He drove her to the Parkhurst shopping complex and watched as her eyes opened wide as she took it all in.

"It's all so big," she said to him, amazed, as they stood in the entrance.

"Stop kidding around," he said. "It's only a glorified mall."

"But there's people and shops everywhere," she said as she spun around, eager to look at everything; taking in every sight and sound, watching as the people pushed past her.

John was puzzled, "But you've shopped at places like this in the past, right?"

Zoe shook her head. "Ricky was pretty strict when it came to places like this. He said I could have whatever I wanted, just name it and he would have it brought in for me. Just like the Jeep. I mentioned to him that I'd like a red Jeep so we could take some off-road trips and have some fun. And then, bang, out of nowhere, a week later I've got one! But he never took me places like this and I've never shopped in any place like this. Usually his guards or staff would pick things up for me."

"But that's horrible," John replied.

"I know."

"You should've tried to get out of that relationship sooner than you did."

She turned to face him, the excitement in her eyes replaced by sadness.

"Believe me, Johnny," she whispered. "I tried. I truly did."

John stood beside her and placed his right arm around her body. He rubbed her side and squeezed her.

"I thought we were here to shop," he smiled down at her.

She hugged him tight and rested her head on his chest.

"You're right," she said. "No more bad thoughts."

"Exactly."

She lifted her head to stare up at him, "Thanks, Johnny."

"My pleasure." He let her go and looked around the complex. "Where do you want to start?"

"I have no idea," she replied. "There's so much to do and see."

"Well, don't get too excited. You're on a budget, remember.""Yeah, I know," Zoe dug deep into her left pocket and pulled out a roll of cash. "I suppose I should count it first."

She opened the wad of money and started to count.

John watched as she counted the notes. They were all hundred dollar bills. He became increasingly nervous as Zoe counted higher and higher. They stood at the entrance of the shopping complex with people charging past on every side.

Zoe stopped counting at four thousand, seven hundred dollars.

"Do you think that's enough?" she asked him, holding the money out to him.

He reached out and rolled it up in her hands, "Put it away before we're mugged."

"Don't worry," she smiled. "I can handle myself."

"Yeah, well, put it away anyway."

"I'm sure I can spend it all in one afternoon without any problem. I've forgotten how exciting it is to shop."

"Hang on," John interrupted. "Is that all the money you have? Don't go spending it all, you'll need it to begin your life again. To buy food or rent a place and other things."

Zoe patted his shoulder, "Don't worry so much. I have my own savings. This is just the money I took from Ricky. It's the only thing that still binds me to him. I don't want the money, so I'm gonna spend it to start my life over."

"Okay, just checking."

"Don't worry so much Johnny." She smiled. "I have lots of plans and dreams I'm going to make sure happen."

"Just don't lose your head when you see all these nice things."

"I won't. Anyway, you'll be there to stop me buying anything too silly, right?"

"Right," he smiled at her.

"And if I ever run out of money, I can go back to making coffees behind a counter at a café somewhere."

He laughed, "Yeah, or research."

"Huh?"

"You know, researching. Being a researcher."

"Oh, yeah, that too." She looked around once more, her eyes dancing from shop window to shop window. "Shall we?" she said.

"Go for it."

* * *

They stopped at a coffee shop just after half past two. Zoe found them a table and began to squeeze all her parcels into the seat next to her. Some of them were too bulky, so she placed them on the table.

"Anything to eat?" he asked her.

"Nah, I'm not hungry. But I'd love a mineral water."

John walked to the counter and ordered a coffee and a mineral water from the waitress.

The shop was dingy and run down, and he was glad they weren't eating any of the food that was slowly being nuked under the heat lamps in front of him. Anyway, they were going to have an early dinner with Helen, so he didn't feel forced to have a meal now. He was more tired than hungry anyway. Zoe had shopped like he had never seen anyone shop before.

He turned to face her while he was waiting for the drinks. She was surrounded by her purchases and they made her seem even smaller as they surrounded her. He wasn't sure how much money she had left, but there couldn't be much.

As he watched, she excitedly pawed through each of the bags, as if checking what each contained.

Maybe she's already forgotten what she's bought, John thought and laughed to himself.

From where he stood he was looking at her from side-on. He could see her ribcage and her muscles as they flexed and stretched while she reached for a bag almost out of her grasp. Her tanned skin looked warm and inviting and so beautiful against her pink top. She looked so feminine and yet so strong. Her legs tensed as she lifted herself slightly off the chair and the muscles in her arms tightened as she pushed through her purchases. The two braids swung in the air as she turned her head, deciding which package she would search through next.

John smiled.

Who could hurt someone so sweet?

He paid for the drinks and took them back to the table.

"Is there enough room here for me?" he asked as he sat down opposite her and placed the drinks on the table.

She smiled at him but said nothing.

"Drink up," he said. "We'd better be leaving soon so we're back in time to get that phone call from Helen."

Zoe nodded and unscrewed the top of her mineral water bottle. She placed it to her lips and took two big gulps.

"Better?" he asked.

She nodded and placed the bottle back on the table. Then she smiled and held out her hand, palm outstretched for him to take.

He tilted his head to one side, but then followed her example. He held out his hand and she clasped it firmly and shook it.

"Zoe Barber," she said. "Nice to meet you."

John's forehead creased in puzzlement.

"Ah, John Murdock," he replied.

She let go of his hand and took another mouthful of water.

"It's nice to be properly introduced, don't you think?" she smiled. "We didn't get around to doing that last night."

"Yeah," John sipped his coffee. "I guess so. Very formal of you, though."

"I'm just an old fashioned girl," she winked back at him.

"Yeah, I can see that."

One corner of her mouth turned upwards in a smirk, "I hope you're not besmirching my reputation with that comment."

"Well, I'm sure old fashioned girls don't wear cut-off jeans and pink tops that cover hardly anything."

"They do these days."

"Or have pierced belly buttons with diamonds in them."

"Do I embarrass you?" she asked, her smirk now growing to the other side of her mouth.

"No, you don't. I'm just saying –"

"I think you're embarrassed being seen in public with me!"

"No, you're wrong."

"Or maybe you're just turned on by it all."

John took a gulp of coffee. It was too hot and burned his tongue.

"Maybe you *like* the idea of being seen with me in public. Maybe you *love* it when other zguys look me over and think to themselves 'Yeah, I'd love to screw her. That guy's *really* lucky to have her.' Maybe you like it all but just won't admit it."

John could feel his cock start to grow hard and push against the inside of his jeans. He just shook his head and tried to look exasperated. But he knew he was failing dismally.

"Am I right?" Zoe leaned closer to him, her eyes narrowed as she whispered. "You're turned on by it all, right? Maybe *you're* the old fashioned one."

He laughed, "Yeah, right. That's me! I'm old fashioned? I don't think so."

"Maybe Helen's held you back," she whispered. "Maybe she's not putting out for you any more. Maybe there's no excitement left in your life. Huh? Am I close?" she tilted her head to one side, as if awaiting a response. "Stop me anytime if I'm wrong, Johnny. I mean, I know you love her and I know you're married to her and all that, but have you ever thought that maybe it could have been the wrong decision? Have you ever wondered if you *hadn't* married her what your life might be like?"

She paused and sat back, waiting for his answer.

John just stared at his coffee.

"Are you *embarrassed* by Helen, Johnny? Do you go shopping with her and bring her here for coffee? I bet you don't. Or do you both live your own separate lives with separate interests and only ever meet over a defrosted TV dinner at home?"

John sipped his coffee and looked around the shop.

"Come on Johnny, I've opened myself up to you, I've told you all my dirty secrets and problems. I *confided* in you Johnny! It looks like it's time for you to confide in me."

John stared back at the coffee.

"It's eating you up inside and you have to speak out. Get it off your chest. I did last night and I feel a million bucks now. Try it, you'll like it. Please?"

She reached out and took his hands in hers. His eyes rose to meet hers while his erection throbbed under the table.

"We've all got our dirty little secrets, Johnny," she smiled. "Sometimes it helps if you tell someone. Care to tell me yours?"

John pulled back from her and removed his hands from the table.

"This isn't helping either of us," he whispered.

"But it would if you'd let it."

"Not here," he said, looking around the lunch bar. "Not now."

Zoe sat back in her own chair and crossed her arms over her pink top.

"Alright," she nodded. "Have it your way. But I want you to remember that I'm here for you, okay?"

John nodded.

"If you ever want to talk, or anything, I'll listen."

"Okay," John said.

"Good," she smiled and finished off her mineral water with one last mouthful.

"But it felt good, didn't it, Johnny?" she smirked. "Shopping with me."

John smiled and then nodded, "Yeah. It made me feel young again."

Zoe laughed out loud and then clasped her hand over her mouth until she calmed down. "Come on, Johnny. Don't go all *grandpa* on me. 'It made me feel young again,'" she mimicked his voice and then laughed again. "You're only three years older than me."

"I don't feel it."

"That's life getting you down," she said. "Stick with me and I'll soon get you regenerated."

John's hands rested in his lap, trying hard to push his erection away from the underside of the table.

"That's what worries me," he smiled.

She smiled back and ran her eyes over his face, as if looking for something she hadn't seen before. Her hands automatically went to each of her braids to check they were still in place and not coming undone.

She looks so hot in those braids and pink top, John thought. *Imagine how good she'd be sitting on top of you.*

Then he wished he hadn't as his erection found new life.

Zoe turned in her seat and started to dive through her packages again.

"I've got a present for you," she said as she searched.

"Really?" John replied, happy to change the conversation and get his mind off other things.

"Yeah, somewhere..." she continued looking. "I picked it up when you went for a browse through the men's section of that last store."

"You didn't have to do that," he said before sipping his coffee again.

"It's a pleasure, and at least this way you'll always have something that will remind you of me."

"Yeah, like I need *reminding*," he rolled his eyes.

She looked at him out of the corner of her eyes. "Don't be naughty or you won't get it," she said.

"Sorry, Mistress," he replied and smiled at her.

She stopped searching through her bags and turned to face him. She was silent for a moment as her face changed with her thoughts. Then she smiled again and continued looking, this time through another bag.

"Ahh!" she yelled with excitement and victory. "Got it!"

She pulled out a small black box and handed it over the table to him.

"From me to you," she said.

"It's not that gold Rolex I've always wanted is it?" he smiled at her.

Zoe slapped her forehead with her hand, "*Now* you tell me!"

John pulled the lid off the box and stared down at a shining silver key ring; at one end was an eye-bolt and the ring at the other end held one single red key.

"Thanks," he said, genuinely surprised.

"See," she reached over and took it from the box. "It's got this handy little bolt thingy at this end which allows you to slip it over a belt loop in your jeans and carry your keys on your hip! You'll have them with you at all times and won't have to worry about leaving them near the front door or losing them or anything. They'll always be hooked to your hip."

John pointed to the red key hanging from the other end of the key ring. It was an odd shape and design, not like a normal door key. It was less sophisticated and had only three large teeth. John had no idea what it was for. He'd never seen a key like it before.

"And that's the key to...?" he prompted.

"My heart?" she smiled. "Or some sunken treasure? Fort Knox?"

John began to laugh.

"Maybe it's the key to disarm all nuclear warheads?" she continued. "Or a prison cell?"

She giggled with him now as she handed him back the key ring.

"Or maybe it's the key to freedom," she whispered.

John took the key ring from her, "Thanks. I really like it."

"I've used it once," she said, her eyes burrowing through him. "Maybe you'll need to use it one day."

John stared back at her, unsure whether she was being serious or just joking.

After a long pause, he said, "Well, thank you, it's very nice and a lovely thought. But you shouldn't have bought it."

"It's my pleasure. And it's solid silver too!"

"Yeah, I can tell," he weighed it in his hands. "Heavy."

"Strong things for strong men," she said. "We petite ladies can't be seen sporting those kinds of things around town."

Zoe giggled again.

"I hope you like it," she said.

"I do, Zoe," John replied. "Thank you."

He tested the eye-bolt a couple of times, drawing back the trigger and watching the catch open.

"Go on," she said. "Put your keys on it."

While Zoe watched, John pulled his keys from his pocket and transferred them from his old key ring to the new one.

"There," he said when he was done. "Easy!"

"Perfect," Zoe beamed. "It'll look so good on you."

He placed the key ring in his left hand and brought it down towards his left hip.

"Hey, hang on," Zoe said.

"Huh?"

"Wrong side," she pointed to his left hip.

"What?"

"It goes on your right hip."

"Right, left," he shrugged his shoulders. "What's the difference? It's the same thing."

Zoe shook her head, "Nope. You're wrong. It's got to go on your right hip."

"But, Zoe, I'd prefer it on my left," John replied.

"You just told me right, left what's the difference! So you shouldn't mind wearing it on your right hip."

"But I –"

"*Please*, Johnny," she pouted. "For me?"

John let out a deep sigh, "Left, right, right, left..."

He took the key ring from his left hand and transferred it to his right. He held up his right hand so Zoe could see the key ring easily and then he pointed to his right hip.

"Right hip," he mouthed silently to her.

She giggled and was smiling once again.

John found the belt loop on his right hip, pulled back the trigger on the key ring to open the eye-hook and hooked it around the loop. He stood up and moved to the side of the table where he modelled the key ring for Zoe; swinging his hips from side to side so that the keys jingled.

"And what does madam think?" he asked in a mock-English accent.

Zoe laughed louder, "Madam is impressed."

"Good," John smiled at her and then looked at his watch. "We'd better get going. It's quarter-past three and we want to be home in time to get that call from Helen."

Zoe nodded. She stood up and began to gather all her parcels together.

"You should have a cell phone, Johnny," she said. "Then we wouldn't have to race home."

"Don't like them," he said. "They give you brain cancer."

Zoe laughed as she turned around to face him with all her bags in her hands.

"And people can always find you," Zoe said.

"That too," John agreed. "Is that why you don't have one?"

"You don't need one if you're stuck in a house all day surrounded by guards," Zoe said. "Ricky always knew where I was."

Her smile disappeared as she looked to the floor.

John took hold of her bags and gave her a quick hug.

"Come on," he said. "Enough of that. Let's not spoil a great day so far."

"Okay," she nodded. "I'll try."

"And I don't want your tears staining my new-fangled key ring, either," he said as he bumped his right hip against hers.

Zoe's laugh drowned out the sound of keys jingling.

"You didn't take the red key off the ring when you put all your keys on it," she said as they walked out of the coffee shop.

"Why would I?" he said. "You said it was the key to free-dom."

"It is," she replied.

"Well, maybe I *will* need it one day," he said.

She looked up at him and smiled.

"You never know," she said.

"That's right," he agreed. "You never know."

<u>Nine</u>

John drove the car along his street with a little less than ten minutes to spare before four o'clock.

The trip home had been a quiet one. Zoe hadn't said much and even though John had tried to start a conversation, he realised that this trip meant the end of the fun and the start, once again, of all the worry and problems with Fox.

He hoped Helen had found out something useful for Zoe. Otherwise she was going to be in this uncertain state for days, maybe weeks.

Where will she go? he thought to himself. *She can't stay here; not for weeks or months. That's bound to cause problems.*

"You okay?" he had asked.

She only nodded and continued to stare out the side window.

"Feel free to put the radio on if you like."

She had turned to him then and smiled, "Thanks, Johnny. I think that just might help the situation."

She reached over and scanned the stations until she found something that she liked.

The music was too loud for John's taste, but he wasn't about to stop her listening to it if it helped her.

The loud beat actually gave them both much-needed time to think.

And before long, John was turning into the driveway.

"And here we are," he turned to face Zoe as he brought the car to a stop in the driveway.

She smiled at him.

John turned down the music on the radio.

"Murdock Tours hope you enjoyed your day," he said with his hands cupped over his mouth. "Please take time to look through our gift shop and pick up some of our brochures detailing other exciting Murdock Tours!"

Zoe giggled and slapped him on the shoulder, "You idiot."

"All part of the service ma'am," he replied as he mimed tipping his hat in her direction.

"A question for the tour operator," she put up her hand and batted her eyelids.

"Yes, little lady, what can I do for you?"

"Are we going to sit here all day or what? A certain little lady has had too much mineral water and needs to use the bathroom."

John laughed, reached over and opened the glove compartment. Sitting inside was a small zip-top leather pouch. He picked it up and handed it to her.

"Open it," he said.

She pulled back the zip and placed her fingers inside, pulling out a handful of keys.

"Spares," he said.

"Great!"

He pushed some keys around until he found the one attached to a chain with a small blue plastic alien hanging from it.

"This is it," he lifted it up for her to take. "The front door key."

Zoe giggled, "You're the best tour operator ever. Such service! And I bet the bathrooms will be spotless."

"Of course!"

He returned the rest of the keys to the pouch, zipped up the top and threw it back into the glove compartment.

"Out you get," he said to her. "I'll bring in your bags."

She smiled and pecked him lightly on the cheek, "And such a gentleman too."

As she climbed from the car, he tapped her on the shoulder.

"One thing," he said.

"Anything."

"Open the garage door for me, please?"

She turned around and smirked at him. "And I thought you were a gentleman," she said.

"Hey I'm bringing in all those large and heavy bags!"

"Ha, ha."

As she ran around to the front of the car, he watched her buttocks jiggle in her cut-off jeans.

Some women just have it all, he thought to himself.

She bent down to open the garage door, pointing her butt in the air and wiggling it as she worked the handle.

"Jesus," he muttered to himself as he watched. "What an ass."

Then she stood and pulled the garage door. It swung up past her and thudded into position in the ceiling of the garage.

"Voila," she mouthed as she swept her hands forward allowing him access to the garage.

He mimed tipping his hat to her again and drove forward into the garage.

He pulled up just short of the back wall and beside Helen's car. He turned off the engine. The music on the radio stopped at the same time. He was thankful for that. A bit of peace and quiet would help him think better than anything else.

He looked in the rear-view mirror but could see no sign of Zoe. She'd probably turned and run straight for the front door to get to the bathroom as soon as possible.

The bags in the back of the car reminded John of the wonderful few hours he had spent with her.

Everything was so easy and simple. She lived only for the moment and could be amused or distracted by simple, everyday things.

Such an easy life, he thought to himself. *Yeah, right. Who are you kidding? She's spent years being beaten every second night by Fox. Yeah, great life!*

But what would she do now?

Maybe she was trying not to think about it, but John knew he had to.

If that prick Fox was dead, then everything was fine and he couldn't come after her. But what if it wasn't that easy? What if some of his guards and employees actually did phone the police and get them involved? Fox may not be hunting her any more, but the police might be. There was no way that he and Helen could hide her out here for long.

They've got a term for that, "accessory after the fact" or "harbouring a wanted criminal" or something, he thought.

And that was the *easy* option.

What if Fox wasn't dead? What if he had only been knocked unconscious and was now on her trail and hunting her down, determined to kill her, and anyone helping her?

And what if Helen came back and said she couldn't find anything? That didn't necessarily mean that Fox was dead or alive. They'd still be in limbo wondering whether he was coming after them or not. That was the worst situation of all.

John rubbed his hands over his face.

Nothing's ever easy, he thought. *Nothing.*

He climbed from the car and shut his door. He stood looking out into the street, focussing on the houses opposite.

"Does everyone have such a complicated life?" he muttered.

Then he turned and stared over at Helen's car. He hoped she would have good news for them. He opened the back door and climbed in to grab Zoe's shopping bags. It looked to him as if they had multiplied in the back of the car on the way home. She brought new meaning to the phrase, "Spending up a storm."

John laughed to himself. "Well, it's her money...or it was."

He dragged out the bags, shut the car door and walked out of the garage. He looked up at the garage door and thought about closing it, but changed his mind. He'd have to put all the shopping bags down to do it, and he couldn't really be bothered. Anyway, they were going to meet Helen in an hour or so for dinner, so he decided to leave the door open.

There's no law against it, he thought as he walked up the paved path towards the front door.

As he walked, he managed to hook his new key ring through the belt loop on his right hip.

"Got to keep her happy," he muttered. "Left, right, what's the difference?"

The bags were beginning to get heavier so he quickened his pace. He looked ahead, hoping to see Zoe coming to help him carry her purchases, but there was only the front door.

The *open* front door.

The door was wide open, the little blue alien hanging from the key.

The key still in the lock.

"Shit," John said as he dropped the bags and sprinted for the door.

<u>Ten</u>

John sprinted up the hallway and found Zoe by the phone in the lounge room.

She turned around with a surprised look on her face.

"What is it?" she yelled.

"Huh?" he said, peering around the room, looking for any sign of trouble.

"Johnny, what's *wrong?*"

He caught his breath, "I was going to ask you the same question!"

"I don't understand."

"Well, I saw the front door wide open and the key still in the lock and I thought…well, I don't know, I thought there was trouble."

Zoe smiled and walked to him. She hugged him hard and looked up at him.

"Are you my knight in shining armour, here to save me?" she whispered.

"More like your unfit friend in trembling terror."

She laughed and swatted his chest.

"Don't worry," she turned and headed for the bathroom. "I had to rush in because the phone was ringing."

John looked around the room once more, trying to convince himself everything was fine.

"Really?" he finally said. "Was it Helen?"

He turned to find himself alone in the room. Zoe had gone.

The bathroom.

John's mind was starting to clear and function properly again. He ran his fingers through his hair.

Calm down, he thought. *Don't go all paranoid all of a sudden.*

He turned and walked back down the hall and outside once more. He swept his eyes along the street. Nothing was

out of place. All looked fine apart from the number of shopping bags scattered around his front lawn.

He hoped no one had seen him make a fool of himself
and was even now waiting for a second performance.

Luckily, everything seemed okay.

He walked down to the bags, bent over and picked them
all up. He turned and headed back to the front door.

Zoe's had enough crazies in her life already, he thought.
Don't add to that tally now.

He placed the spare front door key on the key holder as
he closed the front door. He walked back up the hallway and
Zoe appeared at the kitchen door.

"Coffee?" she asked.

"Yeah, why not." He struggled past her with the bags.
"Where do you want me to put these?"

"Just on the bed, near my suitcase," she said.

"Okay."

John walked across the lounge room and into the main
bedroom. He dropped the bags on the bed, glad to be rid of
them, and headed back to the lounge.

Zoe was waiting for him on the sofa. She watched him
as he came towards her.

He couldn't read the expressions on her face; there was
no happiness or sadness.

"Well?" he asked.

"That was Helen," she said in a low voice.

"I gathered that," he sat down next to her on the sofa
and placed a hand on her bare knee, trying to comfort her.

"And?" he said.

"She wants to meet us at five thirty."

"Ahuh, but did she find anything?"

"That's just it, Johnny," Zoe leaned closer to his face. He
could feel her breath on his lips. "She didn't say."

"What do you mean?"

"She said she couldn't talk now, but she wanted to meet
us at five thirty at the entrance to the Kmart on Elizabeth
Street."

"And that's it?"

"That's it."

"Nothing more?"

"Nothing more."

"She didn't ask to talk with me?"

"No, she just hung up," she replied.

John shrugged. He wasn't surprised. He wondered what he had done with the flowers he had brought home last night. He sighed deeply. He didn't know why he tried anymore.

"But why at the Kmart?" he asked.

"She said it's exactly halfway between here and the hospital," she replied.

John nodded, sat back on the sofa and sighed again.

After a long silence, Zoe turned to face him.

"I'm scared, Johnny."

He pulled her to him and hugged her tight.

"Don't worry, we'll sort it out," he whispered.

I'm scared too, he thought.

They arrived at the car park at quarter past five. Finding a parking spot was easy. The car park was more than half empty, the peak shopping hours well and truly over for the day.

John pulled into a space right in front of the entrance of the Kmart and turned off the engine.

"Well, here we are," he turned to face Zoe.

She hadn't said a word as they drove; thoughts and emotions played across her face while she stared out the window and fiddled with her braids.

"Do you think she's found out anything, Johnny?" she asked in a quiet voice.

"I don't know," he replied. "Only time will tell."

She nodded and turned to face him.

"I'm grateful, you know," she said. "For everything you've done for me."

"That's okay," he said.

"I just landed on your doorstep last night and both Helen and you have been so helpful in every way. I couldn't have got this far without you both."

She reached over and kissed him on the cheek.

"We'll help in any way we can," he said.

She shuddered and rubbed her bare arms with her hands.

"You should've brought a coat, you'll get cold."

"I'm not cold," she replied. "Just scared."

"Don't be."

"It's hard not to be."

"I know."

They sat in the car for a few minutes, saying nothing. They both stared at the entrance to the Kmart.

From where they sat they could see some of the staff behind the counters. Occasionally one or two of the staff would turn and stare back out at them.

A small stream of people continued leaving the complex. John watched people head for their cars with parcels in their hands.

Life is so easy for some, he thought.

He turned to look at Zoe.

She sat staring at the entrance to Kmart. Her breathing was deep and rhythmical, her chest expanding and deflating in a slow, measured action. Her breasts lifted and fell in time with her breath. From side on, he couldn't see the diamond in her belly button, but he could see the ring that held it there.

Such a beauty, he thought. *She deserves none of this crap from Fox.*

He turned back to watch the entrance too.

John looked at his watch: 5:30.

"What will you do?" he asked her.

She shook her head, "I don't know."

"Do you have family somewhere? Or friends?"

Zoe pried her eyes from the entrance and faced him.

"My parents split up when I was little. I lived with my mother. My father just left us. I haven't seen him for years. I don't have a clue where he is, and I don't think I want to know, anyway. My mother got sick and died when I was young." Her eyes fell into her lap. "We had a funeral and everything," she continued. "It was horrible."

John reached over and touched her hand, "I'm sorry."

Zoe shook her head. "Don't worry, it was a long time ago. People forget."

"But the pain never goes," he said.

"No, it doesn't. It was one of the worst days of my life."

"But what about friends?"

"Most of my friends were Ricky's friends. I've got no one else. If I go to them they'll tell Ricky where I am."

"If he's still alive."

"Yeah, if he's still alive."

John took a deep breath.

Here we go, he thought. *For better or for worse.*

"Well, you'll just have to stay with us until this whole thing blows over," he smiled at her.

She lifted her head and looked deep into his eyes. Her face changed from a look of sadness to amazement and then happiness.

"Are you serious?" she asked.

"I certainly am!"

"But...really? What will Helen say?"

She'll kill me, he thought.

"I'm sure Helen will agree with me. You're safest with us at the moment and you can stay for as long as you like."

Zoe's jaw dropped and she jumped in her seat, "Unbelievable!" She reached over and hugged John hard. "You're the greatest, Johnny," she said. "I love you."

"We can't have you facing all these problems by yourself," he continued. "You can stay with us until you work out a plan or set yourself up somewhere. I might even be able to pull some strings at work and get you a job part time or something."

You're going over the top, he thought. *Don't promise her what you can't deliver.*

But it's Zoe! I can't not help her!

She hugged him harder. "You're the best, Johnny."

"It's the least we can do."

She sat back in her seat and checked her braids. Her face clouded for a second.

"But why are you doing this for me?" she asked.

"You're in trouble," he replied. "Friends help other friends in times of trouble."

"It could get dangerous," she whispered.

"You've got a better chance with us than on your own."

"Are you willing to risk all?" she asked, her eyes drilling into him. "Everything you own and everyone you know?"

"Let's hope it won't come to that," he replied.

"It might."

It's worth the risk, he thought.

He didn't know why he would risk it all for Zoe.

Yes, you do, just look at her!

She deserves better...

You can't give it to her, you're already in a relationship.

But I can try and help her.

John looked over to the entrance again and stared back at the staff staring at them. He glanced at his watch. 5:40.

"Where is she?" he said.

"Maybe she's just late."

"She shouldn't be," John continued. "The hospital isn't that far from here."

"Could she have been delayed by something?"

"I doubt it, not from something this important."

They sat in the car and waited.

* * *

At 6pm the police car entered the car park.

John didn't notice it at first, but as it drew closer it caught his eye. When it pulled in next to them, it really got his attention.

A bulky uniformed officer with dark glasses and a moustache climbed from the car, gave them a sideways glance, and strolled into the building.

"She definitely said the Kmart on Elizabeth Street?" John asked as he turned back to face Zoe.

She nodded, "No doubt about it."

He sat staring at her and then glanced at his watch again, just to make sure it was 6pm.

"And she said five-thirty?"

Zoe sighed, "Yes, Johnny, she did. I'm not likely to get those two pieces of information wrong. I'm not stupid."

"Okay, okay," John eased back. "I'm not saying you are. I'm just double checking."

"Is there another entrance somewhere? Maybe around the back?"

"Nope, this is it. I'm sure of it."

"And this is the only Kmart in this area?"

He nodded, "Yep, and the only one on Elizabeth Street, that's for sure."

John swivelled in his seat to look out the back window of the car.

The sun was just beginning its descent.

"This doesn't look good," Zoe said.

"Maybe she *is* caught up at the hospital," John mumbled. "Or went straight home or something."

"But she said five-thirty," Zoe stared unblinkingly at the entrance. "Five-thirty at the Kmart on Elizabeth Street."

"Let's give her a bit more time," John said.

"Five-thirty…"

"She might turn up any minute and we can breathe a sigh of relief."

"Kmart…"

"And then we'll blast her for being so damn late."

"Elizabeth Street…"

The loud rap on the window made them both jump.

Zoe let out a yelp and John's hand automatically went for the key in the ignition.

He turned and looked out the driver's window.

Standing above the car was a man in a dark blue uniform. He was wearing dark sunglasses and his moustache twitched into a half smile. One hand was making a circular motion, indicating for John to wind his window down, and the other was resting on his gun that was still sitting in its hip holster.

"Shit," John muttered as he smiled through the glass and began to slowly wind down the window.

"Evening, sir," the police officer said as he squatted by the car.

"Hello," John replied. "You gave us quite a shock."

The officer tilted his head and smiled at Zoe.

"Hello," he said.

"Hi," Zoe replied in a small quiet voice.

"Didn't mean to give you both a scare," he continued. "But the staff inside are somewhat concerned that you've been sitting here in this spot for almost an hour, just watching them. I'm sure you can appreciate that this has made them a bit nervous."

"Are you serious?" John asked, amazed.

"As I said, sir," the officer continued. "I'm sure you can understand their concern."

John sighed and then nodded. "I understand. But we *are* waiting for someone. They were supposed to be here at five-thirty."

The officer nodded, checked his watch and scratched at his moustache. "Well, doesn't look like they're gonna make it, does it?"

"What do you mean?" Zoe asked.

The officer nodded towards the entrance to the Kmart. "Lady, the staff inside have voiced concerns about you loitering here in their car park."

"We are *not* loitering," Zoe replied.

"I understand," John said, putting up a hand to silence her.

"So I'm going to have to ask you to move on," the officer said. "Just doing my job, you understand."

"But this is a public car park," Zoe continued. "You can't ask us to leave!"

"Look," the officer sighed. "It's Saturday night and there's a game on TV that I ain't gonna miss. I'm not *asking* you to leave, I'm *ordering*. And unless you want me to radio in for backup, I suggest you get moving. *Now!*"

The officer started to undo his holster.

John nodded, "Okay, okay. We understand."

"Good. Wise move, sir. You two have a good evening now," the officer smiled as he stood and walked away from the car.

"I don't believe that. What'll we do now?" Zoe asked.

John shrugged. "Nothing much we can do. We might as well go home. If Helen turns up here late and sees we're not here, she'll just have to drive on home and meet us there."

Zoe sat back into her seat and stared ahead once more at the Kmart entrance. She poked her tongue out at the staff still watching them from inside.

John reached over and touched her leg.

"Don't worry," he said. "Everything will work out."

She smiled and placed a hand on his, "I sure hope so."

John started the engine and backed out of the space. In the rear-view mirror he saw the police officer leaning up against his patrol car and watching them leave. John waved his hand out the window to the officer, but the officer didn't wave back, he just stood there stroking his moustache.

* * *

As they merged with traffic on the main highway, Zoe jumped in her seat.

"Got it," she said.

"Got what?"

"Helen must've found out something really important and it's holding her up. She can't call us because you don't have a cell phone."

"They cause brain cancer," he reminded her.

"She's still at the hospital finding out more details!" her smile beamed at him.

"Probably," he said. "Sounds good to me."

"So, what are we waiting for?" she asked, her arms spread wide.

John glanced over at her.

"You're right," he said. "Let's do it!"

He pulled over to the side of the road and waited for a break in traffic. When the road was clear, he did a u-turn and headed in the opposite direction.

"Parkhurst Hospital, here we come!"

Within five minutes they were sitting in another car park.

The Parkhurst Hospital public car park was dotted with cars, as well as with people and families coming and going as visiting hours were in full swing.

"If Mohamed won't come to the mountain…," John quoted as he turned off the engine.

Zoe giggled, "Do you think Mohamed was ever threatened by a cop?"

John laughed.

"Probably," he said. "You know how pesky those police officers can be."

They climbed from the car and headed towards the hospital entrance.

Zoe shivered as she walked.

"Cold or scared?" he asked.

"A little bit of both, I think."

As they walked towards the entrance, a young couple with two children left the building and started walking towards them. The father held his young son by the hand and the mother held a new-born baby across her chest.

John smiled at the father as they passed by.

"You don't have kids," Zoe said as they continued walking to the entrance.

"No," John mumbled.

"It looks like you want some," she continued, using her thumb to point over her shoulder in the direction of the couple who had walked by.

"I do," he said. "But…well, we tried and…there were some problems."

"Oh," Zoe replied. "Sorry."

"It's not your fault. But it hasn't been easy. Helen's been a bit distant since."

She nodded, "I'm sorry, Johnny. I really am."

He turned to look at her and smiled.

"Come on. Don't worry about it," he said. "Let's find Helen."

They entered the hospital and walked over to the reception area. The clean, sterile smell of the place wafted over John as they walked up to speak with the receptionist.

I hate hospitals, he thought.

And then he wondered if he really did hate them, or whether he hated the memories of bringing his wife home after the operation.

"Your sex life will be back to normal in around six weeks," the doctor had told them. "There's nothing to worry about."

Six weeks, he thought. It had been *three years!*

The receptionist smiled at him.

"Good evening," he smiled back. "Could you tell Helen Murdock her husband is down in reception for her?"

"Sure," the receptionist smiled and picked up the phone.

John turned to find Zoe standing at the hospital gift shop, staring through the window at the toys on display. Her face was full of wonder and excitement.

Who needs kids? John asked himself. *When I have Zoe.*

Her finger pointed through the glass at a large brown bear, then it moved down to a blue elephant, and then over to an overstuffed penguin.

"Mr Murdock?"

John turned around to face the receptionist.

"Mrs Murdock isn't in her office. Should I page her for you?"

"That'd be great," he smiled and walked over to the waiting area where he took a seat on a large leather couch.

He smiled at the man sitting in a hard-backed chair near the couch. The man smiled back and then continued to read his magazine.

As John sat down Zoe swung around and smiled at him.

"I like this one," she mouthed silently to him while pointing at a lounging leopard on the top shelf.

He smiled and nodded to her.

She giggled and quickly made her way across to him. She climbed onto the couch and kneeled next to him.

"Will you buy it for me?" she asked.

"What? The leopard?"

"Yeah," she nodded as she ran a hand playfully through his hair. "It reminds me of you."

John grabbed her hand and placed it on her lap. "I don't think so."

"Please?" she whined loudly.

The man in the chair glanced up from his magazine and looked at both John and Zoe.

"Hi there," Zoe waved.

The man went back to reading his magazine.

"Asshole," she muttered.

"Sshh," John whispered. "Don't be an idiot."

"I want the leopard."

"Why?"

"I want to call it Johnny the leopard."

"Ah-uh. I'm no leopard."

Zoe giggled, "Yes, you are."

"Am I?"

"Sure you are?"

"Why?"

"Because you never change your spots," she whispered as she ran a finger down the side of his cheek.

"Very funny."

"It's true."

"Well, the store is closed now, so I couldn't buy it even if I wanted to."

"Get Helen to pick it up for me."

John laughed. "Yeah, I can see her doing that. 'Honey, could you possibly pick up the leopard in the hospital gift shop for Zoe, she says it reminds her of me.'" John shook his head. "That would go down really well.""Tell her I want it and I'm paying for it."

"Here's an idea," he said. "Why don't *you* tell her you want it and *give* her the money for it?"

Zoe swatted John's wrist and sat back on the couch, "There's no fun in that."

They sat there in silence for a minute or two.

There was very little to do in the reception area. John glanced over at the man reading the magazine. He was sitting straight in the chair and his eyes were concentrating hard on the article. While he sat there, his right leg shook up and down non-stop, like he was trying to keep time with some extremely fast music that only he could hear.

The receptionist waved at John and caught his eye. "I'll page her again for you," she said.

John smiled back at her, "Thanks."

Zoe sighed deeply and reached across him to pick up a magazine from a nearby magazine table. As she did so, her smell enveloped him and her right braid brushed against his cheek.

Just what I don't need, he thought. *Helen walking in and seeing Zoe all over me.*

He pushed her back in the seat.

"I was just going to get a magazine," she pouted.

"Ask and I'll pass you one."

"You won't know which one I want."

He reached into the magazine pile, picked one out and handed it to her.

"I don't want 'Home Beautiful'," she mumbled.

"Yes, you do."

"It's boring."

"You can look for ideas for your new home," he said.

"Very funny," she said as she threw it across him.

The magazine hit the side of the pile and slipped to the floor, taking a couple of others with it.

Zoe shrugged, "Almost."

The man looked up at Zoe from his magazine and frowned.

"Don't know what he thinks he's looking at," she mumbled. "Old pervert."

"That's enough," John said sternly.

"I bet he's got no family or friends," Zoe crossed her arms in front of her, hiding her belly button. "Thinks he can have a free look at something he'll never have."

John sat forward in the couch and turned to face her, blocking her view of the man.

"Please, Zoe. *Enough*, okay? We're here to help *you* so please try to behave."

Her frown turned into a smile as she looked deeply into his eyes.

"Okay, Johnny, I'm sorry. Whatever you say."

"Good."

She grabbed his hand and squeezed it softly.

"What happened?" she asked.

"Huh?"

"Between you and Helen."

"I don't understand?"

"You said there were some problems, that's why you didn't have kids."

"Yeah, we tried. She even got pregnant at one stage..." he couldn't finish the sentence.

"Oh, Johnny," Zoe sat closer to him and rubbed his back. "I'm sorry."

"It went wrong," he whispered.

"I understand," she nodded. "It happens."

"Yeah."

"That's too bad."

"They had to operate so Helen wouldn't have any problems herself."

"I see," Zoe said. "They operated, but she can't have children?" she whispered.

He nodded.

"Oh, Johnny, I'm sorry," she hugged him hard. "It must be hard on both of you."

"Yeah," he said, letting his eyes drop to the floor. "Especially Helen. She hasn't really been the same since it all happened."

"Really?" she took both his hands in hers and held them.

"She used to be so vibrant and so full of life. But it's like they cut it all away from her when they did the operation."

Zoe was silent for a few seconds.

"It would be devastating for her," she said finally.

John looked deep into her eyes, "It was devastating for me too."

They stared at each other.

Her eyes were so richly brown and so deep he could lose himself in them. Her braids framed her face beautifully and her smell was all around him. The scar across her left eyebrow was so small, and yet it was so endearing, just like the bend in her nose and her lovely, inviting lips.

He leaned towards her.

She leaned towards him.

"Excuse me," called the receptionist from her desk.

John's head snapped around to look at her.

"I can't seem to find Mrs Murdock."

John let go of Zoe's hands, stood and walked towards the receptionist. As he did so, he glanced over at the man reading the magazine. His eyes were set firmly on Zoe.

Maybe he is *an old pervert,* he thought.

"I've paged her three times now and she's not answering," the receptionist said as he reached her.

"Could you try her office once more?" he asked.

The receptionist sighed, "I don't think there's much point."

John smiled at her, "Please?"

"Okay, I'll give it a go."

The receptionist picked up the phone and dialled.

As she did so, Zoe walked up and stood next to John.

"No luck?" Zoe asked.

"Doesn't look like it," he said. "She must have gone home."

"Oh, hello," the receptionist said into the phone. "I didn't think anyone was there."

John smiled.

Success!

"I'm looking for Mrs Murdock. Her husband is here."

John's smiled disappeared.

The receptionist nodded, "Ah-uh. Okay." She cupped her hand over the mouthpiece and leaned over towards John. "Carol says she's not here."

"But she must be," John said. "Did she just leave?"

"Hang on," the receptionist removed her hand from the mouthpiece. "Carol? Did Mrs Murdock just leave by any chance?"

John turned to Zoe with a puzzled look on his face. She shrugged.

"Oh, I see," the receptionist said into the phone before turning to face him. "Carol says she hasn't been in all day."

"What?" John said. "That can't be right."

"Well, that's what Carol says," the receptionist replied.

"Can I talk with her?"

"Huh?"

John reached out for the phone, "Can I talk to Carol?"

"I don't know," the receptionist replied, unsure of what to do. "Usually we don't allow –"

"Please," John asked. "I'll only be a minute."

The receptionist thought about it for a moment and then nodded. "Okay," she said. "But only for a minute."

John took the phone from her.

"Hello, Carol?"

"Ah, yeah. Who's this?"

"It's John Murdock, Helen's husband."

"Oh, hi, John. We met at last year's Christmas party, remember? We bumped into each other at the bar and I spilled that cocktail over Maggie Chambers."

"Yeah, I do," he said. "Listen, I'm trying to find Helen. It's rather important I do because she was searching out some information for a friend of ours."

"I wish I could help you John, but I haven't seen her all day."

"But you must have!"

"I wouldn't lie to you about it, John. I haven't seen her."

"She told us she was coming here to do some research," John said, trying to keep his voice calm.

"Well, if she did, I haven't seen her."

"Is there somewhere else in the building she could be?"

"I doubt it. She would do most of her research at her desk PC. Unless she's gone down into the archives or something, but she'd always leave her handbag and other stuff up here."

"She won't be in the archives," he replied. "She's trying to trace something that happened only a few days ago."

"What happened?" Carol asked. "Maybe I can help."

"Ahh, that's okay," John tried to think of a story he could give her, but none came. "I think we've solved it now anyway."

"Isn't Helen at home?" Carol asked.

"No, that's the point. She said to meet her somewhere but she didn't arrive, so I thought maybe she was still here."

"Well, I'm sorry John, but I haven't seen her all day."

"Is it possible she found something last night and went to follow it up at another hospital or library or something?"

"Anything's possible, but I haven't seen her since last night when she said goodnight to me."

Yes! he thought.

"So you *did* see her last night?" he asked.

"Of course, she was here."

"So she was trying to find out something?"

"I don't understand, John."

"You saw her when she came back to the hospital to search for something?"

"Came back?"

"Yes, after she returned to the hospital."

"John, I think you've got it all wrong. Helen said goodnight to me when she finished her shift at five last night. She didn't come back. She went home at her normal time and I haven't seen her since."

John's stomach fell and a feeling of dread ran through his spine.

Something was wrong.

"Are you sure?" he whispered down the phone.

"Of course I am. My shift starts just before hers ends," Carol replied. "She left at five just like she usually does."

Dead wrong.

"I see," John said.

"Is everything all right?" Carol sounded concerned.

"Yes," John said. He nodded as he stared at the receptionist. She had a worried look on her face. "It's fine. I just got my story confused."

"Are you sure?" Carol replied. "Is everything okay, John?"

"All okay," he muttered. "I just got the wrong story. I should've listened when she told me."

"She's not due back until Monday, now," Carol continued.

"Monday, yes. She'll be here Monday."

He turned to face Zoe. There was a hopeful look in her eyes.

"Well?" she asked.

John shook his head.

Zoe's face crumbled and her eyes fell to the floor. She turned and walked back towards the couch in the waiting area.

John turned to watch her.

"And it's a good thing too..." Carol said in his ear.

John noticed that the man reading the magazine had gone.

"...because she won't be too happy when she returns if security don't get their act together..."

John glanced around the reception area looking for the man, but he was nowhere to be seen.

Zoe slumped onto the couch, placed her hands under her chin and rested her elbows on her knees.

"...she'll tear this place apart to find out who parked in her car spot."

John focussed back on Carol's voice.

"Sorry?" he said. "What were you saying?"

"I said Helen will *kill* whoever parked in her car spot. She hates it when someone does that and I've already called security to have it removed or towed away or something. But they only have one or two staff on duty at the weekend and I suppose it's not a priority. But I have made the call and they assured me –"

"Car, what car?" he interrupted.

"The car in her *parking spot*." Carol sounded as if she was beginning to get exasperated. "It's a red four wheel drive."

"A Jeep?" John asked, his eyes focussing in on Zoe.

Zoe's head lifted in a flash and there was fire in her eyes again when she heard him mention the Jeep.

"How the hell should I know?" Carol replied. "It's red, it's big and it's in Helen's car spot and if someone doesn't remove it before Monday, she'll kill them."

John pushed the phone back into the receptionist's hands.

"Thanks," he said to her as he dashed over to Zoe.

Something's not right...

"She's not here," he said.

"She has to be!" Zoe replied.

"She isn't, at least not now. They say she never came back here after she finished work at five o'clock on Friday."

"But that's *crazy!*"

"You told me she came back here," he said, staring deep into her eyes.

"That's right," Zoe nodded. "At least, that's what she told me she would do! After I arrived and told her what had happened she said she was coming back here," Zoe's forehead creased. "And when she called she said she was calling from here. I'm *sure* that's what she said. I know I wasn't thinking straight at the time, but I'm pretty sure that's what she said."

John grabbed her by the arms, "Carol says she hasn't seen her, but your Jeep is in her car spot in the staff car park."

"So she *did* come here, then?" Zoe looked hopeful.

"Looks that way," John said. He felt his world spinning. He was sure he was speaking too fast as he put all the pieces of information in his mind into some sort of order. "So Carol hasn't seen her, but that doesn't mean anything. The Jeep proves she came back here to check out whether Fox was alive or dead."

Zoe nodded, "I get it. But where is she now?"

John shrugged and put his hands on his hips. "I don't know."

"Maybe she left a note on her desk or something."

John shook his head. "Doesn't look like it. Carol seems to think she hasn't been in her office since five o'clock last night."

"So, what do we do now?" Zoe asked, running her hands over her braids.

"We've just got to hope she's found something and has been delayed somewhere and is trying to contact us at home."

"Yeah," Zoe nodded. "Or she might already be home waiting for us."

"You could be right," he nodded.

"But what if she isn't?" Zoe's looked uncertain again. "What'll we do then?"

"One step at a time," he said. "We'll take it one step at a time."

He grabbed her hand and pulled her along with him as they dashed back to the receptionist.

"Where's the staff car park?" he asked.

"I'm sorry," the receptionist looked confused. "I don't think I can –"

"Please!" John raised his voice. "It's important!"

The receptionist sat back in the chair and took a deep breath, "Go down that hallway and follow it to the end. Turn left and take that corridor until you see some double doors. Go through the doors and you're in the staff car park."

John smiled at her, "Thanks."

Holding on tightly to Zoe's hand, they sprinted down the corridor.

* * *

The staff car park consisted of ten rows of car spaces, two cordoned off for doctors and the rest for general staff. About half the spaces were filled but there was no one in the quiet and badly lit area.

"What do you think?" John asked as they stopped just outside the doors.

"It could be anywhere," Zoe answered. "Do you know where she usually parks?"

"No." John shook his head. "Okay, I'll take the front five rows and you take the back five."

"Alright."

John turned to face her. "But be careful, okay? Any sign of trouble, just yell."

She smiled, "Sure, Johnny. I will. First one to find the Jeep wins!"

"Yeah, yeah, whatever. Just be careful."

She giggled and ran off into the car park.

After a few minutes, as John was about to enter his fourth row, he heard Zoe call to him.

"John, I've got it!" she yelled. "Over here!"

John followed her voice and found her halfway down the final row, standing next to the Jeep with her hands on her hips, waiting for him.

He ran up and stopped in front of her.

"This is it," she pointed to the Jeep.

John gave the Jeep a quick glance. It was a standard red Jeep Wrangler with a soft-top and wide tyres, and it was parked with its hood against the wall. It still had its new car shine and looked as if it had just been driven out of the factory. Only the mud-splattered tyres and mud guards proved the Jeep had been driven anywhere. He turned to Zoe when he read the licence plate.

TAMEME

"Tame me?" he groaned.

She giggled. "Yeah, really funny, huh? That's Ricky's idea of a joke. He always thought I was rough in bed and that he was the only man alive who could tame me. So that's why he bought the plates. He had them specially made and everything."

"Subtlety's not his strong point," John replied.

"No," Zoe agreed.

"And they're not very inconspicuous, are they?"

Zoe's smile disappeared. "I didn't think of that."

"Any sign of Helen or a note or anything?" he asked her.

"I didn't look," she said. "I wanted to wait for you."

"Okay," he sighed. "Let's check it out."

John walked down the driver's side while Zoe took the passenger side. The soft-top of the Jeep was attached, so they stared through the plastic windows to look inside.

"Nothing here," Zoe said.

John nodded. The back of the Jeep was empty. He walked forward to the driver's seat and tried the door.

The door opened.

"It's not locked," John said, amazed.

Zoe tried the front passenger door. It came open too.

John bent down and looked at the ignition switch. It was empty.

"No keys," he said.

"Johnny," Zoe said in a low voice. "You better look at this."

John glanced across the Jeep and up at her. He followed her eyes to the driver's headrest.

It was covered in blood.

<u>Eleven</u>

"**O**h my God," John whispered as he reached out to touch the bloodstain. "No!"

"That proves it!" Zoe sat down in the passenger seat and placed her head in her hands.

"Proves what?" John asked as he continued to stare at the blood.

"They're here."

"Huh?"

She turned to look at him, tears in her eyes. "Ricky's here and he's after me."

John reached out and rubbed her hand.

"Let's not jump to conclusions just yet," he said.

"Jump to conclusions?" she replied. "How can we not?"

"I know it looks bad but –"

"It not only looks bad, Johnny. It *is* bad! Helen's blood is all over that headrest."

"I know that's what it looks like, but there could be another explanation."

Zoe stared at him and her head tilted, as if weighing up what he had just said.

"What other explanation could there possibly be?" she whispered.

John stared at her, and then back to the headrest covered in blood.

"I don't know," he mumbled. "But it's not necessarily what we think."

"How can it be anything other than what it looks like? That's Helen's blood – your *wife's* blood – on that headrest. It sure as hell wasn't there when I arrived last night!"

"But – "

"It's obvious, Johnny," Zoe continued. "He's followed me. Or one or more of his thugs have. They've been following me since I left. They must have. And Helen took my Jeep to come here. They probably thought it was me driving to the hospital and they followed her until she arrived here and then they attacked. They thought they were grabbing me but got Helen instead!"

"But you talked to her this morning! And again around two hours ago. So she *was* here and they must have grabbed her as she left to come and meet us."

Zoe nodded. "You're right. I didn't think of that." She looked back at the bloody headrest. "It's the only scenario that makes sense."

John agreed. It was the only logical reason. He looked again at the blood smeared on the headrest. He couldn't tell how much was there, but patches of it hadn't yet dried. Most of the headrest was covered with the blood; it didn't look too thick, but some of it still felt damp to touch and it had seeped right into the fabric. John hoped Helen wasn't wounded too badly. But he couldn't be sure.

My God, he thought. *Now we're* all *in trouble...*

There was a long silence between them.

"I'm sorry, Johnny," Zoe finally said.

"Sorry?"

"For dragging you both into this. Now none of us can escape. If only I'd kept driving last night and not stopped to see Helen, both of you wouldn't be involved in this mess now!"

John rested his head on the roll bar of the Jeep. His mind was spinning.

How can they do this? he thought. *How can they just grab a person off the street in broad daylight and get away with it? If* only *I'd got home a few minutes earlier last night!*

If only...

Events were moving too fast for him. He didn't have time to take it all in, pause, and then work out the next logical step.

This can't be happening, he thought. *But it is...*

"There's got to be a way," he whispered.

Zoe shook her head. "Ricky's getting closer."

"But how?" he asked.

"I don't know," Zoe shrugged. "Somehow he's managed to track me down. I don't know how. But he's here now and he's after me."

She stared at him, confusion and panic in her eyes, "I told you he was powerful. I told you what he could do. Now do you believe me?"

"I always did," John whispered.

At least, I think I do, he thought.

The whole scenario seemed so utterly unreal; just not possible. But now Helen was in danger, he had to see it through.

But is Zoe telling me the whole truth? he wondered.

He would have to bide his time to see how Fox's game would play out to the end.

"Now you can see for yourself what he's capable of. He can't be stopped. He just takes what he wants. He always has."

John nodded.

Things are starting to get very dangerous indeed…

"Then there's only one answer," he said. "We go to the police."

"What?"

"The police can sort out this whole mess."

Zoe let out a strangled laugh, "I don't think so."

"It's the only way!"

"Are you crazy?" Zoe crawled from the passenger seat across to the driver's side of the Jeep. "He's got Helen! There's no way he's just going to hand her over now. Not to you, not to the police. He'll want to make a deal for her. He'll want to use her and blackmail you and me so he gets what he wants. That's what he *does*, Johnny, that's how he makes his *money*. He's not going to be stopped by you or me or the police. The police aren't going to find him. He's too smart for that. He won't let Helen go until he gets what he wants."

"And that is?" John asked. He knew what the answer was going to be, but he felt compelled to ask it anyway.

Zoe's face fell to the floor and her eyes began to tear.

"Me," she said.

"And…?" John searched for more of the story.

"Just me."

John shook his head and reached down to hug her. She kneeled on the driver's seat and placed her hands around his body, hugging him hard.

"I'm so sorry, Johnny," she sobbed into his chest. "So sorry."He hugged her and rubbed his hands on her back. She was cold and starting to shiver.

I'm in this now, he thought. *To the bitter end. Whether I like it or not.*

"So the police are out?" he asked.

Zoe nodded.

They hugged each other for quite a while.

Her unique smell enveloped him again and he thought back to last night and this morning. She was so innocent and yet on the other hand she knew how to get what she wanted. Had Fox taught her to act that way? Or had she developed the skill herself? One moment she could be a woman exuding sexuality and animal prowess, and the next she could be a frightened little child. She was hard to read on some occasions, and yet on others he could see right into her inner-most thoughts and soul.

Right now, she was like a scared little girl, waking up from a nightmare.

Except we can't wake from this one, John thought.

The events of the last twenty-four hours had just rushed out of control. John didn't know what to think, who to trust or who to believe.

But Zoe has no reason to lie, he told himself.

And Helen's blood on the headrest was very, *very* real.

A car drove into the car park and pulled into a space two rows down. John tensed as he listened to the engine die. He readied himself for anything.

He knew now that Fox was a man who couldn't be taken lightly. He was a killer who would take what he wanted, no matter what. He had Helen, and that was enough to convince John that they were all involved in this situation. No matter what.

How quickly your life can change, he thought as he sighed. *And now we have to play Fox's sick, twisted little game.*

He watched as a man climbed from the car and reached in for a briefcase. He looked like a doctor, but John couldn't be sure.

Maybe they dress like doctors, he thought. *Maybe that's how they got in here and attacked Helen.*

His mind played out a scenario of what could have happened to his wife. He pictured Helen walking from the hospital and into the car park towards Zoe's Jeep. It would have been sometime after she called them at 4pm, so most of the car park would probably have been just like it was now.

She would've walked to this spot and climbed into the Jeep and placed her handbag on the passenger seat.

They would've moved fast and been at her door within seconds to stop her from starting the engine and driving away. Did they talk to her? Had someone in a doctor's coat spoken to her before they attacked? Did they threaten her or just hit her in the head with something?

He had no idea what happened, but the scene playing in his mind chilled him and made him feel sick.

They can't get away with this, he thought. *I won't let them.*

Had they tried to get Helen to take them back to Zoe? Or had their plan gone wrong when they realised that the woman in the car wasn't Zoe? Was *that* why they had attacked her? Had they panicked when they realised they had the wrong woman?

The man by the car turned and looked over towards John and Zoe. He stood there for a moment or two, looking at them, and then waved. John waved back. The man turned and headed for the entrance to the hospital.

John sighed deeply.

Calm down, he told himself. *Don't go crazy. Not everyone's the enemy.*

"Okay," John said as he watched the man enter the hospital through the car park doors. He then pried Zoe from him. "We're too exposed here. We have to get somewhere safe and work out what we're going to do."

"No where's safe now," Zoe mumbled as she knelt back in the driver's seat and pouted.

"Well there's places safer than this," John replied. "Fox could be watching us now."

Zoe's eyes grew large and fear stretched across her face as she realised John was right. Her eyes darted all around them and she turned and crawled back into the passenger seat to survey the other side of the car park.

"You're right," she said then. "Johnny, what are we going to do?"

"We'll work something out. You know this Fox guy better than I do. What do you think his next move will be?"

"Whatever it is, it won't be good for us," she paused and stared back at him, "or Helen."

"Do you have any spare keys?"

"Huh?" Zoe looked confused.

"Keys?" John repeated. "For the Jeep?"

"Ah, no." Zoe replied. "I gave my only set to Helen."

"Damn."

"Why?"

"Because leaving the Jeep here will create suspicion. People are going to wonder about a strange car sitting here. They'll start to worry. Carol already knows about it and wants security to move it. If they come over here and find blood, the police will be called in whether we like it or not."

Zoe nodded. "So we need to hide the Jeep?"

That's it, John thought to himself. *Get yourself in deeper and deeper.*

But what else can I do?

"We need to get it back to the house for certain. Maybe we can hide it in the garage and keep it out of sight."

Zoe crawled over to the driver's seat once more and put her head under the steering wheel.

"No problem," she said.

"Huh?"

"Leave it to me," she turned her head to look up at him. "I've got some skills you don't know about."

He stared at her and she smiled.

"Don't worry, Johnny. I'll have the engine purring in no time."

"You mean you're gong to –?"

"Don't look so surprised," Zoe frowned at him. "Girls can hot-wire cars too, you know."

John smiled back at her. "You're a woman of many talents, Zoe Barber."

"You can say that again," she giggled as she turned back to continue her task. "Some of my talents would simply amaze you."

"I bet they would," John nodded as he surveyed the area for any onlookers.

The last thing we need is to be hauled in by security for attempting to steal a car, he thought.

After a few minutes more, the Jeep engine suddenly roared into life.

"Yeessss!" Zoe hissed with delight.

"Well done," John nodded. "I'm impressed!"

Zoe smiled at him as she sat in the driver's seat.

"I told you I'm a woman of many talents," she said.

John placed his hands on his hips and smiled, "And I believe you."

Zoe's smile turned to a frown.

"Now what?" she asked.

"You still have my spare front door key?" he asked her.

Zoe nodded and slapped her hip pocket with her hand. "Yep. I took it from the key holder by the front door as we left. Just like you told me to."

"Good. And you know how to get home from here?"

She nodded again. "I think so. It shouldn't be too hard. I found your house once, I can find it again."

"Okay," John moved away from the driver's seat and shut the car door. "Go there now. Don't stop for anything. Go straight to the house and get inside."

"Ahuh," Zoe bit her bottom lip and wound down the window. "But what if they –"

"No 'what ifs'. Drive the car straight to the house and get inside. We've got no other option."

"What about you?"

"I'll be right behind you in my car. Okay?"

"Okay."

"We'll work out some sort of plan when we get home."

"Okay," Zoe's face changed again. "I'm sorry, Johnny."

John reached through the window and brushed her cheek with his hand. "Stop apologising. It's not your fault. Just start thinking of ways to fix the problem."

He smiled at her and she smiled back. But he could tell it was a fake smile. She was worried. And scared.

So am I, he thought.

"Now go!"

Zoe nodded. She backed the Jeep out of the spot and John watched as she drove it out of the car park.

Helen, where the hell are you?

Once he could no longer hear the Jeep's engine, he turned and slowly headed back through the hospital and to his car.

Now we're all in trouble, he thought again as he walked. *Big trouble.*

He pulled the car over to the curb on Painted Hills Drive.

He stared out the windshield at the road in front of him. The sun had set and the evening twilight was giving way to darkness. There was no one on the street in front of him.

He checked his rear-view mirror as well. No one there either.

Since leaving the hospital, John had been extra careful and was on the lookout to see if he was being followed.

As far as he could tell, no one was on his tail. But he knew that if Ricky Fox or any of his thugs were following him, they weren't going to stand out.

So, he'd taken a detour.

It was a risk, he knew that, but he'd taken it anyway. He had to make sure no-one else got caught up in this mess and got hurt.

And he needed time to think.

He also needed time and silence and an opportunity to put things right in his mind without Zoe around to distract him.

So he sat in the car and tried to put all the events of the last twenty-four hours into some sort of order to find an explanation for it all.

Things had started to go haywire from the moment Zoe had arrived. She'd landed on their doorstep and brought all her troubles with her. First she dragged Helen and then John into this mess.

And now Helen is in danger. Probably more danger than the rest of us, he thought. *And just what can I do about it?*

She had gone to the hospital to help her friend, only to get attacked by the thugs that had been following Zoe.

Helen must've believed her story, he thought.

Don't you?

Yes, I do, I guess… It's just so hard to believe!

But now Helen's missing.

Yeah.

That's a solid fact!

It is.

Whether you believe her fully or not…

I know, I know. I'll have to play Fox's game until it leads us to Helen.

Exactly.

But if they'll go to those sorts of extremes, what chance do we have to stop them? he wondered.

"The police should be involved," he whispered to himself as he looked out the driver's window to the house directly opposite.

105 Painted Hills Drive.

But getting the police involved will place everyone at risk, he thought.

And it could mean Helen would be in even more danger. If they're willing to kidnap a complete stranger to get what they want, there's no reason why they wouldn't just kill her and make a run for it if they're cornered by the police.

"Shit," John said as he thumped the steering wheel.

They needed a plan.

But there wasn't one.

Zoe was the key. To everything.

And she was the only one who knew how to play Fox at his own game.

So, she had all the answers too.

John took the keys from the ignition and climbed from the car. He shoved his hands in his pockets and glanced down both sides of the street.

The street was empty. No sign of anyone.

Slowly, he walked across the road and up the front steps of the house at number 105.

Better make this quick, he thought.

He rang the doorbell and heard the chimes sound deep within the house.

He turned around on the doorstep to survey the street once more.

No one.

But he knew the longer he stood there, the greater the chance of him being seen.

Don't make yourself an easy target, he told himself. *Get back in the car and head for home!*

He turned to face the front door once more.

"Come on," he whispered. "Come on!"

There was no sound of movement from inside.

He rang the doorbell once more and slowly counted to ten.

He glanced up and down the street again.

No one.

"Damn," he said as he finished counting.

He pulled his wallet from his pocket and grabbed one of his business cards. He slipped the business card into the grill of the front wire door.

He waited a few seconds longer, his ears desperately trying to search out a sound from within the house.

But there was only silence.

"Shit," he mumbled as he turned and headed back towards his car.

He kept his head down and glanced from side to side, waiting for someone to call his name or run up to him. But the street was still deserted and there was no sign of anyone.

John reached his car and climbed back inside. As he started the engine he looked back across the street to the house. He could see his business card stuck in the wire door and wondered how long it would take to be found.

As he drove from the street and headed for home, he thought about Zoe and hoped she had made it back to his house safely. Leaving her unguarded for even these few minutes was a risk, but it was a risk he had to take.

Because with Ricky Fox or his thugs on the loose, there was no telling how far they would go, or how many risks they would take, to get Zoe back.

<u>Twelve</u>

John knew something was wrong the moment he drove into the street.

The red Jeep was easily recognisable under the glow of the street lights. As John drove closer, he could see that the Jeep was parked on an angle across his driveway and half onto his front lawn. The headlights were still shining and the front driver's door was wide open.

John's eyes darted up the street, looking for anything suspicious.

Nothing.

Then he peered around looking for Zoe. He couldn't see her.

"Shit," he mumbled as he swung the car into the driveway.

He parked the car just short of the rear of the Jeep and turned off the engine.

Slowly, he opened his door and climbed out. He tried hard not to make a sound; his ears reached into the distance to try to hear any noise in the darkness.

Silence.

Carefully, he walked towards the Jeep.

The Jeep's headlights illuminated the area and made it easy for him to inspect the car for any sign of trouble. Everything looked normal, except the fact that it was parked at a strange angle and the driver's door was open. The engine was silent and there was no other sign of danger.

But why leave it like this unless there was trouble? John thought.

"I shouldn't've left her. Not even for a minute," he whispered.

Taking one last glace at the Jeep and the area around it, John crept towards the front door of his house. He could see from where he stood that the front door was closed. Light was escaping from the crack underneath it.

At least Zoe's inside, he thought.

Then he stopped in his tracks and studied the front door.

"Or someone is," he whispered.

He unhooked the keys from his hip and searched through them until he found the front door key. Holding the key in his fingers, he started walking towards the front door again.

The night was beginning to get cold as the heat from the day evaporated from the air, and all of a sudden John was conscious of his breath fogging the air in front of him.

He climbed the front step and reached out for the doorknob. Slowly, he turned it.

The door was locked.

The silence seemed heavier now, almost unnatural, and it caused John to turn swiftly to one side and peer out into the street once more. He couldn't see much from where he was with the Jeep's headlights shining into his eyes. Suddenly he felt safer for what he couldn't see.

If I can't see it, I can't worry about it, he told himself.

Turning back to face the door, he inserted the key and turned it.

Slowly, and as quietly as he could, he then turned the knob.

The bolt slid loudly and John cringed at the sound it made. He pushed open the door and stared into the house. Light streamed from the lounge room and into the other end of the hallway.

John stepped into the hallway and closed the door behind him.

He stood in silence and listened to the house.

Nothing. No sound at all.

It was then he realised he was holding his breath, trying hard not to make any noise himself. He let it out in one gush and placed his keys back on his hip. They jangled loudly in the silence.

He wanted to call out for Zoe, but he couldn't bring himself to do it. He didn't want to alert anyone laying in wait that he was there, and he didn't want to face the horrible prospect of Zoe not answering his call.

I should've been here, he thought. *I shouldn't've left her for even a second!*

As quietly as he could, he crept up the hallway towards the lounge room.

The closer he got, the more desperate he became.

The lamp from the corner table first attracted his attention. It was lying on the floor by the table; its shade bent to one side, throwing light at an odd angle down the hallway. The corner table had been turned upside down, its four feet pointing to the ceiling.

John's pace quickened as he reached the lounge room door.

The phone was strewn on the floor. The receiver by the foot of the sofa while the cord snaked towards the bedroom door where its base lay.

A corner of the sofa was pulled out from the wall and one of the sofa cushions was standing at an angle near the main bedroom door. The book Zoe had been reading earlier was now sitting open, upside down and spine torn, at his feet just inside the lounge room entrance.

"Shit," he muttered.

Suddenly, he felt weak and scared. The threats that Zoe had warned him about were now becoming real and very dangerous. There was no denying it. Fox was unhinged and he would stop at nothing to get what he wanted.

This is serious shit!

John reached out for one of the dining chairs and pulled it to him. Then he sat down on it with his head in his hands.

What have I got myself into? he wondered.

Events were starting to spiral out of control and he was powerless to stop them.

First Zoe had appeared on their doorstep, then Helen went missing and now Zoe was gone too. Was there any way to stop Fox? What could John possibly do against him?

John began to shake. He couldn't tell if it was from rage or fear, but he suspected from both.

Come on, he talked to himself. *Pull yourself together. Now both Zoe and Helen need you and you can't let them down. They're depending on you.*

But what could he do? Fox always seemed one step ahead of them and knew what they were planning. He read the game so well, probably because they were playing *his game*. He made the rules, he made the plays, he knew the score.

John lifted his head and surveyed the room again.

And if I were Fox, I'd leave a calling card.

He peered around, looking closely at everything once more. He stood and walked into the kitchen and checked in there too.

Nothing.

No note, no threat, no clue.

Just a bunch of dying flowers, left strewn on the benchtop.

He walked back into the lounge room and stared at the closed door of the main bedroom.

His chest felt heavy and fear crawled up his spine as he stared at the door.

He hadn't checked out the bedrooms or the bathroom, and his mind told him not to. It told him to get away from there and put as much distance between him and Fox as he possibly could.

But he knew he couldn't. He knew he had to face Fox in a showdown just as certainly as he knew he'd have to check out the bedrooms and face whatever was inside them; whether that be a note from Fox, or maybe even Zoe's mutilated body.

He had to.

He owed that much to Zoe and Helen.

He stared at the doorknob of the main bedroom. He focussed on it and walked quickly towards it.

Let's get this over with, he thought as he reached the door.

He grabbed the knob and opened the door.

Taking a step into the bedroom, he stared into the darkness and listened to the silence. He could see nothing so he reached across and turned on the light.

The bedroom was unchanged. It looked exactly as it had when they had left it that morning. Zoe's suitcase was still on the bed and the packages she had bought were beside it, exactly where John had placed them.

Their trip to the shopping centre seemed so long ago now, even though it was just a few hours before. John shook his head when he thought about it. They had acted so *normal* then, as if this threat wasn't their concern or didn't affect them. How could they have been so naive and flippant about the whole situation? They had no idea what sort of danger they were all in.

Or maybe Zoe *did* know, and she was living life to its fullest while she could.

She knew Fox would catch up with her, John thought as he switched off the light and turned to walk back into the lounge room. *She knew. But she wouldn't let it spoil the freedom she had just grasped.*

Suddenly, John felt very tired and ashamed that perhaps he hadn't taken her seriously enough. None of it seemed real until he had walked in on the mess in his lounge room. Only then did Ricky Fox become real and dangerous in his mind.

And now it might be too late for both Zoe and Helen, he thought.

John shut the bedroom door behind him and leaned back on it. He couldn't let Fox walk away so easily. Someone had to show him that he can't threaten and do these things to normal people in a normal, safe world. He had to fight back and somehow get Zoe and Helen back too.

He had to see this sick game through to the end.

Someone has got to stop this bastard, he thought. *Fox dragged my wife and me into this, and I'm damned if I'm gonna sit back and not make him pay for crossing paths with me.*

He sighed deeply as his mind began to spin. Slowly, he let his knees bend and he slid down the bedroom door into a squatting position.

"I can't let him win," he whispered.

And then he saw her foot.

First he thought it was just one of her sneakers, but then he realised that it was much more than that.

He stared closely at the space behind the sofa. He could make out a pair of old sneakers and, above them, a pair of legs and knees pulled up in the tight, dark space. Two arms were holding them all together.

John lifted his eyes further and could now see Zoe's head, resting on top of her knees, her face burrowed down between them.

His heart raced.

"Zoe?" John whispered as he crawled towards her. "Zoe?"

As he came closer to the space behind the sofa, he realised she was sitting up in a foetal position, slowly rocking back and forth in the one spot. Her breathing was fast and shallow. One of her braids had come undone and looked like a slowly fraying rope, while the other was tucked somewhere between her head and knees.

"Zoe?" he whispered once more as he reached her. Carefully, he lifted the sofa away from her so he could kneel next to her.

"Zoe, are you okay?" he whispered as he reached out to stroke her hair.

As he touched her, she jumped in fright and let out a muffled scream.

"Get away from me," she sobbed without lifting her head.

"Zoe? Zoe, it's me. John."

There was a moment's silence and then slowly she lifted her head to look at him.

"See? It's me, Zoe. It's John."

Her tear-streaked face tried to smile, but she couldn't manage it. Her half-smile split into a sob and she reached out and hugged him.

"Oh, Johnny," she whispered into his ear. "You're here."

Fear suddenly gave way to relief as John realised Zoe was probably unharmed. He hugged her back.

"It's okay," he said. "There's nothing to be afraid of."

"You're here," she said again.

"Yes, I'm here. And everything's fine."

"You're here to protect me."

"Everything's okay."

"Make them go away," she whispered.

"Huh?"

"Make them go away."

"Who?" John stared into her eyes for what seemed like minutes. Then, he pulled away from her and got to his feet. "Come on," he said in a low voice as he helped her stand. "Let's get to the sofa and you can tell me everything."

John led Zoe to the sofa and then retrieved the cushion from near the bedroom door. He placed it back on the sofa and then sat down next to her.

He took her hands in his and smiled at her.

"Who are you talking about?" he asked.

Her face was a whirlpool of emotions that changed from fear to sadness to relief and everything in-between.

"They came for me, Johnny," she whispered. "Ricky's men," her eyes burrowed into his soul.

"Here in the house?"

She shook her head and ran a hand through the hair that was continuing to unwind from her braid.

"No, not here," she continued. "They followed me."

"From the hospital?"

She nodded. "Yeah, I think so. Maybe. I'm not sure."

"What did they do? Did they try to hurt you?"

Zoe's bottom lip began to tremble. She tried to stop it, but couldn't. She let out a sob and then leaned forward into John's arms. He comforted her as best he could while she cried into his chest.

Fox, you bastard, he thought. *How can you put her through something like this?*

After a few minutes, her crying began to ease and John rocked her back and forth in his arms.

"They're not here now," he whispered to her. "I'm here and they're not. Don't worry. They can't harm you now."

After Zoe stopped crying, there were a few minutes of heavy silence between them. Then, as if readying herself, Zoe let out a big sigh and sat back to look at him. She wiped at the drying tears on her face with the backs of her hands and then tried to smile at him.

"Will you hold me some more?" she asked.

He nodded.

She turned around so her back was facing him and then she leaned backwards onto him. Her head rested on his chest and she stretched her body out on the sofa.

John placed both arms around her and let them rest just above her breasts. His eyes ventured further down her body and came to rest on her belly button. The diamond and the ring holding it there were in clear sight. His eyes watched as the diamond rose and fell in time to Zoe's breathing. Occasionally, the light would reflect from the diamond. It was one of the most endearing things he had ever seen.

God, he thought. *She's beautiful.*

She held on tight to his arms, took another deep breath and said, "Okay, from the beginning."

John didn't say anything. He just waited for her to start when she felt ready. His eyes slowly moved back up towards her breasts.

"I left you at the hospital, right?" she began.

"Yep."

"And I started driving here."

"Okay."

"I'm not quite sure when I first saw them, but I guess it was about half-way here that I realised that the car behind me was travelling way, way too close to me. So, I think to myself, 'Okay, Zoe. Don't have a panic attack. It's probably just one of those crazy drivers you hear so much about.' So I take the next turn and head off on a little detour."

"But they follow you," John said.

"Yeah. But I still don't panic. I take another corner, and another, but they still follow and now they're even closer."

"Ricky's thugs?"

Zoe nodded. "Yeah, that's them. Anyway, I get lost with all these turns and everything and I end up in some dead-end side street. There's nowhere for me to go other than to reverse and drive out the way I came, but they're too close to me for that. So I sit in the car and I think they're going to come and get me, but they just sit at the other end of the street in their car, with their lights on high and they're just sitting there and doing nothing. It really freaked me out. It was like they were waiting for me to make the first move or the wrong move or something so they could come after me."

"*Bastards*," John couldn't believe what he was hearing. He held her tighter. "Go on."

"Well, I'm almost beside myself with fear and I didn't know what to do. All I wanted was to get out of there and get home here and make sure you were safe too. I mean, there could have been another load of thugs after you."

She turned her head to stare up into his eyes.

"No," he replied. "No one followed me."

She smiled and looked back down at her hands.

"Good," she continued. "I'm glad. So, I had no choice. I put the Jeep into reverse and floored it and backed straight up the street at them."

"Really?" John was amazed.

"Yeah, I mean, what else could I do?"

"Good for you. That'll show them you're not going to be frightened so easily."

"But that's the weird thing," Zoe said. "As I started to reverse, so did they."

"Huh?"

"They wouldn't let me get any closer than about twenty-five feet from them. They reversed when I did, they stopped when I did."

"Weird."

"Yeah, like it was all some big game of cat and mouse."

"Some game," he said.

"Yeah. Loads of fun. Anyway, I stopped the Jeep and they stopped their car. I started to reverse again, and so did they. I thought that there was no way they would allow this to go on forever, so I just kept doing it, waiting until they changed the rules. But they didn't. Eventually, I reversed so far that they reversed past an intersection and I was able to drive down it and get away."

"They didn't follow you?"

"Nope."

"They just *let* you go?"

"Yep."

"But that's crazy!" John said.

"I know. But that's Ricky for you. You never know what he's going to do."

"Did you get a look at the car, or the licence plate?"

Zoe shook her head. "One car looks the same as another to me, unless it's a Jeep! It was big and black. And I never even *thought* about looking at plates."

"So then what happened?"

"Well, I speed home here and I'm sure you'll already be here and in a panic because I'm nowhere to be seen, but when I get here, there's no sign of you. Nothing!"

Silence settled between them again.

"Sorry about that," John mumbled.

"Where were you?"

"I...I needed to make sure no one was following me, so I took a detour or two myself to make sure."

"But you said no one followed you from the hospital."

"No one did. But I had to make sure of that. So I took some detours to make certain. They just took a bit longer than I expected."

"Oh, okay. Maybe I should've done the same thing. Anyway there's no sign of your car and no lights on in the house, so I naturally panic and think the worst. I charge up the drive and run inside looking for you, but there's no sign of you anywhere. Then I really get scared."

"And the place was trashed?"

"Huh?"

"This room, it was all messed up when you got here?"

"No, why?"

John was confused, "Well, I thought the thugs must have been here and messed up this room a bit. You know, to scare us."

Zoe shook her head, "No, Johnny, this room was fine."

"So they didn't call by?"

"No."

"But look at the state of this room!"

There was a long pause.

"I did that," Zoe mumbled.

"You?"

She nodded.

"Why?"

Zoe turned to look up at him again. Her dark brown eyes were pools of sadness. "I'm sorry, Johnny, I didn't mean to. I just lost it for a moment."

"Lost it?"

"Yeah, went crazy."

"Why?"

She turned from him and began re-braiding her hair.

"Why?" he asked her again, more forcefully this time. "When I walked in here I thought they had come and taken you away."

"Not yet," she muttered.

"What made you do it, Zoe?" he asked. "What made you trash the room and cower behind the sofa?"

"Ricky," she whispered.

"Ricky?"

"Yeah."

"Ricky was here?"

She shook her head, "No. He phoned."

Thirteen

John kissed the top of her head and hugged her tighter.

"So he knows where you are?" he whispered.

Zoe nodded.

"I knew I couldn't escape him. I should've known better than to try."

"I think you did the right thing."

"But what has it achieved?" she whispered. "He's already found me and I know he's going to make me pay for it."

"Tell me what he said."

Zoe sighed deeply and continued re-braiding her hair.

"Okay, let me think. I was standing here in the middle of the room wondering if you're okay and whether they'd got to you, and suddenly the phone rings. To begin with, I'm relieved because I think it's either you calling to say where you are or Helen calling to say everything's okay. I honestly thought it was you, Johnny."

"I understand."

"But it wasn't."

"It was Ricky."

"Ah-huh. I pick up the phone and he's on the other end."

Zoe fell silent for a few seconds, as if building up the courage to continue.

"Go on," John prodded.

"It's all over, Johnny," she turned to stare up at him once more. "He knows where I am and he knows who I'm with."

"And he has Helen?" John asked.

Zoe nodded. "I talked to her."

"What?"

"Ricky said he wanted me back and I had to follow his instructions and if I didn't he would kill Helen. I just stood there with the phone in my hand and I was frozen, you know, so scared I just couldn't move. I couldn't believe all this was happening and that he had tracked me down. But I managed to tell him that I didn't believe him. It was all I could say. So, he put Helen on the phone to prove it to me."

"Bastard." John said between clenched teeth. "How did she sound? Was she okay?"

"Yeah, she sounded fine. I mean, she sounded scared and all, but she said she was safe and well and that we should follow Ricky's instructions."

John nodded. "Okay," he said. "Do we have any other choice?"

"No," Zoe shook her head. "We don't. I have to go back to him."

John hugged her harder. "Don't worry," he said. "We'll follow his instructions."

"There's no other way."

"But you won't be going back to him."

"Huh?" she looked up at him with confusion in her eyes.

"We'll do what he wants, up to a point, and when I'm satisfied both you and Helen are safe, we'll start playing the game to *our* rules."

Zoe shifted on the sofa and turned her body around to lie stomach-down on him. She rested her chin on his chest and stared into his eyes.

He missed staring at the diamond in her belly button, but her face was no less captivating.

"Are you serious?" she asked. "You have no idea who you're dealing with."

He smiled at her and ran a hand along her braids. "Bastards like him can't get away with things like this. Someone has to fight back sometime."

"You'd do this for me?"

John nodded. "And Helen. I have no other choice."

"But how? What are we going to do?"

He sighed, "I have no idea yet. But we have to fight back."

She smiled and kissed his chest.

"You're the best, Johnny. Even better than I dreamed."

"But to do so, I need to know something," John continued. "What happened to the gun you had last night?"

"The gun?"

"Yes, last I saw of it, it was over there on the hallway floor," he pointed.

Zoe smiled, "Oh, that's easy. It's in my handbag. I put it there when I cleaned up this morning."

"In your handbag?"

"Yes."

"The one you took out shopping with you?"

"Yes," she giggled. "For protection, just in case..."

John sighed, "Well, we'll see what Fox has to say when we pull the ace from our sleeves."

"But, Johnny, he'll have his men around him for sure. You'll be taking on a whole group of killers."

"Don't worry, Zoe," John whispered. "If he can take Helen and use her as a hostage to get what he wants, I'm sure we can take him hostage to make our escape."

"Are you serious?" she asked him.

"*Deadly.*"

"My hero," she said and smiled up at him.

"So," John continued. "What's the plan? What does he want us to do?"

Zoe sighed deeply again and began to fiddle with the buttons on his shirt.

"He told me that I'd been a very naughty girl and that I would pay for it when he saw me again. He said he'd been knocked out by our fight, but not for long and that when he got back on his feet he found my address book on the floor of the bedroom."

"Address book?"

She nodded. "It was by my suitcase. Well, I thought it was. I put it there when I was packing. With Ricky barging in on me and surprising me and probably because of the fight we had, it must've fallen to the floor and I didn't see it when I ran from the room. He went through it. Most of the names in the book are friends of his and there were only a couple of names that were really just friends of mine. So, he got his men to call around to all of the people he knew were his friends. They wouldn't allow me to hide with them anyway. They know what Ricky would do to them if he found out I was with them and they had lied to him. So, that left three names in the address book. Two were friends of mine close by in the next neighbourhood and he sent his men to check. The other name..." her voice trailed off.

"Was Helen's." John finished for her.

She nodded.

"Well, at least that explains how he found you so quickly."

"Yeah. He grabbed a few of his best men and headed out this way. Knowing the way they drive, they were probably here before I was. I mean, I had to stop to sleep for a few hours here and there. They could take turns to drive."

"So they were already watching this place before you even arrived?" John asked.

Zoe's face cracked as tears began to flow.

"I'm so sorry, Johnny," she sobbed. "I've dragged you and Helen into this and I'm so so sorry."

"Ssshh," he rubbed her shoulders. "There's nothing you can do about that now."

"I know, I know," she continued as she wiped the tears away. "But I'm so sorry to have dragged you both into this."

"Well, what we have to do now is drag ourselves *out* of it."

Zoe nodded, "You're right. I just hope we can."

John waited for Zoe to compose herself before he continued the conversation. When she was once more calm, he asked the question again.

"So, they were already here when you arrived last night?"

"Yes. They saw me pull up in the Jeep and watched me as I went inside."

"And when Helen came out to drive off to the hospital they thought she was you?"

"I guess so. They followed her to the hospital, laid in wait and then grabbed her when they could. They must have realised it wasn't me when she arrived at the hospital last night. But I guess they grabbed her as a bargaining chip or insurance or something. They knew that if they could

threaten the life of one of my friends, I'd come quietly without a fuss. And they're right. If I'd been driving the Jeep, they
would've grabbed me and I'd already be back with Ricky and
he'd be punishing me."

"But they got Helen instead."

"Yeah, and I don't want to think about what they'll be
doing to her."

"If Fox is smart, they won't be doing anything. She's a
great bargaining tool, alright. Especially as I imagine they've
been following you all today as well."

Zoe nodded. "They kept looking for another chance to
grab me, but you were with me all day and we were in public places with lots of people, so they couldn't do it."

"But why not try to get you when you were driving back
from the hospital? Why follow you and scare you and then
let you go?"

"Because that's Ricky's style, Johnny. That's what you've
got to understand. He scares and he pushes and he taunts,
and when you're at your weakest, he attacks. That's his
game. He sent those guys to follow me so I *knew* he knew
where I was. And then he makes the phone call. Then, he
tells me the whole story. How he found the address book,
how they followed me, how his men grabbed Helen. He
tells me it all on the phone, like I'm his greatest ally, but
he knows that what he's really doing is scaring me half to
death."

She fell silent and rested her chin on his chest again.
The tears had stopped, but she was pouting and sniffling.

"So, what do we have to do?"

"He wants to swap Helen for me."

"Yeah, I guessed that," John said. "At least we know Hel-
en is okay."

"Yeah, she sounded scared and tired though."

"I bet she is."

"Do you know Hepburn Lakes?" Zoe asked.

"Ah yeah, it's out of town. About a three hour drive. It's
a little country town."

Zoe nodded. "That's where we have to go."

"Hepburn Lakes?"

Zoe nodded. "Ricky said we have to go there. We have to get there by nine o'clock tomorrow morning and then he'll let us know the next stage of his instructions."

"Why there?"

Zoe crawled up John's body so their faces were closer. She continued in a low voice, "Ricky and I took a holiday there once, about a year ago. We stayed at some old church which he had bought and converted for 'business use' as he liked to call it. I only spent the weekend there because he had some business that he had to conduct there the following week. And there was no way I was going to hang around for that."

"What sort of business?"

"I think you know, Johnny. The church is about ten minutes outside of Hepburn Lakes and in the middle of nowhere. There's no one around for miles and it's perfect for the kind of business Ricky wants to conduct. No nosy neighbours, no witnesses, no case."

"I see," John said. "Then it's perfect for us too."

"Huh?"

"We'll meet him on his own turf."

"Are you sure?"

"We'll play him at his own game."

"It'll be dangerous."

"And we'll win."

"I hope you're right, Johnny," Zoe said as she snuggled her head under his chin and hugged him tight.

"So, we get to this church by nine o'clock tomorrow morning, right?"

"Yep. That's what he said. We have to be there by nine."

"And that's where we'll meet him?"

"No."

"No?"

"There's a phone at the church, one of those really old fashioned black ones with a dial and everything. He said he would call at nine o'clock tomorrow morning. If we don't answer..." Zoe stopped talking.

"If we don't answer?" John prodded.

"Helen dies," she muttered.

There was silence for a long while.

"And if we do answer?" John asked.

"Ricky will give us instructions on how to get to the exchange point."

"Okay," John sighed deeply as he tried to take it all in. "Then that's what we have to do."

Zoe lifted her head to look him in the eyes. Their faces were just inches apart. Her forehead creased with ever-changing emotions.

"You'll do this for me?" she asked.

He reached forward and kissed her on the bridge of the nose. He took his thumb and brushed it across the scar in her left eyebrow.

"Yes," he whispered back.

"Why?" she asked in a quiet voice.

"I have no other choice."

"Sure you do," she replied. "You say goodbye to me and let me drive up there alone and I get one of Ricky's men to drive Helen back home."

"I don't think so.""Honest, Ricky said nothing would happen to Helen if we followed the rules. He keeps his word about things like that."

"That's not what I meant."

"Huh?"

"I'm not letting you go back to him. You can't."

Zoe stared into his eyes. It was as if she was boring down into his very soul.

They were both so quiet he could hear her deep, rhythmic breathing.

"Do you mean that?" she asked.

"Yes," he replied. "I'm not letting you go."

Her face changed again; emotions sweeping across her. She smiled. Then the smile quivered and she looked sad, then worried. Finally, the smile returned. Slowly, she climbed off him and stood next to the sofa.

"Then we better get packed and get going," she said as she held out both hands to him.

John took her hands and let her pull him up from the sofa. He nodded his head. "Yes, we might as well."

"I'm sorry, Johnny," she said again.

"Stop apologising," he rubbed her arm. "We'll get you out of this."

"No, this time I mean about the lounge room."

"Oh," John had forgotten about the mess. "It's okay. I understand now."

"Ricky started taunting me, telling me what he was going to do to me once he got me back and how I'm going to pay for what I put him through. I just lost it. I threw the phone on the floor and backed away, I guess I must have knocked over the lamp and the table then. I don't know how the book and the sofa cushions got messed, I really don't, but I just panicked and I started to think about his thugs following me and him knowing where I am and..."

She broke into tears once more.

John stepped forward and took her in his arms.

"It's okay," he whispered and he rocked her. "It's okay, it's not that much mess. I understand now."

"I don't know how I came to be behind the sofa, either. Maybe I blacked out for a while or something. I don't know. I just needed to hide and that's where I ended up."

"It's okay," he said again.

They stood silent in each other's arms in the middle of the lounge room.

It was inevitable, he thought to himself. *A showdown with Fox was always going to happen. It's just happening sooner rather than later.*

I can't avoid it.

He needed Zoe at her best if he was going to beat Fox at his own game, but he didn't know how much longer she could hold up under the pressure. The last thing he needed was for her to break apart once they were confronted with Fox and Helen.

"Do you know how to get there?" he asked her. "To the church at Hepburn Lakes?"

She nodded and looked up at him. At some stage during their talk she had fixed the braid that had been unravelling.

"Yes," she whispered. "I even know where Ricky hid the front door key."

"Okay," he pulled away from her. "Give me a few minutes to get some clothes together and we'll leave straight away."

She nodded.

"Are there beds at this church?"

"Huh?" she looked confused by the question.

"If we leave now we'll get there before midnight. We can try to get some rest and be ready for the call in the morning."

She nodded, "I don't think I'm going to sleep much."

"I know," he agreed. "Neither do I. But we'll have to try."

"Okay, I'll get my things together too," she said as she turned and walked towards the bedroom.

"You won't need anything," he said. "You'll be coming back here with Helen and me."

She turned back to face him and leaned on the doorway to the bedroom.

"I have to take my stuff, Johnny," she said as she tried to smile. "I know you mean it when you say we're going to teach Ricky a lesson. But I have to weigh that against what I know about him and his men. There's every chance that I *won't* be coming back with you and Helen, and I have to face that reality. For me, now, all I can hope is that you and Helen get away free, because it's my fault you were both dragged into this. I can only hope that I can talk Ricky into letting you two go."

"Zoe, you can't think like that. We *will* beat Fox at his own game."

"I know you believe that, Johnny. I really want to believe you too. But I have to ready myself just in case what you're planning doesn't work. I *have* to."

She turned around and walked slowly into the bedroom.

John watched her go and waited until the bedroom light was switched on.

"There's got to be another way," he shouted to her.

"I don't think so, Johnny," came her reply from the other room. "There's no turning back now."

The hardest thing for John to admit was that he knew she was right.

<u>Fourteen</u>

The radio stations began to fade on the dial when they were an hour into the drive to Hepburn Lakes.

Zoe continued to twist the tuning knob, trying desperately to find a station that would still register. As she did so, she juggled the wheel of the Jeep, making sure they didn't run off the side of the road.

John let her continue, even though he could tell the station searching was becoming futile. It was as if she needed some background noise to keep her alert and thinking. Or that she feared the silence would engulf them if the radio was turned off. He thought about talking with her, but realised that if she wanted to talk, she could talk to him. He was more concerned that she kept her eyes on the road as she drove.

He could tell she needed time to think.

And so did he.

The night stretched in front of them, with only the Jeep's headlights shining along the long lonely road. They hadn't seen a car for at least twenty minutes and John didn't think they would see many more at this time of night. Occasionally, in low-lying areas, they would drive through blankets of fog and every time they did, Zoe would crank up the heater one more notch. Even with the removable top secured on the Jeep, the cold night air seemed to seep into the car to surround them.

John wished they had used his car, but Zoe had been adamant that they take the Jeep.

"We've got to take the Jeep," she had said. "Ricky will be looking for it. If we arrive in anything different he might panic and do something stupid."

"But which car surely doesn't matter," he replied.

"Ricky wants me back, Johnny," she had said as she carried her suitcase out from the main bedroom and dumped it on the lounge room floor. "And that means *all* of me. Not just me personally, but also the car, my clothes and whatever else I took from him."

"And his money?"

Her eyes fell to the ground, "Yeah, well, he won't be getting that. There's none left."

She turned and headed back into the bedroom.

"If we don't show up with everything," she called back over her shoulder. "He'll get suspicious and think we're trying to pull something on him."

"That's what we'll be doing," John said.

"I know that," she replied as she walked back into the lounge room with her arms full of the parcels she had bought that day. "But we don't want *him* to know that. Otherwise he could go crazy on us."

She dropped the parcels onto the lounge room floor by her suitcase and placed her hands on her hips.

John smiled at her and realised she was standing there, waiting for him to say something.

"What?" he asked.

Zoe spread her arms in front of her and then spun around on the spot, "What do you think?"

John realised then that she had changed her clothes and redone her hair. He surprised himself that he hadn't noticed it earlier, but he'd been thinking too hard about Fox and the plan that was forming in his mind.

"When did you do that?" he asked.

"Only a few minutes ago, it doesn't take long you know," she smiled at him.

Zoe's hair was now tied in a bun at the back of her head. No strands of hair escaped, it was like a vortex sucking all her hair into one central point on her head. It gave her a slightly harsher look, not as feminine as the ponytail or the braids, but John liked it all the same.

Her cut-off jeans had been replaced by a new black pair that she had bought while they were shopping earlier in the day and she now wore a black t-shirt. It hugged her body and served as a reminder to John of what was under the material. Across the front of the t-shirt was a multi-coloured strip divided into four squares. The first square held a picture of a red dog, the second of a white cat, the third of a blue mouse and the fourth of a yellow piece of cheese. Underneath the design were the words *Natural Selection.*

John thought it looked cute on her.

Everything looks good on Zoe.

Her breasts bulged under the t-shirt and John's eyes were drawn there even though he could see nothing more than mounds of fabric. Along the neck and arms of the t-shirt were dozens of little metal rivets, punched into the fabric to border the whole design. The rivets shone in the light.

"If you want to get there before midnight," Zoe said, smiling. "You're going to have to stop looking at me."

John brought his eyes up from her breasts to rest on her smirking face.

"Ah, yeah, sorry," he mumbled. "I got distracted."

"That's okay," she giggled. "I like it when you're distract-ed. But you did say we should get going soon so we can be there by midnight."

"You're right," he said as he walked forward and picked up the suitcase. "I'll go and put this in the car."

"In the Jeep," she warned him. "I want you to put it all in the Jeep. We're going in the Jeep, comprehendo?"

John nodded. "If you say so."

Knowing he had no other choice, he turned and carried the suitcase down the hall.

Within a few more minutes, all Zoe's parcels were in the back of the Jeep along with a canvas bag filled with some of his clothes and a change of shoes. He didn't know how long they would be at Hepburn Lakes, but he wanted to be prepared one way or the other.

He'd driven his car into the garage and made sure the garage door was locked.

Then they were ready to go.

John stood outside by the hood of the car, rubbing his shoulders from the cold night and mentally running through the facts that Zoe had told him.

Fox better enjoy what time he has left, John thought to himself. *Because he's fast running out of it. I have to try to fix this guy for all of us.*

Zoe appeared at the front door and looked over to him.

"Everything's in the Jeep?" she asked.

John stood to attention and did a quick military salute, "All personal items inventoried and stored, ma'am!"

Zoe giggled. "Okay, I'll only be a minute." She disappeared from the doorway and then just as quickly reappeared. "Hungry?"

John put his hands on his hips, "Yeah, I guess so. Why?"

"Well, unless you want to starve to death on our drive to Hepburn Lakes, I suggest I make a few sandwiches to eat on the way. I mean, we never got to have dinner, did we?"

John nodded, "Yeah, I forgot about that."

"I'll only be a minute," she called.

"Okay. Turn off the lights when you come," he called back. "I'll just check the street to make sure no one's watching us."

John couldn't shake the feeling that someone, somewhere, was watching their every move. Ricky was ahead of them every step of the way.

Well, that's about to change, he thought.

By the time he had checked out the street and found nothing suspicious, Zoe was standing next to him with a bag of sandwiches in one hand and a sweater in the other.

"Can you see anyone?" she asked.

John shook his head. "Nope, I must be getting paranoid."

"Probably," Zoe replied. "You don't have much food in the house."

"Sorry."

"I just hope you don't mind cheese sandwiches."

He smiled, "At the moment, I'd eat anything."

She handed him a sweater.

"What's this?" he asked as they walked back to the Jeep.

"It's a sweater," she replied. "You know, you wear them? Keeps the cold out."

"I know that."

"You'll need it."

"I don't think so," he replied as he threw it into the back of the Jeep to rest across Zoe's suitcase.

"It'll get cold up there."

"I don't think I need it just yet," he replied. "But you should have one."

"Nah," she shook her head. "I'm made of stronger stuff."

"Really?" he smiled.

"Really," she smiled back.

"Are we ready?"

Zoe nodded her head and sighed deeply.

"Yeah," she said. "We better get going."

John walked up the front path to check the front door was locked and, satisfied it was, turned and headed back to the Jeep. Zoe was already in the driver's seat and fiddling with the wires to get the engine to kick over.

"We could take *my* car," John tried once more as he climbed into the passenger's seat. "I even have keys that start the engine."

She looked over at him and pulled a face, "Very funny, mister comedian."

And then the engine roared into life.

"See?" Zoe smiled. "You've got to learn to have faith in me, to trust me. One day your life may be in my hands."

"I doubt it," John replied.

"You never know."

"Still," he crossed his arms and smirked. "They'd be nice hands to put my life in!"

They had both laughed then as Zoe backed the Jeep out into the street.

Now, John turned his head from the road in front of them and watched as Zoe once again fiddled with the radio.

"I think you're fighting a losing battle," he said.

Zoe nodded and stabbed at the *Off* button. The radio went dead.

John looked at his watch; it was almost 10 o'clock. They would be at the church before midnight.

He stared down at the half-eaten sandwiches.

"You want another one?" he asked.

"No thanks," Zoe replied. "I think I've lost my appetite."

John nodded. He knew how she felt. The closer they drove to Hepburn Lakes, the more unsure and nervous he became.

He had no idea what kind of situation they were driving into.

It must have been even worse for Zoe.

He listened to the sound of the Jeep's engine and the low whistle of the night air as it collided against the soft-top.

There was silence between them for a few minutes longer.

John reached into the back of the Jeep, dropped what remained of the sandwiches onto the back seat and grabbed his sweater. He pulled it into his lap and began to climb into it.

"I told you," Zoe said.

John looked at her. She had a smirk on her face.

"Yeah, yeah," he replied. "I know."

"Should have put it on before we left."

"Well, I didn't know I was going to freeze in here."

"It's not cold, it's bracing," she replied.

"Ahuh."

"And I've got the heater on," she pointed to it.

"I know, but it's fighting a losing battle too."

"You look good in that sweater," she said as she took her eyes off the road long enough to look him over.

"Why, thank you," he replied, with mock surprise.

"But I guess you look good in anything."

He smiled and focussed back on the road ahead.

"Or nothing," she whispered.

"Zoe, don't –"

"But I know that already, don't I?" she continued, her eyes glued to the road in front of them. "When I saw you in the shower this morning, I thought to myself, 'God, there's a man I'd like to fuck.'"

"Zoe, please –"

"And fuck hard."

John didn't reply.

"I'd really like to fuck you," Zoe continued.

"We've been through this already," John sighed.

What can I say? he wondered. *I'd really like to fuck you too?*

"Yeah, I know," she continued, nodding her head. "You love Helen and you won't cheat on her la-la-lalala."

A bend in the road appeared in the headlights and Zoe turned the steering wheel to compensate. The Jeep skidded slightly as it turned to the left. John thought she took the turn too fast, but he wasn't about to mention it.

"Is Helen a good fuck?" Zoe asked.

"What?" John turned to face her. "How can you ask that?"

"I just want to know, Johnny. I'm just filling in the time. I don't like it when it's too quiet, and I just want you to help me get through this."

"By asking questions like that? Can't you think of anything else to ask?"

"No, I can't. I'm interested in you and I want to know you're happy."

"I've told you I'm happy," he sighed as he crossed his arms over his chest. "I've told you that countless times in the past twenty-four hours. Shouldn't we be talking about Fox and what we're going to do?"

Zoe fell silent for a minute, as if thinking through what he had said.

"I don't want to think about Ricky," she mumbled finally. "Because when I do, all I can think about are the ways he's going to hurt me."

"He *won't* hurt you."

"Hit me."

"I won't let him."

"Beat me."

"It won't get that far!"

"Rape me again."

John sat back in the passenger's seat, looking over at her. He could see her forehead crease as she tried to hold back the tears.

"I'm telling you, Zoe," he whispered to her. "It *won't get that far.*"

She looked over at him and tried to smile, "I wish I could believe that, Johnny."

"It's true."

"You have no idea what could happen," she said.

"I'm willing to risk it."

"For *me?*"

"For you."

Zoe's chin quivered and she ran her left hand over her hair to make sure the bun was still in place.

"You're a great man, Johnny Murdock," she said.

"I'm just doing what I have to do to get us all out of this mess."

"And you'll do whatever it takes?" she asked him.

"Yes."

She smiled.

"I think I love you," she replied.

"Now, Zoe, I've already said -"

"I know, I know," she turned to give him a quick glance and a smile. "You love Helen. I know. But I love you for what you're doing for me. For what you're about to do for me. That's what I meant."

"Oh," John replied. "Okay, well that's fine."

They both sat and stared as the road unfolded in front of them.

After a while, Zoe turned to look at him once more. She smiled.

He smiled back.

"It must have been hard on you," she said. "The problems Helen had, you know."

Glad for the change of conversation, John nodded.

"Yeah, it was. The doctors said everything would be back to normal within six weeks. That was three years ago. We never got close to 'normal' again."

"You can't blame her," Zoe replied. "It's not her fault."

"I don't. I don't blame her. There's no one to blame, and that's what makes it hard. If it was me or her or the doctors or the hospital, then we could at least blame them and say it's all their fault. But it's none of them, none of us. It's *no one's* fault and that's what makes it so hard."

"It must have been tough on Helen."

"It was."

"And really tough on you too," Zoe reached over and placed a hand on his thigh.

"I know. It was."

He sat in silence, suddenly not wanting to talk. He concentrated on her hand resting on his thigh. He felt the pressure and her warmth and suddenly he was seeing her back on the sofa last night, naked and exposed just for him.

Just for him.

She's willing and able. She wants *to do it with you. She* wants *to* fuck *you*, he thought.

"We haven't had sex in a long, long time," he said.

He heard himself say it, but he couldn't believe he had. He wanted to get his mind off the image of Zoe naked on his sofa, so he had tried to start another conversation. What he had said was not what he expected he was going to say.

"I already had that much figured out," Zoe nodded. "It's fairly obvious."

"Sorry," he said. "I don't usually talk about things like this."

"That's obvious too."

"I don't know why I said it."

"It's okay, Johnny," she squeezed his thigh but kept her eyes on the road. "Don't worry about it. It's good to get things like this off your chest. You'll feel better if you talk about it. Believe me, I know. I'm a good listener and I know I can help you."

"I've never told *anyone* that before."

"Don't worry about it," she repeated. "You haven't told me anything I didn't already know."

"How could you know? Did Helen tell you?"

Zoe shook her head. "She never talked to me about anything like that. You know what she can be like."

"Yeah…"

"But I can figure these things out."

"I don't see how."

"Come on, Johnny. Do you really expect me to believe that you've been all lovey-dovey with your wife? Do you? A girl can tell these things, you know."

John shook his head. "There's no way you can."

Zoe giggled, "Johnny, you *think* you're covering your tracks so well, but you're not."

John's forehead creased and he turned to look at her once more, "What do you mean?"

"Come on, it doesn't take a rocket scientist to work it all out."

"I don't understand."

"You haven't had sex with your wife for ages, in fact, you haven't even *slept* with her for months."

John's jaw dropped.

"*How?* How do you know?" he asked.

"It's easy," Zoe said as she glanced his way. "You haven't slept in that main bed for a long long time. There's no sign that you have. Helen's cosmetics and clothes are all over the room. But there's no sign of anything of yours, except for a skimpy half wardrobe of clothes and a half-empty underwear drawer. Even your smell isn't on any of the bed covers."

"Please, you're kidding, right?" he replied."Yet, in the spare bedroom," she continued. "the bed covers smell of you and I found a drawer full of your stuff – you know, old rings, chains and watches. Add to that the fact that you made no complaints about me taking the main bedroom last night. You went straight to the other bedroom where you'd *already* been sleeping for months! It doesn't take much to work it all out. Plus there's hardly any food in the house. So, it looks like you both eat out a lot – and I'm guessing not with each other."

John sat in a stunned silence.

"Mark one up to Zoe the intrepid broken relationship spotter!"

John shook his head in disbelief.

How did she know? he thought. *Is it all* that *obvious?*

"I'm good at getting to the bottom of things," she continued. "You can't hide anything from me, Johnny. At least, not for long. I can eventually work things out."

She couldn't possibly have just figured it out, he told himself. *Am I that obvious?*

"Don't worry yourself silly about it, Johnny," she continued. "Relationships cool down. It happens all the time. No need to hide it."

"We're trying to fix it," he muttered.

"And that's good. That's healthy. But you don't have to bury it deep down. Talk about it, you might feel better."

"You worked all that out just from those signs?" he asked.

"Yep."

"And Helen didn't say *anything?*"

"Nothing."

John shook his head.

"Zoe, once again," he sighed. "You amaze me."

"Hey," she smiled. "I'm a pretty amazing chick."

"You can say that again!"

"I'm a pretty amazing chick," she giggled.

"Very funny," he replied.

They took another turn in the road, slower this time, and sat in silence for quite a few miles.

"Even though it's no one's fault," she said after a while. "You deserve better."

"There's nothing we can do about it," John replied.

"But don't you see, Johnny?" Zoe continued. "One thing I've learnt about life in the last few days is that you *can* change things. It may hurt to begin with and you may be scared to follow through, but in the end it's better for *everyone.*"

"I don't see how it can be."

"I didn't want to fight with Ricky or drive through the night to escape him, it scared me half to death, but I did it and I feel better for it. Even if we now have to face him and I'm forced to go back with him, at least I know that I *tried* to stand up to him and maybe, just maybe, in the future I can escape from him for good."

"You won't be going back with him," John repeated. "I've *told* you that already."

Zoe nodded and took her eyes from the road long enough to smile at him.

"That's not my point, Johnny. What I'm saying is if you're unhappy, no matter what the reason, you should take steps to fix it."

"I'm not unhappy."

"Come on, you can't fool me. Sleeping in separate beds? *No sex?* And you're *happy?*"

"I told you, we're working on it."

"You also told me it's been three years. How much longer are you going to work on it?"

John sat in silence. He stared through the windshield at the road ahead.

"I'm sorry, Johnny," Zoe continued. "But I think you know I'm right. I'm only telling you what you've been telling me about my relationship with Ricky. If it's not working and it's hurting you, it's time to get out."

"You just don't understand," John replied.

Zoe giggled.

"I understand," she replied. "Seeing you in the shower this morning proved it. You're more hot and horny than you've ever felt in your life, right?"

He didn't answer.

"I know you think about me," she said.

He turned to stare out the passenger's side window.

"I know you want me."

She shifted her hand from his thigh and rested it on his groin. John knew there was no way he could hide his quickly pulsing cock. It began to grow once more.

Shit, he thought.

"I know you want to *fuck* me."

John reached down and placed his hand over hers.

"Okay," he said. "You're right. You make it pretty difficult for a guy to say no, that's for sure. I'll tell you one thing, you're persistent, no doubt about it."

She smiled, "I always get what I want."

He picked up her hand, removed it from his groin and placed it on her lap.

"And there's no doubt that I've thought about you and got all...ah...'hot and horny' as you said, but that doesn't change anything."

"You have an active fantasy life then?" she asked.

"I don't know what you mean."

"Well, you said yourself you were thinking about me. Do you fantasise often about women you can't sleep with?"

"I don't think that's unnatural. All men do it."

Zoe giggled. "That's about right."

"And it's hard *not* to fantasise about you. I mean, you flaunt what you've got – all of it – and leave very little to the imagination."

She turned her head and smiled at him. "I'm only trying to show you what you're missing if you turn me down."

John let out a short laugh. "I already *know* what I'm missing."

Boy, do I!

There was another silence between them, filled only with the constant white noise of the air rushing against the Jeep.

John continued to peer through his side window. Any sign of civilisation had disappeared long ago now. The arc of light from the headlights barely reached to the side of the road. All he could make out were trees and bushes; there were no other lights or signs of life.

He wondered if they really were doing the right thing.

"Do you think I'm beautiful?" Zoe asked.

"Huh?" John was surprised by the question. "Well, Zoe, I think you know the answer to that."

She smirked. "I'm making you uncomfortable again, aren't I? I'm sorry."

"No, no, I'm not uncomfortable. I just think you know the answer, that's all."

"But I don't, that's why I'm asking you."

"You can figure out what I think of you after catching me in the shower today."

Zoe shook her head. "No, that just means you'd fuck me… or want to anyway. I asked you if I'm beautiful, not sexy."

John sat in silence for a moment, thinking about the question.

"Yes, I think you're beautiful."

What else can I say? he thought.

But he realised he truly meant it. She *was* beautiful.

"Really?"

"Really."

Zoe jumped in her seat as she shouted for joy. The Jeep swerved on the road.

"Don't get too excited," John said. "Keep your eyes on the road."

Again, the silence.

John turned to watch Zoe as she drove. Her face was beaming now; she wore a large smile and her eyes were wide. The bun at the back of her head continued to hold her hair, although a few strands had begun to escape. The rivets in her t-shirt were illuminated from the lights of the dashboard.

"Why did you ask that?" he asked.

"Ask what?"

"About whether I thought you were beautiful."

"I just wanted to know, that's all."

"But you must know that already."

She shook her head, "No. I didn't."

"Come on, stop fooling."

"I didn't know it," she glanced over to him. "No one's ever said that to me before."

"Of *course* they have!"

"No, they *haven't*."

"I don't believe you," John replied. "You can't tell me that Fox never said that to you, or one of your other boyfriends or *someone else* has never said that to you."

She shook her head, "They haven't."

"But you've had relationships," John continued.

Zoe nodded, "Yeah, relationships based on sex, Johnny. Nothing more. I know I'm a good fuck, in fact, I'm a great fuck. People have told me *that*, but no one's ever said I was beautiful before. I'm great in bed, on top, on bottom, on my knees, on the ground, 69, you name it and I've done it. I'm terrific no matter what position you put me in, but I've never been called beautiful before."

Her voice broke on her last words and she raised her hand to her face, as if to steady it and to control the tears that were trying to escape.

John reached over and rubbed her shoulder.

"I'm sorry," he whispered.

Zoe pulled herself together and continued. "You see, Johnny, you're the kind of guy who has sex with someone because you *love* them. The guys I've been with want to have sex because you're worth *screwing*. There's a difference."

John nodded, "Yeah, I see that now."

"Do you understand what I mean?"

He nodded and took her hand.

"Yes," he whispered. "And I'm sorry."

"Sorry?"

"Sorry that you've had to deal with all these assholes who want you only for your body."

She turned to him and smiled, "Thanks, Johnny. That means a lot to me."

"You deserve better. You deserve someone who will love you and treat you right and with the respect you should be given."

"I know."

"You need to be as far away from Fox as possible."

She nodded, "Yeah, I know that too. But we're driving straight towards him now. Escaping from him is never going to happen."

"Oh yes it is." John replied. "I'm going to help you get away from him. And we're going to succeed."

She glanced over at him once again. "I hope you're right."

"I'm right."

"I hope we do succeed."

"We will. We'll fight him at his own game and I'll make sure that I leave Hepburn Lakes with both you and Helen. You can stay with us until you get on your feet and then you'll be free."

Zoe squeezed his hand tight. "Thanks, Johnny, that means a lot to me."

"It's the least I can do."

"If there's any way I can repay you," she continued.

"Don't worry about it."

"But you should get *something* in return."

"It's not necessary."

"Maybe I can help you and Helen."

"Huh?"

"You know, with the problems you've been having."

John frowned, "I don't think so."

Zoe had an excited look in her eyes. "Yeah, I could! Maybe I could talk to you both, sit you down and see if we can bring you two closer together."

"You don't have to do anything, believe me."

"Maybe we can work through the problems together. You know, the way we've talked through mine."

"I don't think it's that easy, Zoe."

"Yeah, sure it is! We'll find out Helen's reasons for the way she is and I'll find out yours and we'll work something out."

"I don't *think* so!"

Zoe continued to stare at the road. John followed her stare and watched as the road stretched out before them. He looked for anything different in the small patch of light shining from the headlights in front of them.

It all looked the same.

He wondered where Helen was now, and whether she was okay. He wouldn't let Fox harm her, but there was very little he could do or say about it until they met face to face tomorrow. Then he would teach the bastard a lesson.

At least, he hoped he could.

Hang in there Helen, he thought. *I'm on my way.*

"What about a threesome?"

"*What?*" he turned to face her, his jaw dropping.

"I said, what about a threesome? Would that help?"

John was astounded. "Are you *serious?*"

"Of course!" Zoe seemed surprised by his question. "Maybe a threesome would help Helen feel more relaxed or something. Maybe we can all work it out that way."

"A *threesome?*" John shook his head.

"Yeah, you know. Helen and me and you."

"I *know* what you mean! I just can't believe you suggested it!"

"Why not? It's perfectly natural."

"Natural?"

"Sure! And that way maybe I can bring you two closer together. Guide you both and work things out."

"Ahuh."

"What do you think?"

"I don't think so."

"Why not?"

"I just don't think so, Zoe."

She pouted, "It would be fun."

"I don't think Helen would go for something like that, believe me. She's not *that* kind of woman."

Zoe smirked, "But you would?"

John shook his head in amazement and let out a laugh. He stared at her and paused before answering.

"Don't ask things like that, Zoe."

She giggled. "I thought so. Caught you out there! You'd *like* it, wouldn't you?"

"Zoe, don't –"

"You'd be in a threesome with me anytime, right?"

"Please, can we *change* the subject now?"

"I don't know why you've turned all conservative on me all of a sudden," she threw him a wicked glance. "It's perfectly natural. What three people decide to do in the privacy of their own home is their own business. There's nothing to worry about. You'd sure enjoy it."

"I'm sure I would," John replied. "But it's *not* going to happen."

Zoe laughed. "Come on, Johnny, are you telling me you've never had a threesome?"

"Never."

"Not once?"

"Not once."

"Really?" Zoe looked surprised.

"Really."

"Well, you're missing out on a great time," she said.

"Oh, so I guess you're Queen of the Orgies then?" he asked.

"*Orgies?* Yuck! No way. I'm no orgy girl. A threesome isn't an orgy, Johnny. It's just a lot of fun."

"And how many have you had?" he had to ask.

"Only two," she replied.

"Only two? You sound disappointed."

"I'd like to make it three," she smiled at him. "You, Helen and me."

"No way," he crossed his arms in front of his chest.

"You don't know what you're missing!"

"I think I have a pretty good idea," he replied.

They drove further without saying anything.

This girl is full of surprises, John thought as he shook his head.

Eventually, he couldn't resist. "You've done threesomes before?"

"Yeah," Zoe replied in a matter-of-fact tone. "I mean, first of all, it wasn't my idea. I had a girlfriend who liked having threesomes with her boyfriend and another girlfriend of hers. But then that girl moved to another state. So, my girlfriend asked me if I'd be interested in doing it with her and her boyfriend. Of course, I was a bit nervous to begin with, I didn't just jump in there and say, 'Okay, what position do you want me in?' But after a few drinks I got relaxed enough to try it and then we had a real good time. Eventually though, she and her boyfriend broke up. So, once I talked it over with Ricky, we invited her to join us. She was thrilled with the idea."

"You invited her to have sex with you and *Fox?*"

"I think Ricky was even more excited than she was! Men really seem to enjoy it."

"You knew how dangerous Ricky was, and you invited her to join you?"

"Oh, don't worry," Zoe continued. "She was a long-time friend of Ricky's. She knew the score. In fact, it wouldn't surprise me if they'd slept together before anyway. Or since, for that matter."

John shook his head and sat in silence.

"It's perfectly natural," Zoe continued.

"Yeah, yeah," John replied.

"So what do you say?" Zoe said after a pause. "You, me and Helen?"

"Huh? *No!* The answer is still no!"

"You mean you *seriously* wouldn't have a threesome with Helen and me?"

"Exactly."

There was silence again in the car.

Why have a threesome when I could just have you, he thought to himself.

Then he felt ashamed for thinking it.

Still...

Suddenly, Zoe slammed on the brakes and pulled the steering wheel savagely to the right. The tyres screamed in the darkness and the Jeep swerved and shuddered onto the shoulder of the road.

"Hey, what the -?" John reached out to grab hold of something to steady himself.

The Jeep skidded along the gravel shoulder, the tyres throwing up a dust cloud around them. Eventually they came to a halt.

Zoe unbuckled her seatbelt, turned and leaned forward to face him. Their faces were inches apart.

"So you won't have a threesome?" she asked again.

"No, I've already said that."

"Why?"

"It doesn't matter why."

"Oh, I think it does," Zoe's eyes squinted as she stared into his soul.

"No, it *doesn't.*"

She nodded. "Yes, it does. I'm starting to piece together your puzzle, Johnny."

He sat back in the passenger's seat. Suddenly the Jeep felt smaller; the air hot and dry.

"I don't know what you mean," he replied.

"All the pieces are starting to fit."

"Pieces? What pieces?"

"It's not that you *won't* have a threesome with me," she whispered. "It's that you *won't* have sex with your *wife!*"

John stared at her.

"I'm right, aren't I?" her face broke into a half smile.

John knew he didn't have to answer.

Fifteen

"**I** think it's just over the next hill," Zoe said as they continued driving into the night.

The Jeep shuddered along as the tyres bit into pot holes and bumps. The road had begun to deteriorate a few minutes after they had driven through Hepburn Lakes.

John had been relieved when he saw the sign welcoming them to Hepburn Lakes, as it meant their journey was almost over.

He had looked out the window as the town passed by in the hope of seeing some form of life. But all the house and shop windows were dark and there was no sign of anyone. The general store was the only building with a light burning in the night, and it was blinking on and off. Even the local hotel and bar was closed. And then, within seconds, they had left the town and were continuing along the lonely road.

A few minutes after that, Zoe had slowed down the Jeep and had begun looking from side to side.

"It's around here somewhere," she had mumbled.

Then she spotted the turn off to the left. John was sure that if they weren't looking for the road, they would have driven straight past it just like everyone else.

"We're almost there," she had smiled to him as she turned the steering wheel and drove on.

He wanted to get to the church as soon as possible. He needed time out of the Jeep so he could get his thoughts together. They hadn't spoken much since they had talked about having a threesome and Zoe had worked out he wasn't sleeping with Helen.

Was it that obvious? he thought to himself. *If she could see that so clearly, who else could?*

He needed time to plan how they were all going to escape from Ricky tomorrow, but all he could think about was Zoe. As he stared out the windshield of the Jeep, he pictured her naked on the sofa, then he remembered her on the bed today, spread with his bathrobe around her, her legs apart. Her parted vulva so tantalising.

"I just want to help you, Johnny," she had whispered.

He remembered her pierced belly button and the diamond that sat inside it, and the way she had giggled when she had caught him erect in the shower.

And then he remembered her cowering behind the sofa, scared to move, and the stories she had told him about Fox and the way he hurt her.

That's better, pal, he thought. *Concentrate on Fox and how you're going to turn the tables on him tomorrow.*

They crested the hill and Zoe put her foot on the brakes.

"Yeah," she said, almost to herself. "I think it should be on the right here somewhere. You can't see the church from the road, but there's a steep driveway along here somewhere."

They continued driving slowly. John peered into the darkness, looking for the driveway and hoping that no one was at the church waiting for them.

He hadn't thought about that possibility before, and now that he did, he was suddenly scared to venture any further into the night.

We should've driven up here tomorrow morning, he told himself. *At least then we could see if anyone was already here awaiting our arrival.*

But he kept the thought to himself as he didn't want to panic Zoe with another possible problem. He just made sure that he was ready for anything.

There's no turning back now.

John spotted a gap in the foliage ahead.

"There," he pointed it out to her. "Is that it?"

Zoe glanced to where he was pointing.

"Yeah," she replied. "I think so."

She stopped the Jeep and stared up the dirt driveway.

"You know, a horrible thought just crossed my mind," she said.

"I know," John nodded. "It's probably the same one that just crossed mine."

She turned to face him, "What if they're already up there waiting for us?"

John nodded. "I know. I just thought that myself."

"What will we do then?"

"I don't know. Is it likely that Fox would be up there? Do you think that's the kind of thing he would do?"

Zoe stared back up the driveway and her forehead creased. "No," she replied. "I don't think it is. Fox doesn't need to be sneaky like that. He's got too much power. He's more likely to be standing there waving us up the driveway. I don't think he'd hide and wait for us."

"Okay," John said. "I believe you. If that's what you think."

Zoe nodded.

"Well," he said. "Shall we?"

She turned to look at him once more. He couldn't read her face now. It was a mixture of emotions he hadn't seen before.

"You don't want to go up there now?" he asked.

"No, no," she replied, shaking her head and turning back to stare out the windshield. "I do. I'm…I don't know…just trying to get my thoughts in order."

"I know," John reached out and rubbed her arm. "I've been trying to do that too. But sometimes events move quicker than thoughts."

"Yeah, don't I know it!" Zoe replied.

She sighed deeply and turned to face him.

"This is your last chance," she said.

"Huh?"

"Your last chance to pull out. I can drive you back to Hepburn Lakes now and leave you there. I saw a hotel as we drove through the town. I can drop you there if you like. Once we drive up that driveway there's no turning back."

"I understand," he replied."Do you?" her eyes pierced through him in the darkness. "Do you *really?*"

"Zoe, I've already told you," he said. "I have no choice. I'm here to help you and Helen and hopefully by this time tomorrow we'll be heading back home."

"I know you say that, but –"

"I'm not turning back without you."

She smiled at him.

"Thanks, Johnny," she said. "Even though there's been all this trouble, I'm glad I'm here with you now. You're the only one I need."

"Good. So let's get up that driveway and check out this church while we still have time."

She giggled and turned back to look through the windshield. "Yes, sir!"

The Jeep accelerated towards the driveway.

John stared out through the windows, checking both sides of the Jeep and peering into the darkness trying to spot anything out of the ordinary. He didn't know what he was looking for, but he stayed alert for anything that looked suspicious. But it was too dark to make out anything other than large clusters of trees and bushes. If there were anyone watching them, there was no way John would be able to see them.

The Jeep shuddered as it climbed the steep unpaved driveway.

"Nearly there," Zoe said, her voice vibrating with the vehicle.

John realised he was holding his breath and bracing himself, almost as if he were preparing for something to go wrong or for Fox to spring out in front of their headlights.

They reached the top of the driveway and then the ground levelled out. John let his breath out with a gush and tried to get his bearings. But it was still too dark and he was limited to only that which he could see with the help of the headlights.

"Bumpy," he muttered.

"Thankfully we have the Jeep," Zoe replied as she steered along the driveway. "Imagine getting up that track in your car."

John nodded. *Maybe it* was *a good idea to bring the Jeep,* he thought. *Fox could have us going across some rough terrain tomorrow to get to the meeting point.*

"Yeah, you were right about coming in the Jeep," he said.

"Aren't I always?" she smirked at him.

"I'm beginning to believe that, yeah," he replied.

She giggled again. "It took you long enough."

John turned back to stare out the windshield.

"Now, take it nice and slow," he said to her. "We don't want to drive into something nasty."

"I know," Zoe said. "I'm so nervous, I'm shaking. Who knows what could happen?"

"Just keep your wits about you," he replied. "Look for anything out of the ordinary."

"It's exciting, don't you think?" she asked.

"Huh?"

"All this danger and not knowing what will happen next. Doesn't it make you sort of excited?"

John frowned, "No. It makes me scared and on edge. Not excited."

"But can't you feel the electricity? The zing in the air?"

"No, Zoe," John said in a steady voice. "I feel the cold and the fear."

Zoe shook her head as she continued driving along the path. "No, there's more to it than that. There's a power, a *force* that's guiding us. It makes us strong and ready for anything. It's exciting and powerful."

"Well, whatever. Just keep your eyes open for anything."

"It makes me feel so horny," she said in a deep voice. She glanced over to him.

"Concentrate, Zoe," he said to her. "Please. We don't have time for this."

"I'm so hot, Johnny. I need you."

"Watch where you're driving and concentrate!" he yelled.

And then they were blinded by the lights.

Sixteen

The Jeep was flooded with the lights. They were so strong, John was forced to close his eyes and put his hands up to his face.

"What the -?" he muttered and readied himself for anything; like the sound of gunfire and yelling and people running towards them.

But there was only the sound of the Jeep's engine.

Slowly his eyes became accustomed to the lights and he was able to open them further.

He turned to look at Zoe. She was staring at him with a smirk on her face.

"Don't worry, Johnny," she said. "It's just the security lights. They turn on when you approach. They'll go off soon."

John turned his head to stare out of the Jeep.

They were parked just outside the small brick church. The security floodlights lit up the whole area around them. For the first time in hours John was able to see further than just a few feet from the Jeep.

He discovered they were sitting on the top of a small, well-forested hill. Trees and bushes were closely packed all around them, but the area directly around the church was cleared of everything, leaving only dirt. John looked up through the windshield at the wall of the church in from of him.

It looked small in the surroundings, but was probably a normal size for a brick church that was built maybe a century ago. The wall they were facing had to be the side where the altar used to be, as he could see the outline of a brick cross built into the wall. The cross stretched from ground to roof and the bricks were a darker colour - making the cross look as if it were standing out against the wall of the church.

He couldn't see any windows, but as he dropped his eyes lower, he found the door. It was old and wooden, and its brown paint was peeling badly. Next to the door was an air-conditioning unit and, on the other side, a pile of fire-wood and a shovel.

"Don't think we'll be needing the air-conditioning," he said.

"Nope," Zoe agreed. "But we'll probably need to start a fire. It looks like it'll be a cold night."

"I think you're right," John agreed. "But we don't want to attract attention to ourselves."

"Don't worry," Zoe said. "Ricky knows we're coming here. If he wants to strike tonight he will, whether we light a fire or not."

Zoe turned off the engine.

"Shall we?" she asked.

"I guess so. It looks okay. Very quiet though."

"Well, we *are* out in the middle of nowhere, Johnny."

"Yeah, I know. But it still doesn't hurt to be careful."

"Should I get the gun from my handbag?" she asked.

"No, no," he replied. "Just take it easy."

"Okay," Zoe agreed. "I'm in your hands. What do you want to do?"

John rubbed his chin and realised he hadn't had time to shave that morning. Then he looked at his watch: 11:25pm.

Before midnight.

And then his mind flew back twenty-four hours. At this time last night, he hadn't even met Zoe. He'd been on his way home from work.

How things can change in twenty-four hours, he thought. *Now look where I am! And it's all moving way too fast. I need time to think this through.*

"Alright," he said. "We'll take this nice and slowly. Where's the key to the front door? You said you knew where it was."

"Yep. It's inside the air-conditioning box. There's a little service door, and the key's hanging from a string there."

"Okay, good. We'll get out and you can get the key. Then we'll go inside and check the whole place out. Make sure that there's no sign of anyone around."

"Okay," Zoe nodded.

"Once we've checked that, I'll take a little walk around out here to make sure the same applies outside."

"And I can get the fire started," Zoe continued. "Sound like a good idea?"

John turned and smiled at her. "Okay, sounds perfect."

"A deal."

Zoe turned off the Jeep's headlights and opened her door. The cold night air rushed in at them.

"And let's make it quick," she said. "Before I freeze to death."

John climbed from the Jeep and took a good look at the dark pine trees that were surrounding them before he walked over to the church door to join Zoe.

"It's *so* quiet," John whispered.

"I know." Zoe replied as she bent down and opened the air-conditioning unit. The service door squeaked through lack of use and sounded loud in the silence. "I think that's one of the reasons I had to leave after a couple of days when I came here last year. The lack of noise was starting to make me go crazy!"

"I can understand that."

"Got it!" Zoe yelled.

"Ssshh," John said.

Zoe stood up with the key to the front door dangling from a piece of string in her hand.

"I don't think anyone's going to hear us," she pouted. "We're miles from anywhere."

"You never know," John replied. He pointed to the security floodlights. "And how long do these lights stay on?"

"A few minutes. They're movement activated," Zoe replied. "So, the sooner we get inside, the sooner they'll go off."

John nodded. The sooner they were inside and the lights were off, the better. Just in case someone actually was watching them from the bushes, the lights made it too easy to see Zoe and John. At least with the lights out, the darkness would disadvantage everyone.

If there's anyone out there, he thought.

But he knew he'd have to take a look around the church first, both inside and out, before he was satisfied they were alone.

Zoe placed the key in the lock and turned it. The church door swung open noisily.

"Easy," she whispered.

Darkness greeted them from within.

"Is there a light?" John asked.

"Ah," Zoe took a step inside the church and reached around to the wall. "I think it's here somewhere."

"We should've brought flashlights," John complained. "I didn't think of that."

"Got it."

The inside of the church illuminated. Zoe turned back to face him with a large smile on her face.

"Well done."

"A pleasure," she said. "Now what?"

"We go inside."

Zoe turned to look into the church and then back to look at him. She rubbed her arms as a chill passed through her.

"Ah, you want to go first?" she asked.

John smiled. "Sure."

He stepped forward into the church. The air was musty and cold. The light illuminated most of the centre of the church but left the corners in darkness.

"Okay, you stay behind me," he said to her as he took another step forward. "If anything happens, do what I do. Okay? And if I get into trouble, make a run for the Jeep and get the hell out of here."

"Okay, Johnny."

Suddenly, Zoe's voice sounded small and very frightened.

John took her hand and walked down a short step and into the main hall of the church. The lights were strung up high in the wood-lined cathedral ceiling, and they were positioned in the worst possible place to illuminate the area below. Each of the four corners in the church were in a murky, unsettling darkness. As John walked forward the wooden floorboards creaked loudly under his step.

There was a large wooden table off to one side of the church, where the pews probably once sat, and to the left of the entrance area there was a small kitchenette with a stove and refrigerator. A bench separated the kitchenette from the rest of the church.

Just behind the kitchenette was a door. It was half-open and John could make out a bath and toilet.

At least there's a bathroom, he thought.

At the other end of the church was a wooden railing that separated the far section from the main room. The railing was semi-circular in shape and cut across the room. In the middle of the railing was a gap just wide enough for a person to walk through.

John could make out the shapes of two beds behind the railing.

He squeezed Zoe's hand. She squeezed back.

They walked further into the church and stopped by the long wooden table.

"Everything looks fine," Zoe said. Her voice echoed around the room and sounded loud in the silence.

"Quiet," John whispered.

"And soon we'll be nice and warm," Zoe pointed to the fireplace directly across from them.

It was halfway down the right wall of the church and looked like it hadn't been used in a long time. The black charred bricks were covered in dust and a thick cobweb hung across the fireplace entrance. To one side, sitting on a pile of old newspapers, was a rusty fireplace poker. A half open box of matches rested nearby.

On the other side of the fireplace were two metal chairs. The dust had dulled the shine of the metal and a black substance, that looked like soot, streaked the metal slats that formed the back of the chairs.

Zoe shivered, "So you think I could get a fire started?"

John took one last glance around the church and nodded. "Okay. But be careful."

"I will. There's a pile of wood just outside the door, so I should have it going in no time."

John walked over to the fireplace and picked up the poker. It wasn't much, but it was heavy and he felt safer with it in his hands.

Slowly, he walked around the church, unable to shake the feeling that someone was there with them. He checked the two dark corners at the far end of the church, but there was nothing there other than another metal chair in one corner and some old magazines in the other. As he walked, he glanced out the old stained-glass windows. They were set into the two side walls at regular intervals; there were four on each side. John tried to look out into the night, but the combination of stained-glass and the darkness beyond only allowed John to see his reflection staring back at him. Most of the stained-glass was broken or chipped, and some looked as if it had been fixed at one stage or another. Large pieces of clear tape covered parts of the windows that were broken, keeping the night air out.

He walked through the gap in the curved wooden railing dividing the main room and checked out the two beds. They were both single beds, each with their headboards pushed up against the wooden railing. The ends of the beds almost touched the far wall of the church. The area smelt musty and mouldy.

But still no sign of anyone.

Maybe I'm wrong, he thought to himself. *Maybe I'm just being paranoid.*

But he had to be careful – for all of them.

He turned from the beds and stared back down the church to the front door. Zoe was struggling through the door with some logs in her arms. She smiled at him and he smiled back.

His eyes lifted to the far wall where he spotted the large brick cross which he had also seen outside. John estimated it was at least 20 feet tall and ten feet wide and took up most of the wall inside too.

Why just abandon a church out here? he wondered. *But then again, why build it in the middle of nowhere in the first place?*

Below the cross was a small platform and lectern built out from the wall and raised above the floor of the church.

Probably where the priest would have given his sermons, John thought. *Above his congregation and looking down on them.*

The platform was six feet off the ground and the only way to access it was by using the small spiral staircase near the kitchenette. It connected to one side of the platform.

The sounds of the firewood clanking into the fireplace turned his attention back to Zoe. She was kneeling in front of the fireplace with her back to him. She lifted the firewood and was slowly building a pyre. She looked as if she was concentrating hard and John didn't want to disturb her.

He shivered as he realised just how cold it was in the church. The sooner the fire was roaring, the better.

He walked past the large table set to one side in the middle of the room and inspected it as he did so. It was made of heavy, old mahogany, just like the two long chairs that ran the length of each side of the table. They looked as if they were old church pews that had been converted to suit the table. John moved the fireplace poker to his left hand and ran his right hand along the table as he walked by it.

As he reached the end of the table, his fingers ran over a rough groove. He stopped and turned to study it. It ran deep and directly across the table. It had cut through several layers of the wood, and chips and splinters ran along its edge. John couldn't work out what had caused such a deep groove.

If Fox conducts business *here, I don't want to know,* he thought.

He walked over to the kitchenette and quickly surveyed the refrigerator and the stove. They both looked functional and relatively new. He opened the refrigerator and discovered it was empty. The counter in front of the stove housed drawers underneath. He opened each one. The bottom three drawers were empty, but the top drawer contained cutlery; spoons, forks and knives. An old black phone sat in one corner of the counter.

John picked up the receiver and listened to the dial tone. At least they could call for help if they needed it.

He turned around and stared at the spiral staircase leading up to the platform attached to the wall. It was an old wrought-iron staircase that was beginning to rust in some areas. John put his foot on the first step and tested to see if it would take his weight. It moaned but stayed firm. Satisfied that the whole thing wasn't about to fall on him, he continued to climb until he was standing on the platform and looking down over the church below.

Zoe was still working at the fireplace, balling up the sheets of newspaper and pushing it under the logs.

John walked to the lectern and placed his hands upon an old dusty copy of a King James Bible. The Bible was large and heavy, its leather cover stiff and cracked.

"The Lord giveth," he said in a deep booming voice which reverberated around the church.

Zoe turned around to look at him with a smile on her face.

"And the Lord taketh away," he continued.

"Should we pray for the Lord to watch over us in our hour of need?" Zoe called to him.

"Can't hurt," John said. "We need all the help we can get."

Zoe turned back to continue building the fire.

"Is that fire going to be long?" John asked. "It's cold in here."

"I'm working on it," she replied.

"Okay, I'm going to take a look around outside, just to make sure everything's okay."

"Okay."

"I won't be long."

"Okay."

"Everything looks safe in here."

"Ah-uh."

John watched as Zoe balled up more newspaper and buried it under the firewood.

"If you hear me screaming, that's just me dying," he smirked.

"Okay." She continued to focus on the fireplace.

John shook his head.

Once she's concentrating on something, he thought. *You can't break her.*

He turned from the lectern and was about to climb back down the stairs when he noticed a small square doorway set into the back wall at the base of the large cross. The doorway was no more than three feet high and looked more like an access hatch. But access to what? John bent down, rested the fireplace poker on the floor, reached out and grabbed the handle of the door with both hands. He pulled but the door wouldn't budge. He noticed the small keyhole under the doorknob. The door was either locked or jammed. He pulled at it a couple more times just to make sure, but it wouldn't budge.

"*Johnny!*" Zoe squealed.

John jumped up, spun around and looked down at the fireplace.

Zoe was standing with a scared expression on her face and had her hands covering her open mouth.

"*What?*" he called, his eyes darting around the church. "What is it?"

Zoe ran her hands over her hair and checked her bun.

"Sorry," she said. "I looked up and I couldn't see you. I didn't know where you had gone. Then I heard that rattling noise."

John let out a deep sigh. "It was me. I was up here," he said.

"I know that *now,*" Zoe replied. "But when I couldn't see you I thought maybe, you know, that you'd –"

"Well don't think anything like that. I was only up here looking at some sort of service hatch. It's down at the base of this platform. You can't see it from where you are. I tried to open it, but I think it's locked."

"Strange place for a hatch," she replied with her hands on her hips now.

"I know." John walked over to the staircase and descended back to the church floor. "Now, as I said before, I'm going to have a look around outside. Okay?"

"Alright."

"I don't think you heard a word I said a few minutes ago," he walked towards her.

"When was that?"

"When you were working on the fireplace. I had a whole conversation with you, but you seemed miles away."

She tried to smile, but it didn't work. "I'd like to be miles away from this place," she whispered.

He opened his arms and she stepped into them. He hugged her hard.

Me too, he thought. *With you.*

"I know," he replied. "And soon we will be. All of us. You, me and Helen."

She looked up into his eyes.

"But what if that *doesn't* happen?" she asked.

"Don't think like that."

"But I have to. What if I'm forced to go with Ricky tomorrow? What if he hurts Helen? Or what if he hurts me? Or *you?*"

"You can't dwell on these things."

"I must! I know Ricky and I know what he's capable of. You have to understand that there's a pretty good chance that he'll only let the two of you go, and there's even a better chance that he'll let *none* of us go."She burrowed her head back into his chest.

"I'm sorry, Johnny. But I thought you should know. You don't know who you're dealing with here and tomorrow's going to be very dangerous."

"I understand."

"Probably the most dangerous day of your life."

"I know."

"I just hope you're right and I'm wrong," Zoe replied.

John rubbed her back and let her smell waft over him. She was beginning to shake and John wasn't sure if it was from cold or fear.

"Okay," he said after a moment or two. "Why don't you get that fire started so that when I come back inside it's all nice and warm in here."

She nodded and stared back up at him.

"Okay."

"Good, I'll be back in a few minutes."

She turned and walked back to the fireplace. He watched her as she went.

We'll get out of this, he thought. *All of us.*

* * *

The security floodlights illuminated the moment John stepped out the church door. He waited for his eyes to adjust to the brightness before he took a step further.

Once he could see without squinting, he stared out into the trees and bushes that surrounded the church. He listened for any kind of noise, but the night was quiet. Almost unnaturally quiet. There was no breeze to rustle through the pines, and no sound of any animals either.

The only sounds he could hear were his own footsteps in the dirt and gravel and the occasional cooling sounds of the Jeep's engine. He walked to the Jeep and checked around it, making sure it hadn't been sabotaged by having the wheels slashed or something.

You're getting paranoid!

He checked through the windows too, just to make sure no one was hiding inside, but he could only see the empty seats and luggage in the back.

I better bring in our clothes, he thought. *But that can wait.*

Satisfied that nothing had changed near the Jeep, John slowly began to walk around the church. He walked down the long right side wall first, his path getting darker as he left the security lights behind. He kept his eyes focussed on the bushes and trees around him, looking for any sign of movement. As he passed one of the stained-glass windows, John tried to peer inside, but the warped glass didn't let him see clearly. He could just make out Zoe's head to his right; she was still looking downwards and was focussed on the fireplace.

He turned back and continued to study the pines.

It was at that moment he realised he no longer had the fireplace poker with him. He had no idea where he had left it.

Suddenly he felt a little vulnerable with nothing to protect himself. But he wasn't going back to find it and then have to start this all over again. The only way for him to go was forward.

Let's just hope I don't run into any trouble.

He reached the far end of the church having seen nothing suspicious. More floodlights illuminated the area behind the church and John paused at the corner for a minute or two, just to survey the area and to look out for any movement.

The area behind the church was cleared too, but more so than anywhere else. About thirty feet away and down a slight decline was a smaller building, built to resemble the church. But this building was made of wood.

Quickly, he ran over to the building and began to inspect it. It was half the size of the church and the paint on the wooden walls was peeling. While it resembled the church from a distance, up close John could tell that it was nothing more than a storage or machinery shed. There was a double doorway and one window, both set into the front wall. There were no floodlights attached to the shed, so John had to rely on the weaker light from the church lights to help him inspect the area. The trees and bushes began again directly behind the shed, but they had been cleared on both sides.

The double doors were locked with a small single padlock, threaded through the metal latch. John cupped his hands around his face as he pushed himself up against the window, but he couldn't make much out inside the shed. He could see it was filled with some sort of mechanical equipment, but he couldn't tell what kind. He guessed it was a tractor of some sort, but it was too dark to tell.

Satisfied that the area was safe and that no one was around – at least, as far as he could see – he turned and walked back to the church.

As he walked, he picked up the faintest smell of smoke in the air. He raised his eyes to the chimney of the church and was sure he could see thick wisps of smoke rising from it.

Well done, Zoe, he thought.

Realizing that the night was colder than he thought, John began to jog down the other side of the church, checking from side to side to make sure nothing was suspicious.

In the shadows halfway down he spotted a paved path heading off into the pines.

He stopped by the path and ran a hand through his hair. He didn't want to investigate too far from the church, but he couldn't risk that the path led to someone watching them or to some other building from where Fox was waiting to spring his attack.

John turned back and stared through a nearby church window. But, just as with the windows on the other side, he could hardly see anything inside.

I've got to, he told himself. *For peace of mind!*

He turned and carefully walked down the path. As he did so, he left the comfort of the floodlights and the church behind. Very quickly, the night began to swallow the light and the path became darker and darker.

The silence closed in around him and the cold night air made his breathing heavy and damp.

Just as the last of the light dissipated and he thought he couldn't possibly continue along in the dark, a new set of lights illuminated from in front of him. He squinted for a moment and braced himself for anything, but the night was as quiet and lonely as ever.

The path ended just in front of him and opened out into a large and mostly empty rectangular space. In the middle of the area was a large circular gazebo painted in greens and creams, and directly behind the gazebo were sets of wooden seats. John scanned the area for any sign of life but there wasn't any. He took a few tentative steps out into the area and looked around. The ground underneath him was not paved, but it wasn't dirt either. In fact, it was a clay substance that reminded John of old-style tennis courts.

He looked around once more and nodded his head.

It *was* a tennis court, or at least, was one once. The lines that had been painted on the surface of the court were now almost completely worn away by the weather, but he could just make out fragments of them here and here. Halfway down the court and on each side was a short metal pole, probably once used to hold the tennis net. A metal loop was welded at the top of each pole.

A perfect place to tie the net, John thought as he fingered the rusty loop.

Against one of the wooden seats leaned an old chalk scoreboard.

John walked over to the gazebo and slowly climbed the steps.

No one's played tennis here for a while, he thought as he stood in the centre of the structure.

The gazebo looked new. The green and cream paintwork was not weather-beaten or peeling like the shed or the church door. It had either been just recently built, or renovated.

"I wonder if one of Fox's 'business deals' paid for this," John mumbled to himself.

The wooden seats surrounding the gazebo on two sides were also made from old pews that had probably once resided in the church.

It reminded John of the place where he and Helen had married.

It didn't feel like six years ago. Time had gone so fast. But he still remembered it as if it were yesterday.

The gazebo they were married in was not as large as this one, but on that day it was his whole world. They had been so happy then, kissing under the gazebo in the gardens just outside Parkhurst. They had been married in the full-blown heat of summer and neither of them had sweated so much in their lives. Family and friends had swarmed all around them, making the stifling heat even more unbearable. He remembered Helen saying that she hoped someone had given them an air-conditioner as a wedding present.

John smiled as he stood and stared out at the tennis court.

So happy then.

But this was totally different. There was no heat surrounding him now. In fact, it was the opposite. He had begun to shiver.

Oh, Helen, he thought. *I hope you're okay. Hang in there. I'm coming for you.*

He walked down the steps of the gazebo and took one last look around him.

I've got to get back, he thought. *Zoe will wonder what's happened to me.*

As he walked towards the path to take him back to the church, something caught his eye.

He turned his head sharply to the right and took two steps backwards.

At the end of the tennis court, just past the tree-line, he spotted something at ground level shining in the darkness. Slowly, he turned and walked towards it. As he came closer, he could tell the security lights were reflecting off the metal surface of the object.

When he was just five feet away, he realised what it was.

It was a large metal cross, half-buried in the ground.

John stared at the cross and a chill sliced up his body.

Seventeen

He couldn't work out why it affected him so deeply. After all, he was standing in a churchyard. But perhaps it was the sight of another metal cross next to the one he had seen, and one next to *that,* which had caused him the chill.

He turned his head from side to side and realised there was a whole row of crosses bordering the edge of the old tennis court.

And directly in the middle of them was another path.

Weighing the options of whether to follow the path or go straight back to the church, John decided that five minutes more outside making sure everything was okay was worth it.

He stepped over the crosses and onto the path.

As he walked he realised that the path was lined with metal crosses on both sides. They were all evenly spaced apart, one every four feet. Some still stood erect, while others had toppled over and were lying on the ground.

No one's been looking after this part of the churchyard for a long time, John thought. *Not like the gazebo in the tennis court.*

The further down the path he walked, the darker it became. The lights from the tennis court could just penetrate this far.

His mind continually demanded he turn around and head back for the church. Just as he was about to do just that, the path terminated at an old iron gate in a half-standing wire fence. The gate was rusted and had fallen off its hinges. John had to lift it out of his way to continue.

As his eyes became accustomed to the half-light in the area, John could easily make out where he was.

The small metal crosses gave way to large stone ones which sat atop concrete graves. He surveyed the area and could count over two dozen graves, most with stone crosses, but some with wooden ones and others with gravestones as well. The graves were arranged in two semi-circles, both facing the gateway John had just entered.

The earth smelled different here and the air seemed dank. John rubbed his arms to keep himself warm as he peered around the crosses and headstones, looking for anyone who could be hiding amongst them.

Everything looked darkly charred, but he wasn't sure if that was a trick of his mind or whether the earth around the cemetery was actually burnt. He bent down and ran his hand over the dirt nearby. It came away black and sticky.

While he knelt, John's eyes focussed on six small mounds of earth directly in front of him. These mounds formed a third semi-circle in the cemetery, but none of these had headstones or crosses.

And they looked freshly dug.

"Fox's business associates?" John mumbled. "I wonder…"

Near the mounds were what looked like deep tyre marks. John reached out slowly to touch the closest one.

And then the lights went out.

The twilight that surrounded the cemetery now turned into pitch black. John stood and rubbed his hand on the back of his jeans before turning around and stretching out his hands to feel for the gate.

This is the last place you want to be in the dark and with no flashlight, he thought.

After finding the gate, he slowly made his way back up the path, occasionally walking into the metal crosses as he went. At least the crosses served as a directional device and allowed him to stay on the path.

Gotta keep calm and make it back safely, he thought. *Because if I don't I'll lose it completely.*

He reached the tennis court after what seemed like an eternity. The floodlights reactivated as he approached and the whole area was again brilliantly lit. Not wanting to be side-tracked again, John marched straight across the court and continued up the other path to the church.

Enough of this, he thought. *I can check it all out again when the sun rises.*

The area around the church was dark as he approached, but as he stepped from the path, the church security lights activated once more.

His eyes swung from side to side and he continued to be on the lookout for anything out of the ordinary. He found nothing.

The smell of smoke was stronger now and John could see it rising above the chimney.

He reached the church door, opened it and stepped inside.

Safe!

The warmth hit him immediately, in stark contrast to the cold night air outside. Gone was the cold and stale air of the church. Instead, it was filled with the crackling sounds of an open fire and a slightly smoky smell. The chill John had been feeling dissipated immediately as he closed the door behind him.

He turned and stared into the church.

Zoe was lying on the floor next to the fireplace.

Naked.

Her body was stretched out along the floor. The light from the fire danced across her stomach and legs, and reflected in the diamond snug in her belly button. She looked warm and tender and the dancing flames made her body look alive even though she was quite still.

Zoe was lying parallel with the fireplace and wall. John could see her legs, stomach and breasts, but that was all. The rest of her body was hidden from view.

Her legs were spread wide apart, giving John an excellent view of her vagina once again. He felt himself growing hard as his eyes ran up her legs to her thighs and then beyond.

She never gives up, he thought.

The shadows from the flames danced over her hairless mound and made it come alive, almost beckoning for him to come inside. In the heat of the church and with the firelight, he felt tempted.

It would be so easy, he thought.

John shook his head and smirked.

No one would know...

"Steady," he muttered to himself.

The diamond shone in the light and reflected into his eyes as he took a step towards her. The closer he came to her, the more he could see and his eyes worked their way up past her belly button to her breasts.

Even though he had committed the sight of her naked body to memory, he was once again amazed at how beautiful she was. He let his eyes roam her peaks and valleys as he stood just out of reach of her.

She wants you, he thought. *She's lying there naked waiting for you to take her. To* fuck *her. This could be your last chance. DO IT!*

John shook his head hard, as if to be rid of his thoughts.

"You make a very tempting offer," he said as he smiled.

Zoe didn't reply.

John smile disappeared. "Zoe?"

No answer.

John took a step closer. Now he could see all of her.

Her head was turned away from him and her eyes were closed.

"Zoe?"

She didn't move.

John kneeled down to her and touched her shoulder. It was hot and sweaty.

"Zoe?" He shook her.

She didn't react.

"Zoe!" he called louder and shook her more.

Suddenly, she jerked awake and let out a short scream.

John pulled backwards, a yell escaping from his lips too. Their voices combined and echoed around the church.

She turned to face him, a strange half-scared half-happy expression on her face.

"Oh, it's you," she said.

"Yeah," John replied. "I thought something had happened."

Zoe sat up and stretched her arms above her head. Her breasts jiggled as she did so.

"Nah," she said. "Nothing happening here without you around. I must've fallen asleep."

"Looks like it."

"The fire was so nice and warm and everything. And I guess I was tired."

"It's alright," John replied, rubbing her bare shoulder.

"Sorry if I gave you a shock," she said.

"That's okay."

"I got myself ready for you, but when you didn't come back as quickly as I thought, I must've just fallen asleep."

"Ready for me?"

"Yeah," she giggled. "You know."

"I do?" John replied.

Zoe turned over and sat on her knees. "Come on, Johnny," she said. "Stop playing hard to get. You can drop the game now. We're out here, just the two of us, no one for miles around. I've got the fire going. It's hot in here. Hot and sticky. So take your clothes off and let's *fuck*."

"Zoe, I've already told you –"

"I know, I know." She crawled up to him and placed a hand on his pulsing groin. "But no one's going to find us out here. And Mister Cock down there is alive and kicking and just waiting to blow off some steam."

She began unzipping his jeans with one hand and pushing him onto his back with her other.

"Zoe, no!" John was unbalanced and found himself falling onto the floor. As soon as his back hit the floorboards she was on top of him. Her breath was hot and wet as she kissed his mouth hard. Her tongue darted inside and pushed to the back of his throat. Her breathing was loud, fast and heavy and filled his mouth too.

As one hand ripped open his shirt and rubbed his chest, the other reached down into his underwear. His cock was set free and it bobbed up out of his jeans. Then it was enclosed in Zoe's sweaty hand. She pumped away, making him more erect and ready to explode.

"I told you," she whispered into his mouth. "You wanted this."

John shook his head from side to side.

"Yes, you do," she said. Her teeth clamped down on his bottom lip and bit hard.

John let out a cry of pain as he felt blood flow into his mouth.

"That's it," she whispered as her tongue licked at the blood pooling along his teeth and inside his mouth. "Bleed for me. Bleed for Zoe. Bleed for me and *fuck* me."

"Stop it," John tried to say, but it came out in a muffled whimper.

"*Do it,*" she moaned. "Let yourself go. I know you *want* to. And I want your cock inside me now."

The hand rubbing his chest turned into a claw as she raked her fingernails across him. The nails dug in deep and hard and John could feel the grooves forming and the blood running.

Her other hand tightened on his cock and then ran down the shaft to his balls. Before he knew it, she was squeezing hard.

John froze and stopped struggling.

"Now," she whispered as she moved her mouth to his ear. "Are you going to be a good boy?"

John nodded.

She bit his earlobe.

"Promise?"

"Yes," he whispered.

She sat up and straddled him. She had his blood smeared on her chin and across her breasts. Her buttocks touched the tip of his pulsing cock.

"I thought you'd see it my way," she smiled down at him. "I only want to say thank you for all you've done."

John licked at the tear in his lip. The blood was still oozing.

He shook his head.

"I've told you," he said in a low voice. "You *don't* have to."

She pouted, "But I *want* to."

"I know. But you have to understand, Zoe. I really like you and I think highly of you. Doing this, saying thanks by forcing me to have sex with you will only cheapen the way

I feel about you. I like you as a *person,* not because we can have good sex together."

Her face fell and emotions danced across it with the shadows of the flames. "Remember I said you were beautiful?" he continued. "I meant that. And you said that meant the world to you."

She nodded and her bottom lip started to quiver.

"It did," she whispered.

"So don't spoil it. Don't spoil the relationship we already have as friends."

She looked deep into his eyes for a few seconds and then sighed.

There was a long silence between them.

John held his breath. There was little else he could do. She held the upper hand.

Finally, Zoe climbed from him to stand staring at the fire.

"I'm sorry," she whispered as she crossed her arms in front of her chest.

"Don't be," John replied as he re-buttoned his shirt. He took a second to glance at the five long rake marks across his chest. They looked deep and ugly. The blood was trickling down his chest and stomach. He used his shirt to staunch the flow.

Quickly, he pulled up his jeans. "I just feel that you're doing all this for me and I want to pay you back in some way."

"Well, that's *not* the way," he said as he stood and walked across to stand beside her near the fire. For the first time he noticed the small bandage across the top of her left buttock.

He touched the bandage, "What's this?"

She glanced over her shoulder at the bandage and then met his eyes.

"Nothing," she replied. "I noticed it after you found me behind the sofa. I guess I must have cut myself when I was panicking about Ricky."

"Is it serious?" he asked. "Are you going to be okay?"

"Yeah," she looked back into the fire. "I'll live. It's nothing really."

"I didn't see any blood at the time, on you or on the floor or anything."

"As I said, it's not too deep. Just a scratch really."

"I only want your wellbeing," he whispered in her ear. "I want to make sure you're okay and can get on with your life after this whole thing blows over."

She turned to face him, "Are you sure?"

"I'm positive."

"And that's it?"

John smiled, "That's it."

She smirked, "You mean I can't even tempt you?" She reached out, exposing her breasts to him. "You don't even want to try me?"

You have no *idea,* he thought.

John signed. "Listen Zoe," his voice was firm and direct. "I'm not going to continue to play silly games with you. I've told you already and I'm only going to tell you one more time. Okay? I *can't* and *won't* have sex with you!"

"But, Johnny," she pouted again. "This is our last chance."

"No!"

"This is *your* last chance!"

"NO."

"Our last moments of freedom together before tomorrow!"

"*NO!*"

She turned to face the fire once more. John watched as the shadows played across her. He tried to read her emotions, but for the first time there weren't any.

"You don't want to fuck me," she muttered.

"Exactly!" he replied. "You finally understand. That's exactly right. I'm here to get Helen back and to free you from Fox. But that's it!"

"Why don't you want to fuck me, Johnny?" she asked, still staring at the fire.

"And another thing," he said, his anger rising. "While we're letting all the truths spill out. Don't call me Johnny! I *hate* it. My name is John, okay? No one calls me Johnny!"

Her mouth trembled.

"Do you understand?" he said in a slow, level tone.

She nodded her head slowly.

Finally, I'm getting through to her, he thought.

John pressed on his shirt to mop up the still-bleeding scratches on his chest.

"Shit," he said. "You play rough."

"Do you like it like that?" she asked.

"No, I don't. How the hell am I supposed to explain these scratches when we get Helen back? Shit, Zoe, sometimes you just don't think. No wonder Fox could control you so easily. Use your brain, girl."

The silence between them was heavy. Only the sound of the fire crackled in the night.

John watched Zoe.

She stood still, watching the fire.

John sighed and looked at his watch.

I've gone too far now, he thought.

"Look," he began in a calmer tone. "It's after midnight and we both need to get some rest for tomorrow. Let's go to bed and try and get some sleep, okay?"

She didn't reply.

"Okay?" he took a step forward and touched her shoulder.

She nodded.

"Good. I'll bring in the luggage from the Jeep and then we can get some sleep."

She nodded again.

"We have to concentrate on what we're here for."

"You're right," she agreed.

"We need to be at our sharpest and at the ready for anything to happen in the next few hours, okay?"

She nodded.

"Now, why don't you put on some clothes and I'll bring in the rest of our belongings from the Jeep."

He smiled at her, but she continued looking at the fire.

He sighed and walked towards the church door. As he did so, he listened for any sound behind him, but all he could hear were his own footsteps echoing on the wooden floorboards.

Amazing, was all John could think as he gently poked the jagged bite in his lip with his tongue. *Amazing.*

He opened the church door and the cold night air greeted him. He walked over to the Jeep as the floodlights sprang to life and he felt more aware than ever. The heat in the church had made him feel light-headed and sleepy, but now he felt awake again. The chill in the air seeped into the wounds in his chest and caused them to burn.

He glanced around the night once more. He was ready for anything unexpected to burst out at him, to run from the bushes and attack.

But all was silent.

He opened the back of the Jeep and pulled out his canvas bag and Zoe's suitcase. Eyeing the bushes as he did so, he turned and walked back to the church.

Zoe was standing naked in the doorway.

John walked up to her but she wouldn't let him pass.

"Please, Zoe," he said. "You'll catch a chill standing there in this cold."

She looked deeply into his eyes as if she was searching for something. Then she smiled and moved aside. "Sorry," she said.

John placed the bag and suitcase inside the church door.

"You can move them down to the beds if you like," he said as he turned and walked back to the Jeep.

The cold was making his chest wound hurt more. He didn't want to spend any more time outside than he had to. So he grabbed the rest of her parcels in one hand and her handbag in the other. He closed the back of the Jeep and started to walk back to the church.

He realised quickly he was carrying too many parcels. They blocked his line of sight and he couldn't see where he was going. His foot caught on a rock. He tried to redistribute the parcels and re-balance, but he failed. The parcels and Zoe's handbag tumbled from his hands and fell to the ground, some of the contents spilling into the dust.

"Shit," John muttered as he looked at the mess. "Just what I need."

"Want me to help you?" Zoe asked from the door.

John shook his head, "No, no. Stay where you are. I don't need you catching pneumonia or anything. I'll fix it."

He began scooping her purchases back into the bags.

Most of the items hadn't escaped the shopping bags. It was Zoe's handbag that had spilled the most.

He grabbed the handbag in one hand and started to shovel her make-up, brushes, tissues and receipts back into it.

Women and handbags, John shook his head. *I'll never understand why they carry so much junk around with them.*

He grabbed a compact mirror and lipstick and placed them in the handbag, then he reached out and grabbed her car keys and threw them in too.

He stood and picked up the parcels and smiled at Zoe.

She had a worried expression on her face.

"What is it?" he asked.

"Nothing," she replied.

John walked towards her and entered the church. He bent down and put the parcels on top of her suitcase and held out her handbag.

"Do you want this?" he asked.

She smiled and stepped forward, "Yeah, thanks."

"Sorry about the mess. It's probably all out of order now."

She reached out to grab the handbag.

And John jerked it out of her grip.

He took a step backwards out of the church and tilted his head slightly.

"*Hang on,*" he said, as his eyes narrowed on her.

He took another step back and watched as Zoe stood in the doorway. Her eyes darted from his face to her handbag and back again.

John opened the handbag and rummaged around inside.

"What's going on here?" he asked.

He pulled his hand out of the handbag. He was holding her car keys.

"What're these?" he showed them to her.

She tried to smile, but failed. "They're my car keys."

"But you said *Helen* had your car keys."

"Yeah, well, these are my spares, Johnny."

"Don't call me Johnny," he replied. "You said you didn't have any spares! That's why we travelled all this way in a Jeep that you had to *hot-wire!*"

"I must've forgotten I had them," Zoe shrugged her shoulders. She stepped out of the church and towards him. "Can I have the handbag back, please?"

John stepped backwards. "I don't think so."

"*Please,*" Zoe walked towards him.

John backed up further. "What else have you got in here you don't want to tell me about?"

"Nothing, honest, Johnny."

"Don't call me Johnny! What *else* don't you want me to know about?"

She shook her head, "Johnny, please. *Don't!*"

"Stop calling me Johnny!"

"I can explain everything," she said as she took another step towards him. The security lights shone from behind her, making her bare shoulders shine and causing a dark shadow to fall across her face.

"You better start talking, and talking fast," John replied as he took another step back.

He felt a sharp cold pain in his back and he cried out. The side of the Jeep had slammed up against him and had almost knocked him off his feet. He threw out one hand on the hood to brace himself.

Zoe took another step forward. "Please, can I have the handbag?"

"You said the gun was in here too," he whispered. "But I didn't see it."

John placed his hand back in the bag and started to fumble around for the gun.

He found nothing.

"It's not here," he said.

"I know," Zoe pouted.

"You said it was, and it isn't. Like you said you didn't have keys but you *did.*"

"It's under the seat in the Jeep," she replied. "Honest, it is."

"I don't know what to believe any more," John muttered as he continued to fumble in the handbag. As he did so, Zoe walked closer.

"Please give me the bag," Zoe held out her hands.

"Fine!" John replied as he turned the handbag upside down and shook all the contents onto the ground. They clanked loudly as they fell and hit the dirt and gravel.

Zoe came to a halt and looked down at the mess.

"Sorry," John said as he dropped the now-empty hand-bag onto the ground and kicked it towards her. He let the car keys fall from his hand too. "Looks like I'm clumsy."

He prodded at the handbag's contents with the toe of his shoe, kicking more dust over them.

"Can't see any gun," he replied.

Zoe pouted, "I told you, it's under the front seat in the Jeep."

John eyed her up and down. It was cold in the night air, but Zoe's naked body didn't look as if she was affected by it. Her nipples were erect but she wasn't shivering. Her hair was still tightly held in the bun. The diamond in her belly button was slightly off-centre.

"I don't know whether to believe you or not," he said.

"I'm telling you the *truth*," she replied as she continued to look at her handbag on the ground.

"Well, I'm going to climb in there and get it now," he said. She nodded.

"Don't try anything," he replied.

She looked at him and spread her arms wide. "What am I going to do to you?" she replied.

John edged his way along the hood of the Jeep, not tak-ing his eyes off her. He opened the passenger door and bent inside.

As he did so, Zoe knelt down and started picking up her things and placing them back in the handbag.

John took one last look over his shoulder to check on her before he bent further forward and checked under the seat for the gun.

He reached under and stretched as far as he could, but there was nothing there. He climbed onto the passenger seat and moved across to the driver's seat. He reached under the driver's seat and stretched as far as he could.

Nothing.

He sighed deeply.

Nothing!

He shook his head and climbed out of the Jeep. He turned around to face her with his hands on his hips.

"Zoe, quit playing games," he looked towards the handbag.

It was still on the ground, the contents underneath it.

Zoe wasn't there.

"I have," she said from beside him.

He turned to face her.

He saw the shovel swinging towards him and he tried to duck.

He was too late.

It slammed into the side of his head and the blow rang in his ears.

He cannoned from the shovel into the passenger seat of the Jeep. His head hit the door roll-bar as he fell backwards.

He blacked out for just a second.

When he opened his eyes, Zoe was standing above him.

"Sorry, looks like I'm clumsy," she mimicked him.

She smiled, turned from him and opened the glove box.

John closed his eyes and tried to will the pains in his head to disappear. A high pitched sound began buzzing in his ears. His mind was throbbing and white stars swirled in his eyes. He squeezed his eyes shut tight to make the stars disappear.

They wouldn't.

He opened his eyes again.

Zoe was holding his right arm.

"Now what do you think, Johnny?" she asked.

John tried to mumble, but it came out as a low groan.

"Shit, Johnny," she continued mimicking him. "Sometimes you just don't think. No wonder I could control you so easily. Use your brain, man."

She laughed.

John closed his eyes again and tried to get his mind to settle down; it was spinning like a top.

He heard the clicking sound and felt the cold metal around his wrist. He was then pulled forward into a sitting position.

He opened his eyes and fought for consciousness.

His wrist was attached to a handcuff. The other cuff was securely fastened to the door roll-bar of the Jeep.

John pulled himself forward and out of the Jeep. He tried to stand, but his legs were like jelly. He fell to one side and needed to rest against the side of the Jeep for support.

Why? was all he could think.

He pulled at the cuff on his wrist; it was tightly secured and was starting to bite into skin and bone. He yanked at the chain and tried to pull the other cuff from the roll-bar of the door.

But it was no use.

WHY!

He swung his head around to look for Zoe, but his eyesight wasn't working properly. He was starting to see double and all he could make out were blobs of objects.

His breathing was loud in his ears.

"Don't you get it yet, Johnny?" she was right by him, but he couldn't see her.

"Don't...call...me Johnny!" he said through clenched teeth.

"But I love you, Johnny!"

"Don't...call..." he continued.

"And it's time you realised it."

He couldn't see the shovel as it slammed into his head for a second time.

PART

II

Eighteen

Pounding.
I can hear the pounding.
Footsteps?
No, it's too loud.
It's so dark.
I can't see.
But the pounding is hurting my ears.
A heartbeat?
Could it be a heartbeat?
So loud?
It's not possible.
Run.
I have to run.
There's no other choice.
The sound is so loud I have to get away.
I have to escape.
Escape from the things that haunt me.
And follow me...
Escape before they can catch me.
There must be a way.
There must be safety somewhere.
Why can't I see?
Why can't I run?
I must.
But I can't.
My legs won't move.
What have you done to me?
Why?
Why won't you let me escape?
The pounding.
Louder now, getting louder still.
I can hear them.
Laughing at me.
No, it's not laughter.

They're screaming.
They're screaming too!
Why?
WHY!
Leave them alone.
Do not hurt them.
Hurt me!
You hear me?
HURT ME!
But don't hurt them!
You have no right to hurt them.
Not when it's all my fault.
No!
Leave them alone.
I'll try to stand.
To reach out.
But they're all around me now.
I can't see them.
But I know they're there.
The pounding is louder still.
The screaming is growing.
Leave them alone.
I'm telling you.
LEAVE THEM THE FUCK ALONE!
They've got me now.
The hands are all around me.
Reaching out.
Reaching up.
They have my legs.
What are you doing?
No.
No!
NO!
They're pulling me down.
How?
Why?
You can't!
Pulling me down.
I'm falling.

Falling into the ground.
The ground is swallowing me up.
And the screaming is turning to laughter.
You?
YOU!
You tricked me.
Why did you trick me?
And the pounding is getting louder still.

<u>Nineteen</u>

The pain sliced through his head and neck as he tried to open his eyes.

He lifted his head to look around him, but the double-image of his surrounds only made his head pound more.

Taking a deep breath, he tried to stand from his sitting position, but realised he didn't have the strength.

He squeezed his eyes shut, hoping to wish away the blurred vision. Trying to stop the pounding in his mind.

What...? was all John could think.

He took another deep breath to calm himself down, to get a grip on things.

The pain in his head continued to throb. He leaned backwards and tried to work out where he was – and why.

Slowly, he began to grasp reality once more.

Okay, take it slow, he thought to himself.

His mind slipped into gear, pushing the pain aside as he began to regain control.

He could feel the night air around him, cold and damp.

He was outside.

The pounding he heard matched the throbbing in his mind and, raising his eyebrows, he could already feel the swelling of the large bump on the side of his head.

How did that happen? he thought.

And then it all came back...

Zoe. The Church. Ricky Fox.

The car keys. The gun.

The shovel.

John moved his right hand to feel the bump on his head. He whimpered in pain as pins and needles flooded his arm. He jerked his hand to a stop, sending another wave of pain through him.

His arm clattered against metal.

Metal on metal.

And then he realised his right arm was hanging above him.

He had no choice.

Taking a deep breath, he slowly opened his eyes once more.

Squinting from the light around him, he began to make sense of his surroundings as his vision began to improve.

Trees, bushes and dirt. Okay, I'm outside. It's night. Where is the light coming from?

Then he remembered the security lights on the church. It was all starting to fit back into place again. Slowly, his mind was working through the clouds of unconsciousness.

From the shadows in front of him, he realised the lights were somewhere behind him. He tried to bend his neck to see them, but he couldn't. The stiffness in his neck added to the pain already in his head and the numbness in his arm.

John licked his dry lips; a thin film of dust from the driveway had coated his tongue. He prodded at the wound on his lip once more, and realised the dust had stopped the bleeding. It was now a dry and rough gash that tasted like gritty copper.

He remembered how that had happened now too.

Zoe...

Turning his head more, in spite of the pain, he looked over his shoulder and found he was leaning against the front of the Jeep. His right hand, hanging above him, looked swollen and blue, and was surrounded by the shining polished metal of a handcuff. The other cuff was attached to the Jeep's front grill.

Well, that explains one thing, he thought.

He pulled at the cuff with his right arm, sending a new wave of pins and needles coursing through his body.

The other cuff slipped up and down the grill and clattered loudly in the night as he pulled at it, but there was no escape from its grip.

John raised his left hand from the ground, reached out for the cuff and yanked it a couple more times, but still no success. The more he struggled, the more his body screamed in pain.

The pounding in his head was louder now, and every-so-often his vision would blur again.

He sighed deeply and turned back around, resting his back against the bumper of the Jeep. He looked down at himself. The dirt and dust covered his clothes, and through his half-buttoned shirt he could see the still-seeping claw marks down his chest. They were deep and ugly, with the edges of each wound puffy and black. The dust had covered most of the wound, but there were still trickles of blood descending. The pain from his chest had, for the most part, subsided – or it was being numbed by the pain in his head.

John's eyes focussed on his surrounding area as he searched for something – anything – that could help him out of the situation.

But he could find nothing.

Nothing.

He reached up with his left hand and gently felt the bump on the side of his head.

It was about half the size of a clenched fist and just as hard. It hurt to touch. John closed his eyes as the pain shot through his skull once more.

As he rested his left arm on his lap, he realised his watch was missing.

Why?

Zoe, was all he could think. *Zoe, Zoe...*

Why?

He opened his eyes again and looked around, searching for any sign of her. The pines he faced held no clue to her whereabouts. He turned to survey as much of the area as he could see behind him, but there was no sign of her there either.

He looked for the spilled contents of her handbag on the ground nearby.

Nothing.

John sat back once more. There was nothing he could do. Nothing at all.

Except wait.

He sighed deeply and shook his head. Then he thought about what had happened since Friday night.

If I'd known what I was getting into, I would've stayed at work, he thought. *How quickly life can change.*

He tried to get as comfortable as he could on the ground. His buttocks were starting to go numb from the hard ground and his shoes were doing nothing to stop the night air from freezing his toe.

I'll be completely numb in a few hours if I don't get out of this, he thought.

He sat up straighter in the hope it would relieve some of the pain from his right arm and help keep the pins and needles at bay. And he closed his eyes, concentrating on the pounding in his skull, trying to get it to diminish.

But he knew that wasn't going to happen.

Zoe, he thought through the pounding. *Why?*

He replayed the events through his head, as he remembered them. Finding the purse and the spare car keys, dropping them to the ground, taunting her.

Maybe I pushed her too far, he thought. *Maybe I shouldn't've said the things I did. She's been through a lot and I probably should've been more careful.*

He nodded to himself.

She's just a delicate child.

He looked around once more.

Yeah, delicate... But there's no excuse for something like this.

He shook his right arm, trying to improve the circulation. The cuffs scraped on the grill of the Jeep and the pain bit into his shoulder and side once more.

John realised he had to do something, he couldn't sit here all night and just wait.

He had to, if needed, apologise to Zoe for saying what he said and for doing the things he had done.

She'll understand, he thought to himself. *I'll apologise and say I don't know what came over me and she'll let me go. Then I'll get out of this crazy mess. I don't need this. I don't need to be in a situation I can't control.*

It was a simple plan, and one that was bound to work.

An apology or two, a smile from me, and she'll be fine.

John straightened himself into a better sitting position, ignoring the pounding in his head and the pins and needles in his arm as he did so.

He opened his eyes and stared out into the night. The stars above in the clear night sky shone down unblinking at him.

For the first time, he realised he was shivering. His clothes were wet with the damp night air and his breath fogged in front of him.

He had no choice.

He opened his mouth.

"Zoe…" it was meant to be a call for help, but it came out as a cracked whisper from a dry throat.

He licked his lips and swallowed.

"Zoe…" he tried again. This time it was louder, but not loud enough.

"Zoe…*Zoe!*" Still not loud enough. He could barely hear it over the pounding in his head.

"Zoe!"

That's better, he thought. *You're almost there!*

"ZOOOOOOOEEEEEEE!"

The loudness of his scream surprised even him. It sounded desperate. And it cracked the silence of the night. It echoed into the darkness and caused John's skull to hurt more. Now he could also feel the pulse of his heartbeat throbbing through the bump on the side of his head.

He listened to the night. Trying to hear anything that sounded like help was on the way, trying to divorce the thudding in his head from other noises of the night.

He waited.

He didn't know for how long, but he waited.

Nothing.

He was pinned to the Jeep in a position where he couldn't see the church. For some reason Zoe had turned the Jeep around so the hood faced away from the church. He tried to bend his head backwards and stretch far enough to see, but the front of the Jeep was in the way. He had no idea if Zoe was in the church or whether she could hear him.

He had no idea where she was.

What if she's not here? What if she's left me? he thought. *I could die here!*

John took a deep breath and tried to calm down before panic grabbed hold.

Come on, he thought to himself. *She hasn't gone anywhere, she's not going to leave the Jeep behind.*

He nodded his head and tried to smile. He knew what he was thinking was right.

Or he hoped it was.

She wouldn't leave without him.

At least, he didn't think she would.

Plus, she needed his help with Ricky Fox in the morning. So, she would have to unshackle him soon.

He just needed to play the waiting game.

Yeah, he thought. *That's all I have to do. Let her get her little revenge for how I treated her. Then, when I'm free I'll let her know exactly what I think of her little game.*

He'd wait out her game. He had no other choice.

He sat back and got himself comfortable resting against the Jeep. By moving his right arm every-so-often, he was keeping the circulation flowing and the pins and needles away. The numbness was starting to disappear and the feeling was returning to his arm. But with the feeling came the pain of the cuffs biting into his right wrist, and that pain was adding to the pain running through his head.

He could stand up to ease the pain in his arm, but he wasn't sure his legs would work right now.

He could wait, though.

He'd wait her out. Soon she'd need him and come for him.

But what if you're left here all night? You're not going to be in any fit state to meet Fox on his own terms and beat him. You have to be at your best and you won't be. You'll be tired, battered and sore. He's going to walk all over the top of you, Zoe and Helen.

John shook his head.

Helen, poor Helen, he thought. *Hang in there, girl, I'm coming to get you!*

He hoped he would be able to save her. And Zoe. Although Zoe was starting to wear a bit thin right now…

This is crazy!

Panic suddenly filled him. It rose out of nowhere, almost like it rose from the ground around him, and he knew he had to get out of this mess.

Now!

He filled his lungs.

"ZOOOOOOOOOOOOOOEEEEEEEEEEEEEEE!"

He screamed it at loud as he could. His body shook with the scream, his throat burned, his head pounded. His one-word plea seemed to stretch forever until his throat gave out and the noise stopped. It echoed around him in the night and he imagined it flying across the church, past the tennis court and over the graves – heading right out into the darkness, stretching on forever.

She must have heard this time, he thought as he slumped back down by the Jeep.

All he would have to do is wait.

He tried to get his breathing under control. He closed his eyes tight and tried to fight the pain in his head and wrist.

The pounding sounded louder somehow, clearer now.

And then John was struck by an odd thought.

What if that pounding I hear isn't in my mind?

He tilted his head to one side. The thought came out of nowhere and surprised him.

What if that pounding I hear isn't in my head?

For the first time, he concentrated on the noise, trying to work out its source and whether it was inside or outside his body.

There was no doubt that the bump on his head was throbbing in time to his heartbeat. But the rhythmic pounding that he thought was just in his head could be from an external source. He just couldn't really tell.

If it's not in my head, then what is it?

He listened carefully, trying to match the noise with anything he had heard before, but after a few minutes he realised his efforts were futile.

It's got to be inside my head, he decided. *Not that it matters, I can't do anything chained to this Jeep anyway.*

He sighed deeply.

I just have to wait it out. Play the game and wait it out.

I have to!

He didn't have to wait long.

<u>Twenty</u>

He heard her before he saw her.

First he thought it was the wind through the trees, but as he opened his eyes and looked into the night sky, he realised there was no breeze and the pines were not swaying.

He looked around, trying to pinpoint where the sounds were coming from, but it was too difficult with the pounding inside his head.

Suddenly, the bushes directly in front of him parted and Zoe stepped into the clearing. She stopped walking and stood no more than twenty feet away from him.

He looked at her as she stood there.

She was naked.

And her body gleamed with sweat.

He could see her breasts rise and fall as she took deep breaths, her nipples erect in the cold night air.

His eyes dropped to the diamond in her belly button. It gleamed still; if anything, it gleamed more from the sweat. The sweat streaked her sides and stomach, as if she too had been covered in a fine layer of dust. It created streams through the dust as it rolled down her body.

John realised then he was holding his breath, as if he was waiting for something unexpected to happen.

His eyes dropped lower to the shaved mound between her legs. It was wet and slick too, and ever-so inviting.

Despite the situation, John found himself growing hard.

And then his eyes dropped lower.

To the shovel she was clutching in her right hand.

The shovel.

His eyes darted back to her face.

She was staring at him.

He smiled at her.

She didn't smile back.

She stood there for what seemed like an eternity. John waited for Zoe to say something, or to move. But she didn't. She stared back at him, getting her breathing under control.

He waited in the quiet night.

He wasn't going anywhere in a hurry.

Eventually her breathing returned to normal and her breasts stopped rising and falling so quickly.

She seemed so much taller now, standing by the bushes, compared to John, who was still on the ground by the Jeep.

Taller and stronger.

The scared little girl John had known in the last twenty-four hours as Zoe bore no resemblance to the woman now standing in front of him.

He studied her face, trying to read the emotions he had come to expect would be displayed there. But her face was a blank canvas. She just stared at him.

John didn't know what to do or say.

He tried smiling once more.

Nothing.

Okay, enough of this game, he thought.

"Hi," he said.

It sounded ridiculous in the situation he was in, but he had to start somewhere. And, most of all, he wanted to know what she was thinking and feeling.

Easy does it, he thought.

She didn't reply.

"I seem to be a bit tied up here," he said, smiling again. "Do you think you could give me a hand?"

He shook his right hand to rattle the handcuffs.

Zoe moved the shovel from her right hand to her left. She said nothing.

John sighed and shook his head.

He ran his left hand through his hair, trying hard not to touch the bump that seemed to be still growing on the side of his head.

He looked around and tried to pat off some of the dust from his clothing.

"Look, Zoe," he began. "I'm sorry for what I said before. I was mad and didn't mean any of it. I just lost my cool, that's all, I'm sure you understand. Right? I've been sitting here thinking about it, and I agree, I acted badly and I'm sorry. I really am, I didn't mean to act that way."

He looked back at her. No response.

He pointed to his clothes, "I'm getting all dirty down here and with the cold night air I'm going to catch something. Do you think you could unchain me so I can go inside?"

Nothing.

The cold night was like a vortex, as if it was sucking his words up and away before they were reaching Zoe.

She stared at him.

Still no reply!

"Look, I understand you're upset. Honestly, I would be too if someone said all those things to me. But I didn't mean any of it. I was just letting off steam, you know? I'm not used to this kind of situation and I didn't know how to react. I'm *sorry*, okay? Can you untie me and we'll discuss this properly, like adults, okay?"

Yeah, he thought to himself. *We'll discuss is as soon as I get that shovel off you and find the gun.*

He smiled one last time.

"*Please?*" It sounded so whiney and childlike, but what else could he do?

Zoe placed her right hand on her hip.

Well, there's movement at least!

John refused to say anything more. He'd stated his case – and now he wanted her to act on it.

They stared for a long time at each other in the cold night.

Time's running out, girl, he thought to himself. *Do something or I will!*

He smiled and suppressed a laugh.

Yeah, right! What are you gonna do strapped to the front of a Jeep? Poke your tongue out at her until she caves in to your every wish?

He couldn't help it then. He shook his head, tried not to laugh, but couldn't.

He burst out laughing.

It took her by surprise.

She stepped backwards and a shadow of doubt ran across her face.

Breakthrough, he thought.

He laughed harder.

Soon, tears were running down his face as he rocked back and forth on the ground. The cuffs clattered on the metal grill of the Jeep as he let his whole body convulse.

And then she took a step forward.

He saw her.

And she knew he saw her.

The security lights made the sweat on her body shine, and together with the tears filling John's eyes, Zoe took on an angelic appearance – almost ethereal.

He continued to laugh, stretching it for as long as he could, until she was standing just out of his reach.

"Don't you see, Zoe?" he said as the laughter died away and he began to wipe the tears on his face with his left hand. "If you leave me out here all night in this cold night air, and you stay out here with all that sweat over your body – *neither* of us is going to be in any fit state to meet Fox on his terms in a few hours time!"

Zoe's face fell and she looked to the ground.

"That's why we're here, remember?" John saw the opening and took it. "We're here to help *you.* Now, I can't help you when I'm tied to the front of the Jeep okay?"

He waited for a response, but none was forthcoming.

"Now, I'm sorry for what I said earlier, and maybe I went a bit over the top. But *this* is over the top too," he shook the handcuffs once again. "Don't you agree?"

The clanging of the metal made Zoe look up and focus on him.

Two can play at this game, he thought.

"I'm here for you, Zoe, remember that. But I can't help you unless you help me. I want to help you. In any way I can. But I can't help you like this, now can I?"

He smiled once more.

Finally, she smiled back.

YES! John thought.

"Untie me, *please?*" he asked.

She walked towards him, bent down and stared deep into his eyes.

Her lovely brown pools engulfed him as he looked back at her. He could smell her once more. She smelt different this time – the sweat on her body made her smell more primitive, more sexual.

More *alive.*

John was hard once again.

Zoe leaned forward and kissed him softly.

He closed his eyes and tasted the salty sweat on her own lips.

Then she ran her wet tongue across his lips, wiping the dust from them.

John's tongue shot out to meet hers. They touched and held for a second. Then hers withdrew.

"Untie me, *please?*" he asked again.

She ran a finger down his face and her tongue traced a line from his lips, across his cheek and upwards as she moved her mouth slowly to his ear.

"Not yet..." she whispered.

John's eyes shot open in time to see Zoe take one step backwards.

He lunged for her with both hands, but the handcuffs yanked at him and threw him off balance. He fell sideways onto his shoulder in the dust, the handcuffs holding his right arm and sending pain shooting through his side.

He turned to stare up at Zoe.

She smiled at him.

"Not yet..." she said again as she raised the shovel and brought it slamming down.

<u>Twenty-one</u>

Run.
I have to run.
I can't see but I need to run.
Run before they find me and get me.
A mountain.
It's steep.
But I must.
I must run and run and runrunrun.
They can't catch me there.
They can't get at me there.
I know that now.
If I can make it I know I'm safe.
Safe from the pain and sadness.
From the fear and lies.
I just have to make it there.
I can hear them.
The pounding.
They're behind me.
The screams are too loud.
I have to concentrate.
Concentrate!
I have to get there before they get me.
Help me.
HELP ME!
I can't see.
The rain is tearing through me.
The rain is killing me.
I don't want the rain.
I don't need it anymore.
Help me get to you.
Help me.
Before they cause more pain!
I can't live like this.
I can't live without you.

Help!
HELP!
I'm almost there.
I'm almost at the top.
Yes. YES!
They can't reach me now.
I'm safe.
We're safe.
They can't reach us now.
I can see you.
I can't see, but I can see you.
How?
There you are.
My love, there you are!
Turn to me.
Turn to me and embrace me.
I need you.
I need you so much.
Like I never knew before.
I'm so sorry.
But I'm here now.
And I'll never leave you again.
I'm here with you.
Forever.
That's a promise.
I never promised it before, but I do now.
Now I know.
Turn around and embrace me.
Turn around, my love.
Yes, turn.
Turn to me.
No, NO!
OH MY GOD! NO!
Nonononononono!
YOU!

Twenty-two

He woke strapped to a chair.

The first thing he noticed when he regained consciousness was that his headache was worse. He tried to lift his head, but the movement sent pain splitting through his mind.

Both arms were behind him, pinned down low behind his back, and he could feel the cold steel of the handcuffs around both of his wrists. Gently, he tried to move his arms, but the handcuffs clanked against the back rungs of the metal chair and held firm. The numbness in his shoulders told him he had been in this position for quite some time. Though his arms were numb too, he could still feel the handcuffs biting into his wrists, and his right shoulder ached deep in the joints.

He tried to sit forward and straighten up by moving his legs. They were like dead weights, mostly from the knees down, and wouldn't react to his commands. It was then he realised his ankles were tied, one to each of the front legs of the chair. The rope was tied tight, biting into his skin and making movement impossible.

Damn, John thought, as the events by the Jeep slowly resurfaced in his mind. *I was so close to winning her over. So close...*

At least now he wasn't cold. In fact, he was warm...a little too warm.

Opening his eyes slowly, he was blinded by the lights.

Security flood lights again, he thought. *Weren't they set on a timer? They were supposed to turn themselves off after a preset time.*

He squinted until his eyes adjusted to the light.

And as they did, he realised it wasn't the security lights that were blinding him.

It was the sun.

Risking making his headache worse, John gently lifted his head and began to look around.

He was sitting in the middle of the church, the sun shining on him through the stained-glass windows.

He turned his head to the left and peered through the windows. He could see the sun low on the horizon.

Early morning, he thought. *I've been out for quite a while.*

He turned back to stare straight ahead through the wooden dividing railing and at the two beds at the end of the church.

Both were empty.

Both were still made.

And there was no sign of Zoe.

Where is she? he thought. *If she didn't sleep in the bed, where the hell is she?*

He closed his eyes and concentrated on his hearing, but all he could hear was his own breathing. He tried to slow his breath down, almost to a stop, to give his ears a better chance at picking up sounds.

But he could hear nothing inside the church.

He remembered how the floorboards echoed when he walked over them, his shoes sounding loud on the wooden surface. But he could hear no footsteps now. No sounds at all from inside the church.

Outside, he could hear the occasional bird chirping, but no matter how much he strained his ears, there was nothing else he could pick up. No sounds of any use at all.

Just silence.

He remembered how far out in the country they were, how the church was so remotely located. He tried to listen for cars, but wishing for one wasn't going to bring one.

He let his breath out with a rush and opened his eyes once more.

I'm going to have to get out of this somehow.

He was positioned in the middle of the church and nothing was in easy reach. The long table was to his left and the fireplace, now with the dead embers of last night's fire, was to his right. The shadow cast from the rising sun was high up on the wall. It would be a long time before the shadow would reach him and replace the warm sunlight flooding over his body.

He shuffled his legs forward slightly, trying to judge how much slack was in his bindings, but they hardly moved at all.

Well tied, he thought.

He leaned forward on the chair; the metal rungs on its back had been digging into his spine.

The handcuffs slid upwards as he did so, sliding up the metal until they reached the top rung of the chair.

Well, at least she gave me some room for movement.

Zoe had done a good job, though. His legs were tied tight and there was no way he could remove the handcuffs from behind him.

But why treat me this way? he wondered. *What sort of game did she think she was playing?*

John looked down at his clothes once more. At least now they were dry, the dampness from outside having been evaporated by the morning sun. He was still dusty and grimy, but it looked as if someone had tried to scrape the worst of the dust from his clothing, leaving long streaks down his pants and shirt.

His shirt had been rebuttoned too. He couldn't see the wound on his chest, though it didn't feel as if it were still bleeding.

Lifting his head, he tried to work the stiffness out of his neck by peering up into the ceiling of the church. As he did so, he felt a wetness at the back of his head. He rocked his head from side to side. It aggravated his headache, but he continued anyway. His hair at the back of his neck felt hard and sticky, and the wet feeling felt as if it covered his shoulders.

Sweat? Could I sweat that much sitting here? No. Blood? It must be blood! But why? And how?

He had no idea.

As slowly as he could, he began to twist his head around to the right. With his arms stretched out behind him and by leaning forward, he was able to turn himself slightly so he could see over his shoulder into the back of the church.

Zoe was nowhere to be seen.

But he could see the front door of the church.

And it was wide open.

She's not far then.

He turned back around to the front and took in some deep breaths before turning to his left and peering over his left shoulder. The handcuffs clanked against the chair as he did so, sounding loud in the silence.

The kitchenette was empty too.

Nothing.

Where is she?

He leaned back against the chair, the handcuffs sliding back down, and let his head rest on his chest.

By now, his head was pounding.

Where the hell is she?

The worst part was not knowing where Zoe was, what she was doing or why she was doing it.

Just like last night. The way she stepped out from the bushes, John thought. *Where the hell had she been? Out there in the darkness, naked and with a shovel!*

Maybe I don't want to know.

Sweat trickled down his forehead as the sun's rays shone through the windows. He turned to look out the windows again. The sun was higher than before, and John tried to work out how long it would take for it to rise above the windows to leave him in shadow.

He looked back at the shadow on the opposite wall. It was lower now too. It would make its way to him eventually.

Eventually.

The sooner the better.

Far off in the distance, he was sure he could hear a low hum. He had no idea what was making the noise, but it sounded mechanical.

But it also sounded a very long way away.

Was it the sound I heard last night? he wondered. *Or was that pounding really in my head after all?*

The birds continued to sing outside.

At least someone is free, he thought.

He twisted his hands in the handcuffs. Ignoring the metal biting into his wrists, he twisted one way and then the other, trying to see if there was any way to break free.

But they held tight and bit down further.

His shoulder began to ache again, and his headache quickened in pace with his heartbeat.

He sighed deeply. There was no escape.

But that wasn't going to stop him trying.

It's time to put a stop to this, he thought. *I won't be a part of this stupid little game.*

He leaned forward once more, letting the handcuffs slide up the back of the chair. When he was as far forward as he could go, he closed his eyes and clenched his teeth.

Taking a deep breath, he pulled his arms towards him as hard as possible.

Every muscle in his arms strained with the effort and the muscles in his throat tensed with the pain. He closed his eyes and pulled harder, ignoring the pain pounding through his temples and the biting of the cuffs through the skin on his wrists.

The handcuffs slid slightly up and down the metal back of the chair, giving him false hope that either they or the back of the chair was giving way to his strength.

Slowly, a groan began to issue from his chest. It rose to his throat and eventually escaped between his lips. It was a deep, primeval noise that began as a sound of hope, but quickly turned into a cry of despair before dying out completely.

He didn't know how long he had been trying to break the cuffs through the chair, but it seemed like an eternity.

It was no use.

He slumped back into the chair, puffing hard, his arms aching and head thumping with pain.

"Nice try."

It came from behind him.

He heard it through the thudding pain in his ears, but he was too spent to reply.

"But I'd save my strength, Johnny. Those are metal handcuffs and that chair isn't about to give way either."

He concentrated on getting his breathing back under control. Trying hard not to let her aggravate the situation. More sweat rolled down his face and dropped into his eyes. He shook his head, trying to flick the droplets away, but only succeeded in making his head pound more.

The thumping inside his head merged with the sound of footsteps.

Zoe was coming closer.

"How do you feel?" she asked, her voice much closer now.

He didn't reply.

The footsteps stopped just behind him.

"I'm sorry, Johnny," she whispered.

He stared straight ahead, looking past the beds and at the far wall of the church.

There was silence between them.

Something touched his neck.

John bolted forward in the chair. The handcuffs clattered up the back of the chair and stopped him going any further. The force of his movement tipped the chair slightly forward before he rebalanced and rocked it back into place.

"I was just looking at the wound on the back of your head," she said. "I tried to clean it up, but it looks like it bled a bit more."

John kept himself sitting forward, even though his hands and arms were screaming for relief. He was tense and ready for anything.

"I'm sorry, Johnny," she said again from behind him. "But I had to get you in from the cold."

She paused.

He didn't reply.

Don't say anything. Make her explain it all!

"You were right. You know, what you said about the cold?" she continued. "So, I decided to bring you in here. But I had to drag you. You're heavy when you're unconscious, Johnny."

The pain streaming through his body was almost unbearable. John didn't want to give in to it, he didn't want to fold, but he realised he had to stay conscious. He had to make sure he was awake and aware whenever Zoe was around. He had to keep one step ahead of her in this new game.

Currently, he thought he was about five steps behind.

I'll change that.

Slowly, he let the tension ease from his muscles and he allowed his body to relax. But his headache continued pounding his skull.

"I'm sorry about the scrapes on your back and neck. I had no idea dragging you in here would tear you up like that. It must have been the rocks outside in the driveway."

Yeah, he thought. *I bet it was. Good going, girl.*

He let his hands slide down the chair and the rest of his body followed backwards. Within seconds he was leaning against the back of the chair once more.

He concentrated on getting his breathing under control and tried not to let the anger build in him.

It was anger that got you into this mess in the first place, he thought. *If you hadn't yelled at her last night, things may have been different. Take it easy, don't chew her out, and maybe she'll let you go.*

"It wasn't your fault," he heard himself say.

He felt sick when he said it. But he knew he had to.

"Yes, Johnny, it was. And I'm sorry."

"That's okay," he replied.

I can't believe I'm telling her this is all okay!

But he had to play along. At least until he knew the new rules.

"Are you feeling okay?" she asked.

He almost smiled. Her voice sounded concerned.

"I've been better."

Silence fell between them.

John closed his eyes and tried hard to use his ears for an indication as to what Zoe was doing.

She was still behind him somewhere. And close, he was sure of it. But he wasn't going to give her the satisfaction of turning around or asking to be released. It was up to her to make the moves for now.

He could wait.

But the silence was deep. There was no sound to indicate what she was doing or whether she was still there.

He guessed she was, as he hadn't heard her leave. But he was starting to wonder if she had suddenly disappeared when she spoke again.

"I'm sorry," she said.

"You said that already," he replied, trying to keep the edge out of his voice.

But he failed.

Silence again.

Damn!

Then he heard a rustling close by, just near his ear.

His shoulders tensed and he readied himself for anything.

But then the sound died away and the silence continued.

"I didn't mean it, okay," she eventually continued. "I didn't plan to hit you with the shovel. I want you to understand that."

John remained silent.

The more you talk, the more I know, he thought.

"It's just when you started yelling at me, you know, when we were out at the Jeep and you had my handbag and everything, you sounded just like Ricky."

Suddenly, John felt a sinking feeling.

"That's how he used to talk to me. He'd taunt me, bait me, lead me on until I got really mad. And then..." her voice trailed off.

Suddenly John felt terrible. He had no idea he had put her through that, no idea that he had been sounding just like the man he'd said he would protect her from.

"I just lashed out," she continued. "I didn't mean to and I didn't plan to, but I just did. I've wasted too much of my life dealing with Ricky and his fucked-up games, and I didn't want to start playing them with you."

John shook his head. He understood.

What an asshole, he thought.

"I'm sorry too," he replied.

"Don't be. It's not your fault. You don't know Ricky so you don't know how he is. I planned for so long to get away from him and his mind games, I guess I just went into automatic and did the same thing to you when you started to play them too. I had no idea I had the shovel in my hands. I don't even know when I grabbed it. It was just there and I used it."

"I shouldn't't've taunted you."

"You didn't know you were."

"Still, I didn't have the right," he replied.

She lied about the keys, though, he reminded himself. *Worry about that later. Get her to untie you first!*

"I'm sorry, Johnny," she said again, this time much closer to his left ear. "So sorry…"

Silence settled over them again.

John was amazed. She actually had him feeling sorry for her. Just minutes ago he was ready for anything and was on guard against her every move. But now he understood things from her point of view and he knew that he was partially to blame for the trouble he now found himself in.

In a situation like the one last night, he would probably do the same thing if he was her. What else *could* she do?

After all, he thought. *What would you have done to her last night if she hadn't stopped you?*

He thought about that, and he realised he didn't have an answer.

And that scared him even more.

He didn't want to think that he had any part of Ricky Fox in him. He wanted to believe that Fox and himself were two totally different people and that he could never be like that bastard.

Now he remembered yelling at her and sneering at her, being sarcastic and pushing her over the edge.

But she did *lie! Why?*

Maybe Fox *wasn't* so abnormal. Maybe there was a bit of Fox in every man.

John shook his head.

For once in his life he was truly ashamed.

"It won't happen again," he broke the silence between them and waited for her reply.

There was none.

He waited a bit longer.

"Zoe?" he whispered.

Nothing.

He sharpened his ears to listen for any noise. All he heard were bird songs from outside.

"Zoe? You there?"

He started to turn around.

"I'm here," she replied.

He was sure he could feel her breath on the back of his neck. Was she that close to him?

"I said it won't happen again."

"I know, I heard you." She did sound very close.

"I think I just lost it last night and I didn't mean to. I'm sorry. I'm not usually like that and I can understand why you acted the way you did. It won't happen again."

"Good," she replied. "I'm glad."

John waited for her next move, but none was forthcoming. He started to realise that he didn't like the silences between them any more.

"Do you believe me?" he asked.

"Yes, Johnny," she replied. "I honestly do."

John noticed for the first time that the shadow on the far wall had fallen much further. It was now on the floor, halfway between him and the wall, slowly creeping closer. John turned his head to the left and stared out the windows again. The sun was higher in the sky now, quickly climbing up the stained-glass of the windows.

"I'm glad you believe me," he finally said, trying to make a move. "You can release me now."

Zoe didn't reply.

"Zoe?"

"Yes, Johnny?"

"Will you release me?"

"No, Johnny."

He paused, letting her words sink in.

"What?"

"I can't."

"You *can't?*"

"No."

"Why? I thought you said you believed me."

"I do," she whispered.

She sounded so close to him.

"And I said I wouldn't act that way again, you heard that too?"

"Yes."

"Then why can't you release me?"

There was a moment of silence, and then John heard her deep sigh. Another rustling noise followed before the silence began again.

"I'm sorry, Johnny. I had to tie you up in this chair. Not because of last night, but so you won't try to save me from Ricky."

"Huh?"

"You have to understand, okay?"

"I don't know what you're talking about!"

John felt her hand rest on his right shoulder. She rubbed his shoulder lightly.

"I have to do this –"

"Do what?"

Zoe sighed, "Please, Johnny, just *listen*, okay?"

He wanted to say more, to yell at her and demand to be untied, but he bit his tongue.

Easy...let her talk...

He nodded his head, "Go on."

"Okay, I'm sorry, but you have to stay tied up, okay? You probably don't understand, and I really can't ask you to. But I'm doing this for you. I'm doing it for all of us. I'm protecting all of us from Ricky."

"You're right, I *don't* understand!"

"Johnny, you don't know how violent Ricky can be. You have no idea. I tried to explain to you what he's like and how he acts and how dangerous he is, but I don't think you really understand what you'd be up against. So, when I calmed down last night and brought you back in here, I thought about what was going to happen today, and I decided I can't let you go ahead and help me. I just can't. I've got to solve my *own* problems my *own* way. And I saw last night how upset and violent you can become and I just know that if you lose it when Ricky is around we'll all be as good as dead. He won't stand for it and you won't have the power to do anything about it. This is for the best – for all of us – Johnny."

"You can't be *serious!*" John replied.

"I am."

"You can't face him alone!"

"I have to and I will."

"But you're going to need help," he continued. "You said yourself this bastard is violent. Hell, you *know* how violent he can be! You can't walk in there alone – you'll need help."

"Yes, I probably will," Zoe's voice sounded sad, almost strained. "But that's not how we're going to play it. We'll play it by Ricky's rules and his rules only. It's the only way that there will be hope for you and Helen."

"I can't believe you'd do it this way!"

"I have no other choice."

John turned his head to the left, trying to see her over his left shoulder, but he couldn't.

All of a sudden he wanted to see her.

Needed to.

"Yes, you do. Take me with you. I can stay hidden, or in the background somewhere. I promise not to do anything except what you tell me to do."

Zoe let out a soft chuckle.

"I promise," he said.

"Yes," Zoe replied. "You probably do promise, but I know you won't keep it. I know what will happen. I can see in my mind you and Ricky exploding in each other's faces. I can see it happening. Believe me, Johnny, I've spent all night thinking about the scenarios of how today will play out, and I know for sure that if you go along with me, there's no doubt that you'll end up dead. And so will Helen probably. I just can't let that happen."

Even though she was so close to him, the silence that now blanketed them was deep and long.

John shook his head.

There was nothing he could say.

He tried to think of something, but his mind was spinning out of control. He knew he could try to talk her around, but he also knew that he was currently in a position in which he could do nothing, and he didn't think Zoe was going to untie him now – no matter what he said.

She's already decided, he thought.

"Look," he said after a short while. "Why don't we just wait for Fox to call, see what he has to say – what he wants – and then we'll decide our course of action."

"He already has."

"Huh?"

"He's already called."

"When?" John was confused. "I didn't hear him."

"You were out cold, Johnny. He called about two hours ago."

John turned to stare at the still-rising sun and remembered he no longer had a watch.

"It's past nine o'clock?"

Zoe let out a sour giggle, "No, it isn't."

"He said he'd call at nine a.m."

"Another one of his little games," Zoe replied. Her voice sounded small and childlike. "He called two hours early."

"Oh," John replied. "I didn't know."

He heard her footsteps behind him. And then suddenly she was by his side. She squatted down by him to look him straight in the eye.

"And that's just the point, Johnny," she said. "You don't know him and you don't know how he works. You're going to be out of your depth if you meet him and I don't want you to put your life on the line to solve problems that are mine."

"But – "

"You don't know how he thinks or what he's capable of. You haven't got a clue, so it's safer for you to stay here. If I survive today, I'll bring Helen back with me. If I don't, I just hope Ricky keeps his promise to return her here."

"Will he?" John asked, staring deep into her eyes and watching her face change as a multitude of emotions swept across it.

"He said he would," she whispered as her eyes dropped to the ground.

"Do you believe him?"

She nodded, "I think so."

"Zoe, listen to me," John turned sideways in the chair, as far as the handcuffs would let him. "You can't do this, it's not worth the risk. If you really think Fox is that dangerous and your life could be in danger, then untie me and we'll go to the police and we'll arrive there with them and nail the bastard!"

Zoe looked up into his eyes again. She smiled, and then her face broke into sadness. Tears formed in the corners of her eyes.

"Thanks, Johnny," she muttered. "That means a lot to me. That you're willing to risk all for me makes me so happy. But it isn't going to happen."

"We should let the police handle it all. They're experts in situations like this!"

She shook her head, "All you're doing is proving to me that I'm right to leave you here tied up like this. I can't take you with me and I can't take the risk that you'll follow me. I'm sorry, Johnny."

She stood up and walked past him towards the two beds.

She was wearing a pair of tight blue jeans and a navy top that hugged her sides. Her hair was tightly balled, wrapped in a bun at the top of her head.

She means business, John thought as he watched her walking away from him.

"Is that your final decision?" he asked.

"Yes," she replied as she walked past the wooden railings. "I'm sorry."

"Well, I'm sorry too," he added. "I want to help you, I really do. And I think we could beat this guy together, you and me. But I'm hardly in a position to argue the point."

She reached one of the beds and bent down. Lifting the mattress slightly, she pulled the gun out from under it.

So that's where it is! John thought. *How – and when – did she put it there? Not that it matters, it can't help me now.*

"If this is the way you want to play it, then I accept your decision."

Zoe turned and walked back to him. As she did so, she tucked the gun into the back of her jeans.

"Thanks, Johnny. I'm glad you're going to let me handle this my way."

John let out a crooked smile, "I can hardly do anything about it."

Zoe smiled a sad smile back.

"I'm sorry. I wish I didn't have to leave you like this."

John saw his chance.

"Then don't."

"I *have* to."

"I promise if you untie me I won't follow you. I'll wait here until you return."

"I don't believe that."

"It's true. I mean, where am I going to go? You're taking the Jeep, aren't you?"

Zoe nodded.

"Then I can't follow you!"

Zoe stared into his eyes and tilted her head, as if she was considering his idea. Then she shook her head.

"Sorry, Johnny. I can't. I just can't risk it."

John sighed deeply and nodded, "I understand."

"Good. Please realise, if there were any other way…"

"I know, I know. But I want you to realise that I would have stood by you and got you out of the situation you're in."

She nodded, "I do. But I need to handle this my way. Only I know the games that will be played. I can't risk both you and Helen."

John let the silence settle between them again. He stared at her. The sunlight shone against her right side, casting half her body in golden light and the other half in shadow.

Split in two, he thought. *And there's nothing I can do to stop you going.*

"What did Fox tell you to do?" he asked.

Zoe turned her head and stared through the windows out into the sunlight.

"There's a small town about ten miles further on from here called Redlingford. There's really nothing there, just a couple of farms and a river that runs through the centre. Ricky has a farmhouse there. He used it for business deals and stuff before he bought this place. It's half fallen down and in disrepair now, in fact the barn is in better condition than the house."

"You have to meet him there?"

"Yes," she turned back to face him. "And he made it clear he wants me to come alone, in the Jeep, without anyone else. Okay?"

John nodded, "Okay. I understand."

"He said he'd let Helen go if I was a good girl and followed his orders exactly. He would have one of his men bring Helen back here after I arrive. I told him I didn't trust him and he said that he understood and that I could give Helen the Jeep when I arrive and she could drive herself back here if that makes me feel easier about the whole thing."

"And do you?"

Zoe shook her head and looked to the ground, "No, but I think she has a better chance that way. I can meet her on the driveway and make sure she's clear from the house before I let myself go anywhere near Ricky."

"Does he know you're taking the gun?"

"No, but I'm sure he suspects. He must know it's missing."

John leaned forward to get her attention. Her eyes sprung back onto his face.

"This is suicide, you know," he said.

"I know," she closed her eyes and shook her head. Her forehead creased as she held back tears. "I know."

"If I come with you, you'll have a chance."

"No, Johnny," she continued as she opened her eyes and stared back at him. "If you come it *will be* suicide for *all three* of us. With you here and Helen on the way back to you, Ricky will have to play the game fairly. It's the best chance you have."

This is crazy!

"And you?"

"Don't worry about me."

John looked to the floor. "But I do."

"Oh Johnny," she dropped to her knees in front of him and placed his head in her hands. "Do you mean that?"

"You know I do."

The sadness in her face flashed to joy, but then crumpled back to sorrow just as quickly.

"That means so much to me," she whispered to him.

"I wish you didn't have to go."

"But I do, I have to do this for all of us! I have to see this through."

He nodded, "I understand."

She smiled and kissed the tip of his nose, "I'm glad you finally do."

"Will I ever see you again?" he asked her.

"I hope so, Johnny."

"I'll never forget you, you know."

He was trying to get her to change her mind. But he also knew that he meant what he was saying. Even though she'd knocked him out and tied him up, Zoe was someone he didn't want to see get into any more trouble. And he *knew* she couldn't overcome her problems by herself.

She nodded, "And I'll never forget you."

She ran her hand along the side of his face as her eyes pooled with tears.

"Don't cry."

"I won't," she replied as the tears spilled.

John went to hold her, but the handcuffs bit into his wrists and the metal rattled behind him.

Her hand traced down his cheek and along his shoulder.

"I'm so sorry, Johnny" she said, the tears running down her cheeks. "But I have to do this my way."

"I understand. I really do."

He said it, but he didn't mean it.

She ran her fingers down along his arm and then his side, travelling across his stomach and finally resting on his groin.

"What I have to do is important for all of us," she whispered. "I started this. I got you in to it, and I have to get us all out."

She wiped the tears away, pulled down the zip of his jeans and popped the button.

"Zoe," John shook his head. "Don't..."

"I want to," she replied as her hand pulled his underwear to one side. "As a thank you. Please let me…"

John found himself hard and pulsing as she pulled his cock free from his pants.

He went to pull her away, but the handcuffs bit further into his wrists, sending pain up his arms to his shoulders.

"Just relax," she whispered as she lowered her mouth. "Just let me, *please*."

He could do nothing. He was tied and couldn't move. It was like watching a movie of someone else's life and being unable to change the events.

He was helpless.

And her hot wet mouth surrounded him.

He looked down at her head, as it rose and fell, and he stared hard at the tight bun of hair wound on top. And then his eyes landed on the gun tucked behind her back, sticking out of the top of her jeans. His arms tensed uselessly.

If only I could reach it, he thought. *If only I could stop her.*

Then he looked away, looked around him, trying to find anything he could use to stop her from leaving, anything to help his escape while he had the chance.

But there was nothing in reach, he couldn't even reach Zoe.

And he wanted to.

Her tongue licked him, its soft wet surface running up and down his shaft.

He closed his eyes and leaned his head back. His headache had subsided slightly, but now his heart was working overtime, pumping blood through his veins, reawakening the pain in his head.

His mind thought back to the images of her naked on the sofa, the diamond in her belly button shining invitingly at him. And lower down, the shaved beauty of her vagina; pink, hot and inviting.

He remembered her holding out the towel to him when he was having a shower. And there he was erect in front of her. She'd caught him at a most intimate time.

If he had known how the events of yesterday would play out, maybe he would've acted differently.

If *only* he'd known...

Maybe he should've invited her into the shower. Maybe he should've turned on the hot water and grabbed her and lifted her into the shower with him. Wet and slick and soapy they could have ignited the passion that was between them.

Stop denying it, he thought to himself. *You knew all along there was something between you two. Some spark. Something deep inside...*

And that's where he wished he was now.

Deep inside.

Deep inside *Zoe.*

He thought about that.

Thought about her and what he would like to do with her.

And he exploded in her mouth.

It was fast and reflexive and wonderful.

Zoe pumped more and more, faster now. Drawing out of him every last drop he had to give.

He shuddered as she lifted her mouth along his shaft one more time, licking the tip of his cock as she withdrew him from her.

He sat for a long time with his eyes closed and head thrown back.

It had felt so good, so real.

And I want more.

He wanted to remember this feeling forever, for it never to leave him.

He laid back and just let the feelings flood over him.

He didn't open his eyes until he heard a sound from behind him. He looked down and was surprised to find Zoe no longer in front of him and his quickly deflating cock back in his pants.

The sound came from the kitchenette and sounded like glasses clinking.

"Zoe?"

He heard the tap run for a few seconds and then could hear her gulping down the water.

"You okay?" he called over his shoulder.

"I'm perfect now," she said. "And so are you."

John smiled. *We could be perfect together,* he thought.

Then the weight of the events to follow caught up with him again.

"Let me come with you?" he asked one final time.

"Sorry, Johnny," she said from behind him. "My mind is made up."

He nodded.

The sound of footsteps moved from his left to his right.

"Be careful," he called.

"I will," she replied. "See you soon."

"I hope so."

"So do I…"

He heard the jangle of car keys and then the church door closing.

Shutting his eyes to focus on the sounds outside, he heard Zoe's footsteps on the gravel driveway, then the sound of the Jeep door opening and closing.

There was silence for what seemed like forever.

Maybe she's changing her mind.

But then finally the Jeep's engine roared to life.

John tried one last supreme effort to break the handcuffs through the chair, but it was useless. He only succeeded in making the cuffs bite harder, sending more pain flowing up his arms and neck and into his brain.

Zoe, come back!

The sound of the tyres on gravel disappeared and the sound of the engine slowly became fainter as the Jeep drove away.

John squeezed his eyes shut harder, causing stars to appear in his mind, hoping that would help sharpen his hearing.

He continued to hear the engine even as it became fainter. He hung onto the sound with his very being, holding his breath and willing the Jeep to return.

The thudding in his head matched that of his heartbeat, and his chest started to ache from the lack of oxygen.

And then, suddenly, it was gone.

All was silent again.
And he was all alone.

Twenty-three

This is crazy, John thought as he looked around the empty church.

Zoe had been gone ten minutes, he guessed, but he had no real way to tell. She could have been gone longer, for all he knew.

The sun continued to shine on him through the church windows. It was near the top of the panes now, slowly moving upwards into the sky. The shadow that had begun on the wall opposite was now on the floor near him, slowly creeping closer.

John continued struggling with the handcuffs. He tried every possible way to pull them and shake them, desperately hoping to break through the metal of the chair. But all he succeeded in doing was digging them further into his skin, even though he thought they could bite no deeper.

The pain wasn't so intense now, but he realised that was because of the numbness in his hands and arms.

He looked around the church again, slowly this time. Looking at everything with a keen eye, focussing on objects that now could possibly hold the means of his escape.

Starting from his left, he dropped his eyes from the stained-glass windows and ran them across the long wooden table that stretched for almost the length of the room.

Zoe had left nothing to chance. There was nothing on the table at all.

John's eyes slowly moved across the table and to the beds, at the far end of the church.

So she'd stashed the gun there, he thought as he remembered Zoe pulling it from under the mattress. *Where was it before that? It wasn't under the seats in the Jeep, that's for sure!*

And then the events from last night flooded over him again.

The spare keys, the gun, the way she attacked him.

She lied.

She *lied* to him.

Why?

John shook his head, sending stabs of pain up his neck and into his brain.

Why would she lie to me about those things?

John couldn't work it out. He thought she'd been truthful to him. She seemed to have been telling the truth about everything. So why go to all the trouble of lying about the spare keys and the gun?

What was she trying to hide? And why was she hiding it?

As John scanned the beds for any possible idea to help him escape, he tried to put himself in Zoe's mind, tried to work out why she would lie to him about some things and yet be so truthful about others.

Truthful? What's truth and what's lies? he wondered.

And then it all became clear.

Ricky Fox.

It was so simple, and it all made sense.

Fox, you bastard.

When he thought about it, he couldn't blame her. He realised that she had every right to play her most important cards close to her chest. He would too, if he found himself in her situation.

She's played Fox's game for so long, she was probably used to it. It was normal for her. And John worried that she was playing right into his hands now.

Having found enough courage to finally stand up to the guy who is beating her and treating her like shit, she flees from him and drives half-way across the country to find a friend who can help her. Then, when that friend goes for help, she's left with another guy, a complete stranger, and she has to spend the next few days with him because her good friend has been captured by the bastard she was running from.

I'd be very careful too, John decided.

No wonder Zoe wanted to keep the gun to herself. Even the handcuffs made sense when he thought about it.

Maybe she was going to use them on Fox if she got the chance.

John turned his head to the right and glanced along that side of the church. The fire was dead; the charred wood cold and black. He was sure he could still smell some of the smoke from last night. But then he decided his mind was playing tricks on him.

He examined the fireplace more closely.

Where's the fire poker? Or the shovel?

The poker could help him. Maybe he could lever it between the metal slats of the chair. If he could break them he would be able to get free.

But the poker was nowhere in sight.

Damn!

He slowly turned his neck as far as he dared, gritting his teeth as the pain shot across his shoulders and neck and back. Looking over his right shoulder, he glimpsed the closed front door before a cramp bit into the side of his body and jerked him rigid.

He let out a yell of pain as he tossed his head to the front and stared at the beds once more. Gritting his teeth, he closed his eyes and held his breath until the cramp in his side slowly unknotted and subsided.

After what seemed like an eternity, the pain finally vanished and John opened his eyes once more.

Hurry back, Zoe, he thought. *I don't know how long I can stay like this.*

When he thought about the situation she'd escaped from, literally being a prisoner of Fox for years, he could certainly understand why she hadn't told him about the gun and handcuffs.

But how could she just leave me like this? he thought to himself. *I'm trying to help her and she does this to me!*

After being so truthful about her life and what had happened to her, the events leading up to their meeting, why would she not trust him enough to tell him about the gun and handcuffs? Why leave him bound in the church? Why not believe him when he said he'd wait for her here?

He couldn't help feeling he was overlooking something.

John muffled a short laugh.

Simple, he thought. *I'm a man.*

He nodded his head in agreement with himself.

I'm a man, and she knew I was lying when I said I'd stay here.

Why should she trust any man?

He realised things had changed because of last night.

By taunting her about the car keys, by throwing her handbag in the dust and poking fun at her, by chewing her out and being sarcastic towards her, he had shown her that there was a little bit of Ricky Fox in him.

Maybe a lot.

So, why trust me at all?

It was the only scenario that currently made any sense at all.

And I'm a liar.

He had told her he'd wait here for her to return. He'd promised he wouldn't follow her when she left to meet Fox. But he knew inside that he would have done anything to have kept her from going alone. He would've fought her, restrained her, *forced* her to take him with her. And if she'd managed to get away, he would've stalked through the forest to catch up with her.

Redlingford was only ten miles from the church.

John remembered Zoe saying that to him.

Ten miles.

He could cover that distance in no time.

She'd taken the car, so he guessed he only had to head down the driveway and follow the road that brought them here until he reached Redlingford.

I'd do it if I wasn't tied to this chair.

And that was the reason why Zoe had tied him up. She couldn't trust him to keep his word.

And she was right.

John shook his knees and tried to wriggle his feet. His main aim was to keep the circulation flowing down his legs, but he also wanted to check how tightly bound the rope was around his ankles.

He could hardly move his feet at all. Zoe had tied his ankles tight to the chair, making movement of his feet almost impossible. The rope bit into his ankles and he was sure he could feel blood trickling down his socks.

Useless, he thought. *It's all useless.*

He closed his eyes and tried to focus his hearing once again. He needed to sharpen his ears, as they were his only contact with the outside world. The birds had stopped their singing, as if wanting to help him.

John smiled at that thought.

Come on, pal, he told himself. *Don't go crazy on me yet!*

He listened intently for any sound.

Nothing.

He knew the road wasn't far from the church, he knew the driveway wasn't that long, but there were no sounds of cars on the road.

Nothing.

Don't people use this road at all? he screamed in his mind.

Probably not, he replied to himself. *That's why Fox picked this place. A long, long way from anywhere.*

Sighing deeply at the futility of listening to nothing, and opening his eyes once more, he stared down at his body. As he did so, he noticed the shadow was cutting him in two. His head and shoulders were now out of the sunlight, while the rest of his body was still being warmed by the rays.

John felt like time was dragging, but the shadows cast by the sun proved that time was moving at its regular pace. Soon the sun would slip from his body completely and leave him in shadow.

Even the sun is leaving me, he thought.

He leaned his head backwards, fighting the pinpricks of pain in his neck and the back of his head. He looked upwards into the cathedral ceiling.

He tried hard to relax, tried to force the rigidity out of his muscles, forcing his body to be calm.

It was an almost impossible task. The metal chair was hard and uncomfortable, and the numbness in his legs and arms and lower back made relaxing an unobtainable goal.

John licked his lips. They were dry and flaky. Even the wound on his lip from where Zoe had bitten him felt as coarse as sandpaper.

I need a drink, he thought to himself.

But there was nothing to drink.

They better get back soon. I don't know how long I can stay like this.

He wished he could have another chance at the events of last night. He realised that if he had treated Zoe differently, he would've been with her now, on the way to Redlingford.

On the way? She'd be there by now, wouldn't she? Is it happening right now, as I sit here?

If only he hadn't lost his cool and yelled at her. If only they'd gone back inside the church and discussed things properly, maybe John could've been with Zoe to help her, to play an active part in the rest of her life, and his...and Helen's.

I needed to be there to help her and to get Helen free!

But he realised he only had himself to blame for the situation he was now in. He'd lost his cool, scared her, and now he was paying for it.

Damn!

He sat forward and pulled with all his might at the handcuffs. He closed his eyes hard, held his breath and pulled forward, willing the metal in the chair to buckle and break.

The pain shot along his arms and across his back, through his neck and up into his head, reigniting the headache that was just beginning to subside.

After pulling for as long as he could, he slumped back in the chair, his chest heaving.

It's no use, he told himself as sweat trickled down his face. *You're just going to have to wait it out.*

As the sweat ran down his right cheek, John stuck out his tongue, hoping to lick at it. Any moisture at all would help him right now. But the streak of sweat was out of his reach and continued down to the side of his jaw, where it hung for a few precious seconds, as if to taunt him, before it dropped onto his shirt.

Getting his breathing under control and letting the pain ebb away, John came to the conclusion that there was nothing he could do.

He just had to sit and wait. And that made him furious.

Anger got you into this problem in the first place, he told himself. *So there's no use getting angry now. You don't want Zoe and Helen walking in to find you ready to explode and tear strips off them.*

John nodded to his silent thought.

"You're right," his voice croaked.

He closed his eyes, tried to relax and continued to rein in his breathing.

Slowly, his headache began to subside again. The pain was now a dull constant feeling, not the sharp pulsing pain it had been.

He believed the pain was still there, he was just sure he couldn't feel it anymore.

And for the first time, he was glad that most of his body was numb.

<u>Twenty-four</u>

John opened his eyes and looked around the church.

He had no real idea how long he'd been sitting there.

He didn't think he'd fallen asleep, but he couldn't really tell.

He may have drifted off for a while. Or maybe the dull pain and numbness of his body had lulled him into some sort of meditation-like state.

But his eyes were open now and he was alert. His heart was racing and his body was tense.

Had he heard something?

Did a noise startle him awake?

He listened for anything unusual, any sound that was out of place.

Nothing.

He turned to look out the windows.

The painted glass made it hard to distinguish objects, but he could see the outside world through them and could make out different shapes. He was sure he'd be able to recognise the size and shape of a person if someone was outside. His eyes jumped from one window to the next as his ears pierced the silence, hoping for a sound.

But there was no movement. And no sound.

The sun was gone from the stained-glass now. No light shone directly through the windows and the shadow had completed its journey across the church.

John turned back to stare at the windows on the right wall of the church. No sign of sunlight there yet.

Noon.

It had to be.

Around midday? John thought. *Was I out that long? I must've fallen asleep.*

He sat upright in the chair and tried to move his limbs. He could hardly feel his hands any more as his arms moved lazily. His legs were cold and numb and he couldn't feel the muscles any longer. But at least his eyes told him that his legs were moving back and forth.

He turned his head from side to side, trying to break the stiffness that felt like two metal rods on either side in his neck.

His lips were still flaky with dried skin and his tongue felt dry and swollen.

I need a drink, he thought again.

He tried to swallow in the hope of bringing up some saliva. After a few attempts he managed to coat the inside of his mouth. That would hold off the thirst for a little while longer.

Noon! he thought again. *Where are they?*

Suddenly, panic took hold.

John's mind raced as he tried to picture the events that must've already played out, or were still playing out at the farmhouse in Redlingford.

Redlingford was only ten miles away. Zoe would've driven there in no time. She would've arrived within a few minutes of leaving the church.

He closed his eyes and pictured in his mind Zoe arriving at the farmhouse and stopping the Jeep in the driveway. Dust would be billowing around the Jeep, and she would wait for it to settle before stepping from the vehicle. She would make sure that she could see everything around her, and everyone, before making any move.

He could picture her climbing from the Jeep and standing in the drive, her hair in that tight bun, the sunlight shining on it. She would have a hand on each hip, and she would be standing there waiting for Fox to make the first move.

Her face would carry a look of determination, but he knew that emotions would flow over her as they always did. Fox would know exactly what she was thinking and feeling. She didn't have a good poker face and she wouldn't be able to hide her real feelings through it all.

John could see the gun sticking out the back of her jeans too, and that worried him. What chance did Zoe stand with one gun against Fox and any number of his thugs? She wouldn't have time to grab it and use it, and she wouldn't have the skill.

She would be outgunned, outsmarted and out-bluffed.

John knew then that it was all futile.

Everything.

He'd ruined any chance they all had of escape by yelling at Zoe last night.

By forcing her to knock him out.

By making her tie him up.

It was *all* his fault.

And, handcuffed to a metal chair in the church, there was nothing he could do about it.

He could picture Zoe's face as she stood there in the driveway of the farmhouse in Redlingford. He could see the strength in her eyes as she fought to stare Fox down. He watched in his mind's eye as the emotions flowed over her as Fox yelled something to her. And he stood by as her resolve broke and her face melted from strength to anger to helplessness. Her eyes closed and her head fell forward.

The wind played with her hair, sent strands of it floating above her and to the side. The tight bun holding her sun-golden hair together unravelled and sent her hair cascading down her back.

He watched as she fell forward on her knees in the dirt of the driveway, the gun falling from her hand.

She must've grabbed for it.

When?

She opened her eyes and looked up at him. She tried to smile, but couldn't, a look of pain darted across her face.

"Sorry, Johnny," she whispered as a tear spilt from her left eye; the eye with the small scar across the eyebrow.

She fell forward, face down in the dirt.

And John could see the quickly spreading blood, spilling from the bullet wounds spread across her back.

He knelt down by her.

He turned her over as he took her in his arms.

"No!" he whispered. "No..."

He wiped the tear from her dusty face and looked into the cold lifeless eyes staring up and through him. He closed her eyelids with one hand, gently touching the scar that ran across her left eyebrow.

He leaned forward and kissed her on her cold, lifeless lips.

"I'm sorry, Zoe," he said to her. "So sorry."

The blood flowed through his hands and trickled down his arms onto the dry dusty ground.

So much blood. So much blood...

Twenty-five

John woke in a pool of sweat.

His heart was beating hard and his breathing was fast.

He could still see Zoe's face if he closed his eyes. He could see the tear spilling from her eye.

And he could see the blood.

So much blood...

It had seemed so real, as if he were there, as if those events were really taking place.

But he realised he'd fallen asleep once more and drifted into the world of his thoughts, as if he were in some fevered state of reality.

He tried once more to pull the handcuffs through the metal chair. He was desperate, hoping that by some miracle, perhaps this time they would break through. His hands and arms were now completely numb. The only way he could tell he was actually moving his arms was by listening to the clinking of the metal handcuffs on the chair.

Turning to his right, he could see the sunlight beginning to beam through the windows on the other side of the church.

He hadn't been asleep long, but long enough for the sun to start its descent for the day. He knew it was well into the afternoon now. And the slow countdown to night had begun.

Where are they?

Trying to push the images of his dream aside, he told himself that what he saw in his mind wasn't what had really happened.

It can't've happened like that, he told himself.

Zoe wouldn't be beaten so easily.

Never.

But what if she had been?

What if she was lying dead in a pool of her own blood? What if Helen didn't get away? What if Fox had actually won? What if he took them both with him?

And then it hit John hard.

What if no one's coming back for me?

John sat stunned, his mind totally devoid of any other thoughts.

What if no one's coming back for me?

What if I'm stuck here, chained to this chair?

What if? What if? Whatifwhatifwhatifwhatif?

He didn't know what to think. He didn't know how to handle the situation. He had no idea what to do.

I can't just sit here. I can't sit here forever!

He leaned forward and pulled harder on the back of the chair. Feeling was starting to return to his arms, but it was accompanied by pins and needles, which charged up his arms and neck. He needed feeling back in his body to accomplish what he had to do, but the pins and needles were only going to hinder his attempts.

He sat back against the chair and waited for the feeling to pass.

As he waited, he talked to himself, trying to quell the rising fear in his mind.

Now, calm down. You don't know how long this whole thing will take. Who knows what game Fox will try to play? Or what he has planned? Zoe said she was the only one who knew how he would act and she's the best person to try to get Helen out of there. It has to be left up to her.

But she's dead!

No, she isn't. That was just a dream, you know that. It didn't happen, so stop thinking it did.

But what if it did! *I'm stuck here and no one's coming back to get me. I could* die *here in this chair!*

We'll work something out, don't worry about it yet. Give Zoe some time to come through. You trust her don't you?

Yes.

And you know she's going to look after you?

Yes.

I mean, you know how she feels about you, right?

Boy, do I!

Well, she's going to come back just as soon as she can to get you. Right?

Right.

She told you to sit and wait, and that's what you should do, right?

Right.

You don't want her coming back to find you've gone crazy because you were alone for a few hours. You're made of tougher stuff.

Yeah, I know.

Good, then just sit there and wait for her return.

John breathed deeply, trying to calm himself down. His heartbeat had slowed and the panic had subsided. He looked around the church again, surveying his surrounds, looking once more for something to help him escape. But there was nothing.

Where the hell did Zoe put that poker?

He turned to his right and looked over the fireplace at the windows.

John didn't know if he was actually cold, or whether the numbness in his body made him feel that way, but he was looking forward to the sun reaching out to him and bathing him in warm light once more. Just a few hours to wait, and it would be shining directly on him once again.

Just a few hours to wait...

He hoped Zoe and Helen would be back before then.

He shook his head.

Women!

And then he stifled a laugh.

That's what his college buddy Richard Dunbar used to say.

"Women!" he'd say as he sat hunched over his typewriter, typing out a short story or novel. "Never trust 'em and never get involved with 'em. They just screw you and then they *screw* you. Get it?"

John could remember all the times he had confided in Richard about his most secret thoughts and desires. Richard had always been there for him and always had the answers. John was always amazed how much Richard knew about women, considering that for as long as John knew him, he never had a girlfriend.

"They'll play hard to get, but they only really want one thing," he'd told John once. "And when they get it, they'll slip their hand down there and stroke it, and then they'll go a bit lower. But watch out pal, because once they've got you by the balls, they never let go."

And with that, he would finish a sentence on the typewriter and press the return key and smile at John across the room.

"How do you know all this?" John had asked.

"I just do. It's the experience of life."

"What life? You sit at that typewriter all day every day."

Richard wagged a finger at him, "Now, now, don't let all that pent-up sexual frustration get between you and me. We're buddies, remember? It's not my fault you haven't had a fuck in three months."

"That's not true," John yelled back across the dorm from his bed.

"I know for a fact it is!"

John buried his head deeper into the chemistry book he was pretending to read.

"Well, it's not," he replied.

"You're saving yourself, and I know who for."

"You're talking rubbish."

"It'll never happen, you know."

"Shut up."

"You're fooling yourself."

"I said *shut up!*"

"Whatever," Richard shot back. "No use denying it."

"At least I'm not having an affair with a typewriter!" John yelled back at him.

And Richard had laughed then, long and hard until his eyes had filled with tears.

Eventually, John had begun to laugh too.

And he was laughing now.

Alone in a church and handcuffed to a chair, John couldn't believe he was laughing out loud.

Thinking back to that period in his life, remembering the good times he and Richard had both had, John realised just how dependent on each other he and Richard were. They were inseparable. And even after all these years, John found himself laughing again with Richard.

Happy times...

But that was then.

John looked down at his numb and useless body.

What would Richard say now?

He wished they had stayed in touch after college. They promised each other they would, but so does everyone else. And then life gets in the way.

Life.

John pulled at the handcuffs another few infuriating times.

No use.

Richard, if only you were here to get me out of this mess.

He missed their talks and their secret conversations. Heck, he even missed the old typewriter.

So many things to tell you, he thought. *So many secrets...*

He knew what Richard would say anyway. He had no doubt about it.

"I've told you about women," he would've muttered, shaking his head at him. "How many times have I said it? First they screw you, and then they *really* screw you. Pal, it's not worth the trouble, put it back in your pants and think with your big head, not your little one..."

John found himself smiling again. Maybe Richard was right.

But what would you think of Zoe, Richard?

"Just like all the others."

But she isn't, is she?

"Are you seriously telling me she's totally different to any of the other girls you ever knew?"

Come on, she's had a really rough life. And finally she's got herself on her own two feet, telling this Fox prick where to go. It's not her fault he's all powerful and could track her down and drag her and Helen and me into this mess.

"You really believe that?" John could see Richard's eyes squinting at him as he asked the question.

Of course I do, Richard.

"Are you sure?"

Why would she lie to me?

Richard was nodding, "Uh-huh. And I suppose she's quite unlike any other girl you've ever met?"

John nodded to himself in the middle of the church.

"Really?"

Really.

"I've heard that before, you know."

Huh?

"You've said that before, you know."

Never!

"Yes, you have. I've heard it all before."

Buddy, Zoe's one of a kind!

John could hear Richard laughing in his mind.

"One of a kind?" he said between breaths.

Yes.

"Oh, John, how quickly you forget! You mean you don't honestly remember?"

Remember what?

"Not what, but who!"

Who then?

"Laura Austin?"

A silence fell over the church, or so it seemed to John, as Richard evaporated from his mind and left his final two words dangling in the silence.

Laura…

Laura Austin.

John remembered her now.

How could I forget?

And he even remembered telling Richard that she was unlike any other girl he'd ever met.

Now it all came flooding back.

It was his senior year at college, as far as he could remember. He had no idea why, but for some reason he and Richard and some of his classmates attended a funeral service a few blocks from campus.

The service was probably for a teacher or a classmate; he couldn't remember now. Either way, it didn't matter.

It didn't matter then either.

All he could remember was everyone tried to sit as close to the exit as possible, aiming for the back pews, and far from prying eyes. But it was a crowded room.

Was it at a church?

He couldn't recall. John and his classmates found seats in about the middle of the room; teachers to one side, family members on the other.

And it was during the service, while they all sat there looking bored and thinking about other things, that John turned and looked along his row.

And saw Laura Austin staring back at him.

He didn't know who she was at the time, didn't even know her name, but he suddenly realised he wanted to know her.

Very badly.

She was sitting about fifteen feet away. She had a cheeky grin and she was staring intently at him.

He smiled at her.

She smiled back.

What passed between them was unspoken, but they both knew what they wanted.

John looked around to make sure no one was watching. Suddenly, he found his hands were sweating. He wiped them on his pants.

He couldn't remember what happened then, but somehow he must have gestured to her, or nodded his head or something. All he remembered was she giggled loudly.

Heads turned towards her and she blushed and slumped down in her seat.

Harsh stares were aimed at her, but as she settled back down, the heads turned away and back to the priest, who was giving his sermon.

John continued to watch her, smiling at her...loving her.

He remembered he was hard and pulsing, his cock pushing to break through his pants. The room was hot and he felt almost claustrophobic. Too many people and too little space.

Some more time must have elapsed and somehow between them they agreed without speaking, maybe only with hand movements, he wasn't sure. He couldn't remember now.

It didn't matter anyway.

What happened next *did*.

He stood up.

In the middle of the service, he stood up.

And walked out.

John shook his head now, thinking back.

You heartless bastard, he scolded himself. *I can't believe you did that!*

He remembered the faces staring at him as he made his way along his row, excusing himself time and time again, as his legs knocked the knees of classmates. Finally, he made it to the end of the row. He straightened himself up, kept his eyes on the floor in front of him and walked out of the room.

He remembered there being total silence in the room as he did so. Everyone's eyes were upon him. He wondered if the priest had even stopped his sermon.

John didn't know.

And, at the time, he didn't care.

He remembered, they must've thought they were being so cunning, so sneaky. It was like a plan no one had thought of before.

First he got up to leave.

And then, a couple of minutes later, so did she.

What a plan!

Everyone must've known, John told himself now. *How could they not? First I leave and then Laura? It's obvious!*

It may have been, but John didn't care.

And neither did Laura.

He was waiting outside for her, his hands pushed deep into his pockets as he paced up and down nervously. His heart raced when she ran out to him. She was tall and thin and the most beautiful girl John had ever seen.

She ran to him, her dark curly long locks of hair bouncing on her shoulders and down her back.

"Hi," he said.

"Hi," she had smiled a smile that made him melt.

"I'm John."

"I'm Laura."

"It's real nice to meet you, Laura."

"You too," she replied. "That funeral is such a downer."

"I know."

"I got sooo bored."

"I know, they're not much fun," he replied.

"And then I saw you."

John didn't know what to say. He just smiled back at her.

"And I knew I just wanted you," her voice dropped in pitch to a husky tone as she took a step closer to him.

"Really?"

"I want to fuck you, John. I'm so horny I want to do it now!" she stepped forward and put her arms around him.

She bumped up against his erection.

"And you want to fuck me too, it seems," she said, a wicked look transforming her face.

"Where?" was all John managed to say, looking around for somewhere they could easily hide.

"I know," she replied as she took his hand. "Follow me."

John shook his head as he remembered letting her lead him away. He followed after her without a second thought.

"See?" Richard returned to his mind, shattering John's thoughts and memories. "They screw you, and then they *screw* you. I told you, pal!"

John nodded.

You were right.

"Of course I was! And you hit a new low there, John."

A low? It was wonderful!

"It may have been, but think of the repercussions. There's always repercussions, John, no matter what you do. But you didn't think of that then, and it seems you still don't think of things like that."

I know, I know. You'd think I would have learnt by now.

"Exactly, but you haven't. And remember what happened with Laura Austin?"

John nodded.

"Come on, tell me!"

She left me and –
"Exactly, she left you. Left you for dead."
John nodded.
"Just like Zoe."
John shut his eyes tight as the words sliced into his mind.
John pushed Richard aside, throwing him from his thoughts.
The silence was heavy.
The panic returned.
Just.
Like.
Zoe.

Twenty-six

*I*t's not true, John thought. *She said she would come back, and she will. So will Helen. They'll both return and then we can get out of this place.*

Even as he told himself they would return, a growing feeling of panic began to crawl up his spine.

But what if they don't?

They will!

But they haven't! It shouldn't take this long.

It might.

It should be over by now.

Maybe it is...

John opened his eyes and looked around the church for what must have been the hundredth time. The sunlight streaming through the windows to his right was now slowly making its way across to him. Soon he would be warm again.

He rocked from side to side, working his shoulder joints, trying to keep them from getting stiff and sore. He thought about trying to pull his hands through the metal slats of the chair once more, but there was no feeling left in his arms and he knew that the struggle was futile.

There's got to be another way.

There isn't. You're stuck here for good.

There has *to be.*

You're here until you die.

Forcing the panic from his mind, John looked through the wooden railing back towards the beds at the far end of the church and tried to think about escape.

There's got to be a way. If only I could find that damn poker. Even the shovel might work...where the hell did she put them?

His eyes rested on the beds.

They looked so inviting, so relaxing.

If I could get down to the end of the church, maybe I could tip myself onto a bed and at least rest on my side.

It sounded like a wonderful idea, lying on his side on the bed, taking the pressure off his back and arms and legs, but he knew it would be almost impossible to climb onto the bed from his current position. The beds were high but his chair was low; he had no idea how he would manage to tip himself up onto one of them.

But anything is worth a try. Don't worry about how you're going to get on the bed until you manage to get there.

He licked his dry lips with an even drier tongue. Slowly, he focussed on his body and began by rubbing his hands together. The clanking of the handcuffs on the metal slats behind him told him he could still co-ordinate himself to rub them together.

Next, he moved his shoulders up and down, exercising the joints, waiting for feeling to return. Leaning forward slightly, he started to rock his legs side to side as far as his tied ankles would allow.

His body cried out in a dull agony that would've felt worse if he wasn't already so numb.

I have to do this, he thought. *No matter what.*

Pins and needles started to flow once more in waves down his neck and back. It was a sure sign that the circulation was beginning again and feeling was returning to him.

"Come on," he whispered to himself. "Keep going..."

Even these simple movements were incredibly exhausting. Sweat began to bead on his forehead again, and feeling its touch on his face reminded him how incredibly thirsty he was.

His tongue felt swollen, and his lips were as dry and rough as sandpaper.

Need a drink.

But the kitchenette was behind him and there was no way he would be able to reach the sink.

The beds are closer and if I can get down there and somehow tip myself onto one of them, I could get some rest and take some pressure off my body.

John liked that idea.

Rest.

If he could sleep through this nightmare…
But when will you wake up?
When Zoe and Helen return.
What if you never wake up?
I will.
What if they don't return?
THEY WILL!

John moved his head to the right and looked down at the sunlight making its way across the floor towards him. It had moved quite a distance since he last looked. It was now halfway between the wall and his chair. It would soon be touching his feet and legs, warming them in its rays.

He was torn then, between the warmth of the sun and the comfort of the bed. He knew the sun would eventually reach him. But he couldn't guarantee that he could make it to the bed and be able to somehow lie down on it.

His eyes darted between the beds and the sunlight on the floor.

He never thought a choice would be so hard.

He decided to wait.

At least until the sun goes down. I can wait that long.

If he was still tied to the chair by the time night fell, he would make for the beds.

How?

I'll work that out when I have to.

But for the moment, the warm glow of the sunlight was too inviting. He craved it; he needed it. He wanted it to pour over his body, as if its rays would somehow re-energise him, give him back the strength and stamina he had lost.

He looked back down at the sunlight slowly crawling towards him on the floor. Time seemed to be dragging, like his life was in slow motion, but the sun's tracking through the sky proved to him time was still moving at its normal speed.

But then, sometimes, time seemed to be passing quicker than he expected.

Either way, he was still tied to this chair.

Tied and helpless.

While the rest of the world went on with its normal life.

John wished he could have a normal life again.

"Normal?" Richard's voice returned to his head. "There was nothing ever normal about your life, buddy."

You again!

"Yes, me again. Caught you at a bad time? You all tied up with something?"

John could hear Richard's laughter in his head.

Very funny.

"Sorry, I shouldn't laugh."

No, you shouldn't. You should help me.

"Not much I can do from here."

You were always the one who gave me advice.

"Well, it's a bit late for that now. You're already in this mess."

And I suppose you wouldn't've been?

"No, sir! No way! These women, they're trouble. If Zoe had dropped on *my* doorstep, I would've told her to pack her bags and leave. Sorry, sister, no room at the inn for the likes of you."

I couldn't do that.

"I know, and look where it got you."

I couldn't say no.

"I know that too. That's always been your problem."

Bullshit!

"You could never say no – especially to a pretty girl."

It's not true.

"Led around by your erect manhood all your life."

John didn't reply. He knew where Richard was going…

"Just like with Laura Austin."

John sighed and closed his eyes, letting his head fall forward.

Once again, Richard was right.

He remembered Laura leading him by the hand, dragging him back towards the funeral they had just escaped from.

"Where are we going?"

"Trust me," she said over her shoulder to him.

He let himself be pulled along, his eyes resting on her flowing dark brown curls cascading down her back. His eyes then fell further down to her small, round arse and he watched spellbound as each buttock swayed as she walked.

Before he knew it they were rushing past the funeral service and down the side of the building.

At the end of the building, Laura pulled him through a side-door and into a long corridor. Stopping only for a second to make sure there was no one around, Laura gave him a quick smile and then winked at him as she pulled at his hand. John could feel his cock harden as he stood beside her. They half-walked, half-ran down the corridor, trying to be as silent as they could.

John noticed the corridor ended some twenty feet down and he realised it stopped at the other side of the building. At this very moment they were probably making their way behind the altar and priest who was giving his sermon, right in front of the huge crowd. If they could've seen through the wall, he knew their eyes and thoughts wouldn't've been on the dearly departed.

But for a moment or two he was confused.

Where are we going? he thought.

Then he saw the bathroom signs.

And then he understood.

A smile broke out on his face as his erection beat harder against the inside of his pants.

"Almost there," she whispered.

Behind him, he could hear the monotone of the priest's sermon, penetrating the wall and filtering through to them. But he paid it no attention.

There were more important things to think about.

Laura's pace quickened as they passed the men's bathroom.

John remembered looking at the bathroom door as they rushed past. He assumed they would go in there, but he didn't care. He just hoped the ladies bathroom was empty.

And then Laura pulled him past that door too.

John's face became puzzled. His eyes swept the corridor. There was only one bathroom door left.

The one for the handicapped.

John stopped in his tracks.

"In there?" he pointed to the handicapped sign on the door just three feet in front of them.

Laura turned and smiled at him, "Yeah."

"Why there?"

"Why not?" she shot back.

"What about the others?" he nodded back towards the other bathrooms.

"Too busy, someone might walk in on us. There's less chance of anyone using the handicapped bathroom."

She smirked at him and raised an eyebrow.

"You're not *scared*, are you?" her voice dropped to its deep sexy level again.

"No!" John replied quickly, puffing up his chest.

"Anyway," she continued as the squeezed his hand and pulled him towards her again, "The toilets are special in there. Higher than normal. Easier. Helps us do what we want to do."

She leaned forward and licked the tip of his nose with her hot, moist tongue.

"You ready?" she whispered.

He nodded, "Ready and willing."

"Good."

She turned, walked to the door and placed her hand out to touch it. "No turning back?" she whispered over her shoulder to him.

"No way!" he replied.

She pushed open the door and entered the bathroom.

And, blindly, John followed.

Twenty-seven

"**L**ed by your cock at every turn," Richard said to him. John lifted his head and opened his eyes.

"That's not true," his voice croaked in the silence.

He looked around, half expecting to see Richard standing nearby, or sitting over at the long table, typing away on his next book project.

But Richard wasn't there.

No one was there.

The church was as silent as ever.

John listened for any change outside; for a car motor, a Jeep's engine, footsteps, the sound of voices, Zoe calling to him, Helen calling out his name, a police siren, an ambulance. Anything.

Nothing.

Even the birds seemed to have vanished for the day, leaving him on his own.

He looked down to his right and saw the sunlight was now warming the bottom half of his body. Finally, some warmth was returning to his numb and stiff limbs. Soon, he would be able to feel the sunlight on his face again; to feel the warmth he had been missing for so long.

Sunlight!

He needed a drink badly now.

His tongue seemed to grow each time he thought about it. It was dry and swollen and felt like it was hairy, and the insides of his mouth were just as bad.

He tried to swallow, to bring up some saliva, but it hurt his throat too much, so he gave up. His lips felt parched and swollen, and Zoe's bite wound in his bottom lip felt like a yawning chasm with deep sides and no end.

I need a drink.

And with the warmth returning to the lower half of his body, along with some feeling, he realised something else too.

He needed to go to the bathroom.

He hadn't noticed it before, but now the pressure on his bladder was intense. He hadn't drunk anything since last night, before they left for the church, but he realised he hadn't been to the bathroom in all that time either.

He needed to go.

Now.

But there was nothing he could do about it, except hold on and hope that Zoe and Helen would return soon.

"Not looking very likely, is it?" Richard said to him.

Huh?

"I said I don't think the girls are going to return, do you?"

They will.

"I don't think so."

Just you wait and see. Zoe won't let me down. She'll be back.

Richard laughed, "Yeah, I've heard you say that before too..."

Yeah, yeah...

"Remember? Remember who you said it about?"

Okay, okay, I know.

He remembered the events so clearly now. Even though he hadn't thought of them for years, he could still remember each and every one as if they had happened just yesterday.

Laura spun around and hugged John the moment they entered the bathroom. She reached over his shoulder and slammed the door shut, locking it behind them with one swift movement of her hand.

"There," she whispered. "No one can disturb us now."

They kissed each other hard on the lips. Laura's hands were massaging his groin, rubbing the bulge in his pants.

Before he knew what he was doing, John's hands were holding her breasts. They were soft and wonderful to touch and he could feel the hard buttons of her nipples through her shirt and bra.

And he wanted more.

Her tongue darted into his mouth and wrestled with his.

And then he felt her warm hands massaging his cock. Within a few seconds she had unzipped him and set his erection free.

He was unbuttoning her shirt and pushing her bra upwards, watching as her breasts sprung free from their confinement, bouncing in front of him. Her nipples erect and so beautiful to look at.

Their harsh, quick breathing was amplified in the enclosed space of the bathroom.

Laura unbuttoned John's shirt with one hand, running her hand up and down his chest, while her other hand stroked his shaft and played with the tip of his cock.

He placed his hands over her breasts, cupped them and enjoyed their soft silky feel.

And then he bent down and took a nipple into his mouth, and sucked.

Laura let out a deep guttural moan.

"Yes," she whispered. "I want it so bad..."

He stood upright and kissed her on the lips once again. Her tongue darted with his. They tasted each other.

Then she was turning him, guiding him, pushing him backwards towards the toilet. He shuffled in small steps, his pants and underwear around his ankles. She had a dark smile on her face and she was licking her lips.

"I want you," she said.

She pushed him back onto the toilet. He fell backwards only for a short distance; the toilet bowl was higher than normal. His back hit the wall hard and his buttocks slammed down on the cold porcelain seat. But he didn't care.

All he cared about was Laura.

She bent over him and pulled off his jeans and underwear from his feet.

"I want you so bad," she whispered.

She massaged his cock for a few seconds longer, looking at it intently and quietly moaning to herself.

And then she reached out to his shoulders and pushed him back against the wall again, making him slip down slightly, getting him at just the right angle.

She hitched up her skirt and stepped over him. The taller toilet made the height between them just right.

And slowly she descended onto him.

And the folds of her love swallowed him whole.

Warm, wet and deep.

John could remember the scene clearly in his mind, almost as if it were caught on film. And he was surprised to find that he was erect once more. Even after all these years, the memory of Laura could get his passion to flow.

Only this time, he couldn't do anything about it.

It probably didn't last for more than ten minutes, but John remembered clearly the exact moment when Laura's rocking reached its peak. She threw her head back, her breasts bouncing, her arms reaching out to the hand rails attached to the side of the cubicle, her hands clutching at the shiny metal, fingers stretching and fingernails clawing at the paintwork.

And she moaned deeply as she reached orgasm.

Her whole body shuddered and she tightened her hold on him inside. Watching her quake with such totality and seeing the half-sleepy, satisfied look on her face, John found himself building even quicker.

His orgasm followed only seconds later and he exploded in her lovely soft centre. She rode him hard as he pumped inside her, prolonging his ecstasy, moaning with him as he rode the wave of passion.

And then it was all over.

She leaned forward and placed her arms around him. He did the same and ran his hands through her long curls.

Nothing could be more perfect.

They held each other until their breathing calmed. Then, she climbed from him, letting him slip out from her warmth.

She kissed him once more, full on the lips, but with no tongue.

"Bye," she whispered.

Turning around, she straightened her skirt, placed her breasts back in her bra, buttoned her shirt and left the bathroom.

John remembered sitting there on the toilet seat, watching his erection subside in a pool of his own semen, feeling the warm stream slipping down his legs and dripping into the toilet bowl.

And he remembered being in love for the first time.

"She *used* you," Richard said to him now.

I know.

"You didn't at the time though, did you?"

No.

"You thought she was the girl for you. That you'd both end up together."

It wasn't that simple.

"It never is, pal. You thought it was. But it wasn't."

I know.

"I tried to tell you then."

I remember.

"She *used* you."

I know!

"Like Zoe's using you now."

The silence engulfed him as he opened his eyes and looked around the church.

You're wrong.

"Am I?" Richard whispered, and then he was gone.

"It's not the same," John's voice croaked out into the silence and echoed around him.

It's not the same.

He remembered staggering from the handicapped bathroom a few minutes later, tucking his shirt back in his pants as he dashed out of the corridor looking to catch up with Laura.

The funeral service had just concluded when he came charging out of the hallway, looking for her. But there were too many people and the crowd was too thick to quickly get through. His eyes scanned the faces, hoping to see her beautiful smile beaming back at him. But she was nowhere to be seen.

She had vanished.

He wanted to call her name at the top of his voice, but he could tell that the crowd noise would just swallow his plea for his new love.

She was gone.

Just like that.

In mere seconds.

And then Mr. Healey grabbed his shoulder.

"I want to talk to you, Murdock," he said to him, looking down over the rim of his glasses at John.

John could tell by his face that there was hell to pay.

Everyone had seen him leave the funeral service.

Everyone *knew*.

Had it been that obvious?

John didn't care.

He was in love.

Pure and simple.

Or so he thought.

How wrong can a person be? he thought.

Over the next few weeks, John would manufacture any chance he could to run into Laura, to see her around campus, to have lunch at the same time she did. They would talk and laugh, but the same spark just wasn't there. Never again would she look at him the same way, or do the things she had done to him.

Never again.

And at the end of term, she transferred out of state.

Just like that...

"It's only for one term, John," she had told him in their final conversation the day before she left. "My dad's been transferred to another office for just a few months."

"But you'll be back?" he asked hopefully.

"Of course, silly! Sure, I'll be back," she smiled at him and his heart melted. "Wait for me, won't you?"

"I will. Don't worry, I will."

She had leaned forward and kissed him on the cheek then; a small cold peck of a kiss. Then she had turned and walked away.

And out of his life.

Forever.

She never returned.

But John waited.

He waited for months.

For nothing.

"You're saving yourself, and I know who for," Richard had taunted him after Laura had left.

John tried to deny it. He told Richard he was mad.

But Richard saw through him. He knew John was waiting for Laura's return.

The return that never came.

Just like Zoe.

John refused to believe this was the same situation. He trusted Zoe and knew she would keep her word.

Just like you trusted Laura.

This is different.

Is it?

John turned to his right and stared out the church windows.

The sunlight blinded him now.

He shut his eyes hard.

The sun was setting. The rays he thought would bathe him in warmth felt cold on his skin now. He was either too numb to feel them, or the dying rays had no heat left in them.

Soon, the sun would set.

It would finish its lonely journey and die.

Just like you.

And soon it would be night.

Cold, dark night.

And no sign of Helen or Zoe.

John began to wonder if the dream he had earlier in the day was more truthful than he first thought. Maybe Zoe *was* gunned down. Maybe she *was* lying cold and stiff in a ditch somewhere, or in one of Fox's shallow graves.

Maybe the dream was her final thoughts, reaching out across the countryside to him from Redlingford, trying to tell him he was on his own.

Maybe...

"Or maybe she's using you..." Richard whispered in his ear again.

Fuck off!

"Never trust them, pal..."

FUCK OFF!

"They'll screw you, and then they'll *SCREW YOU!*"

"Fuck off!" John's voice broke as he screamed the words into the silent church. "Fuck off, Richard! Just FUCK THE HELL OFFFF!"

His voice echoed around the church for a long time.

John waited for the echo to die before he listened inside his head again. But Richard had gone – or was at least keeping silent for now.

How did I get myself into this? he thought to himself.

He had thought that before too, many times in the past.

He thought it as Mr Healey dragged him to his office.

But even as he was dragged across campus, John kept his eyes peeled, searching desperately for Laura.

John's precious minutes with Laura had been a life-changing event – both for good and bad reasons. He got to remember the wonderful sex they had together, but also the heartache and misery of loving someone who didn't love him back, and waiting for them to return, only they never did… *Of being used.*

Life can so quickly be thrown upside down, on its head, leaving you spinning.

Just like with Laura.

Just like when he met Helen.

Just like when he found Zoe on the sofa Friday night.

Just like every girl he ever met.

It was always the same.

It was still Sunday, a day he would've spent at home with Helen. They could've spent the whole day together reading or talking or shopping. Looking forward to just being with each other and spending some time together.

Could have…

But didn't Helen have to work this weekend? John wondered. *Didn't she say she was busy doing something?*

He couldn't remember now. He wished he'd listened more intently to her when he had the chance. He wished he could have some of the time back they had spent arguing over stupid things.

Some arguments were worse than others.

He wished he could have that time back to live again.

Maybe it would've been different. Maybe if we'd handled losing the baby differently, things would've been better.

But it didn't matter now. None of it did.

And if she did have to work or had something else to do, he knew he would probably have gone to work anyway. No use sitting at home in an empty, cold house. At least there was always something happening at work and some deadline to meet. Sometimes it was just easier to go in on the weekends and work through it all with no interruptions, no staff, and no phones to bother you.

Sometimes it was easier...

Phones.

My God, the phone!

John sat bolt upright and looked around the church again.

The sun, lower in the sky now, continued to shine through the windows to his right. Its rays blinded that side of the church from his view, but that didn't matter.

He turned to his left, tried to stretch his tired and stiff neck muscles as far as they would go.

He tried to look over his left shoulder, but he couldn't see far enough.

He leaned forward in the chair, the metal of the handcuffs clattering against the chair back and biting deeper into his numb wrists.

But he didn't care anymore.

He twisted himself as far as he could to the left.

His eyes strained as the kitchenette came back into his view.

And there it was.

Sitting on the counter of the kitchenette.

He stared at it for what seemed like ages.

The phone.

Twenty-eight

He made it to the halfway mark just as the final rays of sun disappeared across the horizon.

He didn't know how long he had spent staring at the phone once he saw it, but the sun had dipped below the windows when he finally got his mind into action and formed a plan.

It was so simple, he didn't know why he hadn't thought of it earlier. The phone had completely slipped his mind, and only thoughts of spending Sunday at work had brought it back to him.

He shook his head and stifled a laugh.

You idiot, he thought to himself. *You could have been out of this situation hours ago!*

All he had to do was get to the phone, reach it somehow, and call somebody – *anybody* – for help.

To begin with, it had taken him some time to work the feeling back into his body. Limbering his cold and hard joints, suffering through the countless bouts of pins and needles, gritting his teeth as cramp after cramp racked his dehydrated body, finally he felt there was enough feeling and movement to let him try to make it to the phone.

It would hurt.

But the hurt was worth it.

And so he had begun...

Slowly, using his feet and arms to propel his whole body, he began to make small jumps in the chair. His body was heavy and the chair weighed him down even more, but he found he could slide the chair forward on the wooden floor, ever so slightly, with each jump. The handcuffs bit harder into his wrists and the rope around his ankles rubbed at the already-raw skin, but after a considerable amount of effort and countless jumps, he had managed to turn the chair around to face the phone.

It was no more than twenty feet away from him.

Now he had his goal in sight.

I'll make it.

He drew an imaginary line halfway between where he was sitting and the phone on the kitchen counter. The line ran parallel with the end of the long wooden table.

He would rest when he finally reached that imaginary line. That was the deal he made with himself.

And now, with one last jump and as the sun sank below the horizon, he reached his self-imposed halfway point.

Just in time, too. Night will soon fall.

He slumped back into the chair and tried to get his breathing under control. He was sweating again. This time it was freely running down his face, some of it falling into his mouth and onto his swollen tongue.

His eyes had been focussed on the phone since he began the journey. He had no idea how long it had taken him to get this far, but he was filled with new hope that soon this ordeal would be over.

He thought about Zoe and Helen as he sat there resting his weary limbs; his chest heaving and arms and legs aching from the effort. He wanted to know what had happened to them, where they were, and why they hadn't returned.

He thought he knew why.

Fox.

But he wasn't going to think the worst until he knew for sure.

I have to know for sure.

But the first thing he had to do was get himself out of his own situation.

And now you're halfway there.

His breathing sounded loud in the silence of the church. He looked around for the first time in ages, checking out the section of the church that had been out of his view for most of the day. His eyes searched for anything he could use, but most importantly for the poker from the fireplace. But he couldn't see it anywhere.

Where is it? Did Zoe take it with her?

He couldn't remember her taking it. But he didn't see her leave, as he was facing the other way. So, it *was* possible that she had taken it with her.

But why take a poker if you have a gun?

Backup?

Plan B?

Doesn't look like it did her any good.

John pushed the thought from his mind.

Gotta get out of this first, he told himself. *Worry about Zoe and Helen later.*

He tried to convince himself of that, but he was worried about them more than ever now. He kept wishing that he would suddenly hear the engine of the Jeep. He hoped they would pull into the driveway and walk through the door. They would smile at him, walk to him and untie him.

He wished.

He hoped.

But it wasn't happening.

With the sun gone from the sky, he could look out through the windows once more. Darkness was quickly settling around the church.

John didn't like the idea of being tied up all night in this place.

Cold and alone.

Alone.

Alone with no one.

He took a deep breath once more, refocused his eyes on the phone, and started the second half of his trek.

The jumps in the chair covered little distance. Sometimes, he would push off badly and actually slide backwards instead of forwards. But that didn't happen often now that he had managed to work out the best way to do it. The rest of the distance should be easier and take almost no time to cross.

He had begun by trying to use his feet and legs, but he soon realised the more effort he put into the bottom half of his body, the more chance he had of accidentally pushing himself backwards along the floor.

Instead, he transferred most of the work to his arms and torso. That way he could propel himself forwards, using his feet only as a steadying platform so he didn't topple forward or to the side.

The handcuffs bit even deeper into his raw and wounded wrists, but he didn't care. He had to get to the phone.

His bladder was heavier now, and every time he jumped, he could feel the sharp pain deep within him, as if he were about to burst. He needed to escape quickly so he could quench his thirst and empty his bladder.

He pushed up and forward once more.

The chair scraped forward on the floorboards, the sound echoing loudly in the church.

He stopped and took a quick breath.

Then jumped forward again.

Stop.

Breath.

Push.

Stop.

Breath.

Push.

Stop. Breath. Push.

Again and again.

Again again againagainagain.

Slow, painful, monotonous work.

And every time he jumped, he felt the pain, dull and lower down.

His bladder.

But there was precious little he could do about it anyway.

It was full. He could feel it sitting heavy and swollen inside him.

But he was getting closer. He was getting there.

Slowly the phone was getting closer.

Closer and closer as the room around him grew darker and darker.

Stop. Breath. Push.

He had no idea who he was going to call or how he was going to use the phone when he got there, that was something he would worry about once he got over his current hurdle. But he knew it was his key to freedom.

Key to freedom?

John stopped himself from the next jump and stared down at his right hip.

His key ring was gone.

The key ring Zoe had given him.

The one that held the red key.

The key to freedom...?

That's what she'd said!

The key to freedom...

It was gone.

His mind spun as he thought about the key.

The red key.

Was it *really* the key to freedom?

Is that what she really meant?

Was it the key to the *handcuffs* that currently held him?

And what had she done with it?

He glanced around the church once more, this time looking for his key ring or the red key. He checked out the bench in the kitchenette, the long wooden table, even over by the fireplace.

The night was quickly falling and his eyes could see no further into the back recesses of the church.

He couldn't see his key ring anywhere.

Either way, it didn't matter now. She'd taken it from him, he was sure of that. And she hadn't left it where he could find it.

That would be too easy. Way too fuckin' easy!

And suddenly, anger welled up in John's chest.

How can she treat me like this? Why would she do it? I could've helped her, I could've got her and Helen away from Fox. But no, she has to do it herself and like a stupid fool she does! I let her walk out of here and to her death, the stupid bitch! And now we're all going to die!

"Not me," he said between gritted teeth.

He focussed on the phone once more.

"Not me!"

He jumped in the chair, ignoring the pain in his limbs and bladder, and moved closer to the kitchenette.

I'll show her that I can survive. I'll show them all how someone can overcome anything and still survive.

Stop. Breath. Push.

I will survive. No stupid game is going to stop me!

Stop. Breath. Push.

I have way too much to live for!

The light was almost gone and he squinted through his eyes to keep the phone as his main focus.

Stop. Breath. Push.

Stop. Breath. Push. Stop. Breath. Push.

He was closer now, closer than ever before.

So close to the kitchenette.

No more than two or three feet away from the counter and the phone.

"Almost there," he whispered as the sweat ran down the side of his face.

His body was racked with pain, his arms felt as if they were about to break free of their sockets, his bladder was heavy and his ankles and wrists felt raw and bloody.

Stop. Breath. Push.

Closer, closer now.

His breathing became louder, he could hear it echo in the church. It filled his ears, filled his whole world.

The scraping of the chair on the floor became louder and more constant too, joining his breathing in a rhythmic beat.

John held his breath for one last mighty effort.

Push, push, push.

So close...

Push.

I'll show them, I'll show them all!

"This is it!"

He let out an almighty scream and launched himself at the counter, every fibre of his body straining for extra distance.

His feet pushed, and slipped.

His chair sailed forward, but his body twisted, sending the chair slewing off at an angle, turning him sideways as he flew.

His head cannoned into the side of the counter. It struck the surface hard, hitting him just above the temple.

He saw stars as he fell and hit the floor with a grunt of pain. The impact jarred his body.

The sound of the metal chair slamming into the floor echoed around the church as the air whooshed from his body.

John thought night fell around him suddenly.

It didn't.

He lay on his side on the church floor, limp and still handcuffed to the chair.

A warm wetness quickly spread around his groin, but John didn't feel it.

Consciousness slipped from him.

The phone was above him, still on the bench, and out of reach.

And silence returned to the church once more.

Twenty-nine

Falling.
Falling backwards.
There's nothing I can do.
I'm falling.
I reach out.
Try to grab hold.
Can't.
There's nothing to hold.
Why?
Why did you do this to me?
How could you?
You turned to me.
I saw your face.
It was you.
Laughter.
It's all around me again.
I can hear it.
I can hear you.
You're laughing at me.
Laughing with them.
Laughing at ME!
Why?
How can you?
I tried to help.
I tried to fix things.
Now I'm falling.
And you look on.
Falling further.
You won't help.
You can't help.
You can't help?
Or you won't?
How can you not help me?

I tried.
Tried so hard to help you.
Falling.
Further.
And further down.
I reach out to you once more.
Help me.
Please?
PLEASE!
Help me before they get to me!
Help me before I fall forever.
Before I am lost.
Lost!
Lost without you.
Yes, reach out.
Yes, yes!
Reach out to me.
Help me!
I'm reaching too.
See?
Yes, we can reach!
I can touch you.
I feel you now.
Yes!
Grab hold.
Please.
Yes!
Our fingers entwine.
My falling is slowing.
Hold on.
Please hold on to me.
Yes.
Almost there.
Yes.
Hold me.
Hold me and love me.
Yes.
Love me like I love you.
Love me until I must return.

<u>Thirty</u>

John woke with his face pressed into the cold hard floor. He opened his eyes, but the darkness around him was complete. He could see nothing.

For a few seconds he had no idea where he was, or why he was in so much pain.

And then it started to come back to him.

Zoe.

The church.

The phone!

He remembered now. He remembered his last frantic leap. He remembered slipping and becoming unbalanced, flipping through the air, the pain and then the fall to the floor.

He remembered it all.

Damn it, he thought. *Your best chance, and you blew it! How could you be so stupid as to ruin the best chance you had of escape?*

The pain in his right shoulder was intense and moving it only made the agony worse. He tried to move his whole body, but it was difficult as he was numb and cold and stiff.

He had landed in a heap on the floor, his right shoulder and face pressed hard against the cold wooden floorboards. Behind him, and off to the side at a strange angle, his arms and legs hung in the air. The metal chair pressed down on him from above.

He sniffed. The smell of urine filled his nostrils.

The shock from the fall must have jarred his bladder. He didn't have much feeling in his body, but he was sure he could feel the soaking sticky wetness in his pants and the bottom half of his shirt.

At any other time, he would've been disgusted with himself.

He moved his hands and rattled the handcuffs in the vain hope that maybe they had broken free in the fall. But they were still attached to the back of the chair, still pinned behind him, both hands cold and numb.

He shook his feet and found they were still bound too, although he could really only feel his left foot. He hoped his right foot was only numb from the lack of circulation and nothing more serious. A broken ankle or leg was the last thing he needed right now.

His stomach growled loudly in the silence and he realised he hadn't eaten anything since last night.

Last night?

He wasn't even sure what day it was now.

Is it still Sunday night? Or Monday morning? Or later?

He looked around but could see nothing. The night was so dark that he could make out no shapes or shadows in the church.

For all he knew, he was facing a wall or the kitchenette bench. He had no way of telling.

How long have I been out?

He didn't know.

What time is it? I could have been out for hours!

There was nothing he could do about it anyway.

Except wait, he thought to himself. *Wait. Wait wait wait-waitfuckinwait. That's all I do now. Wait and watch as life slowly goes by me.*

He tried to lift his head upwards, but the weight pressing down on his neck and shoulders wouldn't allow it. He only succeeded in creating more pain for his shoulder.

I can't stay like this. Not all night.

Taking a quick breath, he tried to rock his body back and forth, hoping that somehow he might be able to tip himself on his side, or over completely.

Sharp claws of pain shot through his whole body.

He gritted his teeth and closed his eyes hard, willing the pain away. But it was no use. The chair knocked against the floorboards, its thudding loud in the silence of the night. The legs of the chair stopped John from turning over. The chair was bracing him in his current position.

The best he could do was turn his head to the side slightly, resting his ear to the floor and taking some of the pressure off his cheek.

He lay in that position for a long time.

He tried to think of a way out of this mess, but his brain just didn't seem to be functioning. His thoughts were scrambled, he couldn't think straight.

It was so dark he didn't even know whether his eyes were open or not.

Perhaps I'm blind, he thought to himself. *Perhaps Fox came to the church while I was unconscious and gouged out my eyes.*

John chuckled to himself.

That's crazy talk, he thought. *Hey, the whole fucking situation is crazy!*

He had been so close to reaching the phone. *So close.*

But he'd let his anger get the better of him and he'd dropped his concentration, tried for the big leap, only to ruin the best chance he had of getting out of here.

And now he was cold and hungry. His chest and shoulders had begun to shiver in the damp night. The numbness of the rest of his body made him feel as if he only existed from the chest up. If it weren't for the hunger in his stomach, he would've sworn that only his arms, chest and head existed. Although he was sure he could feel the clinging wetness of where he had pissed on himself.

Maybe Fox has chopped me up, cut me in two or something.

John smiled at the lunacy of the thought.

Yeah, and now I'm in some cage at a travelling freak show or something.

"Roll up! Roll up! Come see the fascinating and horrific! Come see the half man, half metal chair!"

I'd pull quite a crowd.

His smile vanished as he thought about Fox.

There's no doubt now, is there? he asked himself. *Fox has won. It's obvious.*

Zoe hadn't returned to the church, and neither had Helen. Fox's plan had worked and now he either had both Helen and Zoe as his prisoners, or the two women were dead. Killed out at the farmhouse while he sat here in his chair, unable to help in any way.

Fox has won. John told himself. *Did I really think I could beat the bastard at his own game?*

Had Fox decided to leave John here to die? Or had he killed Zoe before she even had a chance to tell him that John was at the church?

Maybe it was just like in my dream. Maybe she was shot before she even had a chance to tell him I was here at the church. That I was her security, and that by being here I would ensure she would be released.

It didn't work.

And Fox didn't care.

John tried not to think about it. He didn't want to think that events had played themselves out like that.

But if things were different, why hasn't Zoe or Helen come for me?

John listened to the silence as if waiting for an answer. None came.

Why indeed? he wondered.

Maybe this was still part of the game.

Whose?

Fox's or Zoe's?

He listened again for an answer.

Silence.

All he received was another bout of rumbling from his stomach.

Hang on in there, he told himself. *Only a few hours to go.*

A few hours to what?

I don't know.

Zoe and Helen aren't coming back.

They might be.

They'd be here by now.

I know.

And you can't escape.

I might.

How?

I don't know, yet.

Yet?

I'm working on it.

But he didn't know what to do. Or what he could do.

And that's when he heard the noises.

They were fleeting and could barely be heard, but if he concentrated, he could make out the scratching sounds.

Animals?

A dog, no…smaller. A cat?

Or worse…

He couldn't even tell whether the noises were coming from inside or outside the church. But they sounded close.

Rats?

John didn't want to know. But there was more than one source of the noise. They sounded like they were all around him, scratching and scampering close by.

In the cold darkness of the night, he found his mind spinning, trying to grab hold of any thoughts that would help him in any way.

But there were none.

Something brushed up against his side. He was sure he felt it. He jerked away from it, but the chair held him tight.

He lay on the floor with a mind devoid of ideas of how to escape.

How can I? In the position I'm in, I can't do anyth-ing!

He lay there waiting. Waiting for something to happen.

"That's my pal," Richard spoke to him again. His voice was loud in the night. "Always waiting for something to happen, always watching as others take the lead. And then you follow."

Go away.

"Hey, now that's no way to speak to your best buddy," Richard continued.

I don't want to talk right now.

"Why? Are you busy? You don't seem to be doing much."

Shut up.

"Looks like you're waiting."

I said, shut up!

"Waiting for others to play your hand for you. Just like the old days."

That's not true.

"Sure it is!" Richard replied. "You used to do it then and you're doing it now. At least you're consistent, I guess."

I'm the one who needs to be in control. I'm the one who has to control a situation.

"Yeah, yeah. I know you *say* that. But events prove otherwise, don't they, pal? You're hardly in control now!"

I don't want to talk to you right now.

"No, I guess you don't. But you're gonna anyway."

I won't.

"Yes, you will."

I won't listen.

Richard chuckled, "Pal, I don't think you're in any position to stop me!"

John closed his eyes hard, trying to wish Richard from his mind.

"I'm still here!" Richard replied after a few seconds.

It didn't work.

Don't mock me!

"Well, don't try to ignore me. It won't work."

Okay, okay.

There was silence between them for a while.

"You've let yourself be led around by your cock again, my friend." Richard continued. "I thought you would've learnt your lesson with Laura, but that seems not to be the case. Even all these years later, you're still doing it."

I don't know what you're talking about.

"Come on, John. How blind do you have to be? Laura screwed you. Remember? *Screwed you!* That's with a capital 'SCREW', okay? She played you, she got what she wanted, she lied to you, and you stand there with your cock hanging out of your pants and believe everything she said. Then she leaves and you watch her go. And guess what? She never comes back!"

It wasn't like that.

"Yes, it was."

I was in control of the situation. I knew what was happening.

Richard laughed long and hard. "Really?" he said as his laughter subsided. "Like you are now?"

Shut up.

"It's the same thing, pal. Don't you get it yet? You were never in control of that situation with Laura and you were never in control of this whole mess with Zoe. No matter what you think. And now, look where you've wound up?"

I'm in control.

"Fuck, pal, open your eyes and look around you. You're nose-down and ass-up, tied to a chair in some shit-hole of a church somewhere. No one knows you're here and no one knows what's going on. And no one's coming to get you out of this mess either! You've even pissed all over yourself! In control? You? Give me a break!"

John pushed his face hard into the floorboards, hoping the pain slicing through his mind would slice through Richard as well and silence him once and for all.

"Ain't that easy, pal," Richard replied. "I'm not going anywhere."

John pushed harder. Stars began to swim in his mind.

"Zoe's been in control of this situation since the beginning. She's shown you a bit of tit and arse and then your little man between your legs stands to attention and tells your brain to take a hike!"

John's headache returned as he pushed his head harder into the floor. But the pain was too intense and the effort was too strenuous. Eventually, he gave up and tried to relax.

It's not like that, John finally replied.

"Yes, it is. Just like Laura."

Stop talking about Laura, it's nothing like Laura!

Richard sighed, "Of course it is! She played you, she screwed you and now Zoe is doing the same thing. You weren't in control then and you're certainly not in control now."

What was I supposed to do? Laura moved out of state!

"You just hung around and waited, didn't you?"

Yes!

"Waited for her to return."

Of course!

"But she didn't come back, did she, John?"

No, but I didn't know that was going to happen.

"But you didn't do anything to change the situation, did you?"

John thought for a second. *No, I didn't.*

"You never found out why she didn't come back, did you?"

No, I didn't.

"You didn't do anything. You just waited."

Yeah, I waited.

"You didn't go after her. You didn't try to look her up. Or give her a call. Or write her a letter. Or anything!"

No, I didn't. I just thought she'd come back.

"You waited and watched life pass you by."

I guess so, yeah.

"Just like you're doing now."

But I can't do anything now, I'm tied to this chair! I'm stuck here. This is totally different!

"Really, John? Is it so totally different? Maybe the scenery has changed; we didn't have stained-glass windows in our dorm. And maybe the furniture has changed; our study desks and saggy old mattresses are gone and have been replaced by wooden pews and metal chairs. And maybe Laura never whipped out the handcuffs and rope and tied you up physically, but what about mentally? Isn't this exactly the same situation?"

No!

"Aren't your emotions, your *feelings*, exactly the same?"

NO!

"I think they are. I think this is the same situation, just years later. And if you don't do something to change it soon, you won't *get* another chance to save yourself, or Zoe or Helen."

There's nothing I can do, I'm stuck here.

"Really?"

Yes.

"Well then, I'm sorry pal. If you don't take control then there's nothing more I can do," Richard sounded disappointed in him. "Are you sure there's nothing more you can do?"

There's nothing, I already told you that!

"Then you're gonna die here, John." Richard whispered in his head. "You'll lay there until you die."

And with those final words, Richard was gone and silence returned to John's mind again.

He was alone once more.

You just don't understand, his mind replied to the silence where Richard had been. *No one does. It's more complicated than that.*

But there was no reply.

The cold night air settled back on John and he opened his eyes and looked around, hoping that somehow he could see more or that perhaps day had broken while he had been talking with Richard.

What time is it? How much longer will it be dark? If it were light again, maybe I could see a way out of this. Maybe I could try again.

Maybe I could take control.

John thought about what Richard had said.

Maybe he was right. I can't just lie here waiting for death. I have to fight, I have to try and get out of here no matter what.

And suddenly John felt a rush of renewed vigour.

I've got to try. I have to!

For me.

For all of us.

I have to!

And if the worst has happened, if Fox has killed Zoe and Helen, then it's my duty to spend every moment for the rest of my life hunting that bastard down, to bring him to his knees and make him pay for all the hurt and destruction he's caused.

I owe Helen and Zoe that much at least!

He licked his parched scabby lips with his dry swollen tongue. He tried to swallow, but found it too difficult.

I have to do something, he thought to himself.

And, taking a deep breath, he began.

"Help."

The sound cracked from his mouth and came out as a dry whisper.

He tried again.

"Help."

Louder this time, but still weak.

He swallowed and swallowed again. The juices were beginning to flow in his throat once more.

"Help!"

Better. Keep going.

"Help!"

Louder.

"Help!"

His voice was echoing around the church now.

For the first time, he could feel some strength return to his lifeless body.

There was hope.

Control. Take control.

"HELP!"

Yes!

"HELP!"

Louder, louder!

"HEEEEELLLLLLLP!"

So loud now, the cry was echoing throughout the church for seconds after he had finished.

"HEEEEELLLLLLLP!"

This is going to work. It has to!

"PLEASE! SOMEBODY HEEEEELLLLLP ME!"

He called again and again into the dark and silent night.

"HEEEEELLLLLLLP!"

Over and over, he waited just long enough for the previous cry to die out before he started again.

Control.

"PLEASE! SOMEBODY HEEEEELLLLLP ME!"

His chest ached from the strain and his shoulder and neck muscles were rigid with every effort. But it had to be worth the pain.

"PLEASE! SOMEBODY HEEEEELLLLLLP ME!"

Again and again and again.

Countless times.

The shuffling around him ceased, as if his voice had scared away whatever it was that was foraging nearby.

He cried out for what seemed like hours, until his throat became raw and his voice began to waver.

He tried to continue for as long as he could.

"HEEEEELLLLLLLP!"

But, eventually, his voice began to give out.

And no one came to save him.

One last try.

"HEEEEELLLLLLLP..." only a hoarse whisper this time.

His voice was gone.

All that came out of his mouth now were the strained whispers of a desperate man.

And there were no sounds of help from outside the church.

Nothing.

Eventually, he stopped.

And as the silence fell around him once more, he plunged back into panic.

This is it then, he told himself. *There's no way out. No one's coming to get me. No one can hear me. I'm going to die like this.*

Slowly, the scratching sounds returned. They were louder now; close by and all around him.

Richard was right.

Die.

Like.

This.

And with that thought in his mind, he began to cry.

<u>Thirty-one</u>

I can't move.
I try.
But I can't.
They're holding me.
Holding me tight.
Too tight.
Let me go.
Please!
Let me GO!
I can see you.
You are so close.
I try to get to you.
Can't.
They won't let me.
Try to get to me.
Please.
Try to reach me.
Help.
Can you hear me?
I'm calling to you.
Can you hear me!
It's the laughter.
Can you hear it too?
Loud.
Too loud!
Can you hear me?
Please!
Open your eyes and look at me.
Can you try?
Please!
Open your eyes.
LOOK AT ME!
I struggle more.
But I can't break free.

It's up to you.
You have to try.
Please.
For us.
Try.
You have to.
You're our only hope.
Try to break free of them for us.
You have to try.
What?
What is that?
I can see it.
It's growing.
Dark.
It's dark.
Look out!
It's growing around you!
It's spreading.
Try to listen to me.
The laughter.
No.
They're screaming now.
Why?
Try to move.
Quickly.
It's growing all around you.
It's swallowing you.
What is it?
WHAT IS IT!!!!
And that noise?
Can you hear it?
So loud.
Over and over and over again.
It's deafening.
Move, quickly.
Try to.
Please.
MOVE!
Oh no!

Is it?
It can't be!
Quickly, try to get away.
Get away.
It's getting bigger.
Bigger.
My God!
No!
It's wet.
Sticky.
No, it can't be.
Please, run.
Listen to me if you can.
Move.
RUN!
Run while you can!
Try to!
You have to.
Get away from here!
Save yourself.
You can't help me now.
But try to save yourself.
No!
It's surrounding you now.
This is your last chance!
Please.
Why won't you listen?
Why won't you listen to me!
No!
It's too late.
Oh my God, it's blood.
BLOOD!
Quickly, leave now.
Try to!
Before the blood drowns us all!
Run.
RUN!
They're taking your blood.
It's leaking.

It's pouring from you.
I can see your wounds.
Quickly, while you still can.
Try to save yourself.
My God, so much blood!
So much blood.
Flee.
Try to escape!
Run while you still can!
Before your blood kills us all.

Thirty-two

The sound of a car engine woke him.

John opened his eyes and could see sunlight shining through the church. From where he lay on the floor, he could see across the church to the closed front door.

He was stiff and cold. And still wet from his urine.

But the sound of the car engine getting closer took his mind off his current situation.

He tried to shake his head, but his stiff neck wouldn't let him. He wanted to make sure that the engine noise he was hearing was real and not a figment of his imagination.

But he was sure of it.

It was a car motor.

And it was getting closer.

He held his breath, praying that it was Zoe or Helen, hoping the car would come to the church and not just drive by.

The engine noise became louder.

And then John could hear the sound of the tyres on the gravel driveway.

Yes, he thought. *She's here. She's back! Zoe's come back!*

Trying desperately to break free, John pulled his numb arms towards him once more, hoping against hope that finally they would break free of his bindings.

But the metal of the chair still held; his efforts were futile.

He didn't want her to find him like this, pushed into a corner, face down on the floor. He wanted to greet her with open arms, to hold her and tell her everything was going to be alright.

But he couldn't.

She would find him this way.

Helpless...

The engine noise was louder, echoing around the church now. John could feel the vibrations through the wooden floorboards.

Everything's going to be alright.

And then the engine stopped.

Yes!

There was silence once more.

John realised he was holding his breath. His ears were straining for any further sounds as he tried to paint a mental picture of what was happening outside the church.

Come on, he thought to himself. *I'm in here. In here!*

But the silence continued outside.

John waited, staring unblinkingly at the front door, almost willing it to open on its own.

Nothing.

Hurry! Please!

Silence settled around him. He tried to look out the windows on the opposite side of the church. But from the ground, he could only see some of the trees that surrounded the church and the blue sky above. There was no sign of any movement.

No sign of anyone.

Please!

John peeled his lips apart and tried to lick them with his parched tongue. He took in a deep breath and readied himself.

"Help," his dry broken voice barely registered above a whisper. "I'm in here."

It was no use. If he could hardly hear himself, there was no chance of anyone outside hearing him.

He was *sure* he had heard the car engine. Almost positive. But as the silence continued around him, he began to doubt himself.

Maybe I imagined it, he thought. *Am I going crazy now as well?*

He closed his eyes, trying harder to concentrate on his hearing.

There has to be something...

The vacuum of silence continued.

Please...

As the silence continued, a tear ran down John's face.

It's over, he thought, finally defeated.

And then the car door opened.

His eyes shot open at the sound and he sucked in his breath, as if any noise he made now would ruin any chances of being saved.

Did I really hear that? he asked himself. *I did. I'm sure of it!*

And then, as if to confirm his thoughts, he heard the car door slam shut.

Yes! Yes, I did! She's back. Zoe! Zoe's here!

"In here, Zoe!" he tried to yell, but his voice failed him again.

Silence.

Again.

No!

He listened again. His neck ached as he stretched his head around further. He stared with burning eyes at the front door.

Hurry, please!

He tried to rock his body in the chair, hoping to make any noise he could to attract attention, but his limbs were too numb and stiff and cold to help. All he succeeded in doing was sending jagged pain through his neck and head.

He stopped rocking quickly. He didn't want to black out – not now.

This is your only chance, he told himself. *Don't blow it.*

He listened.

Nothing.

No sounds.

He began to think his mind had been playing tricks with him again.

Maybe he *was* going mad.

Maybe it would be easier for me if I did...

Then the footsteps began.

He could hear them clearly. There was no doubt. The footsteps sounded loud as they crunched on the gravel and dirt outside.

They were real.

And they were getting closer.

Yes! Quickly Zoe, help me, please!

John's muscles tightened as the footsteps came closer. His body ached but he didn't care. He was straining, trying to reach out for her, wishing he could have his arms out, ready to run to her and hug her. Wanting to greet her and welcome her back.

His neck strained as his ears focussed on the footsteps. His eyes never left the front door as tears of joy began to build in them.

The footsteps stopped.

The light shining from the gap between the front door and floorboards was now split. He could make out two shadows under the doorway.

Yes, it's real. I'm not crazy! I can see her shoes! She's here to save me!

Another sound now, a rattle.

His eyes shot up to the door handle.

It was slowly turning.

Yes, yes! Come to me, Zoe. Quickly, please!

What if it's not her?

It has to be!

What if it's Fox?

No! No, it can't be Fox!

His whole body was quaking now, the excitement and fear making him shake.

It has *to be Zoe!*

The door swung open.

John smiled, ready to greet her.

And then his jaw dropped.

He tried to scream, but his dry, useless throat wouldn't let him.

Things would never be the same again.

Thirty-three

Zoe stood in the doorway, covered in blood.

She leaned against the open door. She was breathing heavily as her eyes, wild and wide, looked around the church, quickly surveying the whole building. One hand was still gripping the door handle, while the other held the doorframe.

John looked at her, and he couldn't believe what he saw.

Her hair was dishevelled. Gone was the tight bun that had held her hair in place when she had left. In its place, her hair was falling around her shoulders and in front of her face, poking up in places and sticking out in others. Streaks of red-pink colour stained her golden blonde locks. It looked as if she had tried to wipe the stain from her hair, but had only succeeded in streaking it more. A few clumps of darker red hung here and there; looking dry and heavy.

Blood?

John didn't want to believe it.

But what else could it be?

John dropped his eyes lower. The navy top that had hugged her figure so tightly now looked loose on her, as if it had been pulled out of shape. There was a rip in the material by the neck-line and what looked like three holes in one sleeve.

Zoe's face and neck were stained pink too, just like her hair.

It must be blood, John thought.

The bloody stain was circular and fanned out, like it had been sprayed there, right across her face and neck. But on her arms and hands, it had been spread into one long stain, as if she had tried to wipe it from her body but had been unsuccessful.

Her blue jeans were totally covered in it too; long patches spread across both legs and down onto her shoes.

John stared at her. He didn't know what to think or say.

Slowly, as her breathing became less laboured, Zoe took a step forward and began to close the door behind her.

As she did so, she turned herself around and her wild eyes looked up at the lectern above her on the wall, sweeping across it quickly as if searching for something.

The hair on the back of her head was also bloody.

What the hell happened?

The door closed with a click that sounded loud in the silence.

Zoe's eyes moved from the lectern to the kitchenette.

Then, her eyes dropped to the floor.

At first John thought she hadn't seen him.

She looked at him but it was almost as if she didn't register he was there.

He didn't know what to do, or say, so he just stared back.

And then she smiled.

The terrified look that had been on her face suddenly vanished and was replaced by her warm smile.

"Johnny?"

He tried to nod but it hurt too much. He smiled back at her instead.

"It's really you?" she asked as she took a tentative step towards him.

He shook his head slightly, it was all he could manage.

But it was enough.

"Oh, Johnny!" she rushed over and knelt next to him. She leaned down and kissed the side of his face. "I thought the worst when I got here. I couldn't see you."

"It's okay," he said in his dry, cracked voice.

"My God," she touched the lump on the side of his face, sending pain through his head. "You're hurt."

"I'm alright."

"What happened?" she asked as she touched his hair and stared into his eyes.

"Long story," was all John could say.

"I'm sorry, Johnny."

"It's okay. Help me up," he said.

"Of course."

Zoe placed one arm under his shoulder, picking him up off the floor, and her other hand grabbed the back of the chair.

John felt better already as his neck and face were lifted and freed from the floorboards.

"You ready?" she asked.

He nodded.

"Here we go, hang on."

And in one fluid movement, Zoe lifted John and pulled him sideways. The chair clattered loudly on the floor and John's body was jarred into place as both he and the chair were returned to an upright position. His head swam from the quick movement, but almost immediately he began to feel better.

Finally, he was in a sitting position again. He rotated his head, hoping to work the stiffness out of his neck. It would take a long time, but he didn't care. He was thankful to be up off the cold wooden floor.

The sunlight was beating through the windows onto his back, its warmth helping his body recover, and it shone on Zoe's fair skin as she leaned over him and looked him in the eyes.

He noticed there were tears in the corners of her eyes. He didn't know if they were tears of joy or sorrow. He guessed he would soon find out.

"Better?" she asked.

He nodded.

She sniffed the air, "You had a little accident too."

"I know," his voice croaked.

Zoe ran a finger across his cheek and along his lips.

"And your voice? Damn," she muttered. "I didn't think to leave you anything to drink. How could I be so stupid?"

She turned from him and walked to the kitchenette.

"I didn't think this through at all, did I?" she said over her shoulder to him.

John took a moment to look around at the church once more. He was sitting between the kitchenette bench and the end of the long wooden table. The phone that had caused him so much trouble was on the bench behind him now.

Not that it matters, he thought. *I don't need it now.*

Zoe returned from the kitchenette with a glass of water.

"Here," she said, holding the glass to his mouth. "Drink this."

It hurt to drink, the mouthfuls felt like blades sliding down his throat. But he finished the whole glass quickly, gulping down its refreshing contents. A cold chill spread throughout his stomach and made him feel slightly queasy, but he didn't care.

"I'll get you another," she smiled at him.

He drank the second glass just as fast.

"Better?"

He nodded. "Yes, thank you," his voice sounded louder as it began to return.

Zoe placed the glass on the counter and stood in front of him. Her eyes were focussed on the floor and her hands were clutched tightly in front of her. She took a deep breath and raised her eyes to his.

"I'm sorry, Johnny," she said. "There was nothing I could do."

He looked at her and studied her face as the tears began to roll down her cheeks, taking some of the dried blood with them. He didn't want to say anything. He didn't want to hear what she had to tell him.

But he knew he had to.

Zoe wiped the tears from her eyes, spreading the moistened blood across her cheeks as she did so. She looked down at her hands and at the stains on her arms.

"Oh God," she said as she rushed to the sink. "It's even worse in daylight!"

She turned on the taps and scrubbed at her hands and arms.

John turned to his right and watched her.

She scrubbed hard at the stains, trying desperately to make them disappear. Water splashed onto the counter and floor.

"I can't get it off my skin," she said as fear spread to her face and she scrubbed harder. "I'll never get it off."

"Zoe."

Her eyes darted to him. The fear in her face changed to a smile, then to sorrow.

"Oh, Johnny," she turned off the taps and leaned on the kitchenette bench between them. She stared at him, her eyes deep brown pools of sorrow.

"Tell me," he whispered. "Tell me what happened."

She shook her head and ran her fingers through her hair.

"It's so bad, Johnny, I don't know where to start."

"Start from the beginning," he said. "I have to know."

But I don't want to...

Zoe nodded. She walked around to him and jumped up onto the kitchenette counter. Her legs dangled over the edge, right next to him, and her hands automatically went to her hair, where she began to braid her bloody strands.

John thought about asking her to untie him from the chair; to finally release him. But his body was more comfortable than it had been when he was on the floor. And it wasn't as important as what Zoe had to say.

Untying can wait, he thought to himself. *I need to know what happened first.*

She turned to face him, "From the beginning?" she asked.

John nodded, "Yes."

"You have no idea what I've been through in the past 24 hours."

"Start at the beginning," he repeated.

"Okay, Johnny," she replied with a deep sigh. "From the beginning..."

Thirty-four

"From the beginning…" she repeated, as if to herself, as a way of getting her thoughts in order.

Her eyes unfocussed as she played with her hair.

She stared past him, out through the windows and into the sunlight.

"I left here and drove up the road to Redlingford. It didn't take me much time at all, maybe a few minutes. But I stopped on the way to make sure the gun was ready to use, that the safety was off, and that I knew what I was going to do once I got there."

John nodded at her, but she wasn't watching him. She continued to stare out of the church and to play with her hair. Her left braid was beginning to form.

"When I got there, Ricky was already waiting for me. But that didn't surprise me. I expected that. He's probably been at the farmhouse for days already, working on his plan and getting his henchmen to do the dirty work of tracking me down."

Her eyes dropped to the floor and she stopped talking.

John waited a few seconds for her to continue.

She didn't.

"Go on," he prompted her.

She looked him in the eye. "Johnny, it all happened so fast. I don't know what to tell you."

"Just tell me how it happened."

"I really don't know. It was all so quick. I was taken off guard and I was out of my depth. I shouldn't really have gone. You were right. I should've taken you with me, or we should've called the cops or something, like you said."

John nodded, "It's too late now for those thoughts."

"I know," she whispered, closing her eyes tight as sadness swept across her face. "I know."

"Tell me," he prompted her. "Please."

She slipped off the table and began to pace up and down in front of him, her hands still braiding her hair while her eyes stared at the wooden floor.

"My God, Johnny," she began. "He killed her...right in front of me...killed her!"

Huh? Who? Killed? Killed who?

"What?"

"I'm sorry Johnny, I don't know what to say. He killed her."

"*Helen?*"

She turned to look at him, "Yes."

No, was all he could think. *No! Not Helen! No!*

"I'm sorry, Johnny," Zoe walked over and kissed him on the lips. Her mouth was wet and warm and soft, compared to his. "So sorry," she whispered.

"But..." John didn't know what to think. He didn't know where to begin. His mind was spinning. Suddenly the situation he was in just got much, much worse. Until then, Fox has been some faceless threat. John knew he was out there and was capable of doing violence, but he was still just a threat. Nothing more. Now he had acted, now he had struck.

My God, poor Helen! No!

Fox was a threat no longer.

He was *real*.

"But, how...?" John continued, trying to find the truth in Zoe's eyes while his thoughts spun away from him. "*Why?*"

She turned from him and continued pacing.

"He said his pain would be yours and that if he were to lose someone, so should you. My God..." she shook her head again. "I've never seen him so mad, Johnny. Ever!"

This is crazy!

"Lose someone...?" John whispered. It wasn't making sense to him.

"I told Ricky I had come back to him. I *told* him that, Johnny. But he wouldn't believe me. I said that if he let Helen go, I'd stay with him. But he said I'd already made up my mind and that I'd left him for good and that we were having sex and..."

"Hey, hang on," John interrupted. "Having sex?"

Zoe shook her head as she paced, her footsteps echoing around the church. "I don't know either. He was raving, I just don't know. Maybe some of his men were watching us at your house. Maybe they saw me naked on your bed in the spare room and they just assumed we were doing it together. I have no idea. But I *tried* to tell him, Johnny. I really did. I tried. I said I was here, I was ready to go back with him, but he just wouldn't listen."

"This can't be happening," John whispered and shook his head in disbelief.

"I know, I know, I thought the same thing," Zoe continued, her hands working on her right braid now. "I thought that as I drove up the driveway. Like I told you I would, I stopped a good distance from the farmhouse. Ricky was already on the veranda waiting for me. I could see some of his men standing back in the fields on both sides of the driveway. They were all armed and I was scared, Johnny. But I stood my ground. I got out of the Jeep and stood in the driveway and yelled at him to bring out Helen."

This game has gone too far. It's out of control!

"Poor Helen," John said in a soft voice. "She didn't deserve any of this."

"One of Ricky's men brought her out from inside the farmhouse. She was in a bad way, Johnny, she looked really beaten up and terrible. She could hardly stand. He'd done her over, I could tell. Just like he used to do to me."

"Bastard."

"I yelled to him to leave her alone and to let her go. I said that I'd leave the Jeep where it was and that I would take Helen's place. I said I'd walk up the driveway and that he should let Helen walk towards me. I'd give her the keys and she could drive out of here and leave and we could go back home and he could do anything he wanted to me."

"He didn't believe you," John whispered as he stared hard at the floor, noticing for the first time the patterns in the wood, as if it were the most important thing to look at right at that moment.

Zoe continued pacing, "No, I don't think he did. He called me a good for nothing piece of shit and said that whores like me didn't deserve to live. He called me a lot of other things too. I told him I was sorry and would do anything for him and then he…"

She trailed off.

John looked up at her. She was leaning against the stove, her arms crossed in front of her as her right braid slowly unravelled. Her eyes were shut as tears fell from them, and her bottom lip was quivering.

"Zoe?"

He watched her, and his heart broke. She'd been through so much. Too much. Things she should not have gone through alone.

I could've helped her more.

"Are you alright?" he asked.

She shook her head and tried to control her emotions.

"I'm sorry," she sobbed. "I really am."

He let her cry it out.

Her deep sobs echoed around the church. And they continued for a long time.

John watched her, powerless to do anything.

When she was finished, she wiped the tears from her eyes, took a deep breath, and continued.

"Anyway, I said I was sorry and would do anything for him and then he…he began to tell me exactly what he would do to me…"

She fell silent as she began to pace again, reworking her right braid.

John watched her struggle with the memories of what had happened to her.

"…and how…and with what…"

"I'm sorry," John whispered.

"It's not your fault," she continued. "I should've seen what he was trying to do. Damn it, I've *lived* with his fucking mind games long enough that I should have known what he was trying to do. But seeing Helen in the state she was in and not knowing what I should do next, I fell for it."

John nodded.

She should never have taken him on alone.

"He was taunting me, making me mad. And I ate it up like the brainless piece of shit I am."

"Don't say that."

"It's true though. He knew what buttons to push, and how to get me angry. And it worked. He stood there on the verandah taunting me, describing how he was going to hurt me when we got home, what he was going to insert in me, how he was going to rip me in half, stretch me until I tore and bled, then have some of his friends over to rip me more."

"He's a bastard, a sick *fucking bastard*."

"I know," Zoe nodded as she paced. "But I fell for it anyway. I lost it. I screamed at him, I called him a fucking murderous sick fuck…"

"Good."

"And I pulled the gun out. And then I started firing."

John stared at her, unbelieving.

Zoe stopped talking, but continued pacing in front of him. He watched her intently, waiting for her to continue, not wanting to force her until she was ready.

The silence stretched between them for quite a while.

"I didn't really know what I was doing," Zoe continued eventually. "I just fired in his direction. I emptied the whole gun. I fired and fired and fired and even when the bullets stopped coming I continued pulling the trigger."

"Did you hit him?"

She shook her head, "I didn't hit anyone. Everyone hit the ground when I started shooting. I don't even know if I was aiming anywhere near them, I just fired blindly and wasted my best chance. I should've got closer, I should've waited until Helen had driven off in the Jeep. But he got under my skin, he said those dirty awful things and I just lost it."

John nodded, "I understand."

He noticed her hands were shaking now, as they continued to play with her braids.

She'd done her best, and that was all he could ask of her.

"And that's when Ricky picked himself up and said that I'd just come here to kill him and that I was no longer his.

That's when he said that if I was going to pick you over him, you would have to lose someone too. That was the deal if he was going to lose me."

John nodded. It was all starting to make sense now.

"I didn't know if he meant it or not. I didn't know if he was bluffing or telling the truth. I just stood there. There was nothing else I could do. I didn't have any other weapon; the gun was useless to me now. I just dropped it in front of me and yelled to him that I was sorry. And he smiled at me then. The sick fucking bastard *smiled* at me and I thought I had a chance. I thought maybe an apology was all that he wanted. I'm such a *stupid* fucking bitch. I thought I'd won him over and I even smiled back at him."

"It wouldn't be that easy..."

"It wasn't. He helped Helen up off the verandah and pushed her down the front stairs. He told her to get out of there and go home and I really thought that I'd won! I began to walk towards her. She was having trouble walking and fell to her knees. I started to run to her, but Ricky yelled at me to stay where I was. That was the first moment that I thought something was wrong. Helen struggled back to her feet and smiled at me. She *actually smiled* at me through all the pain and bruises on her face. And she staggered towards me."

Silence again.

My poor Helen...

John knew he had to hear the rest of the story, but he didn't want to be the one to force her to tell it. He knew it was coming, and he would dread every word.

Zoe finished her right braid and ran her hands over her hair. John could see the shaking had spread to her whole body as she paced.

"She would have been about thirty feet from me..." Zoe continued. "And that's when they opened fire."

"*What?*" John stared at her, but her back was to him. She wouldn't turn around and face him.

"They opened fire, all his men, from all around her. They shot her Johnny, they cut her down in front of me. Like some kind of animal."

John watched Zoe's shoulders hunch over and her hands go to her face.

"There was nothing I could do other than watch as the bullets tore into her," she said, her voice muffled by her hands.

My God, John thought. *Helen! No! My poor girl... You never deserved anything like that. Ever!*

John's head was spinning. He felt sick. The numbness in his body could not override the sickness in his stomach and the pains in his chest. He let his head drop forward as he closed his eyes.

He tried to picture Helen's face.

Tried so hard.

He was ashamed of himself when he couldn't.

Oh, Helen, he thought. *There was so much left unsaid between us. So much I needed to say to you...*

"This can't be happening," he said as he stared back at Zoe.

Zoe turned to face him, her tears had created red-stained rivers on her cheeks. "I ran to her, Johnny. I ran to her and picked her up from the ground. She was bleeding so much..."

Zoe walked to him and held her arms out to him, "This is all her blood."

John nodded and closed his eyes once more, letting his head fall on his chest.

"I know," he said.

"I held her, Johnny. I held her until her eyes closed and she –"

"Stop," John whispered. "Don't tell me any more."

The silence between them was heavy.

I can't go on any more, he thought as the sadness overwhelmed him. *I never wanted things to turn out like this.*

He felt hollow inside, almost drained of all energy. But then, almost without another thought, the anger started to build inside him. His sadness turned to rage. He wouldn't let this go unanswered. He couldn't.

I'll hunt you down, Fox. And I'll nail your sorry motherfucking arse if it's the last thing I do.

John opened his eyes and stared at Zoe. She was leaning against the stove, watching him, her arms crossed in front of her. He couldn't read the expression on her face.

"We have to make him pay," he told her.

She nodded, "Don't think I haven't thought about that. But what are we going to do? We haven't got a gun now, and we've got no other weapons!"

"I know."

"But I understand it now if you want to go to the police," she said.

John shook his head, "Don't worry, Zoe. We're not going to the police. This is between Fox and us."

Zoe's expression changed to a look of worry and then fear.

"You don't want to do that, Johnny."

"I have to. For Helen."

"If I can't beat him at his game, you can't."

"I can try."

"I don't want you dying too, Johnny." Zoe walked towards him, her footsteps loud in the silence of the church. "I can't lose you."

"We have to, Zoe. We have to try and stop this bastard."

"But with what? We have nothing, we can't stand against him and his men who are *armed*, Johnny!"

John shook his head; he didn't want to discuss that now.

"What happened then?" he asked.

Zoe looked surprised by the question, "Huh?"

"After Helen," John paused. "What happened then?"

Zoe ran a hand over her hair and started pacing again.

"Well," she said. "Somehow I got back to the Jeep. I must have panicked and run or something. I don't know if they started firing at me or whether I just turned and ran. But I got back to the Jeep and I was screaming and I was covered in blood and I just drove out of there as quickly as I could. I can remember hearing gunshots, I'm sure I did, and I remember hitting one of Ricky's men who jumped onto the Jeep and opened the door. He tried to pull me out. He grabbed me and pulled. I swerved the Jeep, driving side to side on the driveway, and I hit out at him. One second he was there, trying to pull me out, and then the next he was gone. I guess he fell backwards out of the Jeep when I hit him. I drove and drove and didn't look back for fear they were following me."

"He just let you go?"

Zoe nodded as she paced, "That's the thing about Ricky. I don't know how he's going to play the game now, or if there is even any game left to play. Maybe I'm soiled now, maybe he doesn't want me because I've been with you. Maybe killing Helen is all the revenge he needs. I don't know. But I just drove and drove and they didn't follow me. The next thing I knew, it was night and I was still driving. The clock on the dashboard said 2 a.m. and I had no idea where I was or what I was doing. I pulled over to the side of the road and cried and cried for I don't know how long.

"Once I finished crying, I got back in the Jeep and began to find my way back here. That's why it took me so long, Johnny."

John nodded his head. He couldn't find the words to reply.

"But I still can't believe they didn't come after me. And that's the worst part, because if he doesn't track me down now, I'm going to live my life in fear, waiting for him to step out in front of me one day and smile and then kill me. That's what he's like, he's going to make me sweat, to worry myself half to death, until he's ready to strike."

"We'll strike first," John replied.

"We can't."

"We have to!"

"With that?" Zoe turned around to face him, her face angry now. "Don't you get it yet, Johnny? Can't you see what's going on here? You're out of your depth, you don't know how this game will play out in the end! We can't fight this, it's bigger than both of us! Helen is *dead,* Johnny? Do you understand? She's *dead!* That's who you're up against! You're up against someone who'll kill your wife in cold blood! This whole thing is out of control, Johnny! What do you possibly think you can do?"

John shook his head, "I don't know, I really don't. But we've got to go back there and give Fox some of his own medicine. We have to. He has to finally pay for what he's done. There must be something around here we can use against him."

Zoe put her hands on her hips, "There's nothing, Johnny, or I would've taken it with me when I left. Now, we don't even have a gun. We don't have *anything*."Zoe stopped her pacing and stared at him, "Except..." she said to herself as she walked into the kitchenette and started opening the drawers.

From where he sat, John heard the clatter of utensils in the drawers, but couldn't see what Zoe was looking for.

Zoe tugged on one of the drawers, pulled it from its slot and emptied it on the kitchenette counter. A spray of knives, forks and spoons clattered around the counter-top.

Pushing the utensils one way and another, Zoe searched through them, grabbing at the knives, looking at each one.

"This is all we have," she said as she searched. "Our great hope against Ricky."

Her hand grasped the biggest knife on the counter. It was nothing more than a steak knife with a serrated six-inch blade.

"It's not going to be enough," she said to him as she moved it across the counter and placed it just inches in front of his eyes. "Johnny, we can't fight him with *this*."

John stared at the steak knife, the sunlight reflecting off its blade.

But there has to be a way...

"We need to sit down and work this thing out," he said. "We have to plan an attack and then get whatever we need to wipe this fucker off the face of the earth."

"It's not that easy, Johnny,"

"Unchain me and we'll work something out."

Zoe walked around the kitchenette counter and stood in front of him, shaking her head and crossing her arms over her chest.

"It's not that easy, believe me."

"I didn't say it was going to be easy," John replied. "Just untie me and we'll work it out!"

Zoe bent forward and stared into his eyes. Her blood-stained face was just inches away from his and he could feel her breath as she talked.

"I still don't think you get it," she said to him. "This isn't a game. I don't think you realise that, even now. This is life and death stuff."

"I realise that," he said. "Now, untie me."

Zoe sighed deeply and her hands went to the back pocket in her jeans.

Finally! John thought.

Her hands returned from her pockets. She held them closed out in front of his eyes.

"I think you need to understand," Zoe whispered.

She opened her hands.

Resting in her left palm was a gold chain with a half-heart gold pendant attached to it.

Helen's.

The pendant he had given to her when they were engaged.

The other half of the heart was still hanging around John's neck.

John sat in stunned silence.

"I didn't want to show you this," Zoe continued. "I didn't want to hurt you any more. But I think you need to see it."

John looked at the half-heart pendant. The gold was tarnished, dusty now, and there were specks of dried blood on it. The chain was dirty too, and stained so badly with blood that he couldn't tell if it was really gold any more.

The sorrow welled up in John's chest. He felt as if he were drowning in the sadness of it all.

And all of a sudden, he couldn't stop himself. He closed his eyes tight and let his head fall forward as the tears began to fall.

"I'm sorry, Johnny, I really am."

Zoe was closer to him now, by his ear. He could feel her warm hand on his back, rubbing him, comforting him.

"Helen took it from her neck," she continued between his sobs. "She gave it to me while I held her. Before she died she asked me to give it to you and to tell you that she loved you."

John's sobs grew louder as he let the sorrow flow through him.

Oh, Helen, he thought. *Why? Why did this have to happen to us?*

"I thought it would hurt too much to give it to you," Zoe continued rubbing his back. "But now I think you needed to see it, so you know how dangerous this whole game is. Okay?"

John nodded.

"I'm sorry, Johnny" she said once more.

He cried for what seemed like forever.

Zoe stayed by his side and let him cry out the pain. Holding him and kissing his cheek.

His sobs echoed through the church until finally, he could cry no longer. He was too exhausted, too tired.

This is all so fucking fucked up!

With one last, deep sob, he lifted his head and opened his eyes.

He turned his head to the left and looked into Zoe's eyes. She smiled at him. Her face was still spotted with Helen's blood. Even the scar across her left eyebrow was a deep red colour now.

Her smile filled him with warmth and he was glad she was here by him, to make the pain ease slightly. He didn't want to be alone right now.

He smiled back.

She rubbed his arm and then ran her fingers through his hair.

His eyes dropped down.

He saw the chain hanging around her neck.

Then he saw the half-heart pendant hanging there too.

Confusion crossed his face. His eyes flashed back to hers.

She smiled again.

"Now we can be together," she whispered. "Forever."

<u>Thirty-five</u>

"**J**ust you and me, Johnny," she whispered into his ear as she fingered the half-heart pendant.

"What?" John sat back from her.

"Now that Helen's gone, we can be together."

She leaned closer to him.

"I know it's a bad time to talk about this," she said as emotions swept across her. "I know I shouldn't. But this is our *chance*. At least we still have each other. At least this way we can protect each other and be together now for always."

John stared deep into her eyes.

Is this some kind of joke?

He tried to read her face, to work out what she was thinking, but he couldn't.

Is she serious?

"Zoe, look –"

"I know what you're going to say," she continued. "But I don't want you to think about it now. You're too emotional because of all the events that have happened. I understand that, I really do, Johnny. But I've been thinking as I drove back here. Think of it this way, think that maybe it's Fate that has brought us together. Maybe it was *supposed* to work out this way. Maybe we were *destined* to be together. Did you ever think of it like that?"

John shook his head. "This is *crazy*."

"No, no it's not. See this?" Zoe lifted the half-heart gold pendant from her neck and held it out for him to see. "Helen gave me this, Johnny. She *gave* me this, just before she died. It's a *sign*, Johnny. A sign that we can now be together."

John watched her face. Emotions flowed and changed the way she looked. One second she was like a scared child, and then the next she looked joyous and more excited than ever. But there were other emotions mixed in; emotions John hadn't seen before.

He discovered he could no longer read her as easily as he used to.

Kneeling now, she moved closer to him, until she was by his side and looking up into his eyes.

"I love you, Johnny," she whispered.

John turned away from her.

"Don't talk like that," he said.

"I do. I want you."

"We don't always get what we want, Zoe."

"Some of us do."

There was silence between them.

John turned back to face her.

She was sitting on her haunches, her arms crossed in front of her. Worry crossed her brow, but her mouth was bent into a half-smile.

He couldn't see the half-heart pendant now. He could only see the chain disappearing under her shirt. She had hidden the pendant from his view.

"Untie me, Zoe," John said.

She didn't reply. She just stared at him.

Something's not right...

"Untie me, please, Zoe," John repeated, keeping his growing anger in check.

Zoe shook her head. "I don't think so, Johnny. Not yet."

"You'll untie me!" his voice raised to a yell.

"No, I won't."

"Do it now!"

"Not until you *understand*," she said as she stood up and walked to the kitchenette. "Not until you come to your senses and see what's right."

"I know what's right," John's eyes followed her. "And I know what's crazy."

Zoe stopped at the sink and poured herself a glass of water. She began to drink it, ignoring John completely.

"You'll untie me Zoe." John continued, keeping his anger in check. Trying hard not to lose it and push her over the edge like Saturday night.

She put the glass down on the counter and turned to face him.

"Make me," she said.

"*Huh?*"

"Make me untie you."

Has she lost it? John wondered. *Did the events at Redlingford shock her so much that she's lost her mind? Is she as crazy as Fox? Or worse?*

"I can't," he found himself answering her.

"Well, you'll just have to stay there," she crossed her arms.

"*Zoe...*"

She smiled at him, "Unless..."

"Unless what?"

She walked around the counter and leaned over to him. The sun shone on her hair, making the braids look golden. It brought back to John the warm memories of finding her on the sofa, meeting her, spending time and shopping with her.

Did all this begin just three days ago?

"Unless you tell me you love me," she smiled at him.

"Zoe, don't..." he whispered and looked away.

"If you can't say it, then I can't unchain you."

"I can't," John replied through gritted teeth. "I *won't*."

Zoe's eyes fell to the ground and sadness crossed her face.

John felt sorry for her for a split second. But then the stiffness in his neck and his sore arms and numb body reminded him that she could change the situation they were both in.

But she was choosing not to.

Her eyes darted back to his, as if she could hear the thoughts in his head.

"You'll understand soon," she replied.

"Zoe," John closed his eyes and concentrated on keeping his voice quiet and calm. "This is not a game. We've got some serious problems here and I want to help you. I really do. I want to help you get away from Fox and I want to make sure we both get out of here safely. I can't do any of that tied to this chair. Untie me and we'll talk. We'll make a plan and then we'll hunt down Fox and make him pay."

He opened his eyes.

She was standing by him, leaning against the side of one of the pews running down the wooden table.

"You'd really do that?" her voice sounded different now. "You'd really protect me against Ricky?"

John nodded, "You know I would."

"You'd protect me against such terrible danger?"

"Yes."

"Risking everything for me?"

What can I say?

"Yes," he replied, trying to stay calm.

"So, you *do* love me?"

John sighed deeply.

"You'd do that, you'd fight Ricky because you love me, right?" she said again.

"I'll do it because he needs to be stopped." John continued. "He needs to be shown you can't do this to people. I have to do it because of what he did to Helen. He has to pay. Helen deserves to be avenged for all the pain he caused her. And for all the pain he caused you too."

"You mean that?" her voice sounded small and childlike.

"I do," John stared into her eyes and smiled. "But I can't do it all tied to this chair, now can I?"

She smiled back.

Yes, he thought. *I've got her now.*

She walked over to him and smiled once more. She ran her hand along the side of his cheek.

"You're the best, Johnny," she said. "I'm glad you're here for me."

"Untie me, Zoe," he prompted again.

She stepped to his side and leaned behind him.

He could hear the clatter of metal on metal and could feel the weight of her hands on his numb wrists.

Finally!

She leaned back and placed a kiss on his forehead.

John smiled and pushed forward, bringing his hands free.

He heard the clatter as his arms stopped behind his back.

Huh?

He pulled harder.

His arms would not obey. They stayed behind his back. The handcuffs held tight.

He looked up at Zoe as he slipped the handcuffs up the metal rungs of the chair, searching desperately for freedom.

There wasn't any.

"Zoe..." he whispered.

She took a step backwards.

"What are you *doing?*" he asked.

"Sorry, my love," she said. "I can't. I can't let you go."

"What?" the anger began to build again. "Look, Zoe, this has gone far enough. This isn't funny any more. It never was! Now, *untie me!*"

"I can't," she continued. "Not until I know you trust me."

"Trust you?" John was amazed as he pulled forward with his hands once more. "I'm tied to a chair and you won't let me be free. How *can* I trust you?"

"I'll never hurt you, Johnny," she replied. "Unless you force me to."

John stopped his struggling and stared at her.

What?

She looked totally different to him now, but he couldn't work out why.

"Hurt me?" he was confused.

"I don't want to," she replied. "But you have to realise we need to play this out by my rules."

"Rules?"

Whose game is this?

John leaned forward again, tugging once more at the handcuffs. They bit into his wrists, but he didn't care. He had to get free.

"What rules?" he continued. "This isn't some game, Zoe. This is serious shit. This is life and death!"

"I know," she replied.

"People have *died*, Zoe. This is *serious!*"

She nodded. "I know that, I just wanted to make sure you do."

"Believe me," John shook his head. "I've just been told my *wife* has been killed! I *know* how serious this whole fucking thing is. We need to work together to help each other through this."

Zoe smiled then and her worried face changed.

"I'm just glad you finally understand," she said to him as she walked closer. "I think together we'll be unstoppable."

John nodded, "I agree. We'll work together on this."

"You and me?"

"You and me."

Zoe stopped in front of him and reached over to the counter. She moved his glass to one side and picked up the steak knife.

"I'm sorry for what I did, Johnny," she said as she knelt down in front of him.

"It's okay," John replied.

Is that all you can say?

What else can I say? I have to play by her rules! It's still the only way she'll untie me.

"I thought it was for the best." Her head dropped to the floor. "If there were any other way, you know I would have done it."

"As long as you did what you thought was right."

"I did."

He could feel her hands on his legs. Then he heard the knife cutting through the ropes around his ankles.

Her body shook as she cut through the rope.

John stared at the top of her head, at the pink streaks of blood in her hair and wrapped in her braids.

Helen, so much blood, he thought. *I'm so sorry.*

"You don't blame me, do you?" she asked as the knife cut through the bindings on his right ankle. "You don't blame me for all that happened?"

Freedom.

So close.

"Of course not," John replied. His foot came free from the chair and he rested it flat on the floor. Then he stretched it out in front of him, his stiff muscles screaming for relief.

"Good," she moved across and started cutting into the rope around his left ankle. "Because none of it was my fault."

"I know that, Zoe."

Almost there.

"I did what I had to do."

"I know."

Almost free!

"I didn't know it would end this way. I really didn't."

"I understand."

The knife cut through the rope and John's left leg was free too. He stretched it out next to his right. Both ankles were sore and pins and needles began to flood them. From where he sat, John thought both ankles looked swollen. There was some blood on the top of his shoes, probably from the rope biting through the skin.

Then he noticed the stain from where he had urinated. It reached across his pants to his hip and stretched from the bottom of his shirt to just above his knees. The stain was mostly dry now, but John wanted to get out of the jeans and shirt as soon as the pins and needles passed.

Zoe sat back on her haunches and smiled at him.

"That better?" she asked.

John smiled back.

"Much better, thank you."

"I'm glad. I only want to make you happy."

"Good," he nodded his head.

She smiled at him and reached out and touched his cheek again.

"I'd do anything for you," she said.

John nodded, "I know."

He leaned forward, looked over his shoulder and then looked back at her.

"The handcuffs," he said.

Zoe nodded, "I know."

John waited.

"Can you remove them, please?" he asked.

Her face fell.

"No," she whispered.

John stared at her.

He wanted to reach out and strike her. For the first time he thought about slapping her. He couldn't believe he was thinking it, but the anger was building and he felt he needed to do something to make her see he was in charge.

But I'm not, he thought. *While I'm tied to this chair, she is!*

And he knew that if he did hit her or yell at her, he'd push her to the edge like he did Saturday night. And there was no telling what would happen then.

He didn't want to do that. It was his anger that got him into this situation in the first place. It was his anger that had forced her to leave him here and go and face Fox alone. Maybe it was even his anger that had caused Helen to be killed.

Oh, Helen, he thought. *If only I'd kept calm on Saturday night, maybe I could've been there to save you. It's all my fault.*

He knew he couldn't show his anger. He knew he couldn't act like Fox, even though he wanted to.

Calm down, he told himself. *You're halfway to freedom. Take your time and you'll be free soon enough. Don't ruin your chances again!*

He nodded to himself as he looked at her, trying hard to swallow his anger and calm down.

Don't lose your cool. Play it calm.

I'll try.

Just think about where your anger has led you so far.

I know.

And what you've lost.

Helen, my God. Helen, I'm so sorry. I could've saved you. If only...

If only...

He let his head drop to his chest and he closed his eyes. Suddenly, his sadness returned.

Play the game...

"It's all my fault," he whispered.

"I know," Zoe whispered back.

The world around him spun out of control as her words entered his mind.

He lifted his head.

She was staring at him.

He stared back and found himself lost in her deep brown eyes once more.

She reached out to him.

He waited for her touch.

But the cold steel blade of the steak knife pricked his cheek.

He shot his body back in the chair, his back collapsing onto his arms, causing his shoulder joints to strain, sending pain shooting through him.

Zoe leaned forward.

Her eyes never once leaving his.

She traced his cheek with the blade of the steak knife.

He could feel the cold steel as it moved lightly across his skin. Zoe held the knife firmly, pressing down, but not enough to break the skin and make him bleed. Just enough so he could feel it, and think about what it could do.

She dropped the blade down further, from his cheek across his chin and down his throat, sliding roughly over his Adam's apple and to his chest.

John was holding his breath. He didn't dare breathe.

His eyes never left hers.

They stared at each other, entwined, locked.

The knife traced across his chest, sending dull pain through him as it crossed over his claw wounds.

She's crazy!

"Zoe..." he whispered to her, but it had no effect.

She continued to stare at him.

"*Please...*" he muttered.

She dragged the knife across to his left shoulder. It circled his shoulder once, then twice, before coming to a stop. She held the tip of the blade balancing on its point in the middle of his shoulder.

"How does it feel, Johnny?" she asked him without blinking.

"Huh?" John didn't know what else to say.

"How does it feel to have something you love taken away?"

"Zoe, what are you talking about?" John was confused. She wasn't making any sense.

"Does it hurt, Johnny?"

"Zoe, please…"

"Does it?"

Her face changed. Suddenly it became darker. A snarl formed on her lips.

"Does it?" she yelled at him.

"Yes," he replied quickly. "Yes, it does! It hurts!"

She tilted her head to one side and stared at him. Her brow creased and the small scar in her left eyebrow disappeared as she did so. After a pause, she leaned forward and sniffed at the air.

"Is that fear I smell?" she asked him. "Or just more of your piss?"

"Zoe, what are you doing? What's wrong with you?" he pleaded. "Stop it! *Please!*"

"I don't want you to feel fear, Johnny," she replied, straightening her head. "Not fear. That's not right. I want you to feel *pain!*"

Her right hand moved quickly.

He didn't have time to react.

He screamed.

The left side of his body erupted in agony as she buried the knife deep into his shoulder. The skin and muscle parted like butter as the knife pushed downwards and slipped into his body all the way up to its handle. It jagged off to one side, his shoulder bone deflecting the blade slightly, making the knife stick out at a weird angle.

"You feel that, Johnny?" she asked through his screaming. "Do you feel the pain now?"

He went light-headed as he looked down at his left shoulder and saw the knife sticking out. His brain seemed to unravel. Almost as if what he saw wasn't real.

He couldn't believe it was.

It can't *be!*

But the pain was excruciating.

"Can you feel it *now*, Johnny? Can you *feel* that?"

He was nodding his head frantically. He couldn't talk, his mouth wouldn't work.

She leaned closer to him and sniffed the air again.

She smiled and nodded.

"That's better," she said. "That's pain. You can feel it now,
I can tell."

He was still nodding, looking down at his shoulder as the
blood began to pulse out of the wound, pool around the knife
and flow down his arm. He tried desperately to get his hands
to work behind him, but his back was pressing down on his
arms and he couldn't seem to co-ordinate them properly.

The pain was too much. His empty stomach turned over
and he felt as if his feet were weak and useless under him.
The world was rocking back and forth, and no matter how
hard he tried, he couldn't get a grip on anything.

"This..." he tried to get his words together. "This *can't*...
happen. You're...you're...*crazy*."

Zoe smiled at him.

"We all go a little crazy sometimes, Johnny."

He looked up at her, but he couldn't focus properly. Her
face kept blurring in front of him.

He blinked, trying to regain his focus, but it was no use.
Too hard.

"Why?" he muttered.

Zoe laughed.

He was sure he heard her laugh.

"Why?" she mimicked him. "*Why?*"

He nodded, his head falling to one side.

"I've asked myself that many times too, Johnny," she
whispered in his ear. "Now, it's your turn."

He lifted his head once more, and saw her eyes floating
in front of him.

"You're...sick..." the words were spinning in his head.
"You're...*crazy*."

"No, Johnny," she said. "I'm far from crazy."

He watched her as she reached out and grabbed the
knife handle with both hands.

He nodded, "Yes....pull it out....please."

"My pleasure," she replied as she yanked it from his
shoulder.

Stars exploded in his eyes. Pain tore through him as the
teeth of the blade sliced through skin and muscle again. He
gritted his teeth as tears cascaded down his cheeks.

Only a hollow burning sensation remained in his shoulder.

His breath came out in a rush and he was panting hard.

He slumped forward in the chair, trying desperately to get his hands free from behind him. He could hear the metal clanking sounds. But it was no use. His left arm was numb again and he couldn't get it to work at all now.

"Are you hurt, Johnny?" she whispered the question.

He nodded.

"Do you feel like you want to *die?*"

He shook his head as it lolled forward. "No...." he muttered. "No, I don't...I don't...want to...die."

"Then you don't hurt enough."

Her voice was by his ear, he could feel her breath next to him.

"Johnny," she continued after a pause, letting him catch his breath. "Look at me."

He lifted his head and turned it to his left. His eyes stopped at his shoulder wound and watched the blood pour out of the deep, gaping hole. He glanced away quickly, his stomach turning over once more, and then continued on to her face.

A high-pitched noise began to sound in his ears.

"Zoe..." he tried to focus on her, but couldn't. "Please... I..."

She raised the knife in front of his face. She showed it to him, twisting it around so he could see both sides of the now-stained blade. He couldn't focus on it properly. All he saw was the sun shining off sections of the bloody blade.

"Watch," she said.

He focussed on the blade, trying to keep his head upright, fighting the growing urge to be sick.

The pain in his shoulder was ebbing away, but the blood still flowed.

"And feel..."

She turned the blade upside down, wrapped both hands around the handle once more, and in one fluid movement ripped it down the side of his arm.

John watched as his sleeve split open just below his shoulder wound. He heard the tearing of material. The knife cut through it easily and quickly, slicing downwards and through his elbow, continuing on and coming to a sudden rest near his wrist.

The sleeve flipped open and he stared at the gaping cavern of flesh that stretched all the way down his left arm.

It doesn't make sense.

At first there was just numbness.

Then came the blood. It flooded upwards from inside the dark pit of his arm.

And then the pain.

John tried to scream, but he couldn't.

His head lolled forward as he watched his whole arm turn crimson red.

And then everything went black.

Thirty-six

“**M**r. Murdock?”
John looked up to see the nurse standing above him.

“Yes?” John replied.

“She’ll see you now.”

John slowly got to his feet and returned the magazine to the pile.

He smiled at the nurse; a sad, tired smile.

The nurse placed a hand on his shoulder.

“She’s weak,” she said to him as she guided him along the corridor. “So don’t stay too long. But try to smile and reassure her everything will be okay.”

John nodded and stared straight ahead.

“I’ll try,” he replied.

It had been hours since they had brought her in.

When it had all happened, time had flown so quickly. No time to think, just acting on instinct. But when they’d arrived, he’d let go of her hand and they’d taken her away. From that moment on, time had crawled.

And he was left alone to wait.

All alone.

There was nothing he could say or do.

He just had to wait.

Waiting while other events happened around him that he was powerless to control.

Now the time had come. He walked down the corridor and stopped at the door.

“Remember what I said,” the nurse reminded him. “Look happy, but don’t stay too long.”

John nodded and turned to smile at the nurse once more, but he was alone.

He took his hands from his pockets and walked into the ward. He tried not to look at the other patients as he walked past their beds. He didn't want to make eye contact. He didn't want to talk with them.

He was there for only one thing. And one person.

He looked towards the bed at the end of the ward. It seemed to take him so long to walk down there, as if the ward stretched on for eternity.

And as he got closer, his heart began to race.

He peered down at the final bed. It wasn't until he took a few more steps closer that he realised something was wrong.

The bed was empty.

Empty.

She was gone.

He rushed to the bed, reached out and touched its cold sheets, as if he couldn't believe his eyes.

He turned around and stared back up the ward. All the other patients were watching him, leaning forward in their beds and staring at him.

He looked back to the bed one more time.

Then he called out her name.

No answer.

The whole room was deadly quiet.

And then he ran.

He ran out the ward and down the corridor, looking for the nurse he had talked to. There were so many people out there now. He had to push through and past people as quickly as he could. The crowd was holding him back. Their arms reached out, hands grabbing at him, tearing at his clothes and face.

He called her name again.

"Where are you?" he yelled.

But still no answer.

There was movement all around him, people walking past, staring at him, talking, reaching for him, laughing, screaming, but he couldn't hear any of them.

All he heard in his head was a loud heartbeat.

Over and over again the sound pounded in his head.

He called for her once more.

And then he saw the nurse.

John sprinted up to her and put a hand on her shoulder. The nurse turned to look at him. She smiled at John once more.

"Where is she?" John asked.

"Isn't she in the ward?" the nurse looked confused.

"No, I looked in the bed. She wasn't there."

"You sure?"

"I touched the bed, she wasn't there. The sheets were cold."

The nurse smiled. "She's downstairs then, on the first floor."

"The first floor?" John turned, looking for an elevator. "Okay."

"No, no," the nurse reached out to grab him too. "You can't go there."

"I have to!"

"It's out of bounds. Restricted! You can't!"

John struggled out of the nurse's grip and ran to the elevator.

He got inside and pushed the button to the first floor. The button's sickly yellow light illuminated and the door slammed shut just as the nurse reached out for him again.

"You can't go –" the nurse's voice was cut off by the doors.

John was shaking now. He held his hands out to look at them. They looked cold and grey. He noticed for the first time the deep dark bruise marks around his wrists. He touched them gently but they hurt too much, sending pain up his arms.

The elevator descended. As it did so, the heartbeat in his head became louder and louder.

John placed his hands over his ears and tried to block out the sound, but he couldn't.

It continued as the elevator descended further.

Down, deep down.

Eventually, the ride bounced to a stop and the doors opened.

John peered out into the darkness.

"Hello?" he whispered.

No answer.

Slowly, he walked out of the elevator.

"Anyone here?" he called. "Hello?"

The doors closed behind him, cutting off all his light.

Now he was in total darkness.

He couldn't see anything.

But the heartbeat continued to pulse all around him.

He called her name again. "Are you here?"

He walked forward in the darkness. Even though he couldn't see where he was going, he knew he had to go forward.

I have to keep going forward, he thought to himself. *I have to. I can't stop.*

He walked on, trying hard to keep the heartbeat from sounding in his ears, but knowing it was futile to fight it.

Forward. Don't stop. Keep going.

But going to where?

He continued forward.

He was sure the darkness was getting blacker, if that was possible, and the heartbeat getting louder.

Where am I? he thought. *I really should turn back.*

Something brushed against his leg. He jumped in shock and then looked down. It was too dark to see anything, but he was sure something brushed against him.

Soft and small.

It's too dark. I shouldn't be down here.

He walked on further.

Something else brushed up against him, higher this time. It touched his hip.

He spun around in the darkness, trying to see what it was. But he couldn't see anything. There was nothing there to see.

Just before he began to panic, he saw a light shining ahead of him.

It took a second for John to work it out, but he found himself in a long corridor and the light came from a door at the end.

He called to her again.

No answer.

John turned around to look behind him.

Darkness.

And then his leg was touched once more.

Panic sliced up his spine.

He turned and sprinted for the door.

Quickly! I have to make it!

The faster he ran, the further the door seemed to be away from him. He ran and ran, but the door kept getting further away.

Suddenly, pain shot through his torso. His shoulders began to ache and his left arm went limp. He looked down and found blood pumping from his chest and pouring down his legs.

His head began to hurt badly, as if something were trying to burrow its way out from inside him. John raised his right hand up to his forehead. He was sure he could feel movement under his skull. His hand followed a large bulge as it moved across his forehead and down the left side of his head.

"No!" John screamed as he sprinted harder to the door. "NO!"

The door was further away than ever now. He was breathing hard and quickly losing strength. The blood continued to pour from his body. The thing in his head moved across his face, behind his left eye-socket and bulged out his cheek.

"Help me," he called. "Heeeeellllllp!"

And then he was through the doorway and the bright lights were blinding him.

He put his hands up and closed his eyes, waiting to adjust to the sudden light.

After a few seconds, he slowly opened his eyes. He realised then all his pain was gone. His left arm was working again and the bleeding in his chest was gone.

The creature in his head had vanished too.

He heaved a sigh of relief.

He was normal again.

Only the heartbeat remained. Over and over again it pounded in his head.

As his eyes adjusted to the bright light, he could see the white coat in front of him.

He could make out her figure.

She was bending over some trolleys.

He looked around him and realised he was in an operating room.

So bright, he thought.

But it didn't matter now.

"I've found you," he whispered as he walked towards her.

He grabbed her and closed his eyes, spinning her around before kissing her hard on the lips.

The heartbeat was louder than ever now.

He opened his eyes.

And stared into Zoe's.

No!

He pushed her away from him, and took a step backwards.

"No!" he shouted.

The front of the white coat Zoe was wearing was stained red and bloody. So was her face.

She held up her right hand and smiled at John.

"Hi, Johnny," she said.

"You," he whispered. "I don't want you here."

"I'm trapped here."

"Get out!"

"I can't," she replied. "I have to go through with this now."

"You have to leave, now! Before anyone finds out."

"I can't."

"You *have to!*"

She smiled at him.

"Watch," she whispered to him. "And feel..."

"No, no," he replied. "You don't understand. Leave before it's too late!"

"But I came here for this," she said to him.

John's eyes moved to her right hand.

She was holding a bloody hunk of flesh.

It was beating.

It was beating in time to the heartbeat he could hear in his head.

He looked down at his chest.

Saw the gaping hole where his heart used to be.

Looked back at her and stared at his heart, still beating in her hands.

He staggered backwards, trying to get away. But his legs and feet were trapped, being held by something. He looked around. Arms reached up from the floor, one pair for each of his legs. The hands held him firmly.

He tried to turn and run, but he couldn't.

He looked down at the hole in his chest again. He looked at the ragged edges of skin and muscle, and at the broken bones jagging out from his rib cage.

His eyes darted back to Zoe and watched as she moved his still beating heart to her mouth and bit off a chunk of the bloody flesh.

She smiled at him as she chewed, blood dripping from her chin.

And then he screamed.

Thirty-seven

John woke, screaming.

"Bad dream?"

He looked to his left and found Zoe by his side. She smiled at him and patted his chest.

"Don't worry, I'm here for you," she said.

He was lying down.

Finally.

He closed his eyes and concentrated on getting his breathing under control as well as removing the images from the dream out of his head.

He could feel his heart beating.

At least I know it's still in there, he thought.

Then his mind wandered back to reality. He tried to process all the events of the last three days, but there were too many and he wasn't thinking straight. He knew just two things: he had to get away from Zoe, and he had to hunt down and kill Fox.

But stay calm, he thought. *Be on guard. Don't push her too much. Reason with her. You know what she can be like now, how she can fly into rages. Tread softly.*

John opened his eyes and stared up at the ceiling of the church. The wood of the rafters looked old and charred, as if they had been burnt at some stage.

He turned his head from side to side. The pains in his neck were almost gone; only a dull stiffness remained. He looked up at the windows on both sides of the church and could see no sunlight shining through them, but it was light outside.

Okay, so it's only midday. That gives me some time.

His eyes dropped down to the right as he noticed the glow.

There was a well-built fire in the fireplace.

Huh? In the middle of the day? It's not even cold.

The heat from fire was quite intense. He could feel the warmth on his face and body, and he realised then that he was sweating.

He lifted his head to look around the church.

But as he did so, his headache began to return. Wanting to stay clear headed, he put his head back down, willing the pains in his mind to subside.

There was a strong almond smell in the air. He tried to work out what it was, but he couldn't.

"How are you feeling?"

Turning to his left, he looked at Zoe.

She was smiling at him, her eyes showing a mix of sorrow and concern.

Her hair was tied back in a ponytail, and John noticed that the bloodstains that had covered her were now gone. She had showered and cleaned herself up, and was wearing a white bathrobe.

Almost as if nothing had happened.

"Are you thirsty?" she asked.

He nodded his head.

"I'll get you a drink as soon as I've finished this."

Her eyes dropped to his side and she stepped back out of his sight.

John followed her. Lifting his head until she came back into view, he followed her eyes and looked down at his left arm.

He saw the gaping split where she had stabbed him.

His stomach churned as he looked at the long scar stretching along his whole arm. But it didn't look as bad now. The bleeding had stopped and the wound looked as if it had been cleaned; there were no bloodstains around the gash.

And Zoe was sewing it shut.

She had almost completed the stitches, with just a couple of inches of wound to go.

John looked on passively, unable to believe that he was just sitting there watching someone sew up a wound that stretched from his shoulder to his wrist.

And there was no pain at all.

His whole arm was numb.

Her eyes lifted and met his.

"Sorry," she smiled at him. "I got a bit carried away. I do that sometimes."

John smiled back.

What else can I do?

Just be very careful...don't trust her!

"You're just lucky I could find this needle and thread," she continued.

"Thanks," he whispered.

"It's not the proper thread," she continued matter-of-factly. "I could only find some old fishing wire. But I sterilised it before I used it. So it should be okay."

Fishing wire? John thought. *My God! I've got to get out of here! Now!*

John rested his head back down again and tried to work out a plan.

His left arm was numb and useless. His right arm felt okay, although his shoulder was still sore from being handcuffed to the Jeep. His head ached slightly, but he could live with the headache, and his neck wasn't as stiff as it had been. His chest and body felt good, no longer numb now he was lying down and untied from the chair. The feeling had even come back into his legs.

He could actually wriggle his toes once again.

And that was when he first realised he was naked.

Suddenly, panic gripped him. He tried to sit upright, but he couldn't.

Rope was tied tightly across his chest and legs, stopping him from moving. He lifted his head and stared down at his body.

Naked.

And oiled.

He was tied to the old wooden table, pews on either side of him. Thin coils of rope were wrapped around his chest and hips, and then disappeared under the table. Another two coils were tied above and below his knees. His eyes travelled further down his body to his feet, which were both tied to a long metal bar that sat between them, keeping them a set distance apart.

He tried to struggle; to sit up any way he could.

But it was useless.

He couldn't move.

"Don't, Johnny," Zoe said, still concentrating on finishing her stitches, a frown creasing her forehead. "I'm almost there. Don't ruin it now."

John let his body go limp and he rested his head back on the hard wooden table.

She's crazy, he thought to himself. *How can she talk to me like there's nothing wrong? Like we're having a normal everyday conversation?*

He had to get away from her.

"There," she said, touching his palm lightly. "All done."

John craned his neck and looked down at his left arm. The jagged wound was sewn shut now. The fishing wire snaked back and forth across the puffy red lips of the gash and finished in a small knot down by his wrist.

"It should hold," she said.

"Should?" was all John could manage.

"Lucky I had a friend who taught me how to do that, huh?" Zoe beamed at him. "I think I've done a terrific job."

John's eyes moved back to his shoulder. He wanted to see what she had done to the stab wound she had inflicted there, but it was covered by some gauze and a bandage.

"Don't worry, Johnny," she continued. "I took care of that too. It was quite a mess, but I fixed it all. Lucky you were unconscious. It was probably easier that way. There was a hell of a lot of blood."

His eyes went back to her face.

She was smiling again.

How can she smile at me?

"I'll get you that drink now."

She walked past his head and disappeared from view. John's eyes went back to the ceiling and he tried to turn his body to the side, to somehow wriggle out from the ropes. But he couldn't. They were tied too tight. Any movements he made just aggravated the wound on his chest. The ropes ran directly across the claw marks Zoe had left there on Saturday night.

And now that the numbness was gone, he could feel every bit of pain.

There has to be a way out of here.

John heard the water spill into a glass behind him. He closed his eyes and listened as Zoe's footsteps came closer.

"Here, drink," she said.

He felt her hand under his head as she lifted him toward the glass. His lips touched the cold rim and then tasted the cool refreshing water. He found it hard to swallow at first, as if his neck muscles wouldn't work. It took him a few tries, but eventually he emptied the glass.

"Good boy," she replied.

John licked his lips and swallowed. The dryness in his throat was almost gone. He opened his eyes and saw her face upside down above him. She smiled at him once more. He tried to read what she was thinking, but he couldn't work it out.

This can't be happening, he thought.

Dangling from her neck was the gold half-heart pendant.

And that brought it all back to John.

He knew what was happening. And he seemed unable to do *anything* about it.

He shut his eyes tight, wanting to wish her away. But he knew it wouldn't work.

Helen, what did he do to you? How long did Fox torture you? How much pain did you endure while he hurt you?

But John pushed those thoughts aside. He had to. He had his own problems now. As if trying to avenge Helen's death wasn't enough, he now had a love-sick and unbalanced Zoe to contend with.

Now she thought he was hers forever.

She's mad. Completely mad.

Don't pretend you don't like the idea.

I don't.

Come on, imagine it. Zoe with you, by your side.

Stop it.

She'd be all yours.

No!

Ready…and willing.

Stop it.

That's what you were thinking about when you took her shopping on Saturday.

No, it wasn't.

Now she's all yours.

Shut up!

John opened his eyes again, hoping the light would shatter his thoughts.

He looked around for Zoe, but he couldn't see her.

He sharpened his listening, trying to pinpoint her with sound.

Nothing.

It's so hot in here.

His eyes scanned the fireplace once more. The fire was still roaring, spreading its heat throughout the church, the wood crackling every so often in the silence.

Beads of sweat continued trickling down his forehead.

He realised the almond smell came from the oil massaged into his skin.

He tried to move his right arm, but it was pinned under the ropes by his side. He pulled his feet to one side, trying to work them out of the ropes, but the bar between his ankles made movement almost impossible.

I'm trapped.

He didn't want to give in, but there was little he could do in his current situation.

Play her at her own game, go along with her. Maybe she'll trust you then and let you go.

Yeah, maybe.

And you might even enjoy it a little.

Stop it! Stop saying that!

You know you want to.

Helen's dead, I can't think like this.

She's dead, yeah.

I can't think like this!

She's out of the way now.

John shook his head from side to side. Trying hard to shake the thoughts from his mind.

She's out of the way. And you might enjoy it.

"Zoe!" he yelled, his voice sounding panicked as it echoed around the church.

He heard her footsteps ringing out on the floorboards. They sounded loud now, louder than ever, and were coming from the direction of the bathroom.

He turned his head to the side and to the back, towards her footsteps. He watched her as she approached.

His jaw dropped as she stopped in the middle of the church.

She was almost naked, but she wasn't.

John stared at the outfit she was wearing. It was made of black leather, what there was of it, and it made her look as if she were wearing a large spider's web. The leather straps went over her shoulders and under her arms, as well as around her hips. But between the straps was mostly bare skin.

Strips of leather ran across and under her breasts, pushing them out and upwards, making them rounder and more compact.

A circular piece of leather surrounded her belly button, highlighting it and making the diamond sitting there look like a bullseye. John couldn't help staring there, the leather circle drew his attention to the centre of her stomach, exactly as it was supposed to.

And then his eyes dropped lower.

Two thin strands of leather ran from the circular belly button section and down between her legs.

It left her exposed. Her shaved mound open and easily viewable from where John lay.

She was much taller now too, due to the eight inch black leather stiletto-heeled boots she was wearing.

John followed the boots from the ground and up her legs.

He looked at her vagina again and had trouble looking away.

She was oiled too. Her body shining in the glow from the fire.

"What do you think?" she asked.

In spite of himself, he found he was growing hard.

Zoe tilted her head to one side and smiled.

"Don't say anything, Johnny," she said. "You've already answered my question."

Her eyes stayed fixed on his hardening cock. There was nothing he could do to stop it. It was an automatic response to looking at her.

She looked unbelievable.

Shut your eyes then, don't look!

But he couldn't. He had to.

She looked stunning.

His eyes were split between looking at the diamond in her belly button and the moist folds between her legs.

God, she's a stunner.

She placed her hands on her hips, "Okay, I know you want to tell me. So, what *do* you think?"

John didn't know what to say. His mind raced.

"Impressive," was all he could manage.

She bowed.

"Why, thank you, Johnny. I always dress to impress."

She smiled, turned around and walked towards the beds at the far end of the church.

John watched her as she walked.

The leather straps that had disappeared between her legs came together and ran between the cheeks of her arse, like a thong, before continuing up her back and forming one long strip of leather where the other strips from her arms and hips ended. John noticed the small bandage on the top of Zoe's left buttock and wondered what it was, before he remembered that she had cut herself when Fox had called her at his home.

She walked past the railings and bent over when she got to the beds.

The leather between her arse cheeks pulled tighter, opening them to his view. From the way she was standing, he could see the parted lips of her vagina. Moist and warm and welcoming.

John's eyes darted to his cock. It was bobbing in the air, pulsing frantically. Shining in the glow of the raging fire.

She's oiled me there too? he thought to himself. *When? When did she have time to lift me from the chair, undress me, oil me, clean my wounds and tie me to the table? Just how long was I unconscious?*

His eyes swung across to Zoe as she walked back towards him, her footsteps echoing around them.

There was nothing he could do.

She's just so beautiful…and so eager.

She smiled at him a little lopsided smile as she approached. Both her hands were behind her back as she walked closer.

"Are you thirsty?" she asked him again.

He nodded his head as she came closer.

"Good," she replied. "You want a drink of water?"

He nodded.

She stopped by the table and looked down at him. The half-heart pendant dropped forward from her chest. It hung there in the air, as a constant reminder of Helen and what had happened to her.

John could also feel his own chain around his neck.

I'm so sorry. John thought. *But I have no other choice.*

"Really thirsty?"

John nodded again.

"I'll give you something better than water," she replied as she bent over and ran her tongue around his ear.

She straightened herself up and brought her right hand over his chest. He felt the soft touch as it ran down his body.

He lifted his head and saw the riding crop in her hand. It was black and looked oiled too. The tip was made of leather.

"You're going to enjoy this," she whispered, as she passed the tip of the crop over the head of his pulsing cock.

His eyes came back and locked on to hers; deep and brown, they engulfed him once again.

There's no escape.

"I appreciate the beauty of a fine whip, Johnny," she said in a low husky tone as the whip fluttered down his shaft and around his balls.

"And so will you."

He closed his eyes.

I'm sorry, my love. So sorry.

Thirty-eight

His stomach rumbled loudly.

"You're hungry," she whispered as they lay side by side on the table.

"Yes," he replied.

"There's no food here. I'm sorry. I didn't think of that. I'll have to go and get some."

"That's okay. I'm sure I'll survive a while longer," he replied, running a hand through her hair.

He stared across her bare shoulder at the sunlight as it shone through the windows.

"It'll be dark soon," he said.

"I know."

His eyes fell to the fireplace. The fire was almost out and he was beginning to get cold. The waning heat from the sunlight was the only thing keeping them warm, apart from their own body heat.

They were glued together by their own juices, sweat, oil and semen.

John closed his eyes and stroked her hair with his right hand.

It was a small victory, but she had loosened the ropes around his chest so he could get his right arm free.

Slowly, I'm getting there.

"I don't want to move from your side," she muttered.

"Then don't."

"Can we lie here a while longer?"

"Yes."

She snuggled further into his body. He felt her lips brush his shoulder, her legs rub against his hips.

And then he thought back.

Hours had passed. The setting sun proved that they had spent all afternoon together. But where they had been, time meant nothing.

She had climbed up onto the table and stood above him. She'd placed one foot on each side of his head and let him stare up her long legs to the folds between them.

"I know what you want, Johnny," she had said. "This is what you've been denying yourself for so long. Why say no to this?"

He was in no position to struggle or fight her.

He wasn't sure he even wanted to anymore.

He wasn't going to get away from here without playing her game. And he did need her help if she was going to lead him to Fox. She was his only connection to the bastard who killed Helen.

"I know you're thirsty," she continued in her deep husky voice as she slowly bent into a squatting position. "And I know what you're thirsty for."

She was just inches from his face now. He could smell her, see every detail of her folds, her labia, her glistening pink insides, and her ass.

So close.

Her hand reached between her legs and unfastened a black stud on the back of her outfit. The leather straps between her legs fell away. She unfastened another black stud on the front and removed the leather between her legs completely. She let the leather fall to the floor.

"You want me?" she asked.

He didn't answer. He just stared at the beauty before him.

"I know you do. Your cock tells me."

He lifted his head slightly, trying to reach between her legs.

She lifted herself up, out of his reach.

"Uh-uh, not that easy," she said to him.

He rested his head back down.

The oil shined off her lips and folds; he studied the small pucker of her anus. She was so wet and inviting.

"You want me?" she said again, as she lowered herself back down. "If you do, say it."

John had no choice.

I have to.

"I want you," he whispered.

"I can't hear you."

"I want you."

"Louder."

"I want you!" he yelled. His voice echoed around the church.

There was a pause.

Then Zoe lowered herself onto his face.

"Good boy," she said. "I knew you did."

He was covered by her folds. Smothered by her.

His tongue shot forward and buried itself deep in her. He searched inside her, wanting to feel everything; her soft, silky sides, her wet flaps and folds, her dark tangy interior.

He tongued her with passion. Searching out and finding her hard clitoris and rubbing back and forth, swirling around her nub, sucking on it.

She rocked slowly back and forth on his face, moaning deeply to herself, running her hands down his chest and stomach.

Her juices flowed quicker now, dripping into his mouth and spilling from it, trickling down the side of his face. She was wet and slippery and so good.

Her anus rocked back and forth in front of his eyes, puckering and quivering as her passion built.

"You shouldn't deny yourself," she whispered to him.

He could feel her hands down the side of his stomach, moving towards his hips. They reached further down as she bent forward, her arse tilting more and thrusting her clitoris back onto his tongue. Her nails scraped along the sides of his thighs. Then they traced a path up over his legs and down between them.

She squeezed his testicles and made him jump.

"I like that," she said as she squeezed them again.

She leaned further forward as her fingers grabbed his shaft and massaged him slowly.

And then, as he continued licking at her clitoris, her mouth engulfed him.

Warm and wet, her tongue danced along his shaft. Her lips sucked hard. Her tongue licked at the tip of his cock and then her head bobbed up and down. She started slowly, but quickly built up speed.

He could hear her moaning. He wanted to reach out and grab her, to run his fingers up and down her back, to play with her wet folds, but he was tied and could do nothing more.

She rocked back and forth on his face as she sucked harder and longer.

John closed his eyes and tried to hold his passion back. He didn't want to cum until she was ready. He wanted them to reach orgasm together.

He held on for as long as he could, but he couldn't stop it. Her tongue and lips in combination were too good, too perfect.

Wonderful.

Images of her flooded his mind and danced before him. On the sofa, spread out on the bed, her diamond, her belly button, her breasts, her figure, her hair, and her shaved bare mound.

He opened his eyes once more as he started to twist and turn. Even though the ropes held him down, he began to squirm in ecstasy.

And then he exploded in her mouth.

She kept sucking, kept massaging, making the orgasm last; the pleasure long and exquisite.

His breathing was fast and heavy, and he moaned for a long, long time.

And as his moaning subsided, so did the sucking.

As she licked him, she began to buck faster and faster, rubbing her mound against his face.

Her breathing got deeper and quicker, her anus tighter. She threw her head back, strands of her hair escaping from her ponytail.

She came as she continued to massage him with one hand, and squeeze his balls with the other. She let out a long deep moan that lasted for quite a while and she wiggled her hips as he tongued her more.

Her juices smeared across his face, dripping into his mouth and down his throat.

Eventually, she stopped rocking back and forth. She just sat on his face, breathing hard, until John stopped licking her clitoris. When he did, she moved backwards slightly, moving her clitoris away from his tongue. He sucked on one of her flaps instead, sucking it deep into his mouth, stretching it as far as it would go.

She moaned and leaned forward again, licking the last few drops of cum from the head of his cock.

"That was nice," she said as she lifted herself off his face.

He didn't want her to go.

She turned around and faced him.

"Wasn't it?"

John nodded.

"You still thirsty?" she smiled wickedly at him.

"Not as thirsty as I was," he said, licking his wet lips.

He could still smell her. She was on his skin now. Her juices were still with him, smeared around his nose and mouth.

He licked his lips again.

"Have you ever had it so good?" she looked him in the eye as she lay down on his chest.

"No," John replied without hesitation.

"Honest?"

"Honest."

She smiled and played with some of his chest-hairs.

"Good," she said. "I'm glad. I wanted this to be special for you."

"It was."

"I wanted you to know what you were missing."

"Well, I do now."

"It's only fair, Johnny, for us to get what we always wanted."

He stared into her eyes.

"Life should be all about that," she said. "Getting what we most want."

John nodded.

She lay on him for quite some time.

The heat from the fire kept them both warm.

John wasn't too sure how much time had passed, but eventually she lifted her knee and slid it up his leg, rubbing it across his cock and balls.

"I don't suppose," she smiled. "You'd like some more already?"

With little effort, John found himself hardening again.

"Do *you* want more?" he asked.

She nodded her head.

"I want all of you," she said.

But then her face fell and she said in a small voice. "But I can't have you. I've been bad. I've done bad things."

She pouted and her eyes fell to his chest.

Her hand reached down by his side and picked up the whip from beside him.

"Will you teach me a lesson?" she asked.

Is she serious?

"Do you want me to?" he asked.

"Whip me," she said as her eyes grew with excitement. "Please?"

John nodded, "Okay, if you *want* me to."

"I do," she nodded. "I've been a *bad* girl."

"But I can't, I'm tied down."

He tried to move his left arm, but it was still numb and he didn't want to risk splitting the stitches anyway. So, then he tried to move his right arm, but it was pressed tightly into his chest by the ropes binding him.

Zoe had climbed from him, and loosened the rope tied around his chest. He managed to pull his right arm free and she handed him the whip.

"Whip my ass," she smiled at him as she climbed back on the table. "Whip it hard."

This can't be happening, he thought.

But it was.

She turned away from him and crawled down his body. She stopped when she reached his groin and licked the top of his pulsing cock.

She looked over her shoulder at him and smiled, "You ready?"

John nodded.

"Okay," she turned around and bent forward, taking him back into her mouth.

She crawled backwards slightly, raising her arse in the air in front of his face.

And John had begun whipping her.

He shook his head as he thought about it now. The girl lying next to him so quiet and peaceful was the same girl who had bucked on his face and wanted to be whipped.

This has got to end, and end soon, he thought. *There's too much left to do. Problems to solve and people to find. But if I do what she wants now, she'll help me find Fox!*

The sun was setting, its light getting weaker. Soon it would be gone completely.

He felt guilty for having sex with Zoe, but he was powerless to stop her.

Yeah, right, and you didn't enjoy it one bit.

John felt worse now. But he consoled himself that if he could've stopped it, he would've.

Really? Did she force you to whip her?

I didn't have any other option!

Did she force you to enjoy it?

I had to do it.

Did she force you to cum in her mouth or lick her clit?

John opened his eyes, trying hard to force the thoughts from his mind.

Come on, John told himself. *Concentrate on getting out of here.*

He turned his head to look at Zoe. Her eyes were shut and she had a contented smile on her face. He ran his hand through her hair once more.

So beautiful, he thought. *And so dangerous.*

But maybe it wasn't her fault. Maybe this was normal for her.

Is this what Fox always wanted? Did he teach her all these warped sex games? Does she really think love is about this?

I didn't hear you complaining.

Shut up!

Well, don't call them warped sex games, you enjoyed them.

Gotta concentrate.

And you would do them again.

Gotta work out a way to get out of here.

You'd do her again if you got half the chance.

Zoe's forehead furrowed.

John held his breath as he watched her. He didn't know if she was asleep or not. But if she was, he didn't want to wake her. It could be his only chance to think clearly about what he had to do.

She smiled again then, and he looked at her full, round lips.

A white crusty stain sat in the corner of her mouth.

He reached over and slowly peeled it from her skin.

He lifted the dried film over the side of the table and let it fall to the ground.

And then he thought back.

He had started by only whipping her lightly, but she complained that it wasn't hard enough.

So he had hit her harder. The sound of the whip on her skin had echoed around the walls of the church.

When she began to yelp and the marks on her arse turned blood red, he would ease up.

Eventually, she stopped telling him to do it harder.

Instead, she began to bite his cock.

"If you slow down again," she'd said. "I'll bite down hard, comprehendo?"

John had nodded.

She only had to bite into the base of his shaft twice before he realised she meant it. He had kept the whippings fast and furious then, no matter how she whimpered or bucked.

And the more she sucked and massaged him, the more he whipped her. And the more excited he became. And after a short time, John was peaking again, shooting himself deep into her mouth once more. Enjoying his second orgasm as much, if not more, than the first. It felt different this time, she was doing different things to him. But it was wonderful no matter what, having her lick and suck it all out of him.

And he laid back on the table, exhausted.

His right arm was stiff from the strain of whipping her and his balls were aching with a dull ecstasy.

He closed his eyes and breathed deeply.

She's great, he had to admit it. *She's absolutely wonderful.*

He could feel her as her soft oiled hands continued to massage his cock. The tip of her tongue licking up any last drop of his juices.

After a while, she changed positions and started crawling up over his body again.

She was all soft and so oily, he didn't want her to stop.

Her nose nuzzled his and her hot lips landed on his own.

He opened his mouth and she opened hers.

The warm flood of his semen spilled between them and into his mouth.

At first, he didn't know what it was. It was hot and heavy, sticky and tasted foul.

And then he realised.

He went to close his mouth, but she was quicker.

Her mouth clamped down on his and her tongue danced with his through the thick hot fluid.

She kissed him hard, their tongues sticky and wet. Semen spilled from the sides of their lips, slowly rolling down his cheek and into his hair.

But he didn't care.

Not now.

She pulled back slightly and he opened his eyes.

Her tongue slurped from his mouth and ran over his top lip and up his nose. He could smell his own semen now, strong and nutty. She brought her tongue away from his face and into the air, a long thin stream of semen connecting them still, until it broke and fell across his cheek.

She smiled at him and licked at the spilled liquid, spreading it over his cheek and chin, down his throat and to his chest.

He looked down at the top of her head, watching her tongue eagerly lap at his white fluid. More hair had escaped her ponytail now, some of the strands stuck together in clumps of his juices.

She looked up at him and stared straight into his eyes.

They locked on again.

"Swallow it," she whispered. "Swallow it all."

He did so, without a second thought.

And she smiled at him.

"Good boy," she had said.

He had smiled back.

"You're a hard man to break, Johnny," she'd said as she crawled closer towards him and rested by his side. "You're strong too. Stronger than I thought."

She had rested her head on his arm.

"But I got you," she said as she closed her eyes. "I got you."

John's stomach rumbled louder as he turned to look at the half-heart pendant lying to one side of Zoe's neck.

If only she weren't wearing that pendant, he thought. *This would be a lot easier.*

Why? Conscience starting to prick you?

Shut up!

Why should it start now, after all this time?

SHUT UP!

Why don't you just admit you enjoyed it!

"Stop it," John whispered.

"Stop what?" she said, without opening her eyes.

It shocked him to find she was actually awake.

"Nothing," he replied quickly, running his hand along her shoulder.

His stomach rumbled again.

"My, you *are* hungry!" she said as she smiled. "I'll have to fix that for you."

John saw his chance.

"If you let me up, maybe we could go down to that bar in Hepburn Lakes for dinner."

Her smile grew bigger.

"That's a great idea, Johnny," she agreed as she opened her eyes.

Yes! I've done it!

"But you're not going anywhere," her eyes cut through to his soul.

And with those words, John looked past her to the windows of the church.

He watched as the sun set and the last rays of light died away.

Died away.

Just like his hopes of escape.

Thirty-nine

"I'm not being a good host, though," she said as she climbed off him. "I've got no food for you, and that's rude of me."

His eyes watched her back as she slid off the table and walked away from him towards the spiral staircase. Her arse cheeks were still red from the whipping he had given her and he noticed the bandage on her left buttock had slipped slightly.

"I promise I'll feed you in the morning, Johnny."

"But I'm hungry now," he replied.

She stopped walking as she reached the stairs.

"Don't worry, I'm sure you'll be hungry in the morning too." She turned and smiled at him. "Much hungrier. Anyway, there's just too much to do."

He let his head drop back to the table and he closed his eyes.

The morning? Am I going to be tied to this table until then? he wondered. *I can't. I won't let it happen. I've got to get out of here somehow!*

He heard her stilettoed heels ring out on the metal of the staircase and echo around the church. He opened his eyes and tilted his head back.

She came into his view as she reached the lectern, upside down now because of the way John was looking at her.

"Lucky you didn't manage to open this access hatch earlier," she smiled down at him. "It would've ruined your surprise."

Hatch? For a second John didn't know what she was talking about. Then he remembered the locked access hatch in the base of the cross on the wall behind the lectern. The one he had tried to open on Saturday night, but couldn't because it was locked.

Zoe bent down and disappeared from John's sight.

He heard the sound of keys jangling and then the hatch squeaking open.

She had the keys to the hatch all the time?

With Zoe out of sight, John looked around quickly, trying to spy anything that could help him get out of the ropes that held him to the table. But there was nothing within reach.

His right arm was still free and he tried to slacken the ropes around his chest by pulling at them. But they were still too tight. He wished he had the use of his left arm to help with the struggle. He looked down at it once more and traced his eyes along the puffy ridge of his wound. It looked red and ugly, but the stitches were holding firm. For the first time, he flexed the fingers on his left hand. He readied himself for the pain, but he was surprised that there wasn't as much as he thought there would be.

Maybe there's a chance.

He flexed his fingers again.

At least they work.

Preparing for any sudden stab of pain, he slowly lifted his left shoulder, trying to drag his left arm out from under the ropes.

The dull pulsing pain began to spread through his body, but he thought he could live with that if it meant he could escape.

He lifted his shoulder more.

His arm began to shift under the ropes.

That's it! Come on, a little bit at a time.

The sound of the access hatch slamming shut cut through the silence.

John dropped his shoulder and returned to his lying position.

Damn!

Zoe's footsteps sounded louder than before as she walked down the staircase and back to his side.

She smiled down at him.

"Hi," she said.

"Hi," he said back.

"You're bored, aren't you?" she smiled at him.

"Huh?"

"Sick of lying there on that uncomfortable table?"

John stared at her.

Could it be this easy?

It can't be!

Just play her game and be ready for any chance of escape!

"Yes," he replied. "As a matter of fact, I am."

She nodded, "I thought so. It's time I let you up."

He smiled at her, "Thanks."

"No problem. You deserve it. You've been a very good boy so far."

So far?

John's feeling of unease was steadily growing.

What sort of game is this?

She squatted down and reached under the table. John stared at the top of her head. Her hair was all combed back into her ponytail again. He could feel the ropes move slightly across his chest as she began to loosen the knots.

Keep her talking... Keep her mind on the important things to her.

"We really should be getting after Fox," John said.

"I know," she replied from under the table. "But there's plenty of time for that. We're not finished here yet."

Dread washed over John. He didn't want this to continue.

"Zoe, look," he began. "I've had a lot of fun, really I have, but I think we need to get after Fox while we still can."

The ropes began to grow tight across his chest once more. Tighter than before.

John fell silent.

Don't ruin your best shot! Shut up! Play the game her way, you're almost free. Don't anger her now!

The silence continued.

The ropes stayed tight.

Zoe didn't stand up.

Don't lose it now!

"But you'd be the best person to know what to do," he said finally. "And when to do it. So I'm in your hands. Whatever you want to do, we'll do."

The silence continued for a while longer.

And the ropes began to loosen again.

"I'm glad you said that, Johnny," she said as she appeared from under the table. "You know I only want what's best for you."

He nodded his head, "I do."

Damn!

"And for me."

"I understand that now," he smiled at her, reached up with his right hand and ran a finger around the leather strap that circled her left breast. "I really do. I'll do anything you want, Zoe. You're in control."

Her face beamed in excitement.

What are you doing?

I have to play it her way.

No, you don't!

Yes, it's the only way!

You're enjoying it!

No, I'm not.

"Really?" she asked.

He was spellbound by her beauty once more.

"Of course," he replied.

You are *enjoying it!*

I have to play the game her way!

She leaned forward and kissed him full on the lips. Her breath was hard and fast, her lips soft and warm.

So nice...

"I knew you would, Johnny," she said. "I just knew you would. You understand now, don't you?"

He nodded.

"Yes, I do," he whispered.

Sadness flashed across her face, quickly followed by joy. She looked happier than he'd ever seen her.

"I'm glad," she said as she reached down underneath the table. "It'll be so much easier for us now, Johnny."

She straightened up, her eyes falling to her hands.

"And so much more fun."

She unbuckled the leather dog collar she was holding and connected the black leash to it.

What?

"You had your chance the easy way," she said as her eyes met his once more. "But the hard way is *so much* more fun."

John's eyes dropped to the dog collar. The leather was black and covered with large spiked polished studs. On one end of the collar was a large silver buckle with a padlock attached. The leash wrapped around a small hook at the side of the collar and its loops coiled around Zoe's right arm.

She reached out with the dog collar.

John pulled back away from her, "Are you *serious?*"

I've gone too far!

I've pushed her too far!

A crack appeared in her smile. For a moment, she looked as if she was unsure of herself. But then her resolve returned.

"Johnny," she replied. "Don't fight it."

He had no choice. He wanted to yell at her, to scream, to talk sense into her, but he knew that wouldn't help him get out of this situation and escape. He *had* to play her game, he kept reminding himself. He needed her to help him track down Fox. She was the only one who knew where he was, what he looked like, what he could do. He needed her – *no matter what!*

He smiled at her.

This is crazy!

He leaned forward again, looked deep into her eyes.

I can't believe I'm doing this!

Will it help?

I don't know...

"Please put it on me," he whispered.

Her smile grew and she went to say something, but stopped herself. Tears formed in the corners of her eyes and she bit down on her bottom lip.

In total silence, she leaned forward and wrapped the dog collar around his neck.

The leather was stiff and rough and cut into his throat as she tightened the buckle, but he didn't complain. The padlock snapped loudly in place around the buckle and she tugged softly on the leash, testing it. John looked on passively, letting her do as she wished, his eyes cast low, concentrating on her belly button and the diamond that rested inside.

"Good," she said softly. John wasn't sure whether she was talking to him or to herself. He lifted his eyes and stared at her, a small smile on his face.

She took a step back and looked at him.

"How does that feel?" she asked him.

"Nice," he lied.

"*Really?*" she seemed unsure.

"I like it," he replied. "I could get used to it."

She smiled back at him again. She looked happier than ever.

That's it, pal, John told himself. *Keep it nice and calm and play along with her. Look for an opening, a weakness. Eventually she'll let something slip.*

Zoe tugged on the leash. John's neck and head moved quickly towards her.

"You ready?" she asked.

"For anything, Zoe," John replied.

She leaned forward and reached under the table again. Within a few seconds, the ropes across his chest were loose and he was able to push them off with his right hand.

He sat up.

His head swam slightly as he did so, and the pain in his left arm continued a dull throb. He looked down at the stitches. They were holding nicely. He flexed his fingers again without any problem.

Zoe walked down the side of the table and reached underneath it again, unravelling more of the leash as she did so.

As John slowly bent his left arm at the elbow, testing to make sure the stitches wouldn't break, Zoe undid the ropes around his hips and legs.

She leaned forward and unbuckled the leather straps holding the long metal bar between his feet as well.

When he was free, she turned to watch him as he gently tested his arm.

"Don't worry," she said. "The fishing wire will hold. It's strong stuff."

The pain in his arm grew stronger, but after almost two days of different types of pain, John knew he could put up with it.

His left shoulder was sore now, but the gauze still covered the stab wound.

He looked at her as he rotated his right shoulder, testing that out for any soreness too. It wasn't as bad as it had been.

She walked back towards him, letting the end of the leash run up his legs, over his groin and up his chest.

"How do you feel?" she asked.

"I'm feeling good," he replied.

She nodded, "Care to go for a walk?"

Almost there, he told himself. *Take it easy, play it carefully, and you'll get out of this...*

He nodded his head, "That would be great."

She smiled again and reached back under the table.

John heard the clatter of the metal before he saw it.

He tilted his head and looked at Zoe.

Her eyes met his and her face fell.

"Only for a little while," she pouted.

John sighed deeply.

"I promise," she said. "Be good and I'll take them off. I promise."

He nodded.

Zoe stood back up with the handcuffs in her hands.

She reached forward and began to place them around his wrists.

Now's your chance! Grab her!

John thought about it, but didn't act.

Not yet.

Not yet?

I said, not yet!

The metal teeth bit home around his bruised wrists once more. At least Zoe was careful to keep the cuffs away from the stitches near his left wrist.

"Sorry," she said.

Without taking her eyes from him, she walked to his side and let some of the leash drop to the floor, creating a greater space between them.

"Okay," she said. "Climb down."

Slowly, more for his benefit than hers, John climbed from the table. His feet touched the floorboards and he stood on the floor, testing his legs, making sure he wasn't about to topple. It felt strange to be standing again after almost two days, but quickly his body adjusted and he steadied himself. He could keep silent about the pain in his arm and shoulders, his chest and back, if it meant he had a chance to escape.

You have to!

I know!

And soon!

I know!

He smiled at her.

She tugged on the leash, bringing him forward a couple of steps.

"Come on," she said. "You need to go for a walk."

She turned and pulled on the leash once more, dragging him forward as she marched down the side of the kitchenette, leading to the bathroom.

He followed her.

The stiff leather collar dug into the back of his neck, but he didn't care. With her back turned to him, he had a good chance to look around. A chance to check out the church once more, without being tied to a chair or table. He tried to spot anything that may be of use to him.

Anything!

He tried desperately not to look at Zoe's swinging red arse cheeks in front of him.

It may be your only chance to look!

His eyes scanned the kitchenette. Apart from the cutlery still scattered across the counter, there was nothing else he could use as a weapon.

Grab one of the knives and use it?

They're not big enough to threaten her with.

So use them to cut through the leather!

When? And how? Where am I going to hide it? I'm naked!

The phone was still sitting there too.

If I could get to the phone and make a call...
When?
I don't know when! But I've got to try.
He turned his head the other way, glancing up at the lectern as they passed it. He saw the access hatch in the base of the cross on the wall. The door was shut.
Probably locked again too. There's nothing of use up there anyway.
He turned his head further around as Zoe walked him past the lectern. He could see the large King James Bible again.
Did I really read from that only two days ago? It seems like forever.
And then his eyes focussed on the key ring.
His key ring with all his keys.
And the *red* key.
Sitting on top of the Bible.
His key to freedom.
Damn!
So close, and yet so out of reach.
I've got to get that key!
He almost stopped, but knew he couldn't. The pull of the leash dragged him onwards, past the lectern and staircase.
I have to get it!
She stopped by the bathroom, opened the door, switched on the light and turned to face him once again.
"Inside," she said.
John walked past her and into the bathroom.
"You'd better use it," she said, pointing to the toilet. "I don't want you pissing on yourself like you did last night. I'm not cleaning that up again."
John nodded and walked over to the bowl.
He didn't think he needed to urinate, but once he stood there, he could feel the urge grow in his bladder. He didn't want to wet himself again either.
He pointed his cock to the bowl.
He waited.
But found he couldn't go.
He turned to face her.

She was leaning against the bathroom door, staring at him intently, the leash loose in her right hand.

"Do you mind?" he asked. "This is kind of a private moment."

Zoe smiled, "After all this time and you're *still* shy?"

She giggled as she stepped out of the bathroom and to the side of the door.

"I'm just outside the door," she said, "if you need me to help you with anything."

"Okay."

Go!

John turned from the door and glanced around the bathroom. His eyes swept across the bath and shower, over the toilet and behind him to the sink and cabinet above it.

Anything! Look for anything!

He turned his head and stared at the window to his left. It was dark outside now. He couldn't see anything.

His eyes continued up the window. It was different from the others in the church. It was a newer window that wasn't made of stained-glass, but of a frosted glass that was harder to see through.

Makes sense, it's a bathroom after all.

His eyes travelled up the window and stopped on the latch.

It was unlocked.

Now was his chance. He could open the window and scramble through before she could stop him.

What about the leash?

Cut it with something?

What?

Should've grabbed one of those knives!

Damn!

There's got to be something here, something in the cabinet, something to cut through the leather!

Cut through the leather, open the window, and scramble out? All before she gets in here to stop me?

You can do it!

But what about Fox? Leave here now and she won't be of any use. She won't help me find him.

Shit!

I've got to get Fox.

I know.

So I can't escape!

I know.

This game has got to stop!

"You almost done?" she called from outside the door.

"Ah, yeah," he replied, looking down at his cock and willing it to work.

"Men are meant to be quicker than women, you know," she continued.

He shook his cock with his handcuffed hands; the metal clanked loudly in the silence.

After what seemed like an eternity, the urine began to flow and poured loudly into the bowl.

Gotta wait it out, pal, he told himself. *You've got to talk her around to your side. You* need *her help to get at Fox. Gotta talk her around to* my *game plan.*

Maybe I could get him on my own.

Ahuh, yeah, sure, and where do you start? Huh?

Redlingford, I'd go to his farmhouse.

And if he's not there?

I don't know.

If he's left and gone back home? What are you going to do?

I don't know.

Good plan!

Shut up!

He shook his cock to remove the last few drops of piss, then turned to face the bathroom door.

She was standing there, smiling at him. "Awesome," she said. Her eyes were on his cock and her left hand was rubbing her groin. "There's something about a man pissing. It's so masculine and yet it's coming from such a small roll of skin. Just hanging from your body. Out there in the open and so...*exposed*...so dangerously unprotected."

She raised her eyes to his. She was still fingering herself, her fingers spreading wide the lips of her vagina, her middle finger rubbing furiously.

He looked back at her.

"Intense, huh?" she said to him.

"What is?"

"What we're doing together. Just you and me."

"Yeah, I guess."

She stepped into the bathroom, the light making the diamond in her belly button sparkle. She pulled her left hand away from between her legs.

"Want to go to the edge?" she asked as she lifted her hand to her mouth and licked her fingers.

"Zoe…" John began.

She pouted, "Please? You can't get me all horny and then not let me have any fun."

"We've had fun."

"I want more," her hand returned to between her legs, massaging her folds.

"What about Ricky?" John asked.

Zoe sighed, "Help me and I'll help you." She took a step forward, closer to him. "Do this for me, Johnny, and I'll do anything for you."

John stared at her.

He had no other choice.

He nodded.

And Zoe smiled.

<u>Forty</u>

*S*mart move, pal. You should've taken your chance in
the bathroom!
Keep quiet.
*You should've escaped while you had the chance. That
window was unlocked!*
You told me not to. You said I had to get Fox!
Now look at the mess you're in.
It'll get better.
Really?
It has to.

It was dark. And silent.

Darker and more quiet than he had ever known.

And he cursed himself for going along with Zoe.

To the edge...

But I had no choice!

Ahuh, like you didn't!

I didn't!

You didn't try to stop her.

He breathed heavily through his nose – it was the only
proof he had that he was still alive.

His head and eyes were covered by blindfolds. He had a
soft dark blindfold cutting across his nose and eyes and tied
at the back of his head. He also had a black hood covering
his whole head, which she had put over him and tied off
around his throat, just above the dog collar. He could see
nothing through the material.

The hood was hot and smelt of stagnant breath and air.

And all was dark.

His ears were blocked with earplugs, pushed all the way
in so he couldn't hear anything other than his own breathing and thoughts.

And his mouth and jaw were held open by a tight ball of
wadding which made it impossible for him to close them. The
cloth Zoe had shoved into his mouth was dipped in vinegar,

making him want to vomit, but he controlled himself – he had to. He didn't want to choke and die. If the wadding fell any further back into his mouth he could choke on it, and if vomit erupted from his stomach, it had nowhere to go.

The vinegar stung the wound in his lip, making it tingle and then numb.

His arms were spread above him, tied tightly by the wrists, and his legs were splayed below him, tied by the ankles. He was tilted at a slight angle, the middle of his back resting on cold hard wood and his head leaning on a small soft cushion. His groin burned with heat and his cock hung limp, pain still flowing along it and up his body.

"We don't go back from here, Johnny," she had said as she walked him back from the bathroom. "We'll *never* be the same after this."

He hadn't known what she meant then.

How could I?

His eyes had been concentrating on the lectern as they passed it again. He had to make sure his mind wasn't playing tricks. The red key and the key ring with his keys had to still be there on the Bible.

They were.

I've got to get to that key!

But how?

Zoe had dragged him to the middle of the church. She turned to face him and asked him a question.

John hadn't been listening. He was concentrating on trying to work out a way to get to the red key.

The red key of freedom.

He was sure now that it unlocked the handcuffs. And he was willing to risk everything to find out if he was right.

Gotta get out of this.

Fox.

I have to get away from Zoe.

Fox! She's the only one who can lead you to him!

"Well?" she asked as she tugged on his leash, pulling him forward. "Will you?"

John had no idea what she was talking about.

Gotta get that key somehow!

"Well?" she tugged again.

"Anything," John replied, smiling at her. "For you, Zoe. I'll do anything."

She had smiled and walked towards him then. Her stiletto heels gave her enough height now that she was almost as tall as him. She kissed him hard on the lips.

"It'll be worth it, Johnny," she said. "As I always knew it would be."

She let the extra coils of leash drop between them as she walked behind him, running her hand across the wounds on his chest, down to his hip and around up his back.

"Squat," she ordered.

John stared at the charred and cold embers in the fireplace.

Dead.

It'll be getting cold in here soon now night is here. She should build another fire.

The leash tugged violently at his collar, cutting through the skin of his throat. He started to topple backwards, but quickly regained his balance.

"I said, *squat*," she said again, firmer now, from behind him.

John bent his knees and squatted on the ground.

The leash is long enough. What if I make a run for it and grab the keys on the lectern?

But it's no use.

I can unlock the handcuffs before she reaches me!

But then she won't help you find Fox! If you do anything wrong, she'll refuse to help and then you're screwed!

Aren't I screwed now?

You're screwed either way!

"They'll screw you and then they'll screw you," that's what Richard used to say.

Maybe he was right.

John wished he could discuss it all with Richard now. But Richard wasn't there. He tried to call him into his mind, but he wouldn't come.

He was concentrating too hard on the red key.

Too hard on escaping.

And then darkness engulfed him.

Before he realised what was happening, Zoe had placed a blindfold over his eyes and tied it off at the back of his head. He brought his hands up to his face, felt the material, and tried to pull it off. But he couldn't, it was tied too tightly and his hands refused to work properly as the handcuffs bit into his wrists once more.

"Don't struggle, Johnny," she said from behind him. "You told me you'd do this."

This is crazy!

He almost said it, but he held back.

"Do you trust me, Johnny?" she whispered by his ear.

He nodded.

"Really?"

He nodded again.

"You know I'd never hurt you, don't you?"

Do I?

He nodded once more.

"You trust me enough to know I'd do anything for you?"

"Yes," he whispered.

He felt her cheek by his. Her hair brushed against his ear and he felt her arms around him.

She hugged him tight.

"I know you do," she said. "After all this time, it will be worth it."

"I know," he replied.

I'm crazy.

"I'm only doing what's good for you."

He nodded.

"For us."

"Okay," he whispered.

I'm going crazy!

Fear and anger wrestled for control inside his body.

"I like you naked," she said then. "I like you squatting too."

John didn't reply.

"You deserve the best love a man can have," she continued. "Leather is thicker than blood, Johnny. Don't you forget that."

He nodded yet again.

"I'm going to make you fly, my love," she whispered as she stopped hugging him. "We'll fly together. You and me. And you'll never be the same."

He remained in the squatting position as Zoe left him. He heard her footsteps recede along the floor, echoing into the darkness.

His thighs were starting to strain, and his legs began to shake. But he didn't dare move.

Go now, run!

Run? Run where? I'm blindfolded!

It's still worth the risk.

It's not worth anything! I'm staying where I am!

Her heels clanged against the metal of the spiral staircase.

Play it cool and calm, he told himself. *She thinks she loves you. Hell, maybe she does! She isn't going to hurt you.*

John almost chuckled as he thought back to those events now.

How wrong could I be?

He had no idea. Just as he had no idea how long he had been standing, tied the way he now was.

Hours? Minutes? Days?

His legs were beginning to go numb once more, and his arms ached. His body was sagging badly but there was little he could do about it. His arms and legs ached too much when he moved them. He hoped the stitches in his left arm would survive the strain.

He felt a breeze gently caress his body. His eyes moved from side to side, trying to see, even though he knew he couldn't. The silence was total, apart from his rushing heartbeat.

You had your chance, he thought. *You didn't take it. Now look where you are!*

He could feel the cold settle on him. He knew he was only going to get colder. He would freeze, he was sure of it.

And he cast his mind back once more. Watched as his mind replayed the events in every detail.

She had returned to him after opening the access hatch again. His ears painted the picture that his eyes couldn't see.

"Love doesn't get any more pure than this, Johnny," she said. "I've wanted to do this for so long now. I'm glad we finally have the chance."

There were other sounds he couldn't work out, strange metallic noises and plastic rustling.

"Trust me, my love, no matter what happens. You have to learn to trust me."

They were the last words he heard her speak.

She had walked to his side, placed one hand on his head, and used the other to push the soft earplug into his ear.

John didn't know what was happening, but as the plug expanded in his ear and his hearing disappeared from his left side, he knew what was to come.

She moved around his body, running a hand across his neck as she did so. He listened intently with his right ear, grabbing every sound he could before she inserted another plug.

She pushed it in.

And there was total silence.

She's gone mad!

Don't lose it now. She said she'd help you if you did this. Don't ruin your best chance!

He felt her fingers on his face.

Now that his sight and hearing were gone, her touch became so important to him. Her soft hands moved lightly across his cheeks and stopped at his mouth.

Her fingers opened his lips, touched his gums and teeth. And pried open his jaw.

He thought about resisting, but knew it was useless.

Play the game…

He opened his mouth.

And she pushed the gag inside.

Its foul vinegar taste stung his tongue and the inside of his mouth. Saliva poured down the back of his throat, trying to remove the taste, but it was too overpowering.

He wanted to resist, wanted to stop her, but slowly he found his resolve crumbling. He was squatting in the church, handcuffed and leashed like a dog, but he wasn't able to resist her.

She's won, he thought. *I can't stop her now.*

Then the hood was placed over his head.

His submission was complete.

She's won, he thought again.

It made no difference to his eyesight, he couldn't see anything anyway, but with the material over his whole face, he could now feel his breathing. She tied the hood tightly around his neck, and his breathing soon made the hood hot and claustrophobic.

Totally cut off.

He could see and hear nothing.

He couldn't talk.

Only the floorboards under his feet kept him in touch with the outside world.

He was too stunned to think straight. His anger had vanished. So had his will to escape.

He squatted, empty and numb. Not even the pain affected him now.

Nothing...

His leash was tugged upwards. He unbalanced slightly as he stood up. But from out of nowhere, her soft hand touched his chest and helped him straighten.

She's in front of me, he thought.

The leash was tugged again. He walked forward slowly, not wanting to stumble into anything.

She pulled to the right and he took some steps in that direction. Then she tugged on the leash to stop him and they stood still for a moment or two. John's ears reached out, trying hard to pick up any sound. But he heard nothing other than his breathing.

The collar moved slightly on his neck. He readied himself to walk. But the movement stopped and he stood there, dumb, waiting for his next command.

She's won.

Then the leash was tugged to the left.

He followed her lead.

A few steps more.

Where am I now? Do I have any idea?

A stronger tug pulled on the collar. He walked forward.

By the fire? No, I'm facing the other way, I think. Am I?

He didn't know.

Another few steps forward, then a pause, then a few more steps before the toes on his left foot kicked something hard. He toppled, the weight of his body propelling him forward. He lifted his arms, trying to put out his hands to balance himself, but the handcuffs made it almost impossible as they bit into his wrists.

But she was there again, her hands on his chest, stopping him from falling and straightening him back up.

She tugged on the leash again.

He lifted his foot, and stepped onto whatever it was in front of him.

Then he followed with his right foot.

Another step up? Where am I?

It wasn't until he'd taken a few more steps, that he realised there was gravel and dirt under his feet.

I'm outside?

He could feel the cold night air around his body.

Yes! I am! She's taken me outside!

He smiled to himself under the hood.

She can't trick me.

Yeah, great victory, Sherlock!

I told you to shut up!

And look where it got you...

And then he wondered exactly where she was taking him.

The Jeep?

Am I going to meet Fox?

Why? Why do that? What's really going on here?

Panic began to build, but he quashed it. He couldn't believe that she would be taking him to Fox. There was no reason to. She hated Fox as much as he did. They would work together to get Fox just as soon as she finished her little game.

This is no game, he told himself as he was led further forward, walking off the gravel now, the cold dew from the grass under his feet.

The leash led him blindly on.

Sometimes he would stumble. On other occasions sticks and prickles would get under his feet, digging in and hurting, making him jump or stagger. Tree branches and shrubs would brush against his bare chest or legs, but Zoe pulled him forward without stopping.

She didn't come to help.

Only the pulling of the leash kept him on track.

It was a slow process and the night air felt cold and made his wounds itch.

And it felt as if they walked for miles.

But he was powerless to do anything about it.

The leash pulled him on and on.

He tried to concentrate on the ground under his feet. It was mostly wet, slippery grass. But on more than one occasion, the grass gave way to gravel and then something that felt like brick. Eventually, he walked onto another surface he couldn't work out. It was soft and smooth, and felt spongy. It wasn't as cold as the grass had been, and there was very little dew on the surface. He couldn't work out what it was.

He didn't have time.

He was pulled onwards by the leash.

Where is she taking me?

His breathing increased as their pace picked up. He could hear his heartbeat rushing in his head.

He walked faster as the leash forced him to.

He took a few more steps on the flat surface and then cannoned into Zoe's arms. She held him tight.

What? What's happening?

His head swivelled around by instinct, even though he couldn't see anything.

Her hands went to his chest, and she pushed him back slowly.

He took two steps backwards before the collar tightened on his neck.

He stood still then, waiting for the next command.

Slowly, the leash tugged on him.

He moved forward carefully.

His right foot hit the first step.

He lifted it and placed it on top of the step. Then he re-peated the process again with his left foot. He did the same thing for the next step, and the next. He repeated his actions until all the steps were climbed.

He continued walking forward, realizing the ground under his feet was flat and dry. There was no dew here and the coldness was gone too.

Her hands touched his chest again and stopped him walking forward.

He stood still.

And waited.

He shook his head as he thought back now.

You should've tried. You should've tried anything! he thought. *To run while she left you standing there. That was your chance! Maybe your* last *chance!*

But he didn't know that at the time.

He didn't know what was to come.

If he had known, he would've fought. He would've struggled. He would've tried to escape.

Instead, he just stood there, and waited.

And that's when Zoe lost it completely.

<u>Forty-one</u>

John had no idea what she was doing, he couldn't see or hear her movements, but when she had unlocked the handcuffs and set his hands free, he thought that finally the game was at an end.

But he had been wrong.

As the cold steel of the cuffs slipped away from his wrists, he rubbed both of them, feeling the chaffed skin and the imprint that the teeth had made.

Now that his hands were free, he was able to run them up his arms, trying to warm himself from the cold night air. Although, he was still careful not to touch the wound in his left arm.

Maybe this is it, he thought. *The game* is *finally over.*

She touched his chest, pushing him back two steps.

The middle of his back hit something hard and cold.

John leaned forward in shock, the wadding in his mouth muffling his yell.

But her hand was on his chest still, pushing him backwards again.

He relented and felt his body tip slightly backwards.

He rested against the cold wood and he thought it strange that the wood didn't cover his whole back. The wood was only in the middle of his back, with two arms stretching below and above; like some huge X-design.

Her hand reached to his forehead and pushed him backwards. He leaned his head back, and found a padded cushion to rest on.

It's not over, he thought.

Then run.

I can't see!

Grab her, force her to let you go.

I can't see where she is!

Something tugged at his left thigh, pulling him backwards against one of the legs of the X. He touched cold wood as a leather strap wrapped around his thigh. He could feel her hands moving over his leg now, buckling him into the leather strap.

He wanted to tell her to stop, but he knew his voice wouldn't escape the wadding in his mouth.

He was powerless.

She moved further down, inching his leg out slightly, buckling another strap by his knee, and one lower down by his ankle.

John's hopes for an early end to her game were quashed. *It's not over yet.*

There was nothing he could do.

He just stood there, and let her continue.

After buckling his right leg in the same manner, Zoe lifted his right arm above his head and to the side.

He knew what was coming.

He didn't flinch as he felt the cold heavy metal chain wrap around his wrist. The chain bit tightly into the skin, pulling his wrist and arm against the cold surface of the X. He waited as she did the same to his left arm, hoping that it wouldn't affect the stitches that kept his wound closed.

She wouldn't've gone to all that trouble to stitch you up only to let it all unravel now, he thought.

He should've been in pain as he stood there, mirroring the wooden X he was tied to, but the cold night air was biting hard and he wondered if that was the reason he could feel no pain.

Or am I just used to it now? he wondered. *Is it easier to submit than fight?*

He tried to move his arms and legs, tried to see if he had any flexibility in his bindings, but he didn't.

He moved his head from side to side, as if looking for Zoe. But the blindfolds gave nothing away and the earplugs made sure the silence was total.

Only his thoughts accompanied him.

He waited for a long time, or so it seemed to him. He stood tied there, leaning back on the X, waiting for Zoe's next move. But it didn't come.

After a while, he started to wonder if she was still there.

The cold night settled on his shoulders. He could feel the dew in the air and on his skin.

But she didn't touch him again.

His hands and arms started to go numb, and with his feet splayed apart, his heels and ankles began to lose all feeling as well.

"Now *this* is a good look," he heard Richard say in his head.

Shut up!

"No, I mean it. All tied up and nowhere to go!"

Very funny.

"Oh, this isn't funny, John. This is serious stuff. She's got you and there's nothing you can do about it."

I know that.

"You're going to have to follow this through, play it out to the end with her, if you want her to help you."

I know that too"It could be dangerous."

Do I have a choice?

"No, doesn't look like you do," Richard agreed.

I shouldn't've yelled at her Saturday night. I got her mad. That's what got me into this mess.

"It certainly looks that way."

If I had kept calm, maybe Helen would still be alive and we would be home by now, everything back to normal.

"That's possible."

I just shouldn't've said what I said. Or acted the way I did towards her.

"Always shooting off at the mouth before thinking," Richard chuckled. "You don't change, John. It got you into trouble when we were young, and now it's still getting you into trouble."

Huh?

"You've got to learn, pal. You've got to think of consequences. Things you do, they can come back to haunt you down the track."

I don't know what you mean.

"I'm sure you'll have plenty of time to work it out. You're not going anywhere for a while, it seems."

Tell me, please?

"Pal, you've got to find this out for yourself. So many lies can build up in a lifetime. Some you put there on purpose, while others accidentally appear. In the end, you start to believe the lies too."

I don't understand.

"I know, that's part of the problem." Richard replied. "But you will."

Huh?

"Just think about it. I mean, *really* think about it. You're believing *everything* Zoe is telling you!"

Yeah, of course!

"Why?"

Why shouldn't I? I have no reason not to.

"No reason? Come on, you've even had some doubts yourself! What about the car keys?" Richard reminded him. "She said she didn't have them, but then you found them. The gun? She said it was in the Jeep but it wasn't."

John stayed silent, leaning against the X.

"Now she says Helen is dead. Do you really believe her?"

John was stunned by the thought.

Huh?

"Do you really believe her?"

John's chest burned with hope.

Helen could still be alive?

"Isn't that a possibility?"

Helen! It could be true! But why would she lie to me?

"Why not? She wants to have sex with you, she wants to do all this stuff to you. She couldn't get you to do it while Helen was still around, so she tries something else. If you think Helen is dead, maybe it will be easier to get you to agree."

Yeah.

"And, Jesus, it looks like it worked, huh?"

But she has the gold pendant!

"Come on, think about it! You can buy them just about anywhere for peanuts."

That makes a lot of sense.

"Of course it does! Remember, pal? They'll screw you and..."

..and then they'll screw *you.*

"Exactly. It's all a game!"

A game... So, where's Helen?

"I don't know."

But you just said she was alive!

Richard chuckled, "Did I? That's my whole point, buddy. Once you start weaving your lies, you can't tell what's truth and what's fiction any more. You can't tell them apart."

But I don't understand. Now you're saying she isn't *lying?*

"I'm not saying anything. I'm just reminding you that the facts as you see them may not actually be the facts at all."

Damn you, stop playing with me.

"Remember, it could all be an elaborate game, full of half-truths and lies."

You're playing with my mind, stop it!

"You should know all about that, John."

Shut up.

"Seems you've started to believe your own lies too."

Huh?

"Why don't you be honest with her, and maybe she'll be honest with you."

I don't understand!

"Oh, I think you do..."

And then Richard was gone from his mind.

The silence returned.

Fuck you!

But Richard didn't reply.

Fuck you, you bastard! Stop trying to fuck with me! FUCK YOU!

John's hands turned to fists and he pulled on the chains above him.

If you were here now I'd –

But he didn't get time to finish his thought.

A hand touched his groin.

John's mind froze and his breathing stopped.

The hand was soft and warm, and began massaging his limp cock.

Zoe!

He breathed a sigh of relief.

It's Zoe!

He had no idea how long she had left him alone, but it seemed like forever.

But now she was back.

Are you sure it's her?

Huh?

How do you know it's Zoe?

It has *to be!*

But you don't know for sure.

No...but –

Then you better hope it is *her!*

Fear started to grow in John's chest.

Of course it's her. Who else would it be out here?

Who else...?

Despite the situation, her hand felt so good on him, so warm.

He began to grow again.

Within seconds his cock was hard and pulsing.

Then he felt her mouth around him, hot and wet.

So good.

Her hand continued to massage his balls as her lips engulfed him and sucked deeply.

John tried to relax on the X, but it was difficult to do so with the angle he was on and the cold of the night. His thoughts returned to the idea that maybe it wasn't Zoe standing there massaging his cock.

Who then? Who could it be?

Still, his breathing quickened and after a few minutes he began to reach climax. His body tensed and readied for the moment.

And then her mouth left him.

He was hard and ready, but she was gone. His cock was wet and pulsing, and left to the cold night air. His balls ached deeply. His orgasm denied.

Why?

It was then he found out.

At first he thought it was some kind of soft cloth or cotton. He could feel it as it was placed around his groin. It started above his erection and then spread to the side and below. He felt it around his balls and back towards his anus. But he couldn't work out exactly what it was.

Zoe's arms knocked against the insides of his legs as she applied it to him, and as it sat there heavy on him, it began to slowly slide towards the ground.

What the hell is it? What is she doing to me now?

And then he felt the cold steel against his hip.

His body tensed as the image came into his mind.

One of her hands rested on his stomach. She patted him softly, as if trying to reassure him.

Very slowly, he released his tension and tried to relax.

The hand stopped patting him, and the blade made its way from his hip to his groin.

He held his breath.

And Zoe began to shave him.

He didn't dare move. He tried not to breathe. His erection quickly subsided.

What had she said to him in the bathroom?

"There's something about a man pissing. It's so masculine and yet it's coming from such a small roll of skin. Just hanging from your body. Out there in the open and so... exposed...so dangerously unprotected."

Unprotected!

Oh my God!

All he could feel was the blade, cutting through his pubic hair, sweeping closely by his manhood, moving slowly and so dangerously in a sharp dance.

One slip and..., he dared not think of it.

She shaved above his cock first, then to the sides. Then she held the tip of his cock between a finger and thumb as she moved the blade over the top of his balls.

This is crazy, he thought. But he didn't move.

She shaved the sides and then underneath his balls, shaving as far back towards his anus as the angle of his legs permitted.

After what seemed like an eternity, the blade left his body. Her hand returned to his stomach and she patted him once more.

She didn't do it, he couldn't believe it. *She had the chance, but she didn't cut it off!*

For the first time in a while, John allowed his breathing to return to normal.

His panic subsided and gave way to anger.

I can't believe she did that.

She did!

She's crazy!

But you need her.

She just shaved *me!*

But you need *her!*

His crotch burned in the cold air. The stinging bare feeling of naked shaved skin made him even more uncomfortable and vulnerable.

He waited for Zoe to continue.

Continue with what?

I don't want to know!

Maybe she'll let me down now, untie me and set me free.

But nothing happened for a long time.

The burning around his groin began to subside, but the numbness in his limbs remained.

This has gone far enough.

He bit down hard on the wadding, trying to make it smaller. Maybe he could spit it out if he really tried.

Spit it out where? The hood would stop you anyway.

I've got to try something!

But the chewing didn't help. Biting into the material spilled more vinegar onto his tongue and down his throat.

Don't vomit! You can't afford to!

He stopped chewing.

No use.

He rested his head on the padded cushion.

You're beaten.

Broken.

Suddenly, he sensed someone was near him. He didn't know how he knew, but he tensed his body.

Her hand touched his chest.

Are you sure it's Zoe?

It IS!

Positive?

Shut up!

Slowly, her fingers snaked across the claw marks and down to his stomach. One fingernail circled his belly button twice before her hand slipped lower.

He was growing again.

He wished he could control it, but his erection was automatic.

Zoe's hand grabbed hold of his cock, and started to massage it once more.

With his pubic hair shaved, John felt smoother now. Every sensation was heightened, intense, stronger than before.

And her mouth was around him again. Her tongue danced across his shaft, licked his tip and sucked at the pre-cum that dripped there.

Even with the wadding in his mouth, John moaned deeply as his excitement began to peak.

And that's when Zoe lost it.

She went mad.

At least, that's what John thought now.

She had gone too far.

In the space of only a few seconds, as he began to peak, she removed her mouth and grabbed his cock tightly with her hand.

John hardly had time to notice. He just thought she was trying something different to give him a new experience.

A new experience, he almost laughed at that now as he thought back.

Her fingers had pulled at the skin on the underside of his cock, pulling it away from the shaft.

But he didn't care.

He moaned loudly again, trying to get her to continue. He pushed his hips out, wanting her to continue massaging him, stretching to rub his cock against her.

And then the pain sliced through him.

It felt as if the skin around his cock split. The pain rolled down his shaft and groin and through the rest of his body.

Ecstasy turned to agony and his moan of pleasure turned to a scream of terror.

He bit down hard on the wadding in his mouth, squirting more vinegar down his throat.

She held on tight to his cock as the pain continued.

His cock and balls pulsed uncontrollably.

He tried to move his arms and legs. He wanted to grab her, hit out at her, kick her. His back arched off the X, trying to squirm out of her grip.

Anything to stop the pain.

But his bindings were too tight.

His orgasm exploded through the pain; the cum shooting from his cock and into the night.

But the pain continued.

He could feel her pulling at the skin.

He could feel it sliding against his shaft, moving one way, and then reversing.

He felt like she was slicing through him, but he knew his fears must have been amplified in the dark.

He hoped they were.

Prayed they were.

She wouldn't do that to me! She wouldn't!

He felt something sharp drag his cock skin the other way again, and then he felt the snap as it clicked closed.

She let go of him then, his erection already subsiding in all the terror and agony. The last drips of cum oozing from his tip.

His head fell forward and his back slammed against the X. The cold hard wood now a comfort to him. The wadding in his mouth had moved further down the back of his throat as he had tried to scream. He used his tongue as best he could to push the wadding forward in his mouth again.

He waited for more.

He waited for her as the pain ebbed through him.

But that was the last time she had touched him.

And now it felt like hours ago to him.

John's arms were completely numb, as were his legs. The burning sensation around his groin had changed to a dull warmth. But he could still feel his pulse through the pain in his cock. And with his cock limp now, he was sure he could feel the cold touch of steel resting on his balls.

He wasn't sure of it, but he could make a good guess.

She had pierced his cock.

And inserted a ring.

He was sure of it.

Now, he was hers.

<u>Forty-two</u>

The muscle cramps spread up John's legs and back. They arched through his whole body, slicing through his shoulders and ramming into his brain. He bit down hard on the wadding in his mouth, willing the cramps to stop.

Even though the air around him was cold, he was sweating as the cramps attacked him yet again.

How long? he wondered. *How long do I have to stay like this?*

He'd begun counting the seconds, trying to judge time. But it was no use.

His brain didn't want to work properly. He couldn't concentrate on anything for more than a few seconds. Even though he was tied to the X and had nothing to do other than think, he found it increasingly hard to keep his thoughts in line.

He wanted to keep track of time, to try and work out how long he'd been tied there, but his brain wouldn't co-operate.

How long now?

He had no idea.

It was dark when we started this. I remember seeing the sun set. That was while Zoe and I were both still on the table.

He remembered the sex then. He could picture in his mind her puckered anus and the warm inviting folds of her vagina as she sat on his face. He could still taste her and smell her.

He began to grow hard again.

And the pain pulsed through his cock once more, slicing up his body.

Think of something else, quick!

His mind swirled, trying to sprint but managing only to stagger.

There was the bathroom. Then she blindfolded me and brought me here. How long did it take? How long?

He didn't know.

It had felt as if he'd walked for miles to get to where he was now. But he realised it couldn't have been that far.

It had to be near the church.

Zoe had left him twice while he was tied here.

Did she go back to the church?

Yeah, she must have.

How long was she gone?

I don't know.

Try and work it out!

How?

He shook his head from side to side.

It was Monday night. That was all he was sure of.

Or maybe Tuesday morning.

Tuesday.

A whole weekend gone.

Three days out of his life that he was powerless to control.

Powerless.

How quickly lives could change…

If only I'd known all this was going to happen Friday night, I would've stayed at work. I wouldn't've gone home. I would've –

Work!

Tuesday!

Possibilities started to roll around in his mind.

Work! They would've missed me! They would've wondered where I am! I didn't show up, so they'll have started looking for me.

They have to!

He prayed they would.

He *knew* they would.

"And what good is that gonna do you?" Richard asked.

Huh?

"Well, I know you work with some pretty special people, but I don't think they're going to start calling up all the churches in the countryside to find you."

I know that.

"They're not going to know where to look for you."

Of course not. But they'll call home, and when they get no answer, they'll call the hospital and when they find out Helen hasn't arrived for work either, they'll get suspicious!

"Really?"

Of course!

"You have great faith in your fellow workmates."

That's what they'll do!

"And then what will they do?"

Huh?

"After they've made this great leap of logic, that you're in trouble and need help, what are they going to do?"

I don't know.

"Call the police? And tell them what?"

I don't know.

"Search your house for clues? And find what?"

I don't know.

"Well, looks like they'll be here later rather than sooner," Richard concluded.

Just shut up.

"They're not going to find you."

They'll know something is wrong.

"Really? How will they know that?"

They just will.

"I see." Richard continued. "But to me it just looks like a husband and wife have gone off together for a little un-planned holiday. Maybe a dirty weekend. They all know things have been strained between you and Helen. They'll understand. They might be a bit miffed you didn't tell them about it, but they'll get over it. No one will think it's strange."

Yes they will.

"Why?"

Because that's not like us, it's not like Helen and me.

"No, it isn't, is it?"

No, that's what I said.

"Not like you to do anything risky..."

Exactly.

"And you wouldn't lie to cover your tracks while you do something else, now would you?"

No I wouldn't.

"Wouldn't, huh? My, we have changed."

Shut up.

"Just helping you pass the time, my friend. You'll be here for a while yet."

John pulled at the chains around his wrists. His hands were cold and numb, but he could still feel the chain bite his wrists as he tugged on them.

I've got to get out of this.

"Good luck, buddy. But at least you pass the say-something-obvious test."

Very funny. I don't see you helping me.

"You don't see anything at the moment."

Quit with the wise cracks.

"Oh, I'm deadly serious. You've got yourself tied up in a real mess."

I told you to stop trying to be funny.

"And those blindfolds aren't the only things stopping you from seeing."

Huh?

"Come on, John. Use your mind. Push through the years and try to divorce your fact from your fiction. We all make mistakes, I know that, but don't believe everything you've been told."

I don't understand!

"That's part of your problem. Don't believe everything Zoe's telling you, you have no reason to. Not after she lied about the car keys and then the gun."

I have to believe her.

"Do you think she's believed everything you've told her?"

John thought about that for a few seconds.

Probably not.

"Well, there you go. She doesn't trust you, so why should you trust her? If she trusted you, why would she tie you up like this?"

This is what she likes.

"What *she* likes?"

Yes.

"Really?"

This is what Fox taught her sex was all about.

"There you go again!"

I have to trust her. I need her help.

"I know that. But start thinking for yourself. Really, try *thinking* for a change."

I am. I AM! That's ALL I'm doing!

"Try to sort the lies from the truth."

I can't. There isn't time!

"Isn't time?" Richard laughed his throaty laugh. "Pal, you're tied up and going nowhere. You have all the time in the world. Heck, you've probably got all night!'

Zoe will be back.

"Yeah, I know that. But probably not until morning."

It could almost be morning now!

"It could, but you don't really believe that, now do you? You've got hours to go. Plenty of time."

For WHAT?

Richard sighed, "You're not just fighting her, pal. You're fighting yourself too."

I don't understand.

"Pal, that's the whole *fuckin' problem!* I keep saying that over and over again!"

Silence returned to John's head.

His stomach felt heavy. It had stopped growling from hunger pains, as if it had given up trying.

John wondered if he were starting to get delusional. He'd only had a couple of glasses of water for the whole day. He was sure that if the wet cloth weren't in his mouth, he'd be dry and thirsty. Instead, he had the sour taste of vinegar that was keeping his tongue and throat wet.

How long can a man survive without food before he goes mad?

He knew he should be embarrassed about his situation. He knew he should try to get away or to take back control. But his body wouldn't allow it. His willpower was sapped. He didn't know if it was the lack of food or drink, or whether Zoe's games had taken a toll on his mind.

Either way, he needed to try and get his mind into gear and start planning ahead.

He had to be at his best when he met Fox.

He had to teach the guy that he'd gone too far this time.

He needed to *kill.*

He recognised that now as he stood there in the cold night with time to think.

I want to kill Fox.

I want to force him to beg for his life and then I want to kill him slowly.

As the cold bit into his wounds even more, and his numb body started to shiver, he began to work it all out.

Tomorrow has to be the day. She knows I'm going to be missed at work. They'll get suspicious if I don't show at work two days in a row and don't contact them. She must realise that. If she doesn't, I'll tell her. She has to let me go then.

His mind was clearing now. Thoughts and ideas were forming fast.

We'll wait until Tuesday night. That will be our best chance. We'll take the Jeep and drive to Redlingford and surprise Fox and his gang. We don't have any weapons, but I'm sure we can fake him out somehow. There's got to be something around the church we can use. That old machinery shed. Yeah, there must be something in here we could use – even if it's just sharp metal of some kind. Sharp and dangerous.

John smiled underneath the hood.

But what if he's got guards posted?

Even better. We'll pull over before we get to the farmhouse and we'll walk the rest of the way. Maybe we'll find one of his guards. We can overpower him. Zoe can distract him with her body, show him her breasts or something, come on to him, and I can knock him out and take his gun. Then we'll be armed.

John's smile grew bigger.

And ready to fight.

John thought about Zoe. She'd seemed so scared, so terrified, when they first met. Now she was in control, giving the orders, telling him what to do. A regular little general.

A general in leather.

And half naked.

God, what a body! And what a performer!

John felt the cold metal move on his balls. His cock was starting to grow.

And so did the pain.

No! Stop thinking about her. Think about other things!

The pain grew more intense.

I've got to talk her into helping me get Fox. I have to.

But he knew the mere mention of Fox's name could see her defences crumble, and that was the problem.

I have to get her to come with me, but as she is now. Powerful and in control. There has to be a way.

But he knew that wasn't very likely. She'd gone to face Fox herself and had crumbled in front of him. Her plan had fallen to pieces around her, scattered in the dirt of the driveway along with Helen's life.

Or so she said...

John pictured the way Zoe's face gave away her emotions, no matter how hard she tried to hide them.

He knew the plan wouldn't work.

But it was the only one he had right now.

But it's not going to work!

His smile fell along with his hopes.

His mind emptied of thoughts and his body sagged against the wood behind him.

We're all beaten. Each and every one of us.

He knew that now.

We can't get out of the traps we've laid for ourselves. Eventually everything catches up with us.

Everything.

It had happened to Zoe.

And now it was happening to him.

Poor Zoe...

He was her only real friend now.

Friend?

Then why, Zoe, why treat me this way? he asked the darkness.

Because she loves me.

John knew that for sure now.

And he knew the events to come would be hard on them all.

He just hoped they would survive them.

Forty-three

The hood was pulled roughly from his head and the blindfold was untied.

John tried to open his eyes, but the sunlight was blinding. He squeezed them shut again until they adjusted to the light.

The dew on his body had evaporated sometime earlier as the temperature had risen and the coldness in his bones had been thawed by the warmth of the sun.

The earplugs in his ears were removed, and the sound of life flooded back to him.

Everything sounded so loud; the breeze in the trees, the birds chirping. He even noticed things he'd never heard before, small sounds in the underbrush and movements in the scrub. His mind reached out, desperate to hear everything it could to fill the void of silence of the past few long hours.

"Good morning, my love," Zoe said, her voice loud in his ear.

He opened his eyes and turned towards her.

She was standing next to him, smiling.

She reached forward and pulled the wadding from his mouth. His stiff jaws slowly closed and John's tongue ran around his mouth, trying desperately to lick away the remaining vinegar taste.

"Here," she said as she reached down and picked up a glass of water. "Drink this, it will help."

John drank slowly, making the water last and letting his tired jaw muscles relax.

"Thanks," he whispered, his voice sounding hoarse.

He looked around for the first time.

He could see the clay tennis court spread out in front of him. The sunlight reflected from the clay, warming his face and body. He was standing in the gazebo on the tennis court and he looked up at the wooden roof over his head.

His mind flashed back to Saturday night when he had walked out here in the darkness, surveying the area for Fox's men.

It all looks so different in the light of day, he thought. *Bigger. And less threatening.*

Glancing to his side, he looked at the large wooden X he was tied to. The frame was painted green and looked almost new. The paint was shining and there were no scratches or scuffs anywhere that John could see. The frame itself was bolted to the wooden railings supporting the roof of the gazebo.

But this wasn't here Saturday night. I'm sure I would've seen it if it were.

John turned back to look out of the gazebo once more. The sets of wooden seats on either side of the gazebo looked old and dusty in the sunlight, and certainly not stable enough to sit on. From the shadows on the ground, he realised the sun was high in the sky. But the day wasn't hot. The cool breeze was keeping the temperature down, and from what he could see of the skyline, clouds were blowing in on the horizon.

But at least he wasn't as cold as last night.

Somehow, he seemed to have survived through it all.

He was glad that sleep had finally overtaken him.

Sleep?

Or exhaustion?

He turned to face Zoe.

She was still smiling at him, running her eyes up and down his body.

"You made it," she said.

"I did?"

She nodded excitedly. "I'm proud of you, Johnny."

"I'm glad."

Her hair was in braids once more and she was wearing a checked shirt that looked three sizes too big for her. The top three buttons were undone and John could see the mounds at the top of her breasts. Helen's gold chain still hung around her neck and glinted in the sun. She was also wearing a pair of black jeans and an old pair of sneakers.

No matter what she wears, she looks sexy, he thought.

He looked down at his body.

His eyes slid over the crusting claw marks on his chest and then fell further.

Down to his cock.

And the gold ring that pierced it.

Her eyes followed his.

"How does it feel?" she asked.

"I don't know," was all he could reply as he looked at the ring. He could only see a portion of it as the rest was hidden between his cock and balls.

As if reading his thoughts, Zoe bent down, reached out and turned his cock to the side, showing him the full ring for the first time. It shined golden in the morning light. The ring was about one inch in diameter and it entered his skin just below the head of his cock. The skin looked red and puffy, but he couldn't feel any pain.

"The swelling will go down," she said matter-of-factly. "As long as we don't play with it too much."

She smiled at him.

"That's the downside," she continued. "We can't use it for a while. At least, you shouldn't fuck me for a couple of days. But we can do other things to make me cum."

A couple of days? I can't be here that long! I have to get out. Now!

"Does it hurt?" she asked.

"No," his shook his head. "Not really, not much anyway."

"Good."

She straightened up to face him again.

"Had enough of the X-frame?" she asked.

It took a second or so before John realised she was talking about the wooden X that had held him.

He nodded.

She took a step forward, and began untying the straps around his legs.

John watched her as she undid each buckle around his thigh, knee and ankle on his left leg.

Her braids swung against her shoulders as she jerked each buckle open. Then she dug her fingers between the leather and his leg, and pulled. The leather gave way easily each time and soon his leg was free.

Almost there.

He waited until she had unbuckled his right leg.

She straightened herself up and placed her hands on her hips.

"Can I trust you?" she asked with a tilt of her head.

Play it calm, John thought before replying.

"Of course," he smiled back.

"Really?" she was unsure.

"You have my word, Zoe," he replied.

She nodded.

"Good." she smiled as she leaned forward.

Finally! John thought.

But instead of untying his arms, Zoe reached out past his hip. He turned his head and looked down, following her hand.

He saw the collar and leash as she grabbed them from the gazebo railing.

"Zoe," he said in a firm voice. "You don't have to."

Their eyes locked as she took a step backwards.

"Just to be sure," she replied.

"But you know you can trust me now, don't you?" he asked.

She nodded.

"I know. But I promise only the collar and leash. Okay? I really shouldn't've taken the hood off until the end of the scene. But I had to see your face this morning. I've missed you so much." She smiled then. "So I'll do a deal with you. No more blindfolds, hoods or earplugs if you let me put the collar back on you. Okay?"

It was outrageous, but he accepted.

At least you'll be able to see and hear things as they happen!

He nodded his head, "Okay."

Zoe smiled.

"You're the best, Johnny. You really are."

She looped the leash around her arm and then reached up with the collar and began buckling it back around his throat.

Now! Kick at her or knee her in the stomach.

And then what? I'm still chained here.

You've got to try while your legs are free!

I'm waiting it out. I'll get my chance.

When?

I don't know. Soon...

The leather tightened around his throat and bit into his skin. John lifted his chin to relieve the pain and get more comfortable as Zoe finished buckling him in.

"There," she smiled. "You're one sexy man in that collar."

"Thank you," he replied.

Zoe looked up into his eyes. Without the stiletto heels, Zoe was once again much shorter than John. The sneakers didn't give her much height, so she stretched up on her toes to kiss him on the cheek.

"Seems a shame to untie you," she said to him. "It's such a turn on seeing you tied to the X-frame."

John stared back at her and smiled.

What can I say?

Play her game...

"It was a turn on being tied here."

Her face beamed, "Really?"

He nodded.

I can't believe you said that.

Shut up!

That's your plan for getting us out of here? To play along with her?

Keep quiet!

Zoe stepped backwards, a bounce in her step now, her face all smiles.

"I *knew* you'd like it," she said to him. "You just didn't know it until you tried it."

"Thanks for showing me a side to myself I didn't know I had."

Zoe giggled, "We've all got dark sides, Johnny. It's just some of us won't admit it."

"I feel completely different now," he said.

She stepped forward again, her eyes looking deep into his.

He was mesmerised once more.

"And there's so much more we can do," her voice dropped. "This was the edge for you. But it won't be now you've done it and liked it. You'll want more. You'll want to go further. There's plenty more edges out there."

More?

You've blown it now.

Quiet! It could still work.

"I'll go anywhere with you guiding me," he said to her.

The tears formed in the corners of her eyes as her face changed from happiness to sorrow and then back again.

Yes, keep going!

She looked to the ground.

"You mean that?" she asked in a small voice.

"I really do."

Her eyes met his once more.

"I love you, Johnny," she said.

"And I love you too," he replied.

Silence fell between them.

Zoe walked forward and stretched upwards. Taking a small key from her shirt pocket, she unlocked the padlocks that held the chains around his wrists.

After a few seconds, his hands were free.

Something had shifted between them. Suddenly John had some control in the game. He could feel it.

Yes... I'm getting there...

Slowly, John lowered his arms, working his sore shoulder joints and rubbing them hard to kick-start the circulation again.

He looked at the stitches in his left arm. They continued to hold even though the wound still looked red and puffy. John was beginning to grow confident that they actually *would* hold his wound together, just as Zoe had said.

"Thank you," he said as Zoe stepped away from him.

"No problem. You earned the privilege," she replied.

John stood in the gazebo, looking our across the tennis court.

"Nice day," he said.

"They're expecting rain later," she replied.

The weather? You're talking about the fucking weather?

Leave this to me!

Get out while you still can!

I'll play this my way, as always.

Yeah, as always...

"Hungry?" she asked.

John thought about her question. His stomach wasn't complaining like it had been, but he wasn't going to take a chance on refusing food.

"I sure could use a bite to eat," he smiled at her.

She nodded, "So could I! Ready to go?"

"Yep."

She unwound the leash from her arm and reached out with its tip.

John stretched his arm, holding his palm out to her.

She froze, unsure of what he was doing. Her head tilted to one side, and her brow furrowed.

Then she smiled and handed him the end of the leash.

Another step closer to freedom.

She's trusting me now...

John took the cold slip of leather and reached up to his collar. Finding the hook, he fed the leash through. He then tied it off for her.

"How's that?" he asked, showing her his handiwork.

She checked the knot. "You're learning," she replied. "I'd use a running loop knot, instead of that bow knot, but it'll do for now."

"I still have much to learn, it seems," he replied.

She smiled at him.

"Don't worry. The knots are very important. But I'll teach you."

"I'd like that."

She smiled, turned away from him and walked from the gazebo. John watched her go, waiting for the leash to lengthen and grow tight. When he felt it tug on the collar, he followed her lead and walked forward across the gazebo and down the steps onto the tennis court.

He followed her at a distance, watching her braids swing in the air as she turned her head from side to side, looking around her.

What's she looking for?

The sun shined and warmed his whole body now. The numbness and cold from last night had completely evaporated from him. Although the constant dull pain from his injuries remained.

But playing her game was starting to pay off. Soon she would make a mistake and John would be free.

Soon they were on the paved path heading back towards the church. John looked down at the pavers and concentrated as he felt them under his bare feet.

Was this the way we came last night? It feels like it. But the pathway is too short. It took much longer to get to the gazebo, I'm sure of it. Even though I had the hood on. We must've gone a different way. But why?

The path rose up a slight incline.

I don't remember walking down a decline last night. We couldn't've come this way! It's not possible!

John turned his head, looking for any sign of another path nearby that he may have missed Saturday night in the dark. But he couldn't see one. He slowed down as he did so, and paid for his lapse of concentration by a sharp tug on the leash.

He stumbled forward and continued walking. His eyes fixed on Zoe's back as she pulled him along. He watched her arse jiggle from side to side as she walked and that brought back memories of how she looked naked, how she felt yesterday as her wet hot flaps covered his face.

Soon, they reached the clearing and John could see the side of the church in the sunlight for the first time. It looked older than he expected, more weathered. Moss and vines covered much of the stonework, but had been pruned from around the windows. The roof was rusting in places.

He was relieved to see the church again as he knew that it housed his best chance of escape.

Zoe tugged once more on the leash and they began to walk around the side of the church.

The sunlight continued to shine and the rays reflected off the stained-glass windows, blinding John as he walked past them.

He looked up into the sky to find the sun overhead.

Probably around midday.

Half of Tuesday gone already.

He wondered if anyone had missed him. He wondered if there was a panic at work.

There would be.

I hope so.

Someone must be panicking.

And what about Helen? People will wonder where she is when she doesn't arrive for work again too.

Yes! That's right.

Helen! Oh, my poor Helen.

How could that bastard just kill you like that? I swear to you, Helen. I'll avenge you if it's the last thing I do. I owe you that much.

Zoe stopped at the front door of the church.

John walked the few feet between them and then stopped by her side. He looked over at the Jeep. It was facing down the driveway and away from the church. Its mud guards and tyres were covered in dust and dirt.

Zoe opened the church door, turned to smile at John, and then stepped inside.

John followed.

It was cooler inside and it took John's eyes a few seconds to adjust to the darkness. As he walked to the centre of the main room, he turned his head around, surveying everything as quickly as possible.

It all looked the same as yesterday. The cutlery was still spread on the kitchenette counter, the glass he had drunk from was there too, and the phone.

The phone!

The ropes still hung limp around the large wooden table and the metal chair sat nearby with the handcuffs draped across one of the arms. He looked across past the wooden railing dividing the main room and the bedroom. Neither of the beds had been slept in.

Zoe turned to face him.

"I've got to leave you now, Johnny," she said.

"*What?*"

"Not for long," she replied, pulling on the leash and dragging him towards the wooden table.

No, not that again!

"Why?"

"You're hungry, and I've got to get you some food," she replied as she reached the table, turned around and jumped up to sit on it. "I went down to the store at Hepburn Lakes earlier, but it wasn't open."

Here's your chance!

She looked at him with a strange expression. John almost believed she had heard his thought.

"Why do people in these country places insist on having totally weird shopping hours?"

John shrugged his shoulders, "No idea."

"So, if I head back now, they should be open," she continued. "And I'll get us both some food. But that means I have to leave you here."

John's eyes dropped to the ground. "I wish you wouldn't," he said in a soft voice.

Zoe nodded, "I know, I know. But it won't be long. Twenty minutes, half an hour at the most."

Damn it, here's your chance!

John raised his head and met her eyes, "You promise?"

She smiled back a wicked smile and bit her bottom lip, "I promise."

John nodded, "Okay. I *am* slightly hungry anyway."

Zoe giggled as she slid off the table and walked towards him. She reached out and touched his cheek lightly, and then turned around and slapped her hand on the table.

"You better climb up," she said.

John took a step backwards.

Zoe jerked on the leash.

"*Climb up*, I said," she ordered.

John looked into her eyes.

"Please, Zoe," he begged. "Not the table again."

"I said," she continued slowly. "Up on the *table*."

"But I was on that yesterday and I've been standing all night. I'm exhausted. My legs and feet are killing me."

"So?"

"Couldn't I lie down, even for a few minutes, on one of the beds? Please?"

Zoe turned her head and looked over at the beds.

She's thinking about it!

"*Please?*" he asked again. "If you're only gone for twenty minutes, that could be twenty minutes I can use to relax and rest. Then, when you get back we can start again."

She turned to face him, her eyes cutting through him as her smile grew.

"You promise?" she asked.

John nodded.

"I'll have to tie you up still. Probably to the bed and the railing."

"I know."

"And I'll only be gone twenty minutes."

"I understand."

"You promise to be here when I get back?" she asked, worry creeping onto her face now.

He nodded.

"Promise?" she asked again.

"Zoe, where am I going to go?" he stepped towards her. "You'll have the Jeep. I'm not going anywhere because there's nowhere to go. I want to stay here. I'll be here when you get back, I promise."

"Really?"

"Really! I want to be here when you get back. And we can do anything you like."

She smiled at him then.

"Anything?"

"Anything!" he smiled.

You're mad!

Shut up, I know what I'm doing.
"Okay," she said.
John sighed deeply.
She tugged on his leash and walked towards the beds.
John smiled and followed her.
This is my best chance.
So don't blow it.
I won't.
You better not.
Trust me, nothing can go wrong. Nothing!
But John was dead wrong.

Forty-four

"It's all about love, Johnny," she began as she tied his ankles to the end of the bed; running the rope around the bed legs and then tying them off at his ankles. "What we can have and what we can't."

He didn't understand what she was talking about, but he let her continue as he relaxed on the soft bed. The mattress held his weight perfectly and he found himself relaxing and closing his eyes. His body needed the rest.

Keep alert.

I am.

Concentrate!

Just let me lie here for a minute or two, I'll be alright.

"It's like the key ring I gave you," she continued as the knots grew tighter around his bare ankles.

Key ring?

John was listening intently now.

"You wear your keys on your right hip to prove you are mine. I wear my keys on my left hip, to show I own you."

"I've got nothing to wear them on at the moment," he replied.

She giggled, "Don't worry, Johnny. You won't be naked forever. Even though I'd like you to be. Your clothes are in the hatch up by the lectern. I'll get them for you when we're finished here."Good," John replied as he opened his eyes and watched her. "And I get the key ring back too?"

She nodded as she walked along to the head of the bed.

"Good," John replied. "Right hip?"

"Right hip," she smiled down at him. Her braids fell forward.

"Okay," he smiled back.

"Do you want a blanket or something?"

John thought about his answer for a second or two and then shook his head. "No, I should be fine just laying here.

It's so comfortable. I think I'll fall off to sleep as soon as you leave."

"It'll be only a short nap."

"That's okay, I think I need it anyway."

He lifted his hands up to her and held them out ready. She took them and pushed them back over his head. His knuckles hit the wooden railing of the room divider and she pushed them down.

"Anyway, the key ring is like the ring in your cock," she continued. "It proves we belong to each other."

He felt the cold steel of the handcuffs bite into his left wrist and heard the clattering sound of the teeth as they locked into position.

You're crazy letting her do this!

I know what I'm doing.

"I was going to pierce your belly button last night, just like mine, so we could be exactly the same," she said as she pulled on his wrist some more.

He heard the metal snake through the wooden railing and felt his shoulder muscles tense as he was stretched further up the bed.

"But then I saw your cock. It was so inviting, so beautiful just sitting there. I had to pierce it instead. Manhood caged and controlled. It's such a wonderful thing."

The metal teeth snapped around his right wrist.

"So now we belong to each other. We'll be together forever. We're nearly the same." She pulled on the handcuffs to make sure the wooden railing would hold. "You'll get used to it sitting down here. It'll be such a turn on when we fuck again. You're not going to believe how good it feels inside me, rubbing up and down."

"What about the diamond?" John asked, curious now. "I don't have one of those."

Zoe smiled at him. "The diamond is just for me."

"Oh?"

"It serves as a reminder," her face clouded.

"Of what?"

"Of past events," her voice sounded small. "Of horrible things that I won't let happen to me again."

"I see," John nodded.

Your time is running out, Fox. I'm going to come and get you for what you did to Zoe and Helen.

"It's there to remind me of the day I decided to take matters into my own hands and control my own life."

"Well, it's beautiful," John replied, lifting his head and staring at her checked shirt. "Pity I can't see it right now."

She smiled at him, "Don't worry, Johnny. You'll see it again, plenty of times."

"Good," he replied. "Well, I'll see you when you get back."

He closed his eyes.

Sleep could be so easy now.

Fight it!

"One more thing," she said.

"Hmmm?" he said softly, keeping his eyes closed.

He felt her touch his cock again.

She lifted it up.

John smiled to himself as he started to grow once more.

"Any pain?" she asked as she massaged him, being careful to place her fingers under the ring.

"I can't feel any," he said, keeping his eyes shut. "It feels okay, actually."

"Good," she replied.

She touched the ring, pulled on it slightly.

Two pinpricks of pain charged along his shaft.

John gritted his teeth. But he wasn't going to tell her it hurt.

She pulled the ring harder.

He could feel the skin lift away from his shaft. As it did so, his erection began to wane and his breathing increased.

Still, he said nothing.

Then the ring shook from side to side violently. He gasped as the pain ran through him.

Opening his eyes, he lifted his head and looked down along his body.

Zoe was tying the leash to the ring.

Her eyes were on his as she did so.

"Sorry, Johnny," she said. "I just have to make sure you won't go anywhere."

No!

After knotting the leash to the ring a couple of times, she lifted the rest of it down between his legs. She walked to the end of the bed and bent down. He could feel the vibrations through the ring as she began tying the leash to the end of the bed.

"You don't have to do this," he told her.

"Just as a precaution," she said.

"Please, don't!"

She didn't reply this time.

His body was stretched fully along the bed. There was nowhere for him to move, nowhere to go. The handcuffs held his hands tightly above his head, and his feet were tied, one to each corner of the bed.

The ring pulled more.

His now-limp cock stretched with it.

The leash pulled again.

John gasped as the pain shot through him. He arched his back, but it didn't help. It felt as if the skin were being ripped from his cock.

"No," he gasped. His cock stretched more, the ring pulling the skin further.

Then the pulling stopped.

John heard her footsteps as she walked back up the bed.

She came into his view once more as she leaned over and kissed his forehead.

"I won't be long, my love," she replied.

He nodded.

"Okay," he whispered through gritted teeth.

He closed his eyes, trying to will away the pain coursing through the skin of his cock.

It wouldn't go.

All the relaxation the bed had brought was gone now. His muscles tensed as he stretched his body, trying desperately to move down the bed, to give some slack to the leash pulling on his cock. But it was no use. The handcuffs refused to give another inch as they clattered against the wooden railings, and the rope around his ankles was tied too tightly around the legs of the bed to help him.

He concentrated on the pain and tried every small movement to relieve it. But no matter what he tried, the constant
pulling on the ring remained.

He didn't open his eyes until he heard the car engine.

Help? It's arrived already?

He looked around for Zoe.

She was gone.

Then he realised it was her. He listened as the Jeep's engine roared. He heard the tyres on the gravel driveway, and
he held his breath until the engine sound died away.

Silence returned to the church. Only the occasional bird
chirp and the sound of the breeze in the trees outside could
be heard.

He was alone once more. Tied and bound again.

And he needed to escape.

But he realised he couldn't.

Zoe had won again.

Forty-five

The pain was excruciating.

"You can't just lie here, pal."

Richard's voice entered his mind.

What else can I do?

"She'll be back soon!"

I know that.

"This is your best chance to escape."

I can't get out of this. I can't! Can't you feel the pain in my cock?

"So?"

SO? What do you mean by that? I can't escape now!

"Always thinking with your little head instead of your big head, John," Richard replied.

I can't do anything about this situation. I'll just have to wait.

"Isn't a small amount of pain worth it if you can escape?"

I don't think ripping the skin off my manhood is worth anything!

"Oh no," Richard mocked. "Heaven forbid if you cause a bit of pain to Mr. Happy. Can't have him spilling any blood, now can we?"

Shut up, Richard. I don't need your help.

"You need something…"

Quiet, I can win this on my own terms.

"Really? Looks like Zoe has all the cards at the moment. And if you think this is extreme, can you imagine what she has planned for you when she returns?"

Shut up!

"Pal, you've got to do something, and do it quick!"

I can't!

"This game's life and death. This is *serious!* You've got to do something!"

But what? *I can't!*

"Can't? Or won't?"

I told you to keep quiet!

John's shoulder muscles began to ache as he tried to stretch further. The pressure on the ring in his cock was the same and the pain continued to ebb.

"I think you want to be dominated by this girl."

That's not true!

"I think you're enjoying it."

That's certainly one thing I'm not *doing!*

"Yeah, yeah. I know, pal. They've got a word for that, you know. It's denial."

Shut it, Richard.

"I think you're liking every minute of it."

I'm not!

"But you tell her you are!"

John's body tensed more.

Shut the fuck up!

"And you're saying, fuck Helen, fuck everything I've ever cared about or worked for. Fuck you, world. I'm gonna let this little nympho screw my brains out."

I'm not saying that at all!

"I want her to screw me, to fuck me until I bleed. I love it!"

I will not!

John's arms tensed. The pain in his cock intensified.

"Then *do something!*"

I am!

"You're not trying hard enough."

I am!

John's hands turned into fists.

"You're pathetic, John. She's walking all over you and you're letting her. You're a man, but she's in control. And you're *loving* it!"

Fuck you!

"No, fuck *you*, John. That's what she's doing! Screwing you and *screwing you!* Big time! You've become her little doggy fuck slave."

No, I haven't.

"You have, John."

No!

"Woof woof!"

No! NO!

"Bark for me, John. Bark!"

Fuck you, Richard. Fuck the hell off!

"Or do you only bark for your bitch?"

The yell built in his chest and exploded outwards. Despite the pain, John screamed deep and long; primeval. He pulled at the handcuffs around his wrists. He tugged at the rope tied around his ankles. The pain in his cock didn't matter to him now. His whole body cried out for release.

His scream died away to the echoes in the church.

And his handcuffs slipped forward.

John froze on the bed for one still moment.

He was sure of it. The handcuffs had slipped forward, but only for a second.

The pains in his chest, arms and legs were intense, and his cock felt swollen and hot. But he didn't care.

Not now.

He tilted his head backwards.

The chords in his neck strained as he pushed the top of his head down into the mattress.

The pain was growing by the second, and he could feel a muscle cramp building in his back, but he didn't stop. He couldn't.

Everything he saw was upside down now, with his head tilted back at such an angle. He could see his hands, the handcuffs around them, and the chain link that ran between the cuffs and around behind one of the vertical wooden slats that made up the partition.

The vertical slats had small crosses cut out of them, one on top of the other, each about two inches apart.

That would weaken the wood, he thought.

But the wood was top quality and wasn't going to bend easily.

The thick hand-railing ran horizontally along the top of each of the slats. The slats were held in position by a small groove cut into the railing, one for each slat. John tried to rattle the slat the handcuff chain was wrapped around, but it didn't move. It was held tight by its groove and the hand-rail.

But the handcuffs moved! They slipped forward somehow, I'm sure of it!

Ignoring the pain in his legs and back, and the pulling of the leash on his cock, John flexed his arms and got ready to pull.

Slowly, he pulled forward on the handcuffs.

The metal chain scraped across the wood.

But nothing else.

They moved forward, damn it. I know they did!

He pulled harder, the pain growing in his body.

The vertical slats held.

How? How did the cuffs move forward?

He braced himself and took a deep breath for one last try.

He pulled hard. Every ounce of strength he had left poured into his arms as he pulled down on the handcuffs. The chain scraped the other way, across the slat once more. He twisted his body, trying to force the slat to break or at least move.

The pain intensified. A back spasm bit hard and sudden, causing him to jerk sideways. The ropes held him in place but he didn't take his eyes off the railing. The leash pulled harder than ever now, his cock quickly numbing to the pain.

The handcuffs slid upwards towards the handrail.

No, that's further away!

He arched his back more, trying to create more reach, but the muscles in his back cramped and his body stiffened as the pain took hold.

And just before he shut his eyes to scream in agony and let his body crash back to the bed, he saw the handcuffs shoot up higher to the top of the slat.

They cannoned into the underside of the hand-railing.

And the hand-railing lifted up.

Huh?

It was a slight movement, but he had seen it!

As he lay on the bed, waiting for the pain and the cramps to subside, he played the images over in his mind.

Yes, I did see it. The hand-railing moved. I raised it! And the slat moved forward slightly in its groove. It did! I saw it!

He didn't know how long he stayed there, unmoving, waiting for his breath to normalise and for the cramps to disappear. It felt like a long time. But in that time, he worked out exactly what he would do.

He waited until the pain became more bearable. The constant painful tugging by the leash on his ring had made his cock go numb, and John wanted to use that to his advantage.

If I can't feel it, I don't know what damage I'm doing until it's too late.

When he was ready, he arched his back again and tilted his head backwards. He watched as he lifted the handcuffs as far as he could. They slid up the wooden slat, but it wasn't enough to reach the underside of the hand-rail.

He arched himself further.

The ropes bit into his ankles as he stretched and the dull pulling on his cock continued.

The handcuffs slid slowly higher on the slat, passing one of the cut-out crosses.

He was two crosses away from the handrail.

He stretched more; every millimetre higher was a small victory. He set his mind on reaching the top of the second cross cut out of the slat.

When he got there, he breathed a sigh of relief. He waited for a second, using the weight of his body and the chain between the handcuffs to hold his position high up on the slat. And then he started inching up the final cross.

Slowly.

Ever so slowly.

His body screamed for relief, but he wouldn't allow it. Beads of sweat formed on his forehead. His eyes darted across to the wound along his left arm; sweat beaded around the tear in his skin.

Those stitches better hold, he told himself.

The chain nudged against the underside of the handrail.

Finally! Yes!

Breathing through his nose, trying to control his ever-increasing breath, John readied himself for the final hurdle.

The sweat rolled down into his hair.

John licked at his lips.

Just a little further.

He stretched and pulled the handcuffs upwards.

They inched up, taking the handrail with them.

Yes!

He did it again.

The handrail lifted more.

Yes! I did it. Not much more now. Please, not much more!

The railing was only two inches thick. That had to mean the slats could only sit an inch or less into the railing.

An inch or less to freedom! Come on!

Another back spasm tightened on his muscles.

No!

He arched his back more to fight it, but it bit harder, shooting pain through his whole body.

No, not when I'm so close!

He gritted his teeth, fighting the pain.

Not now.

He slid upwards more.

Not now, when I've almost won!

A cramp bit into his thigh, twisting him to the left.

"NO!" he screamed as his body flexed, arching him even more and lifting him from the bed.

He pushed with his ankles, using whatever small extra reach he had, and made one last lunge.

He reached forward, his hands stretching upwards.

The chain slid higher.

The railing jumped.

And the slat popped out.

It fell towards him with a clatter as his hands shot forward, above his face, landing forcefully on his stomach.

The air whooshed from his chest and the metal of the handcuffs felt cold on his hot sweaty body.

He closed his eyes and let his body go limp.

Free.

The pain and cramps rolled across him.
He let them.
They're free. My hands are free.
And slowly the pain ebbed away.
Free. I'm free...
At last.

Forty-six

I can't just lie here.

He knew that. But he wanted to let the pain ease. And the bed was so comfortable.

She could be back at any minute!

He knew he had to act, and act soon. He had no idea how long Zoe had been gone.

Or how long he had been laying there since freeing his hands from above him.

She could be driving back up the driveway now!

He sat up in the bed, ignoring the complaints of the muscles in his back. He had to get moving as soon as possible. The quicker he could get away from here, the better.

He listened for the sound of a car engine. There wasn't one.

He looked down at his cock. The leash was knotted tightly to the ring. John could see the tears in the skin where the ring had torn away when it had pulled hard. There was some blood, but not much.

He pushed himself down the bed, bending his knees for leverage, relieving the tension from the leash. He reached down with his cuffed hands and began to undo the knot.

But what about Zoe and Fox?

What about them?

You need her to get to him.

I can't worry about that now. I have to save myself.

You swore revenge for Helen!

I know.

You promised her.

I know! But this is different now.

Different?

There are other ways.

How?

I'll call the cops!

Do you think that will work?

I don't know.

You mean you don't care.

I can't worry about that now. I have to get out and save myself first.

Save yourself?

I have to.

Again?

I have to!

Coward!

Don't call me that!

The leash knot unravelled in his fingers and he gently pulled it out from the ring. His cock sprang back and rested on his balls, the pain a dull throb.

Almost there.

He pushed himself forward and over the end of the bed. Quickly, he began untying the ropes around his ankles.

Gotta do this quick. Gotta get out of here.

And go where?

Anywhere but here.

As he untied the knots around his ankles, he kept his ears sharply focussed on the noises outside. The breeze was blowing stronger now, through the trees, and he could hear the rustle of the leaves. He didn't know how much time he had left, but he had to make the most of it. Zoe could be back at any moment.

The knot around his right ankle unravelled. He started on the one around his left ankle.

His hands moved feverishly even though he told himself to calm down. The handcuffs made movement difficult, the chain and the thick metal of the cuffs not always allowing his hands to do what he wanted.

But eventually the rope untied and his left ankle was free.

He took a moment to rub his ankles with his hands, massaging away the rope burns and flaked skin.

As he did so, he looked around the church, double checking Zoe wasn't there, hiding in some corner.

She left in the Jeep.

I know that.

So there's nothing to check, get going.

I'm just being careful.

There's no time for that. Go!

He stood up from the bed, walked past the railing and crept into the middle of the church.

His eyes darted around him as he did so, looking for any sign of trouble. He peered out the windows as he passed them, expecting to see Zoe's face staring in at him. But there were no faces pushed up against the stained-glass.

He ran to the lectern, his bare feet slapping loudly on the floorboards.

Quickly, he climbed the spiral staircase two steps at a time.

His eyes darted to the King James Bible.

His key ring was gone.

No!

He stopped dead in his tracks.

NO!

His eyes searched the top of the Bible, but there was nothing there.

But I saw it!

He searched the whole lectern, checking to see if the key ring had fallen down somehow, trying to find a hiding spot, some secret compartment.

There wasn't any.

It was there! I saw it.

There was no sign of the key ring or the red key.

The key to freedom.

He looked down at the handcuffs attached to his wrists.

Damn her, she must've seen me looking at them. She must've moved them somewhere else!

Or she took them with her.

Yeah, that's possible.

So what now?

John's eyes moved to the access hatch. It was closed. He climbed the last few remaining stairs and squatted down in front of the hatch. He reached out and pulled the handle. It was locked.

She said my clothes were in there.

No chance of getting them now.

I'll just have to go without them.

He turned around and stood by the lectern, looking out across the church below him. His eyes scanned the whole room, but there were no keys to be seen anywhere.

I could break into the access hatch given time.

Yeah, time you don't have!

John turned to the stairs and climbed back down them.

Time was precious, he knew it, and he wasn't going to let his best chance of escape slip through his fingers.

I'm not going to waste it.

He marched across to the kitchenette, reached out with his handcuffed hands and picked up the receiver of the phone. He placed it to his ear.

He heard the dial tone, and breathed a large sigh of relief.

Yes!

Holding the receiver in both hands, he began to dial.

Forty-seven

"John Murdock's phone."

"Hi, listen, it's me."

"John? Where the hell are you?"

"Look, I can't talk for long. Just listen, okay?"

"Oh, okay. But we were all wondering where you were, not showing up for work and all."

"Yeah, I know. I'm in Hepburn Lakes."

"Where?"

"Hepburn Lakes!"

"What are you doing all the way out there?"

"Look, I can't talk for long. I'm being held captive by a woman out here."

"Yeah, yeah, good one!"

"Listen, I'm *serious*! I know it sounds ridiculous, but it's *true*! I'm out in the middle of nowhere at some small church about 10 minutes from Hepburn Lakes. Now, I've got to get out of here. So I'm heading down to the town, there's a hotel there, some kind of bar. I saw it when we drove up here. I'll try to head for there. It'll take a while to get there because I have to go on foot, but I'll get there. I want you to drive up here and get me."

"Hey, John, a joke's a joke, but this is going too far!"

"I'm *serious*, okay? When have I ever *lied* to you? I've got to get out of here now. And you *have* to come and pick me up. Okay?"

"Where's your car?"

"Huh? Back at home."

"Can't Helen come and get you?"

"No, she can't. I don't really know where she is."

"*What?*"

"Look, just trust me on this, please? I need your help!"

"Hey, you *are* serious!"

"Yes, *fucking deadly* serious!"

"I mean, I thought something was wrong when I found your card stuck in my wire door on Saturday night. I tried to contact you, but there was no answer. You should've waited, I was only down at the 7 Eleven. And then I couldn't contact you yesterday and –"

"I've got to go. Hepburn Lakes. The hotel, okay? You just sit out the front in your car. I'll come to you."

"It'll take me hours to get there."

"I know. But you have to come."

"I mean, it's *miles* away."

"I *know* that. I don't care. I can wait. This is *important,* okay?"

"Are you okay?"

"I really don't know."

"Can't you call the police or something?"

"It's not that simple."

"No, I didn't think it would be. It never is, huh?"

"I'll be at the hotel."

"Alright, I'll see you there as soon as I can."

Forty-eight

John hung up the phone and took a deep breath. He re-alised he was sweating and that his hands were shaking.

Hang in there, you're almost there.

Finally, something had gone his way and he would soon have some help.

All I have to do is make it to that hotel.

He realised it would take him a while to cover the distance back to Hepburn Lakes, but he knew if he ran part of the way and walked the rest, he should be able to make it in ample time. He had about three hours to complete the distance before any help arrived.

Easy.

I'll just stick to the road.

You can't! Zoe will drive by and see you.

Good point. I'll stay near the road to follow it, but I'll track through the scrub so no one sees me.

It'll be tough with no shoes.

I have no choice. I'll just have to put up with it.

He grabbed the empty glass off the counter and walked around to the sink. He turned on the tap and poured himself a glass of water. He drank it quickly.

Better take a quilt for clothing. Don't want people seeing me naked and ringing the police.

Would that be such a bad thing?

Placing the empty glass in the sink, he turned around and looked at the cutlery on the counter.

I need a weapon.

His eyes danced across the knives. There was little choice. They were mostly butter knives, with a few scattered steak knives and peeling knives too. None of them looked particularly threatening, or sharp.

None of them are going to help me.

But then he thought about the steak knife Zoe had held. And what it had done to his arm and shoulder.

He glanced down at the stitches. They were holding nicely.

He grabbed a steak knife. It felt light in his hands. He ran his thumb across the blade. It was sharp at least.

It's not a lot, but it may be just enough to help me out of a bad situation if I run into one.

You will if you don't hurry!

Okay, I know. I'm trying not to panic.

Just GO!

I'm trying to think clearly!

He turned and walked back towards the beds. His eyes scanned everything around him, looking for anything else that was useful.

John looked at the table, the metal chair, the fireplace.

The poker.

He still couldn't see it.

I wish I knew where it was.

He reached the beds and pulled the quilt from the one he had been tied to.

He wanted to wrap it around himself, like a cape, but it was too difficult with his hands still handcuffed together. He couldn't hold it properly and it was too heavy to throw onto his shoulders. The cuffs made it too hard to manoeuvre.

Damn it, why did she have to take the key?

In the end, he gave up wrestling with the quilt and he let it drop to the floor.

He turned the steak knife around and placed the handle in his left palm with the blade pointing towards him. He then threaded the blade between the cuff and his wrist. He poked himself only once as he did so, but the knife didn't draw any blood. The blade held tightly between wrist and cuff. At least that way it wouldn't fall out of his grip and he could conceal it if needed. It could also be produced quickly at any time, if he was in trouble.

As long as it doesn't accidentally snag on my stitches...

He looked down at the quilt, debating whether or not to take it with him.

This is wasting too much time!

I'll have to go without it.

What if someone sees you?

So what? I've been through enough humiliation in the last couple of days, another person seeing me naked isn't going to matter.

It might attract attention.

That might be exactly what I need.

Leaving the quilt on the floor, John eyed the church one final time.

Stop wasting time!

I'm not, I'm being careful.

Go while you can!

I will.

Or do you want to stay?

No, I don't want to stay here.

Do you want her to catch you?

No! I have to get out.

Then move!

I am!

Move move MOVE!

John ran across the church, heading straight for the door, as panic began to rise in him.

His feet slapped loudly on the floor. The muscles in his legs and thighs ached, especially from where the cramps had taken hold earlier, but he could live with any amount of pain.

As long as I get out.

He climbed the step to the door.

As long as I can get away from her.

And he opened the door.

The warmth of the sun greeted him and the breeze ruffled his hair.

He took a deep breath and felt stronger than ever.

Life was returning to him.

Yes!

Freedom!

Freedom at last.

Freedom from everything.

The game was over.

He had won.
And then he heard it.
No!
He heard the engine.
NO!
He held his breath, concentrating on his hearing, willing the sound to go away.
But there was no doubt.
It was the sound of a car engine.
No, it can't be!
And it was getting closer.
He took a step backwards, panic charging up his spine.
Run!
No, it's too late!
RUN!
She's too close!
He stood paralysed in the doorway, the sound of the engine becoming louder, getting closer by the second.
Move! RUN!
I don't know what to do now!
RUN!
He slammed the door shut, spun around and dashed across the church.
What are you doing?
I can't make it!
Yes, you can!
There's not enough time!
You could run and disappear into the bushes before she knows you're gone!
He reached the beds and grabbed the quilt from the floor.
He spread it back on the bed as fast as he could with his handcuffed hands, while he listened for the sound of the engine.
The noise was muffled now that he was in the church with the door closed, but there was no doubt about it. The car was getting closer.
It was Zoe.
It must be!
You can't be doing this! You don't have time!

He sat on the end of the bed, bent down, and grabbed the ropes. His hands were shaking and his breath was fast. He willed his hands to work, trying hard not to feel the pain as the handcuffs dragged against his skin.

Then he realised it was the steak knife biting into his wrist. He sat up and carefully withdrew the blade from underneath the cuff on his left hand. The blade sprang away from his skin.

His eyes flashed to the counter.

Gotta put it back.

No time!

He looked at the steak knife. Then back to the counter on the other side of the church.

You've got no time! You can't put it back now!

He reached over to the side of the bed and slipped the knife under the mattress.

Then he bent back down and grabbed the ropes.

Quickly!

He wrapped the ropes around his ankles.

I hope this is right. I can't remember how she did it.

You should've looked when you untied them!

I didn't know I was going to have to tie them back up, did I!

He tied the rope tight around his left ankle, then changed his mind and loosened it slightly to give himself more slack.

Then he did the same with his right ankle.

I'll need it.

You'll need more than that!

The engine was loud now, the noise vibrating around the church.

She's almost here!

He reached down to the leash, loosening the knot that tied it to the end of the bed, giving himself a couple of extra inches that he would need.

He lifted his cock and fed the leash through the ring.

Sweat dripped into his eyes. He swabbed it away with his arm.

Quickly, quickly!

The engine was outside now, he was sure of it, just outside the church. He could hear the tyres on the gravel driveway.

The knot around his cock ring was complete. He rolled to his side and pulled himself up the bed. The ropes around his legs and the leash attached to the cock ring pulled at him, but not as much as before, and the pain wasn't so intense. They were still tight, but the extra few inches of slack gave him room to move.

He just hoped Zoe wouldn't notice.

He laid himself flat on the bed and tilted his head backwards. He was sure he could still do it.

He grabbed the vertical slat that had fallen forward earlier, slipped the chain of the handcuffs behind it and pushed it back towards the horizontal handrail.

The tyres stopped moving on the driveway outside.

Come on!

The slat hit the handrail. John tried to bend it with his hands, to see if he could bow it and guide it back into its groove. But the wood was too strong, it wouldn't give.

The engine died.

Silence returned.

Quickly! Just do it!

John stretched further, the ropes giving him the extra inches, just enough space to reach higher.

With his left hand holding the slat, he slipped his right up to the railing. The handcuff chain stretched upwards. He was running out of inches to manoeuvre. He held the slat firmly against the handrail. He pushed upwards with his right hand.

The railing bowed slightly.

But not enough.

He heard the Jeep door open.

He pushed again, with more strength.

The railing bowed again, lifted up higher. The slat inched closer to its groove.

Please! Please go in!

The car door slammed.

I'm running out of time!

His right arm strained with effort as he pushed it higher. The railing bowed more, creeping higher than before. John pushed with his left hand, trying to force the slat back into place.

It slipped under the railing.

Yes!

His hands began to sweat as he inched the slat towards the groove.

Come on, just a bit further.

The handcuff chain was stretched to its limit. John couldn't move his hands any further apart. He needed precious millimetres he didn't have. He moved his right arm slightly, trying to bring it closer to his left.

The railing slipped from his grip and dropped back down with a muffled slap.

The pressure was enough to force the slat from under the railing. Even with John's left hand holding it, he couldn't stop it as the slat popped back out from under the railing.

No! NOOOOOO!

He could hear her footsteps now.

Last chance.

He arched his back and clenched his teeth.

The ropes and leash pulled on him, but he didn't feel them.

This has to work!

He lifted the railing one last time, pushed back with the slat.

It slipped under once more.

The footsteps closer.

He held the railing steady, trying hard not to let it slip again. His hands were wet with sweat now, making it harder to control what he held. His whole body shined with sweat and beads of perspiration rolled down into his hair.

He lifted the railing higher.

One...

He could hear the sound of the door handle turning.

Last...

He gave the slat one final slap with the palm of his hand.

Chance...

The slat jumped into the groove with a snap.
John let go of the railing.
And Zoe walked through the door.

<u>Forty-nine</u>

Luckily for John, Zoe entered the church backwards, carrying an armful of grocery bags.

"I'm back!" she called over her shoulder.

It gave him the time he needed to straighten himself out on the bed and try to calm down.

But the sweat continued rolling from his forehead and his breathing was deep and hard.

"You miss me?" she asked as she turned around to face him.

"That was quick," he replied.

"Quick?" she said as she used her back to push closed the door. "I was gone nearly an hour."

An hour!

You wasted it!

An hour?

You could've been away from here. So far away from this place! You wasted a whole hour!

"They had so much stuff," she said as she walked down the step and to the kitchenette. "I didn't know where to start. Or stop."

She giggled as she used her arm to sweep some of the cutlery to one side of the counter.

John bent his neck to watch her through the wooden railing.

"I'm a bit of a shop-aholic," she smiled as she placed the bags on the counter. "You probably know that by now. And there was some interesting stuff to buy."

She opened a drawer and picked up the cutlery, dropping it into the drawer with a loud crash, handful by handful.

"Maybe I should shop around here more often," she giggled.

She started pulling food from the plastic bags and placing it on the counter.

John used the time to get his breathing under control and to wipe the sweat from his forehead using the sides of his arms.

"You hungry?" she asked.

"I think you know the answer to that."

She giggled again.

"You were really gone almost an hour?" he asked.

"Yes," she nodded. "Why?"

A whole hour!

"It didn't seem that long," he replied. "I must've fallen asleep."

She smiled at him, "A short rest will do you good. You'll need your strength."

"Will I?"

"You will."

In a couple of minutes, all the food had been removed from the bags and the bags were empty, except one. Zoe pushed that bag to the side.

She crunched up all the other bags and threw them into a cupboard.

John couldn't clearly see what she had bought, but he could make out the greens of vegetables and the bright colours of fruit. There were some large packets too, but he couldn't read the writing from where he was.

Zoe scanned the counter, then turned to the sink where she picked up the glass.

John froze.

My God, I left the glass in the sink!

Stupid!

I didn't put it back on the counter!

You've blown it! She'll know.

My God!

Zoe lifted the glass to the tap and poured herself a glass of water.

She drank quickly, gulping it down in a matter of seconds.

She turned to him.

"You want one?" she asked

John nodded, not daring to speak.

She hasn't noticed.

She must have!
She hasn't!
But I moved it.
Maybe she doesn't remember where it was. Maybe she's forgotten it was on the counter.
Maybe...

She poured another glass of water, turned and started walking towards him.

It was then he heard the jangling.

His eyes searched for the source of the noise, trying to pinpoint it.

The noise got closer as Zoe did.

His eyes traced her body.

And he found it.

Hanging from her left hip was his key ring. The red key bouncing against his other keys and her hip, making the noise as she walked.

My key to freedom.
And she's got it.
Damn her!

She walked closer, smiling at him, holding out the glass of water.

Keep calm, he reminded himself. *Play it her way.*
Still?
Yes!
When are you going to play the game your way? Or don't you want to?

He smiled back at her.

She walked around the railing and stopped at the end of the bed. She let her eyes linger over his body, especially his groin, before she continued towards him.

"You're all hot and sweaty," she said. "You getting ready for our next scene?"

He laughed, but he knew it sounded false.

"I won't even have to oil you," she smiled as she leaned forward and placed a hand behind his head.

She lifted him forward to drink from the glass.

John gulped it down. He wasn't really thirsty, but he didn't want to refuse the glass of water. She might get suspicious.

Or deny him future drinks when he may need them.

Suspicious? As if the sweat and the glass weren't enough to make her think something happened while she was gone.

He finished the water and she laid his head back down on the bed.

"Thanks," he smiled up at her.

"It's the least I can do," she replied.

She swung around in front of him, the key ring on her left hip flying out to the side, the red key whizzing past his eyes.

So close!

She walked slowly back to the foot of the bed, her eyes tracing along his body.

She stopped for a few seconds when she reached the end of the bed. Her back was to him. He couldn't see her face.

He realised he'd give anything to know what she was thinking right then.

But there was nothing he could do.

"They had some interesting things at the general store," she said to him without turning around.

"Really?" he replied.

"I was quite impressed."

"Well, I imagine that's their job," John said.

"Things you'd never think they'd have."

"Well, that's why it's a general store."

"The man was *very* helpful."

"Was he?"

"Would you like to see what I bought?"

"Yes," John said slowly, unsure of where the conversation was leading.

She turned around to smile at him.

"Okay, I'll show you."

She went to turn away but changed her mind, turning back to him instead.

"The question is," she said as she tapped the rim of the glass on her chin. "Should I feed you now, or later?"

John nodded, "Zoe, I *am* hungry. I haven't had a thing to eat since Saturday night."

Zoe nodded and her face fell, "I know, that's my fault and I'm sorry."

"It's okay, but I would like something. Even just a sandwich?"

She nodded. "I know, but that would reward you."

John stared at her.

"And I don't know if I want to do that," she said in a soft voice.

"Huh?"

She smiled at him a wicked smile.

"Seeing you all wet and sticky has put me in a punishing mood," she said as she leaned forward and grabbed the leash between his legs.

"And I think you should be punished, Johnny."

She pulled hard on the leash. His cock pulled forward, the ring bit into his skin.

"And I've got just the equipment to do it."

<u>Fifty</u>

Zoe placed the egg scissors around his erect cock. The sharp teeth closed around him and bit into the skin just below his cock ring. Her little finger slipped inside the ring and pulled hard.

John was past screaming. He knew it wouldn't do him any good, it just exhausted him more. His eyes were tightly closed, his teeth clenched.

"Crack for me," she ordered. "I want to see your egg white. Cum for me, spill your creamy white. I want to lick it."

She twisted the egg scissors to one side. Its teeth tore across his skin.

John's back arched with the pain. His hands pulled at the handcuffs, but he was powerless to stop her.

The quilt below him was doused in his sweat. He could feel the cool wetness as he fell back to the bed.

The latest round of pain faded.

Too far, he thought over and over again. *She's gone too far. Too far.*

His mind went blank and he found himself floating back.

He didn't know how long the torture had been in progress, he had no idea. It seemed like forever.

He had looked out the window at one stage, looking for the sunlight, hoping that would give him an idea of the time that had lapsed.

But there was no sunlight, no shadows. Just a grey miasma. The clouds had filled the sky completely, blocking out all rays of sunshine.

All rays of hope…

He knew he had no chance to stop her when she had pulled on his leash after saying she planned to punish him.

He didn't know whether it was because she had noticed the glass in the sink, or whether she thought he had been trying to escape. Or maybe this was just the next level of the game. Either way, it didn't matter now…

Zoe had gone back to the kitchenette, grabbed the extra plastic bag she hadn't unpacked and returned to the bed with it.

"Trust me, Johnny," she had said. "You're going to love what I bought for you.

She then sat on the edge of the bed, placing the bag on her knee.

"Ready?" she smiled at him.

He didn't want to, but he nodded.

And she'd shown him everything she had bought at the general store.

First was the wooden rolling pin.

Then came the egg scissors.

And then the branding iron.

He was surprised to find that fear and panic didn't overwhelm him as she brought each of the items out of the bag.

He had watched them with passionless eyes. He looked at all three items, taking them in, logging them in his mind, but he felt nothing.

She had smiled at him then.

"Tell me what you're really hungry for," she had asked.

He said nothing.

"Tell me you want me, that you hunger for me," her eyes sliced into his very soul.

"I want you," he heard himself whisper.

"Tell me you want me to hurt you."

"Hurt me," he repeated. He heard his voice, but it sounded detached from him.

She leaned forward and kissed him hard; her wet lips on his, her tongue forcing forward, touching his. Her breathing was heavy and as she pulled away from him she streaked her tongue along his cheek and up over his forehead.

"Yum," she said as she pulled away. "You're sweaty."

She licked him some more, letting her tongue trace down his nose, across his other cheek and down to his earlobe. She bit the lobe hard, tugging on it with her teeth.

That was the first time John didn't cry out.

There was no point.

She's won. The game is over.

"I'll be right back," she had said.

She ran across the church to the spiral staircase and climbed the stairs, disappearing behind the lectern. He heard a key scrape into the lock and the hatch open.

He'd been so close.

Was she using the red key from the key ring? If only she hadn't taken it with her when she had gone to the store! I would've been free by now.

The hatch slammed shut and the noise echoed around the church.

Her head then reappeared above the lectern.

She turned around, leaned forward for a moment and then smiled at him.

Within seconds she had climbed back down the stairs, run across the church and was back by his side. She was carrying the leather outfit she had been wearing the day before, and also the King James Bible. John's eyes flashed down to the key ring on her hip once more.

So close.

She got undressed in front of him. Slowly, she unbuttoned her checked shirt. Her belly button appeared once more, this time near his face; the diamond dancing before him as she moved. He tried not to look at the half-heart pendant still hanging around her neck, but it was hard not to. She turned around and unzipped her jeans, pulling them down as she bent forward, her arse moving towards him, so close to him he could smell her. He could see her wet vagina, and as she stepped out of the jeans, she moved her legs further apart, giving him a better view of her moist folds.

And despite everything, he began to grow again.

And the pain returned.

She saw his erection pulsing and she turned around to face him, a smile on her face.

"I turn you on so easily," she said. "That makes me so happy."

She leaned forward and kissed him.

"I tell you what," she said. "If my naked body can do that to you so fast, I won't even bother with the leather. I'll stay totally naked. Would you like that?"

He nodded.

Her smile stretched wider and she looked so happy.

And then she'd reached down and undid the knot holding the leash on his cock ring.

The pain was intense as she undid the knot, but it soon passed once he was free from the leash.

"There," she said once it was untied. "That should free you up."

"Thank you," he'd replied.

"If you're a good boy, I'll untie you even further."

"I'd like that."

"I know you would."

He had closed his eyes, willing the pain to go away.

She climbed onto the bed and ran a hand down his side, across his stomach and over his shaved groin.

"So smooth," she whispered. "So nice. You like being shaved?"

He nodded automatically.

"Me too. We're so alike, you and me."

She grabbed his pulsing cock and kissed the tip.

"I want you so badly," she said.

Her hands went underneath his arse and she lifted him upwards. The ropes around his ankles bit deeper. The handcuffs pulled harder.

He didn't try to fight it. He didn't have the strength.

After a few seconds, she lowered him again, but his buttocks didn't return to the quilt. They stopped six inches in the air as they rested on something hard. He opened his eyes and looked down his body. His hips were tilted, pushed upwards into the air, as was his groin and ass.

"Who would've thought an old Bible would come in so handy?" she said as she looked at him from between his legs.

She was kneeling between his open legs now, one hand massaging his cock, the other straightening the Bible underneath him.

"It's a perfect height," she said.

"For what?" he asked.

"You'll see," she had said with a wicked grin.

And then she'd reached for the rolling pin.

John thought back to that now as he remembered her oiling the wooden handle, pushing it deep inside herself while she knelt on the bed.

"It's got to be just right for you, Johnny" she had replied as she pushed it into her vagina with both hands, rotating her hips to help it slide in and licking her lips as she did so. "I'll make it just right."

She had pulled it out after a short while. The wooden handle of the pin was stained a darker colour, wet from her juices.

She'd then bent over between his legs, pushed his arse cheeks open, and inserted the handle into his anus.

The handle slipped right in – right up to the hilt – and he gasped loudly.

"You like that, huh?" she asked as she slowly pushed and pulled on the pin.

John braced himself as she did so. It felt as if his whole insides were moving, being dragged back and forth with the force of the pin.

His hands clenched and pulled hard on the handcuffs, but he was powerless. There was nothing he could do.

His eyes were closed tight. He was trying to will her to stop.

No, stop it, please. Stop it, please.

But it was no use.

As one hand pumped the rolling pin into his ass, the other rhythmically massaged his cock.

John had no idea how long it all went on. His brain wasn't working properly. It was almost as if his thoughts were running through molasses. Time meant nothing to him now. He was nothing.

Nothing.

And he was powerless.

Through all the pain and terror, John found himself rising to a climax. He didn't want to, he wanted to deny her the satisfaction and so he tried to stop it, tried to hang on. He concentrated on holding back.

But just as he thought it was too late and he was going to lose it all, Zoe stopped massaging his cock. It pulsed automatically, wanting to explode, but her hand didn't return.

She then pulled the rolling pin out. The pin popped out with a slurp and his anus closed tightly. But to John, it still felt as if it were open wide, his insides torn from him.

"A true sign of perfect lovers," Zoe had said to him from between his legs. "Is that they can tell when an orgasm is near. You were about to cum, weren't you?"

John had nodded and opened his eyes, looking down his body to her.

She smiled.

"I knew it," she replied. "I know you so well, Johnny."

She crawled from the bed, taking the rolling pin with her.

"And the truest sign of love," she continued as she picked up the egg scissors. "Is denying your lover the release he so dearly wants until the time is just right."

John had shut his eyes tight, and readied himself for the pain. But nothing could quite prepare him for the agony as the egg scissors tightened around his pulsing cock and the teeth tore into the skin.

"These are good for cracking open eggs," she had muttered. "I wonder if they'll crack you."

And then she had begun the next round of slow torture.

John opened his eyes now and looked towards the windows. It was darker outside, almost night.

It can't be! Has it been that long? Has this been going on for hours?

From what he could see of the sky on the horizon, the clouds were dark and heavy. Maybe it wasn't as late as he thought. But he had no way of telling.

Zoe moved on the bed, rocking it slightly as she pulled on the egg scissors, their teeth cutting into the skin of John's cock once more.

She was bent over him now, the cock ring between her teeth. She pulled on the scissors and yanked the ring with her teeth. As she did so, she let out a low guttural growl.

But he was numb to it all now, he couldn't feel it anymore and he didn't want to.

Thoughts slid on the surface of his mind.

She's mad, totally mad.

But you need her!

Need her? What the fuck for?

To get at Fox.

I don't care anymore.

Yes, you do. For Helen.

Helen. Poor Helen. I'm so sorry.

It's not your fault.

Yes, it is.

Don't blame yourself.

There's no one else to blame!

"We're almost there, my love."

John heard the voice, and for a moment thought it was Helen. But then it filtered through the fog in his brain and he realised it was Zoe.

John looked down between his legs. But she wasn't there. She had moved.

When? How?

Why?

She was standing by the side of the bed. Her hands and arms all bloody. She looked down at them, and at the blood-stained egg scissors in her hands.

John's eyes moved across to his slowly deflating penis. It was a mound of broken skin and blood and almost looked as if it had been chewed by some ravenous dog. He looked at his cock through unfeeling eyes, as if it weren't even part of his body anymore. The warm wet stickiness between his legs meant nothing. He felt no pain, no sorrow. Not even anger.

He was just empty.

Empty.

Nothing.

Zoe dropped the egg scissors on the floor. They clattered loudly and echoed around the church.

Her eyes darted back to his cock and a worried look passed across her face.

"Oh Johnny," she whispered. "What have I done?"

He looked at her but said nothing.

She raised her hands in front of her face, her eyes staring at the blood on them.

"What have I done?" she repeated.

John noticed the diamond in her belly button was hanging off-centre.

She reached down by the bed and grabbed her jeans. Then, she turned from him and sprinted across the church and up the spiral staircase to the hatch.

John watched her go, his eyes following her small round arse cheeks as she ran from him.

He heard the hatch open and slam shut, but his brain was working in slow motion. Sounds were as sluggish as his thoughts. He heard the hatch, but it didn't register with him until she was almost back standing by his side.

And then she was bending over him, the jeans in her hands, the material brushing the side of his face, the half-heart pendant dangling before his eyes. He could hear the rattle of the handcuffs and could feel his arms shaking.

But his brain couldn't process what was happening to him.

And then his arms came free.

Huh?

Zoe removed the cuffs from each wrist and brought his hands down from over his head to rest by his side.

She smiled at him then.

"Is that better?" she asked.

He nodded.

She threw her jeans to one side. The sound of the keys hitting the floor echoed around the church. The handcuffs fell from her hands a few seconds later, echoing loudly in the silence as well.

"You have to help me," she whispered to him.

He nodded, not understanding. Not thinking.

"I've gone too far this time," she said. "Here."

She placed some gauze in his hands.

"Help me fix you up."

John stared at her for a second, then he lifted his head and looked at the gauze.

"I'll get some water and a towel," she continued.

John turned his head to stare back at her, but she was already gone, running towards the kitchenette.

The slapping of her feet on the church floorboards slowly reached him through the mist in his brain.

Carefully, John lifted himself up into a sitting position. He looked down at the rest of his body; his hips pushed into the air by the bible, his blood-red flaccid cock.

Still the pain didn't register.

The pins and needles flowing through his arms as circulation returned was all the pain he could handle for now. He just sat there, waiting for the stabbing pinpricks of pain to subside.

John tried to think straight. He tried to get his thoughts back in order. But his mind wasn't working properly. Time had ceased to flow. The events that happened before him now only registered in a stop-start manner.

Sounds were divorced from actions.

Actions were stilted.

Then Zoe was back by his side, dabbing a towel at his cock.

Cold and wet.

The towel was white, quickly turning pink from the blood.

John held the gauze, looking on, passing it to her when she asked.

The pins and needles soon disappeared, only to be replaced by a dull deep ache between his legs. John sat still, watching her work in front of him, staring at her braids as they swung in the air.

And then his cock was bandaged.

He watched as the bandages began to turn pink too.

This is wrong.

A random thought made it through the minefield of his mind.

She was talking to him.

He turned his head and watched her lips move. But the sound didn't come until a few seconds later.

"....I truly am, Johnny," she was saying.

Huh?

"...planned. But it will soon be over."

He closed his eyes tight and shook his head, trying to clear his mind. He raised his right arm to his head and rubbed his temple.

"…and I love you…"

Have to concentrate.

Have to.

"And now you'll be mine forever."

He opened his eyes once more and stared at her.

She smiled.

She held the branding iron in her hand.

"Forever," she whispered again.

The branding iron…

John looked down at the bed quilt and slowly shook his head. He used the colours in the quilt to try and focus his mind, to concentrate on what he had to do. He tried to find the words to explain. But they wouldn't come.

His eyes wandered across to his bandaged cock. The wrappings were pink and wet now and John could see the tip of his cock-ring poking out of the top of the bandages.

He lifted his head and opened his mouth to speak to her.

But she wasn't by his side.

He turned his head and tried to focus.

He stared across the church and found her.

She was standing by the counter at the kitchenette, the branding iron in her hand.

She was saying something, he could see her mouth moving, but his mind wasn't processing properly; the sounds weren't getting through.

She turned to look at him with a strange expression on her face.

He held out a hand, trying to explain to her something that he had now forgotten, but his mouth wouldn't work.

She placed the branding iron on the counter and then put a hand on her naked hip.

He tried to talk, to get his thoughts into line.

I must, I must. Fight it!

She shook her head and said something more.

John tried to concentrate, to get the sounds he heard into some sort of order.

"...maybe I'm just going crazy."

He heard her say it.

Yes. Fight it. You're winning!

His mind was starting to work again.

He was fighting the cloud of unconsciousness. And he was winning.

Fight it!

"Zoe," he heard himself say.

Yes!

She turned to him and smiled, picking up the branding iron again.

But then just as quickly she lost the smile and looked away from him. Emotions he couldn't read flowed across her face.

He followed her gaze.

His eyes stopped at the open door to the church.

And the person standing there.

"You!"

PART

III

<u>Fifty-one</u>

"**Y**ou!" Zoe repeated.

John's eyes focussed more. His head started to clear as he looked at the person standing in the doorway.

Sherrie.

She'd made it!

And just in time.

Her lips were moving, but John's mind was still too sluggish to put the words in the right order. His eyes darted between Zoe and Sherrie as he fought to clear his mental fog.

Zoe was shaking her head. Her mouth wide open and her hands on her hips.

It was the loud clatter of the branding iron hitting the floor that finally snapped him back into gear.

The iron had slipped from Zoe's hand, falling onto the floor. The loud metallic ring echoed around the church.

Sherrie took a step further forward into the church. Her head turned as she looked around, surveying the room.

And then her eyes met John's.

"John?" she asked, a look of shock stretched across her face.

He opened his mouth to speak, but nothing would come out. He sat on the bed, nodding slowly.

Sherrie took a step closer to Zoe as her head turned to meet her eyes.

"What's going on here?" she demanded.

The words were making sense to John once more.

Zoe stared back at her. For a long moment, no one moved or said anything. Then, Zoe's face crumbled as emotions swept across her. She glanced to the floor as her forehead creased.

Sherrie continued to look at Zoe, not breaking her stare.

John's eyes darted between both women.

And then, slowly, Zoe backed away until her buttocks met the kitchen counter.

The silence continued.

Zoe just leaned there, staring at the church floor, slowly shaking her head back and forth.

"Sherrie?" John's voice croaked. He held his hand out to her.

Carefully, while keeping her eyes on Zoe, Sherrie made her way across the church to him.

John's eyes continued to jump between the two women.

Zoe still hadn't moved. She continued leaning against the kitchen bench, her eyes to the floor, her braids hanging over each shoulder.

And then Sherrie was by his side.

"John, what's happened to you?" Her face was a mixture of disgust and shock. "What's been happening?"

"Not now," he replied. "I'll tell you later. Just get me out of here. And quick."

Sherrie started to untie the ropes around his ankles. As she did so, John's eyes moved back to Zoe.

Her whole body was rocking back and forth now. Her arms crossed her chest, as if she wanted to hide her breasts. Her face looked confused; emotions he couldn't read spread across it.

Is she just going to let me go?

John's left leg was free.

"I don't believe this," Sherrie whispered as she turned back to check on Zoe.

John found it hard to take his eyes from Zoe. He didn't trust her. He expected her to come at them any second, filled with rage, brandishing the branding iron and ready to stop both of them from leaving.

But she didn't.

She just stood there, rocking back and forth.

As Sherrie completed removing the ropes from his right leg, John bent over the side of the mattress and slipped his hand underneath. He kept his eyes on Zoe still, just in case.

Don't let her out of your sight.

But she wasn't watching either of them.

Slowly, he ran his hand up and down the mattress.

Within seconds he felt the handle of the knife.

Yes!

He pulled it out from under the mattress and laid it on the quilt.

Sherrie's eyes met his, and then slipped down to the knife. She looked puzzled.

"We may need this," he said. "To get out safely."

She nodded. Her eyes swept across his body and stopped momentarily at the claw marks on his chest and also at his bandaged cock.

"My God, John, what's she *done* to you?"

"No time now," he said as he swung his feet from the bed and onto the floor. "I'll explain later. We've got to get out *now*."

"Where are your clothes? You can't go like this."

John pointed across the church and past Zoe. "They're in a cupboard behind that lectern."

"I'll get them," Sherrie said and she went to walk away.

He reached out with his left hand and grabbed hers. Dull pain coursed through his arm.

"No," he said, his eyes darting back to Zoe. "It's too dangerous."

And as he said the words, Zoe turned to look at him.

John felt a chill down his spine.

I knew it wouldn't be that easy...

Zoe's face was wet with tears, her mouth was down-turned and her bottom lip was quivering.

She went to say something, but nothing came out.

"Careful," he whispered to Sherrie.

Sherrie's head turned to face Zoe.

They all stared at each other.

No one moved.

"We can't just stay here," Sherrie replied.

"I know," John replied. "But let's take it slowly. We don't know what she could do. She's dangerous."

"I know that," Sherrie said, turning to face him and running a hand along the wound on his left arm. "Just look at the state you're in."

"Don't worry about that now," John replied. "Let's get out of here first."

He squeezed her hand.

Zoe took a step towards them.

John felt Sherrie's hand tighten around his.

He found himself holding his breath, waiting for Zoe's next move.

Play your hand...

But she just stood by the kitchen bench, her arms crossing her chest. She stared at them with a look of sadness on her face. Her head tilted to one side, as if she were deep in thought.

The pendant around Zoe's neck glinted in the half-light.

Helen's pendant.

Poor Helen...

His right hand moved up to the necklace around his neck. He held his half of the heart between his fingers for a few seconds. John's eyes then slipped down to the diamond in her belly button.

You have to get out of here!

I know.

You have to make it to the door.

I know!

Well do it! You don't want her hurting Sherrie, right?

Right.

Then GO!

John took a deep breath.

"Come on," he said to Sherrie. "We have to make a move."

Slowly, he stood up from the bed. His legs were wobbly at first, but he quickly steadied and took a small step forward.

Zoe stepped closer too; one step closer to the middle of the room. One step closer to blocking off their escape to the door.

John's eyes darted to the windows. It was dark out now and no light was coming through. So dark. That would help them hide from her, cover them in the trees outside the church.

We just have to make it that far...

"Where's your car?" John whispered to Sherrie.

"At the end of the driveway," Sherrie kept her eyes on Zoe. She squeezed his hand. "I walked the rest of the way. I didn't know what to expect."

John nodded.

"Okay," he said. "We have to get out of here and then to the car."

"You need clothes," she replied. "It's cold out there and you need to keep warm, especially for those wounds. You look like you're near death."

John turned to face her and he realised she was telling him the truth. After three days of bondage, he realised he must look as exhausted and drained as he felt. His wounds would certainly look bad to anyone who saw them.

Not a pretty sight, I'm sure.

"I'll get them," Sherrie continued.

"No!" John said, holding her hand firmly. "You don't know what she'll do."

His eyes darted back to Zoe.

She stepped closer again. She was in the middle of the church now.

"We *can't* stay here." Sherrie replied, squeezing his hand reassuringly. "There's only one of her and *two* of us! We have to make a move."

She let go of his hand and turned to face him.

"Behind the lectern?" she asked.

He sighed and then nodded. "It's locked though."

"She has the key?" she asked.

John nodded again.

The key!

John's eyes dropped to the ground.

Zoe's jeans were piled on the ground next to where he was standing, along with her leather bondage outfit and handcuffs. And attached to the belt hook of the jeans was his key ring – and the keys.

"The keys," he pointed them out to Sherrie. "They're down here! One of the keys on this ring opens the cupboard!"

Zoe moved forward again, a puzzled expression on her face, her head tilting more.

John realised then she was trying to hear what they were saying.

"We have to move *fast*," he whispered.

But he didn't know what to do.

Or what Zoe would do.

He had a strange feeling that with every step Zoe took towards them, she was regaining her confidence. They had to do something quickly.

And before he had a chance to formulate any ideas, Sherrie had let go of his hand and bent down in front of him.

John kept his eyes on Zoe.

She stared back at him.

John could hear the clatter of the keys as Sherrie undid the key ring from Zoe's jeans.

Within a few seconds, she was standing by him again.

"Can you keep her busy?" Sherrie asked.

John nodded.

With his right hand he picked up the knife from the quilt and held it out in Zoe's direction.

"Stay where you are!" he called to her in a level tone.

Zoe's head stopped tilting. Her eyes dropped to the knife. She seemed surprised. Her mouth opened once more, but she said nothing. She stood straight, didn't move, and stared right back at him.

It looked as if she were about to cry again.

Don't let her fool you again!

Remember what she's done to you!

"I'll get your clothes," Sherrie said. "You make your way to the door."

"*I'll* get the clothes," John replied. "If she tries anything, I'll be able to handle her."

Sherrie turned back to face him. "You're in no condition to do anything except head for the door. I'll get your clothes, you just make sure I have plenty of warning if she tries anything."

"What if she attacks you?"

"I don't think she will," Sherrie replied. "Now let's *do* this and get out of here!"

John nodded. There was no better plan.

He watched helplessly as Sherrie began walking around the railing and towards Zoe.

John's eyes darted back to Zoe to watch for any signs that she might do something unexpected.

Of course she's going to do something unexpected.

I have to stop her.

You can't.

I have to protect Sherrie!

John continued to watch.

Sherrie walked closer to Zoe.

The silence in the church was overpowering. Although occasional gusts of wind blew outside, rattling through the old roof and interrupting the silence.

Emotions rolled across Zoe's face.

I wish I knew what she was thinking.

Zoe's eyes darted to Sherrie as she got closer.

John looked across to her, but all he could see was her long flowing brown hair. He couldn't see her face as she walked away from him.

He looked back to Zoe.

Zoe was still looking at Sherrie.

Is that hate or terror in her eyes?

And then Zoe made a move.

John went to dart forward, but then stopped himself.

Zoe had taken a step backwards.

What?

As Sherrie approached, Zoe took a step back. She tried to half-smile, but it didn't work.

And then John saw her mouth move.

She said something to Sherrie!

She whispered it and John had no hope of hearing it.

He leant forward, but that didn't help.

Sherrie's head turned as she passed Zoe.

Everything moved as if it were in slow motion.

John was sure he saw Sherrie reply, but he couldn't hear what she said either.

And then Zoe took another step backwards.

And another.

Her hands moved up and she buried her face in them.

Sherrie continued past, walking faster now, reaching the spiral staircase in seconds.

She didn't look back to check on Zoe.

Whatever she said had its desired result.

A quiet sob echoed around the church.

John watched Zoe, waiting for a trick or for a sudden movement. Waiting for her to change the game again. But she didn't. She backed into the long wooden table. Her hip hit the corner of the table hard, dislodging the gauze that had been covering the wound she had received back at his house on Saturday.

So long ago now...

The gauze fell to the floor and he could see the fine red slice of the cut in her skin.

How did she do that again?

He couldn't remember.

She stumbled as she cannoned off the table.

John's eyes darted to Sherrie.

But she wasn't on the stairs.

He couldn't see her.

For a moment, panic sped through him.

Then he heard the sounds of the keys in the lock.

She's trying to find the right one. She's up there now!

John focussed back on Zoe.

She was staggering backwards between the table and the kitchen bench.

He stood and watched as she slammed into the wall of the church. Her back slapped the cold surface hard.

Another sob echoed around the church.

He watched her as a low roll of thunder broke the night.

He waited for a reaction from Zoe. The thunder was loud, but her face was still buried in her hands, and she shook her head back and forth.

Come on, you've got to get moving.

Huh?

To the door!

John dragged his eyes from Zoe long enough to check the door to the church was still open.

He only had to get there.

It's not that far!
But it seemed a long way away.
Freedom was so close.
I need Zoe.
Huh?
To get to Fox!
Worry about that afterwards!
I have to know the truth.
Sherrie will help you. Just get out of here first.
I have to make Fox pay for what he did to Helen.
Later! You can't worry about that now!
I need to make him pay for what he did to Zoe too.
LATER!
Slowly at first, John began to move around the railing.

He kept his eyes on Zoe, but she was still standing by the wall, her sobbing becoming louder.

As quietly as he could, he moved another step closer to the door, edging his way down the bed.

And then his foot landed on cold metal.

It clanked on the floor as he did so, but the sound was muffled and not very loud. He checked Zoe hadn't heard the noise before he looked down at what he was standing on.

The handcuffs.
Yes!
You don't need them.
Yes, I do.
Why?
I can get Fox. Use them on him. Show him what it's like to be tied up and tortured.
Are you serious?
Revenge!
You can't do it!
I have to – for Zoe and Helen.
Don't be crazy!
He deserves to get a taste of what he gives to other people.
You can't beat Fox!
I can try!

John bent down and picked up the handcuffs. They were cold and heavy. And strong.

Perfect!

He stood up.

His eyes darted to Zoe.

She wasn't there.

Shit!

He took another step forward, quicker now, panic building again.

Where is she?

He could hear the keys still being tried in the hatch lock.

Come on!

Another wave of thunder rolled across the sky.

He froze until the sound had disappeared and silence had returned.

Where did she go?

He heard the click of the lock.

Yes!

Another step around the railing. Then another. Quicker now.

John's eyes searched the church, looking for Zoe. He tensed himself, ready for her attack at any moment. He wanted to call out to Sherrie, but he didn't dare risk it.

And then he heard another sob; loud and deep.

John stepped further into the middle of the church.

He saw her.

She was sitting on the ground, rolled into a tight ball, just as she had been after she received the call from Fox at his home on Saturday night.

She was rocking back and forth, squeezed into the little space between the table and the kitchen bench. The exact same spot where he had spent one long lonely night tied to a chair and face down on the floor. She'd slipped down the wall and just crumpled.

Her sobs were louder now and her whole body was shaking.

John took a step towards her.

Get AWAY!

She's CRAZY!

Leave now!

John took a step closer to her. Her body was shaking with each sob. He could see her ribs through her skin.

He moved closer.

Lightning flashed through the nearest window for a second, reflecting off the tears on her cheeks and the gold pendant around her neck.

He reached out with his left hand.

"John!"

He swung around and looked up at Sherrie at the lectern.

She was holding his clothes and shoes.

"I've got them," she said.

He nodded.

She started down the stairs.

"Quick, let's go."

John turned to look back at Zoe.

She was staring up at him now. Her face streaked with tears. She was trying to smile at him, but it would disappear as the next sob took hold. The scar across her left eyebrow looked longer and milky white.

John's hand was still reaching out to her.

He let it drop.

Sherrie was by his side now. She threw the clothes and the key ring on the table.

"Quick," she said, taking the knife from him. "Get into them and we'll leave."

John turned from Zoe and reached for the clothes. He put the handcuffs on the table as he began getting dressed.

The clothes felt uncomfortable and heavy on him. He couldn't believe how alien they felt after only a few days without them.

But he knew they would also be warm, and that was something he was craving.

Sherrie stood no more than six feet from Zoe, watching over her with the knife.

They stared at each other.

Zoe's sobbing had subsided and she just sat with her chin on her knees and her eyes looking up at them.

I wonder what Sherrie's thinking...

You probably don't want to know.

John watched them both as he dressed, just in case either did something they would regret.

They were all silent. The night was getting darker, illuminated only by the poor lighting in the church and by random lightning through the windows. The thunder clashed once more, louder this time.

Getting closer.

As John completed dressing, Zoe opened her mouth to speak.

Sherrie jabbed the knife in the air.

Zoe closed her mouth and said nothing. Her brow furrowed.

"You ready?" Sherrie asked without turning to look at him.

John nodded.

"We're going," Sherrie said to Zoe.

Zoe's bottom lip quivered and she looked to the ground. She nodded.

"Come on," Sherrie said as she turned and headed for the door.

John stared at Zoe.

She raised her eyes, looked back at him and tried to smile once more.

He wanted to say something, but he couldn't think of anything.

"It wasn't meant to happen like this, Johnny," she whispered.

John tried to smile, but it didn't work. The ebbing pain in his cock wouldn't let him.

"John," Sherrie called from the doorway. "Quickly."

He turned to face her.

Sherrie was waving for him to follow.

"*Now*, while we can!" she called.

John turned back to Zoe.

She had buried her head back in her hands. She was rocking back and forth again.

"This is wrong," she was whispering to herself. "This is wrong. Wrong. Wrong. This is all wrong."

Over and over again.

John turned to leave as lightning flashed through the windows.

He spotted the key ring and handcuffs on the table. He reached over and grabbed both of them.

Fox will pay. I promise you, Zoe.

He turned and headed for the doorway.

Freedom. At last!

He smiled at Sherrie as he walked towards her.

She smiled back, but she kept an eye over his shoulder, making sure Zoe wasn't going to try anything.

Thunder rumbled around them.

As John walked to the door, he slipped the handcuffs into the back pocket of his jeans.

They'll keep safe there until I'm ready to use them on Fox.

He climbed the step to the doorway and walked out into the night.

It was cold and dark, but he didn't care.

He took another step into the darkness and the security lights came on, flooding the whole area with bright light.

"Thanks for dropping everything to come all the way out here to help," he said to Sherrie as they stood outside the church.

"Looks like you needed it too!" she replied.

They kissed.

"Come on," she said as they broke away from each other. "Let's not hang around here. My car is at the end of the drive."

Quickly, they headed off past the Jeep and down the driveway.

John fought the temptation to look back over his shoulder to see if Zoe was watching or following.

He didn't want to know.

All he needed to do now was leave.

They left the safety of the security lights behind them and headed into the darkness beyond, followed only by momentary flashes of lightning and the broiling sound of thunder.

And as they walked, John hooked the key ring to the belt hook on his right hip.

<u>Fifty-two</u>

"**I** was so worried about you when you didn't come to work," Sherrie said as they sat in the car.

"I know."

They stared into each other's eyes.

"And leaving your card in my screen door freaked me out too. I didn't know what to think. You come to see me, leave the card and then disappear! I was worried sick. I thought maybe you'd left without me."

John ran his hand through her long curly hair and stared into her green eyes.

"I'm sorry," he said. "But there wasn't much I could do about it."

Sherrie nodded. "I know."

"I'm just so glad you picked up my phone when I called."

"Naturally," she said. "I was hanging around it like a hawk. You had me beside myself with nerves."

They sat in silence for a few moments, looking out into the darkness of the night, watching as the lightning flashed intermittently.

The car was parked over at the side of the road to Hepburn Lakes and at the end of the driveway to the church.

"Then I waited and waited down at the hotel." Sherrie continued, staring out into the night. "Once it started to get dark and these storm clouds came over, I thought something must've gone wrong. I knew you'd said something about a church just out of town, and luckily this is the only one. A guy at the hotel gave me directions."

"I'm glad you asked him."

"Me too."

"I don't know how long I would've been tied up in there."

Silence fell between them again.

John looked up at the sky. The clouds looked dark and heavy. It felt like midnight, but the clock on the dashboard said 7:18pm.

"Did…" Sherrie paused. "Did *she* do all that to you?" She looked at his wounded face and gently touched his left arm.

John nodded. "Yeah. I've been up here since Saturday night."

"And Helen?" she asked in a quiet voice.

John let out a deep sigh. "I really don't know any more. I think she's dead."

"*What?*"

"Well, the girl up there says she's dead. And I think I believe her. I don't think she'd lie to me about that. But then again, I don't know what to think now. This whole thing is too confusing. I don't know what to think anymore."

"*Dead?* How? *Why?*"

John turned in his seat and took Sherrie's hands in his.

"It's a long story, my love. And it's complicated."

"It always is with you," she replied as she smiled a sad smile.

"And I don't really know where to start."

"Probably from the beginning."

"I know, but I don't know if we have the time. There's a madman on the loose out here. I think he killed Helen. At least the girl in the church said he did. I think he's also the one responsible for the mental problems that girl has. And we have to stop him!"

"Madman?" Sherrie looked worried. "What are you talking about?"

"Fox. His name's Ricky Fox and he's some hit man who makes money by causing pain – or worse. He's the one who killed Helen! He's got her at a place called Redlingford. It's about 10 minutes from here."

"Can't we call the police?"

"It won't work. He'll get away with it if we do that."

"The cops will take care of it."

"No, he knows ways around the cops. You don't survive this long as a hit man unless you know who to bribe."

"John, this is *serious* shit," Sherrie's face was pale and determined. "I don't think you're in any fit condition to confront this guy."

"I have to!"

"No, you *don't!*"

"Yes, I do. I have to pay him back for all the people he's hurt and killed in the past."

"You don't have to play hero, John."

"I know that, Sherrie. Believe me, I don't want to. But I owe that much to Helen. If he *has* killed her, I have to make him hurt."

"Ordinary people don't have to play hero, John."

"I'm *not* playing hero. But I have to do *something!*"

"But I don't want *you* hurt or killed in the process."

He leaned forward and kissed Sherrie on the cheek.

Such a soft, smooth, lovely cheek...

"I know that, my love. But we have to do what we have to do."

She nodded. "You always say that."

"We have to follow this through. I mean, what if Helen's still alive up there? I have to save her."

"Do you believe she is?"

"I don't know..."

"And how will you explain me?"

"That's not important right now."

"It is to me," Sherrie sat back in the seat.

John sighed. "You know what I mean. You mean the world to me, you *know* that. But I don't want to see Helen hurt if I can save her. And...well...if I'm too late, I can at least do something to make her...I don't know...to make her last resting place..." He trailed off and swallowed hard. He didn't want to think about those kinds of things.

Thunder rolled across the car.

"Either way," he continued after a minute or two of silence. "I have to pay Fox back for what he did to her and the girl up at the church."

"Are you sure you know what you're doing?" Sherrie asked.

John nodded, "I don't think I have any choice."

"We always have choices, John. Some of us just choose not to make them."

"I've got to do this, Sherrie. But I understand if you want to drop me off in town and just leave me to fight my own battles."

She smiled then and squeezed his hands.

"Looks like you've been fighting your own battles for far too long. And I don't think you've been winning. I'm in this with you now. You'll need my help."

"You sure?"

"I'm sure," she smiled. "I have to make sure I protect you and that you come back in one piece."

He leaned forward and kissed her lips, "Thanks, honey." *She smelt so good...*

"I don't want to lose you," she whispered.

"And I don't want to lose *you*," he replied.

"But I think we should head back to Hepburn Lakes first. Get you cleaned up and rested before we do anything else."

John nodded his head. "Yeah, that's a good idea. I don't want to stay here any longer than I have to."

"Me either," Sherrie said as she started the engine. "There's no telling what Zoe might do next."

John nodded.

Sherrie swung the car onto the road. She put the car in reverse and began a u-turn to head them back in the right direction.

"Hepburn Lakes," she smiled at him. "Here we come!"

Fear sliced through John. His mouth dropped wide open.

"How did you *know*?" he whispered.

Sherrie stopped the car in mid-turn.

"Know what?" she asked.

"That the girl in the church is called *Zoe*?"

Sherrie looked the other way to check the road for traffic.

"You must've mentioned it," she said.

"I didn't."

"Well, you *must* have."

Sherrie gunned the engine. The road was empty.

"I didn't!"

Silence.

A slice of lightning illuminated the inside of the car. A deafening clap of thunder followed immediately after it.

John sat back deeper in his seat.

"You *know* her!" he said.

Sherrie turned around to face him. She sighed.

"I – "

Her words were cut short.

The car jolted violently.

John was thrown forward in the seat, the side of his body slamming into the dashboard, the air whooshing from his lungs, pain exploding inside him.

He heard Sherrie's scream above the noise of twisting metal and breaking glass. Her scream stopped suddenly as she was hurled into the steering wheel.

The car rolled forward slightly, then jerked to a stop. The headlights died and so did the engine.

John could hear the tinkling of broken glass outside the car.

He opened his eyes. Turning slowly to minimise the pain, he looked out his side window. He could make out the shape of another car just a few feet away from his window.

Damn it, someone drove into us! Didn't they see us turning on the road?

And then the headlights came on.

The bright light blinded John for a moment. Then the left headlight blew, leaving the right one shining up at an angle, through the broken glass of its lamp.

The engine roared.

"Sherrie? You okay?" he called over his shoulder.

There was no reply.

John was trying to force air back into his lungs. He pulled the door handle, but it wouldn't work properly. His door was jammed shut.

The other car was backing up.

And as John's vision cleared, he could see the car was a Jeep.

A red Jeep Wrangler with TAMEME licence plates.

A flash of lightning lit up the night.

He stared across and through the Jeep's windshield for those few split seconds.

The flash of lightning was gone, but the imprint on his mind was still there.

Zoe was sitting at the wheel.

And she was smiling.

Fifty-three

John turned around and looked at Sherrie.

Her body was slumped forward and she wasn't moving. Her forehead rested on the steering wheel. A trickle of blood ran down the side of her face.

"Sherrie?" he shook her shoulder. "Honey, please, *wake up!*"

She moaned.

John glanced back out the window. The Jeep was still reversing, its engine roaring in the night.

"Sherrie, *please,*" he shook her again. "We've got to get out of here!"

Lightning flashed.

He looked past Sherrie and out her window. The forest was so close. The impact of the Jeep had forced the car sideways and forward, towards the edge of the road. The trees were no more than fifteen feet away from the driver's side of the car.

Gotta get into the forest. Gotta get away!

He reached past Sherrie and grabbed her door handle.

As he did so, light filled the car. He heard the Jeep's engine gunning.

It was getting closer.

He closed his eyes, hunched down in the seat and held onto Sherrie, bracing for the impact.

This is it. It's all my fault and now this is it! If only I'd acted earlier and not dragged everyone into this mess oh God ohGodOHGOD!

But the impact never came.

Thunder rumbled outside the car.

After a few seconds, John opened his eyes and turned to stare out the window.

The headlight was there, right by his window.

Shit!

The Jeep had stopped right at his door, only inches from his face.

With another flash of lightning, John could see Zoe was staring at him through her windshield.

My God! She's playing with us!

He stared back, trying to work out the emotions on her face.

What does she want?

They sat staring at each other for quite a while. John didn't want to make the first move, just in case it was the wrong one.

Play your hand, Zoe. Let me see what you've got!

Sherrie moaned behind him.

"*Sherrie?*" he whispered, not taking his eyes from Zoe. "You okay? You awake now?"

He got no reply.

"Sherrie?" he asked again, his voice pleading with her to wake up.

Thunder rolled heavy and loud through the night air.

You can't stay here!

I know that.

You've to get out before Zoe gets to you.

You don't want to end up back in the church.

I KNOW!

Then DO something!

He had no alternative. He had to act. They couldn't sit in the middle of the road all night, waiting for Zoe to finish playing with them and jump on her prey.

The Jeep's engine gunned in the night.

"John?" Sherrie moaned quietly.

"Honey, you okay?" he fought the urge to turn around and look at her.

"What happened?" her voice was quiet, scared.

"Zoe ran into us with the Jeep," he replied. "And she's out there now. Just sitting watching us."

"Zoe?" Sherrie sounded confused. "Zoe did this?"

"Yes."

John continued staring out the window.

Zoe smiled back at him. She had seen his lips moving. She knew he was talking to Sherrie.

Zoe leaned forward and placed both her hands on top of the steering wheel. Then she rested her chin on her hands.

She's just going to sit there, John thought. *Sit there and wait for us to make the first move!*

"What are we going to do?" Sherrie asked.

John felt her hand on his shoulder, but he didn't dare look around at her. He had to stare Zoe down.

Lightning flashed into the night.

I need a weapon of some kind.

Something to protect us with.

What?

I don't know.

There's nothing here to use.

"Don't make any sudden movements," John said. "I don't think she can see you from where she is."

"Okay."

"Keep low and out of sight."

"I'll try."

"I want you to see if you can start the engine."

"Okay."

"If it starts, you need to be ready to take off as quickly as possible."

"Alright," Sherrie sounded scared.

The Jeep's impact had pushed the car to the side of the road. It was sitting on an angle, half on the road and half on the gravel shoulder. They were still facing away from Hepburn Lakes, but at that moment John didn't care. There was enough room to the side of the Jeep to drive past Zoe if they had the chance. As long as they got away from her, they could work their way back to Hepburn Lakes through back roads if they had to.

We need to be anywhere but here.

Thunder rumbled outside.

"Just let me know when you're ready," he whispered.

John stretched back with his hand, found Sherrie's thigh and squeezed it.

He felt her hand on his. He could feel her fingers shaking.

"I'm ready," she replied.

John continued to stare unblinkingly at Zoe.

"Right," he said. "Let's do it."

"I hope this works."

"So do I."

Zoe was peering back at him from the Jeep.

Lightning again, two flashes this time, and John could see the pendant around her neck.

Helen. I'm so sorry...

Her head tilted to one side, almost as if she knew something was happening, or maybe she was getting bored waiting.

Just a little longer...

Over his shoulder, John heard Sherrie's keys clink against each other and he braced himself for whatever was to come.

"Here goes," said Sherrie.

The ignition clicked.

The engine kicked over.

And a double wave of thunder crashed down upon them, loud and long.

Zoe continued to stare.

She can't hear it! The thunder's masking the engine noise!

He knew they only had seconds to move.

Zoe moved forward in her seat, tilting her head more.

Damn!

She broke his stare and glanced to the front of the car.

He followed her eyes.

The car headlights were on!

"Sherrie!" John turned to her. "Kill the headlights!"

But it was too late.

Starting the engine had turned the headlights back on full. Even with the sound of the thunder hiding the engine noise, Zoe had realised what was happening.

John turned back to her.

She was shaking her head, a look of disappointment on her face.

We can still make it!

She leaned over to the passenger side of the Jeep and disappeared out of sight for a split second.

We have to.

"Sherrie, quick! Drive!"

Then she sat upright again and stared back at him, a look of sadness on her face.

She mouthed something to him. But he couldn't work out what she said.

Then she raised the gun.

And started firing.

Fifty-four

The first bullet shattered through the Jeep's windshield as Zoe fired and a split second later lodged in John's door.

The second bullet shattered his window.

The third ricocheted off the metal edging of the windshield and disappeared into the forest.

"Shit!" John dived backwards and grabbed at Sherrie. *"Get down!"*

She pulled him towards her as the fourth bullet tore the side mirror from John's door.

John looked at Sherrie as lightning lit up their surrounds.

"Keep your head down," he said. "I don't think she's an expert with guns."

John reached up to push Sherrie's head down below the dash, but she resisted and pulled his hand away.

She had a determined look on her face.

"We're not taking this *shit* any more," she said to the night.

She gunned the engine.

"I've had *enough!*"

"Huh?"

"This has got to stop. It has to end *now!*" Sherrie said between clenched teeth.

Yes, John thought. *Drive! Let's go!*

He braced himself and looked out the windshield.

He didn't hear the next shot; it was blocked by thunder. But he knew it had come when the windshield shattered in front of them. Glass shattered outwards and some of the fine shards fell back into the car, over the dashboard and over their feet and legs.

John watched as Sherrie put the car in gear.

She pressed down on the accelerator and the car shot forward.

He held on to the dashboard.

Finally! Yes!

They drove down the road, the headlights shining in the darkness.

Freedom!

Another shot whistled past them, missing completely.

Sherrie slammed on the brakes. The tyres locked on the road and the car skidded slightly to the right as it came to a halt.

"Damn it, she's following us," Sherrie said.

John opened his mouth to say something, but he didn't have time.

He watched her change gears.

And put the car into reverse.

Huh?

Reverse?

Sherrie turned in her seat and looked over her shoulder.

"This has gone far enough," she said.

She pressed down on the accelerator. The car reversed wildly. Sherrie struggled with the steering wheel to keep the car straight on the road.

John tried to grapple with his thoughts, but everything was spinning out of control and he was unable to stop it.

"Hang on," Sherrie said.

And a second later, the car collided solidly with the Jeep.

John had been ready for the impact, but he still bounced back off the seat and hit the dashboard hard. Pain sliced him in two and he felt as if his insides were trying to escape.

Sherrie's foot continued pressing down hard on the accelerator. The car engine was roaring, blocking out any noise from outside. They were moving backwards slowly, inch by inch now.

John looked out the back window.

Now both headlights of the Jeep were broken. Part of the red grill was mangled and destroyed, no longer shiny and new.

I was handcuffed to that...

From where he sat, he couldn't see if Zoe was still in the driver's seat.

He guessed she was when a bullet shattered the back window, spraying glass over both of them.

Sherrie put the car into drive again. They jerked forward quickly as she drove a few feet from the Jeep.

John could now see the Jeep's front licence plate was twisted. It swung back and forth, held on by only one screw.

TAMEME.

Sherrie paused for a second to look out the shattered back window before she reversed again.

John braced himself once more. The seconds before impact seemed to stretch for an eternity.

The car collided with the Jeep again, with more force this time. Metal and glass collided in a symphony of destruction. The Jeep rolled backwards in an arc across the road and came to rest hitting the embankment on the other side.

Sherrie reversed again, cannoning into the front of the Jeep, pushing it further into the embankment. The metal grill of the Jeep pushed higher, popping the hood loudly and bending it out of shape. The metal folded as easily as paper, folding back and in on itself. The front of the Jeep pushed into the back of the car, jagging upwards and lifting from the ground, metal screaming.

Putting the car back into drive, Sherrie pulled away from the twisted metal. Both cars remained entwined for a few seconds before they gave way and the Jeep slid from the back of the car. It shook heavily as the front tyres bounced back on the ground, glass cascading to the road's surface.

Sherrie stopped the car in the middle of the road, then she backed it up a little so they could both stare across at the tangled mess of the Jeep. John heard her let out a deep sigh.

He turned to face her. "You okay?" he asked.

She nodded. "I think so."

He could see she was scared; he could also hear it in her voice.

"I think I lost it for a second," she muttered, shaking her head.

He took her hands and kissed her.

"That's okay. We all go a little crazy sometimes."

Sherrie looked back at the Jeep and John followed her glance.

There was no movement. No sign of life.

The Jeep looked like a dark, dead shell.

"I think we should be going," she said as she ran a shaking hand through her hair.

John nodded. "You *sure* you're okay?"

Sherrie turned to him and her face changed in a second. Strength and determination flashed across it before being replaced with fear.

"Oh, John," she sighed. "What have I done?"

He rubbed her shoulder.

"Don't worry about it now," he comforted her. "You did what you had to do. And *now*, we need to leave."

Sherrie shook her head, "I can't. I mean…it's not right. What if I've *killed* her? What if she's hurt? I can't be responsible for all this!"

John leaned forward and hugged her.

"Listen, you can't worry about those things," he whispered in her ear. "It's more important we get back to Hepburn Lakes. We'll arrange for help there and they can send an ambulance or someone out to take care of this."

He pulled back and looked deep into her eyes.

"But we *have* to get away," he said. "And now. Do you understand?"

She nodded.

"Can you drive?" he asked as he held her still trembling body.

Lightning flashed.

"I…I don't really know," she replied.

"Okay," he nodded. "Slide over and I'll drive."

She moved towards him.

John grabbed the door handle and pulled, but the door wouldn't open.

Shit, I forgot about that.

Sherrie looked at him strangely.

"The door's jammed," he explained.

Thunder rolled all around them as he reached out and pushed the remaining splinters of glass from the side window.

"John…?" Sherrie whispered.

"Don't worry. I'll only be gone for a few seconds."

When the window was free of all the glass shards, John reached up and pulled himself up and out through it. As he did, he ignored the dull aches and pains of his body. He didn't have time to worry about his wounds now. He kept his eye on the wreck of the Jeep. It was still sitting at the side of the road, squashed into the embankment.

Steam was beginning to waft from the engine, and the motor was still running, but just barely. It was coughing and idling erratically.

Slowly dying…

John held himself half-in and half-out of the car.

He waited.

"*John?*" Sherrie's voice sounded worried.

"I'm just being careful," he called back to her.

Finally, the lightning came. Everything around him was white-bright for just a split second.

Long enough for him to peer into the cabin of the Jeep.

It was empty.

He couldn't see Zoe. She didn't seem to be there.

Shit!

John quickly climbed the rest of the way out of the window.

The wind was stronger now, and colder. The night was beginning to settle in.

Gotta move fast!

Once he climbed from the car, he took a moment to steady himself. He turned back and looked at Sherrie's Ford. The passenger side was almost unrecognisable. The metal was gouged and dented all along the side with red paint scars from the Jeep. Long grooves stretched the length of the car, deep into the metal. The back of the car had been pushed right in, and the passenger-side indicator-light was hanging on only by its wires.

He turned back to the Jeep.

No movement. No sign of life.

Steam was pouring from under the crumpled hood now.

He didn't want to make any quick moves. He didn't want to do anything stupid.

Slowly, he backed up and started walking around the car.

As he reached the mangled trunk, he stared in through the shattered back window. Sherrie was staring back out at him.

He smiled.

"You've done quite some damage here," he said. "I don't think the insurance company will be too impressed."

"I don't care right now," Sherrie replied.

"You could lose your no-claim bonus."

"I think I can live with that better than some other things I've done."

Thunder crashed loud and long above them.

John looked up into the dark sky.

This storm's close.

Too close.

That's the last thing we need.

Sherrie screamed.

John's eyes darted to her.

"It's only thund –"

But she was looking away from him. Across the road.

He followed her eyes.

The Jeep lurched forward slowly.

No!

The engine roared.

NO!

The tyres bit into the gravel and the Jeep shot forward. Straight towards them.

Fifty-five

John shouted to Sherrie.

But there was no time.

No time to do anything.

He found himself trying to wave down the Jeep, trying to stop it somehow.

But he couldn't.

Its motor revved.

It wasn't going to stop.

As it charged towards them, he stood between the Jeep and the Ford for as long as he could, hoping he could make Zoe change her mind.

But the Jeep kept coming.

John dived out of the way with seconds to spare.

The Jeep flew across the road and smashed into the side of Sherrie's car.

Metal on metal.

Sparks flew as lightning caught the whole scene in one split-second collage.

The ear-piecing scream of twisted metal and steel colliding filled the air.

As John tumbled on the road surface, he could hear the Jeep's motor roar, the tyres screech on the road, the breaking and twisting of steel under pressure, and the sickening crash that ended it all.

There was silence for a few seconds before another clap of thunder vibrated the night.

He looked up from the road and glanced at the destruction.

The Jeep had Sherrie's car pinned at the side. It had collected the end of the car and pushed it across the road and into the pines of the forest. The Jeep had come to rest impaled in the passenger side of the car.

Oh my God! Sherrie!

The rest of Sherrie's car had been crushed against the wall of pines in the forest. It was sandwiched between the Jeep and the forest.

John stood slowly. His knees were bleeding and his jeans were torn in a couple of places. He was limping as he walked, but he didn't care. He felt his left arm, making sure the stitches were still holding. He could feel no gaping hole, so he assumed they were.

But none of his wounds mattered anymore.

He had to save Sherrie.

As lightning struck, it illuminated the crash and John didn't like what he saw.

The twisted bodies of the two cars, wrecked beyond belief, made him wonder about the state of the people who were in them.

Is that blood pooling on the ground?

Or something else?

Smoke was pouring from the Jeep's crushed hood and he could hear something dripping somewhere.

Gotta move. And quick.

He ran across the road.

Peering into the Jeep as he approached, he looked for any sign of Zoe. The back door of the Jeep had popped open and was hanging wide. The soft canvas top was split along the side, flapping in the wind. The frame of the windshield had broken off and been flung forward, now hanging off the twisted metal of the hood.

And the driver's door was open.

But there was no sign of Zoe.

John turned and looked around him.

Maybe she was thrown clear or jumped before impact.

But he couldn't see her anywhere.

He opened his mouth to call her name.

Then stopped himself.

Suddenly, he was on edge again. Something wasn't right. He was sure of it, but he didn't know what exactly it was.

He wished he could find Zoe, he needed to know where she was. Not knowing made him panic.

He walked further forward, to the front of the Jeep where it pinned Sherrie's Ford to the tree.

Bending down to look in the side window, he called to Sherrie. First in a low voice, and then louder when she didn't reply.

A cold wind cut through him then. It seared his bloody knees and made him start to shiver.

The inside of the car was a crushed mess. There was very little left that resembled the insides of a car. He looked into the front seats, but Sherrie wasn't there either.

Broken tree limbs stuck through the windshield and low-growing branches pierced the roof of the car.

"Sherrie!" he called.

Lightning flashed around him.

It was that split-second of illumination that showed him the driver's door was open, swinging out between the trunks of two pines.

She got out!

He hoped he was right.

Thunder reverberated around him.

Maybe she got out!

She must have!

He straightened up and turned around to check the Jeep once more. As he did so, a double-fork of lightning stretched across the sky. He could see no one was in the Jeep. He could also see the puddles of liquid on the ground.

Fuel?

I hope not.

And then he realised he was standing in it. The fuel was running from underneath the Jeep and was pooling in several places, including around his feet, soaking his shoes.

"Shit," was all he could manage.

Quickly backing away, he dashed into the forest, moving quickly around some of the pines to the other side of the car.

"Sherrie!" he called once more.

It was darker with the pines around him. While the trees gave him extra cover, they also made it harder for him to see.

His eyes slowly began to adjust.

Thunder rolled through the night, louder than before, shaking everything around him.

When the silence returned, he came to a halt to catch his breath and to listen to the night.

The breeze was almost a steady wind now, and it rustled the trees as it blew, making it harder to hear other sounds. The creaks and groans from the cars sounded unnatural and eerie, like some mechanical beast on the prowl, and didn't help him calm down.

Control yourself. Sherrie needs you now. Keep a level head. Don't lose it all now!

He tried not to think about the fuel leaking from the cars, or the fact that he had been standing in it.

This side of the road had a slight decline, and he knew if enough fuel pooled around the cars, it would eventually run down in this direction. Straight towards him.

And Sherrie.

"Sherrie!" he called again.

And this time he heard a muffled reply somewhere up ahead of him.

Was that her? he asked himself. *It had to be! I'm sure it was!*

But what if it's Zoe?

I have to find out. It must be her!

But what if it isn't?

John trekked on in the dark with his hands out in front of him, feeling for the pines all around him.

The forest was densely populated with the pines; their trunks standing tall and bare, with most of the foliage starting on branches more than ten or fifteen feet above his head. The ground was covered with a blanket of dead pine needles, softening his steps as he walked.

At least Zoe won't hear me approach.

He smiled at that idea.

And you won't hear her either!

His smile disappeared.

After what seemed like an eternity, John made it to the open driver's door. He took one more look into the crumpled wreck, just in case Sherrie was in there. But the car was empty.

Lightning struck, illuminating the interior of the car. There was no doubt she wasn't in there, but there was blood on the steering wheel and the door handle.

No!

John turned around to look back into the forest.

She couldn't have gone far. She's injured.

But what if she was carried? What if Zoe's got her!

"Sherrie!" John shouted this time. He had to risk it. He *had* to find her.

He heard the quiet moan again, just before another wave of thunder erupted in the sky.

To the left. I heard it. I did! She's off to the left!

Walking as quickly as he dared, he set off to the left, walking a few feet and then stopping, hoping his eyes would catch something that looked out of place.

He didn't have to walk very far.

Within thirty feet of the car, he found her.

Sherrie was sitting at the base of one of the pines, her back pressed against its trunk and her head in her hands.

A flash of lightning showed the blood running down the side of her head.

John dashed to her, "Sherrie!"

She looked up with a dazed expression on her face. "John?"

"Yes, it's me," he replied as he knelt down next to her.

"I thought you were…" she trailed off, shaking her head.

"Don't think about that now," he said as he hugged her. "Are you okay?"

She nodded. "I think so. I'm really not sure. I don't even know what happened, or how I got here. I don't remember much."

"That's okay, as long as you're alright."

"And you?" she looked into his eyes then, a worried expression on her face.

"I'll live," he tried to smile.

It didn't work.

Sherrie looked around and into the night.

"Have you seen her?" she asked.

John shook his head. "No, I haven't."

"We've got to get out of here," Sherrie said as she began to stand. "She's crazy."

"I know," he helped her up. "But are you okay? Can you walk?"

Sherrie took a couple of small steps. "Yeah, I think so."

Then she let out a yelp of pain and doubled over holding her side.

John reached for her and helped her steady.

"You sure?"

She took in some deep breaths and then straightened back up. "Yeah, I think so." Pain flashed across her face. "We'll just have to take it slow."

"Okay," he helped her walk a few more steps.

"How's the car?" she asked.

"It's a write-off."

Sherrie nodded, "I figured as much."

"We'll have to make it on foot."

"Okay," she replied.

"You think you can make it?"

"Back to Hepburn Lakes?" she turned and smiled at him. "If I'm with you, yeah."

Lightning flashed.

"We're not going back to Hepburn Lakes," he said in a deep voice.

"Huh?" she pulled away from him.

Thunder rumbled like a deadly beast.

"We're heading to Redlingford."

Fifty-six

"What?" Sherrie replied in a shocked voice.

"That's where Fox has Helen," John explained.

"I know, you told me that," she replied. "But you said she was dead."

"I think she is. But I have to know for sure." John looked deep into her eyes. "Zoe said she's dead and Fox killed her. But I have to know. I have to see for myself before I can really believe it."

"You think Zoe lied to you?"

John hung his head and looked to the ground as lightning lit up the area. Images of the past two days flashed through his mind.

She came back covered in blood.

She was wearing Helen's half-heart pendant.

Would she lie?

First they screw you, then they screw *you!*

Was Zoe telling him the truth or was it all lies?

"I don't know," he said finally, turning to face Sherrie once more. "But I need to find out. And if Fox is still there, I have to make him pay."

Thunder rolled long and loud through the night.

Sherrie stepped closer, put an arm around his back and hugged him hard.

"I understand how you feel," she replied. "I think it's a bad idea, but I don't think I have any choice other than to go along with you. I'm *not* walking back to Hepburn Lakes by myself."

"I don't want to get you involved in this, honey," he replied.

"Too late," she smiled at him and pointed to the blood on her face. "I already am."

He nodded and sighed deeply.

"We better get moving," he said as he reached out and wiped the blood from her temple. "Can you walk?"

Sherrie nodded. "How far is it?"

"Zoe said it was about ten miles from here."

"Ten?" Sherrie sounded exhausted already.

"It's going to take us some time to get there," he replied. "Do you think you can make it?"

She nodded. "I'll have to."

"You can stay here. We'll find a good hiding spot if you like."

Sherrie shook her head vigorously. "No way. Uh-uh. I'm sticking with you this time. Safety in numbers. I'll be okay."

The wind blew strongly through the pines and lightning flashed.

At first, he thought it was the sound of the wind. But the noise got stronger and louder after the wind died.

"Jooohhhnnnyyy!"

John turned to Sherrie to ask if she heard it. But she was already looking at him, panic on her face.

She heard it too!

"Jooooohhhhhhnnnnnnyyyyy!"

The cry started low and built up as it stretched for seconds.

John turned in a circle, trying to pinpoint where the voice was coming from.

Zoe!

Another roll of thunder drowned out Zoe's voice.

"She's here," Sherrie whispered, squeezing John's hand while her eyes darted around them.

He nodded. "But where? It sounds like she's all around us."

The wind blew through the pines again; branches bent and needles rustled, combining with the eerie call.

"Jooohhhnnnyyy!"

"Let's get out of here," Sherrie pulled his arm. "This is starting to freak me out."

John backed away towards Sherrie, his eyes wide and searching through the darkness.

Lightning split the night sky.

For a second, John could see clearly around him. His eyes danced, trying to spot Zoe somewhere.

But he couldn't see her.

"Jooohhhnnnyyy!"

She sounded closer now as her voice floated on the wind. Closer, but still issuing from all around them. Almost as if the wind itself was calling his name.

Where the fuck is she?

Sherrie pulled him further into the forest.

"I hope this is the right way," she said over her shoulder.

"Don't worry," John replied, his head still darting back and forth in the darkness. "Let's just put some distance between us and her. We'll work out where we are later."

He squeezed her hand and they set off blindly through the pines, moving deeper into the forest and hoping they were leaving Zoe far behind.

Thunder growled around them.

"Jooohhhhnnnyyy! Don't goooooo!"

Zoe's voice sounded just as loud.

Just as close.

Can she see us?

Does she know what we're doing?

The hairs on the back of John's neck stood on end as fear skittered up his spine.

They soon came to a halt and looked at each other.

Both John and Sherrie were thinking the same thoughts.

"Did that sound closer?" Sherrie asked.

"I don't know."

"I don't want to run straight into her."

"I know."

"I just don't know where it's coming from!"

"We have to take our chances," John replied.

"Jooohhhhnnnyyy! Doooon't leeeeeeave meeeeee!"

John shook his head. If he were out in the forest alone, he would probably think he was going crazy; the stress of the last few days, the dehydration and hunger, the pain. But Sherrie heard the voice too. Sherrie proved it was real.

We have to get out!

"Can you run?" he asked her.

"Yes, I can try," Sherrie nodded.

"Okay," John replied. "Well, just keep running. No matter what."

She nodded.

The wind blew stronger through the trees.

"Jooohhhnnnyyy! Come baaaaaaack!"

Zoe's voice crept through the night and cut through John's soul.

Go back for her.

What?

Go back for her!

You can't!

She can help me get to Fox.

You know where he is.

She can bargain with him.

It didn't work last time.

She can help me!

Yeah, like she already has!

John thought about his wounds. The scratches on his chest bit at him in the cold night air. His arm was still dull with pain, but he could feel the stitches were still holding. He could still feel the lump on his head and the tight wrappings around his cock, and the dull pulling of the cock ring.

She did all that to you.

Yeah, you're right.

She almost killed you.

Yeah, she did.

I owe her nothing! *Not after all that has happened.*

John turned to Sherrie and kissed her hard on the lips. He could smell her now. The sweet scent of her perfume enveloped him. He knew the scent; he'd given her the bottle the day after Christmas last year. Her long curly locks brushed against the side of his face and forehead as the wind blew around them.

Her hot full lips kissed him back with passion.

They embraced as lightning flashed in the sky.

"I love you," she whispered as they pulled apart.

"And I love you."

"Nothing's changed," she said.

John's head tilted to the side. "And nothing's changed with me either," he replied.

She smiled at him then. It was the first time she had done that in a long while.

Thunder deafened them.

"Come on," he said, grabbing Sherrie's hand. "Let's get out of here."

And as they dashed through the pines and into the heart of the forest, Zoe's voice followed them.

"Jooohhhnnnyyy! Coooome baaaack! Youuuu dooooon't understaaaand!"

They ducked around trunks of trees, stepping carefully where they could.

As they ran, John was sure Zoe's voice was fading into the distance.

But that could've been because of the wind. Or his heavy breathing.

Either way, he didn't care.

Gotta get out of here.

He kept that thought rolling over and over in his mind.

Gotta get out of here. Gotta get out of here. Gottaget-outofhere!

"Jooohhhnnnyyy! Pleeeeeasssse!"

They ran into the night.

And Zoe's voice began to waver; lost in the wind and in the thunder.

And when the sky opened up, Zoe's pleading was swallowed in the rain that followed.

It fell hard and heavy.

John welcomed the rain.

Maybe it could wash away all the events of the last few days and give them the cover they needed to get out of here.

Maybe it could help him get to Fox and teach the bastard a lesson he wouldn't forget.

Maybe...

Fifty-seven

He didn't know how long they ran or how much distance they covered. But it was slow going just the same.

They had to be careful where they ran and they stopped constantly to try and listen to the night, trying to convince themselves that Zoe wasn't following them.

The rain cut down their vision and that slowed them down more. They couldn't risk running into a tree trunk or heading blindly into danger.

They had run deep into the forest for quite a while, heading further down the descending slope, and would have continued in that direction except for the wide river that cut off their escape.

The river was at least twenty feet across and was flowing rapidly in the rain. In the heavy downpour it was hard to see the bank on the other side.

John could make out some rocks in the middle of the river, and there were pines at the water's edge, some of their branches stretching out into the water. A few dead pines poked out of the river, their ghostly white trunks looking like skeletal hands in the darkness.

"What do you think?" he asked Sherrie as they stopped by the river bank.

"I don't…know," she said, as she caught her breath. "Do we really…want to risk it?"

John shook his head as lightning flashed.

"I don't think so. No telling how deep it is."

"We can't go back," Sherrie said, looking over her shoulder.

"I know."

"And we can't stay here. We'll *freeze* to death!"

John placed his arm around Sherrie and rubbed her shoulder. She was shivering.

He realised he was cold too. The wind was colder than before, or at least it felt that way. Their rain-soaked clothes and bodies didn't help matters either.

We've got to get out of this rain!

"Come on," he said, smiling and taking her hand.

"Where to?"

John pointed up the river. "We'll follow it. See if we can cross somewhere. If not, we'll work our way back to the main road and head for Redlingford."

"Do you think that's a good idea?" she asked.

"No."

"Then why do it?"

"Because I have to find out for sure. Plus, I think Zoe said there's a couple of farmhouses up there. Maybe we can get help. At the very least we can find shelter for the night and get away from this storm."

Thunder rumbled and the rain came down harder, hitting them with force and stinging them like a thousand bees.

"Can we walk for a while?" Sherrie asked.

John nodded, "I think we should anyway. It'll be safer. I haven't heard Zoe for some time now."

He was right. Zoe's voice had disappeared with the storm. She wasn't haunting them now.

And since she'd stopped calling, John had been able to think clearly once more. And he knew what he had to do.

He looked towards the river and watched the water rush by. Usually it would be a tranquil image for John, but right at this moment, all he saw was the turmoil and violence of the current, and all he could think about was making Fox pay.

I have to see this thing through to the end. Now!

They followed the river as it snaked through the darkness. Occasional flashes of lightning lit their path, giving them a chance to see further ahead. The pines along the bank gave them some shelter from the wind, but the rain still made it through, falling hard and heavy about them.

They walked in silence for quite a long time.

John hoped they were heading in the right direction.

We have to be.

You gonna kill him?

If I can find him, yeah.
How?
I don't know.
He's a strong guy. He'd have to be. Can you do it?
I don't know. But I'll try.
For what he did to Zoe?
For what he did to Helen and Zoe, yeah. And for any-one else he ever hurt.
Are you sure you want to do this?
No. But I have to.
And you'll survive it?
I hope so.
What about Sherrie?
I know, I know. She's the last person I want hurt.
Can you risk her safety?
I have to DO this!
What if Fox gets Sherrie?
He won't. I'll hide her somewhere. She'll be safe.
And Zoe?
I don't know. She's not my concern.
Will she be safe too?
I don't know! She's not my concern now!
So, if you win...
Ahuh...
And beat Fox...
Yeah?
What about Zoe?

"John?" Sherrie's voice startled him out of his thoughts.
He turned to face her as they walked.
"What happened?"
Shit. Not now!
He turned from her and stared across at the river.
"Can you tell me, honey?" she asked. "*Please?*"
"I don't know," he replied.
"It might make things easier."
John shook his head. "I don't know whether you should hear this."
He felt her hand on his shoulder.
"I *want* to know what happened."

There was silence between them.

"And how."

They walked further along the river. The rain continued to pelt down.

"You may not like what you hear," he said eventually.

"I think I can handle it. I'd rather know and not make up my own wild stories."

John nodded.

Like anything could be as wild as the truth?

She has a right to know. She'll find out eventually anyway.

He ran his hand through his soaking hair.

"Where to start..." he said to himself.

"What about at the beginning?"

He turned to face her as lightning flashed.

She was smiling at him.

He smiled back, full of confidence and hope.

"I love you, Sherrie," he said.

She nodded. "I know."

"And I never want to hurt you."

"I know that already, John," she replied. "Now, tell me what happened. From the beginning."

Thunder rolled in as he took a deep breath.

"Okay," he nodded. "From the beginning..."

<u>Fifty-eight</u>

The rain was hard and heavy, worse than before, almost deafening now.

They had stopped by the river under two large pines whose branches intertwined and provided some cover from the heavy downpour.

The storm showed no sign of abating and the river flowed faster, the murky water bubbling and frothing as it crashed into the rocks and over the dead pines strewn through it.

John hugged Sherrie, trying to keep her warm and to stop her shivers.

The thunder rolled off the earth towards them.

Now they had stopped walking, John felt weak once more. He realised he still hadn't eaten since Saturday.

You should've grabbed some food from the kitchen bench before you left the church...

Thankfully he was no longer thirsty. The rain saw to that.

It was hard at first to tell Sherrie everything that had happened. But as he talked, he started to feel better, almost relieved to be able to share what he had gone through with someone so she could understand. And she did.

"I'm so sorry, John," Sherrie whispered.

He leaned back, looked into her eyes and smiled.

"You have nothing to be sorry for," he replied.

She nodded, "Yes I do."

Lightning split the darkness.

He could see her gorgeous green eyes. He ran his hand through her long wet hair, which was plastered on her head now.

"You couldn't've done anything to change the situation. Hell, you didn't even know what was happening until I called you on the phone."

She nodded, "I'm just so glad I was there to pick it up."

"So am I."

"I got here as fast as I could."

"I know that," he smiled again.

"I just wish I hadn't waited at the hotel for so long. I could've saved you from what she did to you."

John hugged her again. "Don't worry, you weren't to know."

"How could she *do* all those things to you?"

"It doesn't matter. We're together now, sweetheart. *That's* what's important."

"She's *crazy*." "I know."

Silence fell between them. He didn't want to push the subject, but he needed to know.

"You and Zoe know each other," he said.

Sherrie nodded and sighed deeply, "Yes, John. But it's a long story."

"Care to fill me in?"

Sherrie's eyes stared off into the distance. "I don't know where to start."

John smiled, "I usually start from the beginning."

She turned to him, a half-smile breaking across her face before soon disappearing, "I know. But I don't feel safe here. She could still be close." Sherrie rubbed her arms for warmth. "I can't tell you here. Can we find somewhere safer to talk? Somewhere I can tell you everything?"

John nodded. She looked cold and scared.

I need to know.

Don't push her.

"That's okay," he said. "Tell me when you feel it's right."

"I will," she replied. "I promise."

The rain eased slightly as thunder shook the night.

John looked up into the dark sky, hoping to see if the clouds were lifting, but he couldn't tell.

"We better get moving," he said.

Sherrie nodded.

"We've walked far enough to be a long way from the church," he continued as he took her hand in his.

"It feels like we've been out here for hours," Sherrie muttered.

"I don't think it's that long."

"I know."

"Let's start heading back up towards the road."

"Do you think that's safe?"

"Yeah, I think so. We have to find the road. It'll take us to Redlingford."

"I'm scared, John," she whispered.

He nodded.

So am I.

"We'll be okay," he replied. "We have the advantage, this bastard doesn't know we're coming."

"But what about Zoe?"

"I think we've lost her. She can't possibly find us out here."

They walked out from the protection of the pines.

The rain continued to fall.

Lightning jagged above them and the thunder followed almost immediately, echoing around the whole area, vibrating the ground they walked on.

They headed back into the forest, leaving the fast flowing river behind them.

"I hope this storm lets up," Sherrie said. "I'm freezing."

"That's the least of our problems."

"Huh?"

"Let's just hope we can find the road and get to Redlingford. We'll find some shelter there, I'm sure. And then we'll sit out this storm."

"Good idea," Sherrie said.

They walked in silence for a long time, through the forest and around countless pines. John looked towards Sherrie every now and again, trying to read the emotions on her face. But he couldn't. She looked deep in thought.

Or shock.

He wanted to say things to her, but with the thunder and the rain, it made it almost impossible.

He didn't really know what to say, anyway.

They walked on.

Two claps of thunder broke through the night.

John jumped at the deafening sound as the trees and ground shook around them.

"This is one *hell* of a storm," Sherrie said as she looked at him. "You okay?"

"Yeah," he smiled. "That thunder caught me off guard."

"It was loud alright."

"And we just *have* to be right in the middle of it."

She rubbed his back, "Don't worry, honey. A little rain isn't going to kill us."

"The lightning might."

She smiled. "Life's a game of chance, John. You play the game to see who wins."

"Yeah, just what I need…" he muttered.

"Huh?"

"We're out in the middle of nowhere running from a psycho and heading towards a killer, and you get all philosophical on me."

Sherrie's smile disappeared and she turned from him.

"When you live your life waiting, John, all you *can* do is be philosophical. You have a long time to think about things on the cold nights when you're alone."

John ran a hand through his hair and stopped walking.

Damn! Me and my big stupid mouth!

He sighed deeply.

"Sweets, I'm sorry," he replied as she turned to face him. "I shouldn't've said that."

Her eyes left his and fell to the ground. She didn't say anything.

He sighed again and looked up into the night.

"You know it was a difficult situation."

She didn't move.

He bent towards her and lifted her chin so she would look into his eyes.

"And you know how much I love you."

Her mouth quivered between a smile and a frown.

"You knew that when we first got into this thing."

She nodded.

"I told you it would take time," he continued. "I couldn't just walk out on Helen."

"I know," she replied.

"We'd been through some tough times. I couldn't just leave. But I was working on it. And things were coming together. It was just going to take a little while longer."

Sherrie nodded.

"I meant everything I said to you, honey. Know that and believe it."

He tried to smile, but the sad look on her face broke his heart.

"I know," she replied. "But now all this has happened."

John nodded.

Sherrie took a step forward and hugged him.

"I'm so sorry, John," she whispered into his ear.

He ran his hands up and down her back.

"That's okay, sweets. We just have to finish this off. Make those who are responsible pay."

"And then you'll be mine?" she asked in a small voice.

He pulled back from her and found her lips. He kissed her hard and long, letting his tongue play with hers.

The thunder and lightning crashed around them.

The rain pelted down on them but they remained embraced.

The world disappeared for a few seconds and nothing else mattered.

"I'm already yours," he whispered once they unlocked themselves.

Sherrie smiled and nodded. "I already know that."

"Come on," he said as he looked up to the sky. "Let's get moving. This storm isn't about to let up."

He took her hand and they continued through the trees. The ground was drenched now, the pine needles squelched underfoot as they walked on them.

And they walked for a long while in the night.

John moved faster now, hoping that soon the road would come into view. He had no idea how far down the decline they had walked, but walking back up the slope was tiring.

The road can't be much further.

He hoped that the road continued straight and didn't turn off or curve at any stage before they met it.

We could be walking right past it!

Don't think like that.

But what if it's true? We could be out here walking for days.

It won't happen.

We could be lost!

It WON'T happen!

We could die out here. They won't find us for weeks!

The storm will pass, the sun will rise, we'll be FINE!

They continued walking through the rain.

Lightning flashed.

The thunder rolled in once more, seconds later.

The hard pitter-patter of the rain was all around them in a deafening cacophony.

But now they hardly noticed it. It was the usual, it was the norm.

They walked further through the forest.

John stared straight ahead.

This is all your fault, Fox. The whole fucking mess. And I'm going to make you pay for it. Somehow. Somewhere. I'll make you pay. Bastards like you who get pleasure out of hurting women don't deserve to live. I will *make you pay!*

Even if it's the last thing I ever do!

<u>Fifty-nine</u>

They slogged on through the soaked forest as the rain drove down, heavier than before, blinding and hard. Their breath fogged in front of their faces as the night turned colder.

Pushing on through it, they walked through the forest that never seemed to end.

Neither of them spoke.

Walking apart from each other and both lost in their own thoughts, they took their own paths through the pines.

Will this ever end? John thought to himself as they continued up the incline.

Lightning flashed, giving him a chance to look ahead. His eyes searched for any sign of the road.

Just more trees.

More and more trees.

He turned to look at Sherrie. She wasn't too far away. She'd dropped off the pace slightly and was walking behind him now. She didn't even seem to be trying to keep up.

I hope she's okay.

Thunder rolled in the night.

John faced forward and kept walking.

"What do you think she's thinking about?" Richard asked in his head.

You again!

"Pretty girl in the woods…got you all tied up and naked. *And* horny… She must be wondering about that."

I was tied up for days! Put through pain and tortured!

"And you enjoyed every moment of it," Richard said.

Not true.

"Oh, I think it *is*, pal."

It's NOT true!

"Deny it all you want. But I was there. I saw how much you tried to escape."

I did try!

"I know how much you *wanted* to escape."

It was just impossible.

"I *know* it was the best sex you've ever had!"

Zoe's crazy. I mean, she's totally lost it!

"Doesn't matter, pal. Maybe *you* are too. Maybe that's why you didn't try to escape. But any way you slice it, you *loved every moment.*"

You're wrong. I escaped! How do you think I got here?

"You got *here*," Richard continued. "Because Sherrie *rescued* you. You didn't escape. You were *rescued!* Comprehend the difference?"

You're talking shit.

"If it weren't for Sherrie, you'd still be at the church and in Zoe's power."

Not true.

"Letting Zoe bend over you and sit on your face until she cums."

You're wrong!

"Don't deny it, pal."

Not TRUE!

"You can't re-write this one. I was there, remember?"

You've got it all wrong!

"More lies, John? When are you going to stop hiding behind your revisions of history?"

I don't want to hear this.

"But you *need* to. Someone has to tell you!"

Go away!

"Lies come back to bite, pal."

GO AWAY!

"And they bite hard. Especially big ones…"

NOOO!

John shook his head as thunder and lightning clashed.

Sherrie yelped.

John spun around to look at her.

She was running towards him.

John's eyes darted, looking for the danger.

"That one scared me," she said as she stopped next to him, a little out of breath. "I didn't think this storm could get any closer to us."

He nodded. "I know what you mean. It's right over us."

"Is it ever going to end?"

"Eventually," John said, running his hand through her wet hair. "Just like this night and all our troubles. Eventually."

She tried to smile, but couldn't.

"How much further?"

"I have no idea. It can't be far."

"Walking uphill instead of down makes it seem *so* much longer."

John nodded. "But at least while we're out here, Zoe can't find us."

"I know. But if she doesn't get us this storm will. Remember the head-cold I had the last time we were out in weather like this?"

John smiled, casting his mind back. He'd forgotten about that.

It would have been six months ago now. They had met at the car park of a local market at Parkhurst one Saturday evening. Helen was working late at the hospital and John had told her he'd be out at a movie.

That's what their lives had become.

Separate in all ways, but they had still shared the same house. Just like boarding with a room-mate, but with a marriage certificate to make it all legal.

At least you can just walk out on a room-mate...

He remembered the thrill he felt as Sherrie drove up in her car; the smile and wave she cast his way, the excitement and *energy* in her eyes.

"Hiya," she'd said as she climbed from the car. "Ready?"

He had nodded towards her and climbed back into his car.

As he watched, she opened the trunk of her car and pulled out a huge picnic basket overflowing with treats. He spotted the two bottlenecks of wine poking out from the top of the basket.

She climbed in his car.

"Midnight picnic," she said as she closed the door and smiled at him. "You game?"

"I thought we were seeing a movie," he smiled. "I picked a nice romantic one too!"

She shook her head, "Nope. Let's go somewhere nice and quiet and dark, and have our own little romance. Who needs films when you can have the real thing?"

He bent forward and kissed her then. Her soft, sweet, full lips sending a charge right through his body. Her smell enveloped him; the smell he craved so much.

When they parted, he turned to start the engine.

"Where to?" he asked.

"Just drive," she smiled.

And he had done just that, for hours, until they pulled off at the side of the road and found a deserted picnic spot. It was cold and damp but they didn't care. They ate and drank.

And talked.

They discussed a lot of things that night; the future, their lives together. They laughed and cried. They kissed and hugged.

And on the big red and white picnic blanket they made love before falling asleep in each other's arms.

It wasn't until four in the morning that they woke.

Cold and stiff and shivering, they jumped back in the car and headed towards town, laughing all the way.

But they weren't laughing so much when Sherrie's head cold hit a few days later and she was off work for a week.

It was painfully hard for John not seeing her in the office; spotting her smiling face and hearing her voice. He had visited when he could, but Helen was keeping track of him then. Watching him and calling him constantly, making sure he was at work and asking him when he would be home.

She hadn't believed his excuse when he got home that morning after the picnic. She was sitting up waiting for him. He said that he'd worked longer than he thought, time had slipped away, and he ran out of fuel on the way home. He'd told her he had to walk a few miles for the fuel, but she didn't believe him.

She asked what film he had seen, but he'd forgotten all about his film excuse. She'd noticed the surprised look on his face when she'd asked the question. There was nothing else for him to say. And she was in no mood to believe any story he told anyway.

So then she started checking on him.

He couldn't risk even a few minutes with Sherrie. And he knew how that made Sherrie feel.

But there was nothing he could do except promise her things would get better and hope beyond hope that they would.

It took some time, but finally Helen's calls stopped. Eventually she started working late again, and her strange looks and questions ceased.

Finally.

He'd promised Sherrie at that midnight picnic that he would leave Helen soon.

Six months ago. It seems like just yesterday. I promised her my heart six months ago.

But you're still with Helen!

Yeah.

Or you were...

I know.

If Zoe and Fox hadn't got involved, would you have left Helen?

I don't know.

You still love her.

I know.

But you love Sherrie too?

Yeah.

And Zoe as well?

I can't think about these things.

You have to.

I can't!

You love her too, don't you?

She nearly KILLED me!

You loved being with her.

Yeah, I did. But it got too weird.

She turned you on.

Yeah.

She was fast and hard, and so was sex with her.

I know. I've never had it like that before.

And you liked it?

Yes, but look what she did to me.

You loved it?

Yes, I did. But she nearly killed me!

"Look, over there," Sherrie grabbed his shoulder and pointed through the pines to the right.

John followed her gaze, but he couldn't see anything other than rain and a wall of trees.

"What?"

"The road!" Sherrie continued. "Didn't you see it when the lightning flashed?"

John shook his head. He was so deep in thought, he didn't even register the lightning.

Thunder growled once more and the rain eased off momentarily into a shower.

"I'm *sure* I saw a road sign and next to it the road rising over a slight hill."

She pulled John in the direction she was pointing.

"I sure hope so," he replied.

As if in answer to him, the lightning struck again. A double fork lit up the sky and the forest around them.

John peered through the trees.

He saw the sign through a small gap to the right.

And he breathed a long sigh of relief.

REDLINGFORD 3 MILES.

<u>Sixty</u>

John squeezed her hand as they came over the hill. He stopped walking and looked through the thinning trees, down the slope and into the night.

Lightning gave him the illumination he needed.

Down in the valley below them, no more than a couple of hundred feet away, were two old farmhouses.

"Is this it?" Sherrie asked by his side.

John searched the night, waiting for the thunder to pass and for another strike of lightning. He didn't have to wait long.

The farmhouses were set away from each other by a distance of about 80 feet. They looked identical, except that the first farmhouse looked in much better condition than the second. Each house sat in the middle of a cleared field. The pines thinned out as they reached the properties, where they stopped altogether. A fence divided the area between both houses and John could make out the dirt driveway running up to the second farmhouse.

They stood in silence, waiting for another flash of lightning.

Was that the driveway? Was that where they killed Helen?

Thunder broke the silence.

The next wave of lightning was not far behind.

John got another look at the second farmhouse in the split-second flash. It was old and looked uncared for. From where he stood, there didn't seem to be any front door, and some of the roof looked as if it had rotted through years ago.

To the right of the second farmhouse, and set just behind it, was a barn.

Just as Zoe described it!

The barn was totally different to the farmhouse. It looked well-kept and newly painted. At least, he thought it did.

But he couldn't be certain of anything, not from this distance.

Zoe wasn't lying!

I knew it! She wasn't lying after all!

John nodded and turned his head to face Sherrie.

"That's it, alright," he said as thunder broke the night. "Just as Zoe described it."

Sherrie looked back into his eyes, "You sure?"

"Yep."

"And you *really* want to do this?"

John sighed, "I've already answered that, honey."

The rain began to fall heavily again, splashing hard into the puddles that were already at their feet.

Sherrie nodded sadly.

"At the very least," he continued. "We can get out of this rain and find some shelter down there."

"Okay," she said. "I'm just scared for us, that's all."

"I know," he squeezed her hand. "So am I."

They started down the hill towards the farmhouses, being careful not to slip over and tumble, their footsteps squelching in the undergrowth below them. John took one look behind him as they left the road and the weather-beaten old sign.

WELCOME TO REDLINGFORD.

These two farmhouses were the only ones they could see. There was no other sign of life.

It was just as Zoe said it would be!

The road disappeared from his view and soon the sign was lost to the rain and darkness.

He didn't want to leave the safety of the road, but he knew he had no other choice.

"And you *really* want to do this?" he heard Sherrie's voice replay in his mind.

No, I don't. But I have to.

Sherrie had asked him the same question as they stopped by the road sign that read REDLINGFORD 3 MILES.

"Do you *really* want to do this?"

John had turned to face her as they rested.

"We don't have any choice," he said.

"Of course we do!"

"Honey, I have to know, okay? I *have* to know! I've told you that already. The last few days have been totally crazy and I don't know what to believe any more. Zoe says Fox has Helen. Zoe says Helen is being held up here. Zoe says Helen is dead. I don't know if she's telling the truth or whether she's lying. But either way, I *have* to find out and I *have* to find out now before we can leave here and get on with our lives."

Silence. Rain fell between them.

"Do you understand?" John asked.

"Yeah, I do," Sherrie replied. "I just don't want you hurt."

"I won't get hurt," he rubbed her shoulder.

"You can't promise that," she turned away.

"I can only try my hardest," he replied. "I can't promise anything."

"I know…you never can…"

They had stared at each other in the rain for a few seconds before he leaned forward and kissed her on the cheek.

"You *know* I love you," he said.

She nodded and blinked the rain from her eyes.

Was it rain?

"And I love you. That's *why* I don't want to lose you."

He took her hand.

"Come on," he said as they walked up the road. "Only a couple of miles to go."

And now we're here.

This is it.

It's time for all the answers.

Are you gonna like them?

I don't know.

They walked through the wet and mushy undergrowth. The pines fanned out, becoming fewer as they walked towards the farmhouses.

John thought again about turning around and heading back to the road.

We could get on the road and walk back to Hepburn Lakes. Get help there and be gone within hours!

Not that easy, and you know it.

I wish it were.
Life never is.
Or death.
Lightning flashed around them and John realised how wide open the area was becoming. The further they walked, the fewer pines there were around them.
If we can see those houses this easily, anyone who's inside can see us as well.
You need cover.
But where?
Apart from the two houses and the barn, there was very little else to hide behind. They'd stepped out into the open and he looked behind him and saw the final row of pines they had just left.
Turn back and wait.
Wait for what?
He wished the forest continued all the way up to the farmhouses. Even a few pines dotted here and there would've helped them get closer without being seen.
Thunder rolled down the valley as they walked closer.
I've got to get closer. Got to see if anyone is there.
What if Fox has gone?
Worry about that later.
No, worry about it now. If he's left, you've lost.
I haven't lost.
You HAVE! He's won!
If he's left, we'll just have to think of something else.
What?
Don't worry about it NOW!
The rain continued falling. It dripped into John's eyes and made his chest and arm wounds itch.
He focussed on the farmhouses again. Something struck him as odd.
He was sure Zoe said Fox had guards stationed around the house, but there were none to be seen.
Are they hiding?
No, guards would be patrolling, not hiding.
He guessed with a storm this heavy, the guards might be pulled back inside the house.

Would Fox do that?

Doubtful.

He looked for any cars in the driveways, but there were none.

Maybe they're out the back.

Or in the barn.

Maybe Fox doesn't want people to know he's here.

Good point.

Maybe he only comes out here to do his business and then goes back into Hepburn Lakes.

I didn't think of that.

Maybe you should've headed for the town! He could be there.

Gotta check this out first anyway.

What if Helen isn't here?

She has to be.

He looked for any sign of life as the lightning struck again, but he couldn't see any. There was no sign of anyone.

Weird…

And then he realised there were no lights shining through the windows of either farmhouse.

No lights.

All dark.

Nothing.

"Which one?" Sherrie said as they walked across a dirt track that connected both driveways.

He turned to her.

"Which one do you want to go to first?" she continued.

John eyed both farmhouses again. He remembered Zoe saying that Fox's house was run down and dilapidated. So he guessed that was the house on the right, and that the other house was maybe owned by someone else.

A good place to start.

"Let's try the one on the left," he pointed.

"Doesn't look like anyone's home," she replied. "At either place."

"Good, then we can use one of them for shelter and get out of this rain. I'm exhausted and need a rest and I think you could do with one too."

Sherrie nodded, feeling the small bump on the side of her face. "Good idea."

They continued down the dirt track, skirting the muddy pools of water caused by the storm, and began walking up the driveway.

You're walking up the driveway.

I know.

What happened to a surprise attack?

Don't panic, keep calm.

You're walking up the fucking driveway with no weapons, no protection, no hope of escape!

We'll be okay.

They could cut you down like they did Helen!

I'm handling it.

Like you did Zoe?

I said, I'm HANDLING it!

"If anyone comes out," he whispered to Sherrie as they walked towards the farmhouse, "our car's broken down on the road and we need to use a phone."

"Okay, that old excuse," she nodded, stepping closer to him and wrapping her arm around his. "We're not honeymooners, are we?"

He smiled. "Not yet."

"Not a fun place to spend a honeymoon," Sherrie continued, squeezing his arm.

"Depends who you're with," John smirked.

They walked closer to the farmhouse.

Sherrie still held his arm. But she was silent now.

The wind blew colder than ever down and across the valley.

John's stomach turned over and he wondered whether it was from fear or from hunger.

Gotta get some food soon...

Maybe there'll be some in the farmhouse.

Lightning turned night to day for a moment in time.

The farmhouse looked like any other nondescript country shack. The timber frame looked solid, but old and weathered. The heavy wrought iron verandah spanned the front of the house, and the peeling paint on the hand railing showed the house had stood in the valley for quite some time. The rock steps up to the front deck were pitted and pock-marked, proving they had probably weathered storms and winds like this for countless years.

As they got closer to the house, the verandah loomed over them like a dark cloak, ready to swallow them in its darkness. The windows looked like the deathly black eye sockets of a long-forgotten skull.

Anyone could be watching us from those windows and we wouldn't even know it.

The rain fell harder.

Thunder echoed through the night.

Lying on its side on the edge of the deck was a dead cactus poking out from a terra-cotta bowl. It looked like it had died from lack of water.

Too bad you couldn't hang on until tonight, John thought.

Sherrie grabbed his hand and pulled him to a stop just as they reached the front steps.

"I've got an uneasy feeling about this," she whispered.

He turned to face her. The rain was running down her face, pooling on her chin and dripping off.

He smiled at her, "I know. But it'll be okay."

"You sure?" she smiled worriedly.

He couldn't lie, "No."

Her smile disappeared.

"I wish I could be," he added.

The wind gusted and blew through them, sending its cold fingers through their bodies.

Metal scraped loudly in the distance; the noise echoing through the valley.

John snapped his head around, following the noise. He peered into the night and towards the other farmhouse.

Did it come from there?

The wind died and the sound disappeared with it.

"Did you hear that?" he whispered to Sherrie.

"Yeah," she said in a small voice.

"What *was* it?"

"I don't know," she came closer to him and whispered in his ear. "Just some loose metal flapping in the wind?"

"I hope so."

"Me too."

He turned to face her.

"Come on," he said. "Let's see if anyone's home."

"I love you, John," she said to him.

He smiled at her, "I love you too."

They walked up the steps and onto the deck.

"Here goes everything!" he muttered.

As lightning and thunder clashed around them, he knocked on the door.

And the sound of metal scraping somewhere in the valley echoed loudly around them once more.

Sixty-one

Sherrie cupped her hands around her face and peered in the last window along the deck.

"Nothing," she called to him. "The place looks empty."

John straightened up from looking in his window. He could see very little through the glass anyway. He could make out the rooms inside, but not much more than that. There certainly wasn't any furniture and no sign anyone had lived there for quite a while.

"I know," he called to her from the other end of the deck. "It doesn't even look like it's been lived in for years."

Thunder rolled above them and the house and verandah creaked with it.

They had knocked on the door three times.

But no one answered.

The house was as dead as it looked.

"Strange that the door was locked," he continued. "If the place was abandoned, why lock the door?"

Sherrie chuckled, "Force of habit?"

John turned to her and smiled, "I don't think so, somehow."

"Well," Sherrie said as she walked back towards him. "At least we're out of the rain."

"For now, yeah."

John turned from her, placed his hands on the railing and looked across the field to the second farmhouse.

No luck here...

Does that surprise you?

No. I think he's in the other one.

Do you really think he's still there?

I don't know. Either way, I have to find Helen if she's still there. Or at least find out what happened to her.

Zoe told you already.

I know.

Don't you believe her?

Yes, I do. I think so.

You don't believe her?

I don't know. Something doesn't feel right. It never has. Not since Friday.

The wind gusted again and he could make out the same metallic noise creaking in the night. Echoing like a metal death call.

What the hell is that noise?

Sherrie was by his side then.

"Well, one building down. Two to go."

He smiled and turned to face her.

She looked up at him and smiled back.

That smile, the face framed in her long curly locks, her bright shining eyes and gorgeous voice…he knew how special she was to him.

He had no doubt about that.

Never did.

He had felt that way from the first moment they met, almost two years ago.

And if it weren't for Fate or good luck, he may never have met her.

But he was so glad he did.

He never made a habit of visiting Helen at the hospital. Most times she was too busy to talk or was off somewhere and couldn't be contacted. But on this particular occasion, he wanted to call by and see how she was.

They'd had an argument the night before; he couldn't remember about what now, as all their arguments blended into one whole dark pit of despair. He had found himself in the area as he came back from a meeting with some suppliers for a new project he was beginning at American Eagle Electronics.

He'd dropped by to see her.

Spur of the moment….

Without thinking.

As if drawn to the hospital.

He'd parked his car out front and walked past the gift shop to reception. He smiled nicely at the receptionist and asked for Helen. The receptionist paged her, but when she didn't come within a couple of minutes, she placed a call through to her office.

Carol wasn't sharing an office with Helen then.

Someone else was.

Sherrie.

Sherrie had told the receptionist that Helen was in a meeting and that John could come through if he liked and could wait for her.

John agreed.

He followed the directions the receptionist had given him and walked down a series of corridors to Helen's office.

And that's when he first set eyes on Sherrie.

He opened the door and she was standing there, waiting for him, a large smile on her face.

"It's *so* good to finally meet you, John," she said as she walked over and shook his hand. "Helen's told me *all* about you."

John smiled. He didn't know what to say.

His voice wouldn't work.

He just stood and looked at her. Brown curly hair flowed around her face, her smile was radiant and her sharp green eyes pierced through his soul.

She was slim and attractive in her business suit, which consisted of a brown jacket and cream blouse, and a short brown skirt that showed off her sexy, smooth legs.

"Have a seat," she said as she turned away from him. "I'm Sherrie, by the way."

Her cute small arse was cupped nicely by her skirt.

John fumbled for the seat. He needed it.

"Nice to meet you," he replied finally.

"Anything I can do for you?" she asked.

John's mind wouldn't work. He smiled.

He knew what he wanted, but that's not what she meant.

"No thanks," he said. "It's okay. I'm just waiting."

"She won't be long," Sherrie replied. As she sat behind her desk, her legs disappeared from view.

"Huh?"

"Helen? She won't be long."

"Oh, okay, fine," John looked towards the window, trying hard to think of other things.

They were silent for quite a while.

"Helen's told me all about you," Sherrie broke the silence.

John looked at her in surprise, "Really?"

Sherrie smiled, "Well, actually, no. She doesn't talk much about her home life."

John nodded. "That doesn't surprise me. She never talks about work at home either."

"Doesn't she?" Sherrie leaned forward, her green eyes so inviting.

"Nah, she likes to leave work behind when she comes home."

"So she's never mentioned *me?*" she asked.

John shook his head, "No, she hasn't."

Sherrie's smile fell, "Oh…"

"But I wish she had," John continued.

Sherrie smiled as she jotted something down on her desk pad. "Thanks," she said.

"No, I mean it," John replied. "Maybe I *should* take a more active interest in my wife's work."

Sherrie looked back at him and placed the pen to her mouth. "Maybe you should."

They had both smiled then.

Their conversation was interrupted just a few minutes later when Helen returned from her meeting. She seemed agitated and angry.

For a while John couldn't work out why.

To begin with he thought it was because he had arrived unannounced, but then he soon realised it was probably because he and Sherrie had been alone together.

They were both smiling when Helen entered the office.

That was bad.

And when John couldn't give her a good reason for why he called in, he could see that she was already thinking the worst.

Helen had been like that ever since losing the baby. Almost as if she were afraid someone would steal him away from her and pull them further apart. She never seemed to realise she was doing all that herself.

John dropped in a few times after that, always around the same time, always hoping Helen was in a meeting.

But she never was.

And that just fanned her suspicions even more.

But who could blame her?

I didn't fire her. I didn't kick her out of a job two weeks later!

No, but Helen did.

She fired Sherrie for no good reason.

Except spite.

And it wasn't until John risked another visit the following week that he found out the news.

"Sherrie at lunch?" he'd asked Helen in the middle of a conversion.

Bad move.

Real. Bad. Move.

"No, she doesn't work here anymore," Helen replied, her look sending daggers through him.

"Oh, she moved on?"

"No, I fired her."

"*Fired* her? What for?"

"She wasn't very good at her job," Helen replied, and quickly changed the subject.

But he knew.

They *both* knew.

Things had never really been the same after that.

And it was almost as if Fate interrupted their lives again when he saw Sherrie walking down the street near his office a couple of weeks later.

He invited her for coffee. She agreed.

They had lunch. He apologised for his wife. She said it wasn't his fault.

He offered her a job as his personal assistant right there and then. And she accepted.

The timing was perfect as his boss had mentioned the idea of getting him a personal assistant only a few days earlier.

The money wasn't as good as she was used to, but John helped out when he could.

And he *never* told Helen.

"As long as I'm with you," Sherrie whispered to him over his desk on her first day. "I don't care about anything else."

And everything fell into place perfectly.

Until last Friday.

Until Zoe.

Things could never be the same again.

John turned to Sherrie and ran his hand up her back, trying to warm her from the cold.

She smiled at him.

"We better get going," she whispered.

He nodded.

They walked from the decking, back into the rain, and down the driveway to the other farmhouse.

<u>Sixty-two</u>

John's unease grew with each step they took towards the second farmhouse.

You shouldn't be doing this.

I HAVE to!

He thought about running for cover, hiding until the storm dispersed and morning came, but he knew he couldn't wait.

If anyone's watching us, they'll have seen us by now, anyway.

They continued walking up the driveway.

Show Fox you're not scared of him. March right in there and meet him face to face.

The driveway was long and muddy, and when the lightning flashed above them, John checked the ground for signs of the Jeep's tyre tracks. And Helen...

Or anything...

Just something to confirm in his mind he was doing the right thing.

But the rain was too heavy and had been falling too long. The driveway was awash with thin streams of water, rushing downward towards the dirt road, and taking the lose dirt and gravel of the driveway with it.

Sherrie stepped closer and hugged his arm as thunder rolled down the valley.

We shouldn't be here.

You're risking everything now.

Everything that's left of your life.

John didn't even know if he was angry anymore. He didn't feel as angry as he thought he would. The events of the last few days had exhausted him, and with no food since Saturday, he felt like he was walking on auto-pilot.

He *had* to find Fox and beat him.

Kill him.

Win the game.

Had to...

But he had no plan, and no energy to see it through.

This is wrong.

And now he was dragging Sherrie into it all.

Sherrie...

They walked closer to the farmhouse through the sleeting rain.

John's legs felt heavy and numb from the cold and his wet shirt rubbed against the claw marks on his chest.

He turned to look at Sherrie.

Her hair was clumped into long wet cords down her head, shoulders and back. She looked miserably cold and forlorn.

He wished he could say something to her.

She's with me through this. She's by my side supporting me.

Helen never did that.

Don't think that way.

But it's true. She's here for me, no matter what. She'll stand by me through anything.

That's what true love is.

And that's what I have with her.

That's why I love her more than anything or anyone else.

John turned away and surveyed the fields that were surrounding them. When lightning broke, he peered off into the darkness. There were no signs of Fox's guards anywhere in the fields.

No sign of anyone.

Maybe that's the idea, he thought. *Maybe Fox has them hidden, waiting just for the right moment for the crossfire...*

Just like they did with Helen...

Don't think like that.

It's true...

They walked on.

The rain continued to fall.

John couldn't believe they had walked so far and for so long out in the open without being stopped or seen by someone. Was Fox really *that* sure of himself?

He won't be soon.

A few feet closer.

Lightning lit up the sky, a double fork that spread its glow for seconds.

As John looked to the farmhouse, his heart sank and so did his hopes.

The lightning told the story.

The farmhouse was a ruin.

John saw enough of it in those split-seconds to know for sure that Fox wasn't here.

And that realization cut right through him, sending his mind reeling in the stormy night.

No! It can't be true!

Thunder clashed and another flash of lightning confirmed what he had seen.

The old wooden farmhouse was almost falling down. Part of the wooden-slated roof was missing, leaving a large hole over half the house. The planks of wood making up the walls were old and dirty. The paint was peeling and some of the wood had come away from the frames, falling to the ground or with one end just hanging in the air. There was no glass in the three windows facing them. There were two doors along the front of the house; the first one was wide open and swinging in the wind and the second was resting on the ground, having fallen from its rusted hinges.

The verandah, or what was left of it, was being propped up with two old weather-beaten pine trunks that must have been cut from the forest for that exact purpose. The iron sheeting on the verandah was loose and flapping in the wind, held on only by a few remaining nails. The gutters that ran across the verandah were twisted and rusted and, in some parts, missing completely. The rain poured right through them, bending them under the force. Weeds and grass had grown up the front steps and through the decking, almost covering it completely and hiding it from view. The brick chimney on the side of the house had fallen over backwards, spilling its bricks into the grass beyond, leaving a huge hole in the farmhouse wall.

No one could live here...

But could they kill here?
Probably.
"Not very inviting," Sherrie said as they stopped in front of the house.

"I know," John agreed.

"I don't think anyone's home. Do you?"

John shook his head.

"Should we?" Sherrie asked. "You know, should we go *in*?"

"With the rain like it is, I think it's our best option."
She nodded and held out her hand.

He took it and smiled.

She's by my side. Even now. And she'll never leave it.
And I'll never leave her...
Together they climbed the rickety steps to the decking. Each sodden weed-covered wooden board under their feet seemed to creak and moan, and sag under their weight.

"Not the safest house..." Sherrie muttered as she squeezed his hand harder.

They walked up to the front door and pushed it aside.

John peered into the house.

A putrid wet smell overpowered him and he quickly began breathing through his mouth.

"Ick!" Sherrie said from beside him. "What *is* that stench?"

"I don't know," he replied. "But it's pretty foul."

John peered into the darkness, trying to make out anything that he could. Lightning lit up the night sky and the inside of the house.

The house was just as badly weathered inside as it was outside. The walls were stripped almost bare, the drywall soggy and crumbling to the ground. Large gaping holes remained in the wooden frames of the walls, allowing John to see almost all the way through the house.

Rain fell heavily into the rooms where there was no roof, and trickled into rooms that had some of the wooden slats still in place above them.

Thunder rolled, shaking the house as it did so.

John grabbed the doorframe until the vibrations subsided.

The wind blew directly through the house, entering from where the chimney and fireplace used to be. It blew through to the other end of the house where the only wall consisted of two large sheets of metal, nailed together and flapping in the wind. There was enough space at the side of the metal sheets for John to see out into the night and across to the barn.

The rain became heavier, pounding down on the roof in a deafening dance.

Lightning flashed again, filling the house.

And in the middle of the house he saw it.

An old green door.

It was shut.

There's another room!

Another room behind the green door.

There has to be.

John took a step into the house.

"Be careful," Sherrie whispered to him.

"I will," he let go of her hand. "You stay here, okay? This could be dangerous."

"Okay," she said in a quiet, scared voice that was drowned out by the rain and thunder.

He looked at the floor to watch where he was stepping. Another flash of lightning showed him that some of the floorboards were missing. There were complete gaps in the floor where floorboards had rotted away, while other areas still had enough flooring to get him to the green door.

Careful, don't do anything stupid when you're this close...

Slowly, he zigzagged his way across the floor, stepping cautiously across the gaps and testing each board he stepped on. Some groaned and some sagged, but they all held firm.

He moved from what once was the entranceway through to what he guessed was the lounge room. Each step took him closer to the door. The rain hit him hard as it fell through the hole in the roof over the lounge room.

He braced himself as he stared at the door.

It could open at any time. He had to be ready for anything – or any*one* – to come out at him.

But the door remained shut as he walked closer. He could see the paint on the door was peeling, and the old yellow wallpaper that had once brightened the room now sagged and slowly disintegrated. In one section of wallpaper, just to the right of the door, John could see dozens of small pockmarks.

Bullet holes?

Thunder growled above him.

There's so many!

After what seemed like an eternity, he made it to the door.

Carefully, he reached out to the old rusted doorknob and grasped it. It felt cold and rough to his touch.

"Here goes everything," he whispered to himself.

He turned the knob and pulled.

The door resisted for a second or two, but then swung open with a loud creak of its hinges.

John only opened it a few inches before he peered inside.

He waited for his eyes to adjust to the extra darkness.

The room behind the green door was dry and weatherproofed. The roof was intact and the walls looked solid. The overpowering smell, however, was stronger in this room compared to the others.

No ventilation to clear it away, he thought.

Lightning flashed outside a few seconds later, illuminating the room through two windows on each side.

These windows had glass in them.

He opened the door wider.

The wallpaper was yellow and old, but it was complete here, as was the flooring. There was no space for the rain or wind to get in, no leaking roof or bullet-ridden walls.

John took a step inside the room.

Thunder clapped outside, but it sounded muffled from where he was standing.

The room looked like a normal room in any house. It was a bit damp and the strange smell was nauseating, but it could've passed for any room in an old farmhouse.

Weird...

Lightning flashed through the windows again and the darkest corner was illuminated for only moments.

He saw the mattress for the first time.

And the clothes piled on it.

He turned, walked over to the corner and knelt down.

It was a small double mattress, covered with a moth-eaten blanket and the small pile of clothes.

He grabbed the clothes and held them in his hands.

It was too dark to make out exactly what he was looking at. So he knelt in the night, waiting for the next flash of lightning to strike.

Soon they came.

He was ready for the flash, and when it came he made good use of it.

He was holding in one hand a suit top and a blouse, and in the other, a skirt and bra.

Leaning forward, he smelled the bra.

My God!

There was no doubt about it. It was Helen's smell. It was Helen's bra!

These are Helen's clothes!

Nooo, please no!

Zoe was right!

Oh God, oh GodohGod!

It happened here, right here, just as she said it did!

Thunder rolled through the valley outside.

The clothes fell from his hands as he stared down at the mattress, his mind reeling as all the facts fell into place.

Everything Zoe said was true.

It's all true!

His mind was spinning in the darkness. He staggered to his feet. Lightning struck again, flooding the mattress with light. It was a dingy, flat mattress laying on the dirty floor. Its stuffing was falling out in places and there were stains all over it.

Stains John didn't want to think about.

Thunder echoed around him.

Oh, Helen. I'm so sorry.

Oh God!

No, it can't be true! It can't happen like this!

*You fucking bastard, Fox. I'll hunt you down, you fuck,
no matter how long it takes!*

He kicked hard at the mattress.

Kicked again.

And heard the metal scrape loudly in the night.

Huh?

He bent down over the mattress and felt around it carefully.

His heartbeat was as loud as the rain hammering on
the roof.

He didn't want to run his hands through the moth-eaten
blanket. But he was sure he heard something clank against
the wall.

He could find nothing on top of the blanket, but he felt a
hard shape underneath it.

In the dark, he pulled the blanket back and ran his hands
over the mattress itself. It was cold and damp and sticky.

The chill of fear spread up his spine.

Eventually his hands came across the cold hard metal.
He picked it up and felt its shape in the dark. He didn't need
any lightning to tell him what it was.

Some kind of shovel? A small shovel or spade?

I don't get it...

Lightning flashed.

Illuminated the mattress and his hands.

And the red stain that was on both.

Reflecting the streak of lightning, the blood gleamed in
the night.

All over the mattress.

All over his hands.

John let out a yelp and staggered backwards, pushing
himself away from the mattress and the dark corner.

The shovel flew from his grasp as he pushed back.

Blood! Oh God, no!

The shovel clattered loudly to the floor.

"John?"

It didn't register at first. His eyes were still glued to the
bloody mattress in the dark corner.

Thunder surrounded him.

So much blood, oh my god, somuchblood!

"*JOHN!*"

He heard Sherrie's voice then, but he couldn't call out. He had no time. Words wouldn't form in his mouth.

He heard the running footsteps.

He heard the crash.

And he heard Sherrie scream.

<u>Sixty-three</u>

John grabbed at the walls.

The door!

He swung around in the dark, searching frantically.

The door!

His nails tore at the wallpaper, reaching out, trying to find the door.

Lightning struck as the rain fell harder, almost blocking out Sherrie's screams altogether.

He was at the wrong wall. He saw the door out of the corner of his eye as the lightning flashed.

He turned and rushed to it in the dark.

His foot hit something as he ran, and it clattered away into another corner.

Sherrie screamed again.

John grabbed the knob of the door and turned it.

The door was stuck.

It must've closed behind me or blown shut or something!

Or it's locked from the outside.

No!

Sherrie screamed again as thunder shook the night.

He pushed harder.

The door gave a little, creaking as it did so.

Harder still.

The door flung open and he staggered out into the lounge room.

At first, he couldn't see anyone, but he could still hear Sherrie screaming.

The rain poured down onto him through the hole in the roof. He pushed it from his eyes as he looked around the house.

"Sherrie?" he yelled. "Where are you?"

"Here," she called back, fear and pain in her voice. *"Quickly!"*

John zeroed in on her voice. It was coming from near the doorway, but there was no sign of her.

"Where?" he called.

"Here, in the entranceway!"

He looked but he couldn't see her.

Not until the lightning flashed again.

And fear rippled through him.

He saw her hands first, and then her head and shoulders. But that was all.

The flash of lightning was all he needed.

Sherrie had fallen through the floorboards and was wedged up to her chest. Her arms swung in the air frantically, reaching out across the room to him.

Carefully he walked towards her, making sure he didn't make the same mistake she did.

He couldn't afford to put one step wrong now.

"What happened?" he asked as he came closer.

"I thought you were in trouble," she said as she stretched for him.

"*Me?*"

"Yeah. You were in that room so long. There was no sound or anything and then I hear this crash of metal or something…and I guess I just panicked. I thought they'd got you or something had gone wrong and I was coming to get you."

John nodded as he knelt by her.

"You've got to watch these old floorboards," he said to her. "Half the floor's missing."

"I know that!"

"And the other half is very dangerous."

"*Now* you tell me!"

He reached out to her as thunder and lightning struck.

Sherrie noticed the stains on his hands.

"What's that on your hands?" she asked.

John pulled them back quickly.

"Nothing," he said, wiping them on his jeans. "Just some oil. It was in that room. I accidentally stumbled onto it."

"Yuk."

"Yeah, I know."

He leaned forward and she lifted her arms higher so he could reach behind her.

"Are you hurt anywhere?" he asked.

"No, I don't think so. I'm just stuck," she replied as she wrapped her arms around his neck. "And embarrassed."

"That's okay, honey. It's good to know you're willing to be my hero."

"Yeah, some hero," she muttered. *"You're* the one saving *me!"*

John lifted her. She rose slightly and then gave out a yelp of pain.

Not that easy...

Quickly, he lowered her back down.

"You *sure* you're okay?" he asked.

"I thought so," Sherrie said, her hand disappearing under the floorboards and touching her side. *"Ouch!"*

"I don't think you are," he replied.

"Well, I can't just sit here," she said. "I'm already in a puddle of something I don't want to think about. Its all scummy and awful under here."

John nodded as he stood and looked around, "I know. I'll get you out somehow. I just don't think pulling you out is going to help if you've bruised or cracked some ribs."

"Yes, Dr. Murdock," she replied.

John turned to stare at her. "I want you in one piece when we leave here. We've got a long walk back to Hepburn Lakes. And I don't want to leave you to go and get help."

"Well, that's one thing you *won't* be doing," she replied. "You're not leaving me here all alone like this."

"Exactly."

Sherrie put both hands on the floorboards and tried to lift herself up.

She let out another cry of pain.

"Shit," she muttered as she slumped backwards. "I'm stuck down here!"

"Sure looks like it," John nodded as he turned back to her. "We need something to lever you out."

"Don't happen to have a can opener on you?" She tried to sound cheerful, but it didn't work.

John knelt back in front of her and pulled at the floorboards surrounding her body. The rain fell hard on his back and head and ran into his eyes.

He pulled, but each of the boards stayed firm.

"Looks like you picked the worst spot to lodge yourself," he said to her.

"Thanks for the pep talk, coach."

"What can you feel down there?" he asked her.

"Cold and numb," she replied. "Although, I guess if I'm numb I can't feel anything…"

"No, I mean what's holding you down here? Is it just floorboards?"

Sherrie's hands disappeared under the floor for a few seconds.

"The floorboards are around me," she said as she felt around. "But there's like this huge beam or something running the other way across my legs and hips. I'm stuck under that."

"It's the support for the floorboards," John nodded. "How did you fall?"

"Awkwardly," she muttered.

John smiled, "I mean, which way?"

"Feet first, obviously," she replied.

"I *know* that. But you must've fallen at an angle to wedge yourself like this."

"Well, honey," she was sounding agitated now. "You're the engineer! I didn't have time, as I wedged myself down here, to check the angle of my fall or the velocity of my re-entry into the earth's surface via the circumference of the radius ring or whatever."

Silence fell between them then.

Only the rain continued.

John leaned forward and kissed her soft wet lips.

"We have to get you *out*," John said as they parted.

"Sure, Sherlock. That was my plan too," she agreed.

"I'll try pulling you up one more time, okay?"

She reached upwards as he stood and came towards her. She wrapped her arms around his neck again.

"Tell me as soon as this hurts, okay?"

"Okay," she whispered in his ear.

She sounded scared.

John couldn't blame her.

Lightning flashed as he pulled.

She moved upwards, slightly higher this time. He could hear her breathing increase and he knew she was hurting. He kept pulling. Her arms tightened around his neck, slipping slightly as he pulled.

One more try.

But it was no use.

She was stuck.

He lowered her once more and stepped back to look at her as thunder drummed the night.

She was in pain, he could tell from her face.

She just doesn't want to say it.

"No good, huh?" she said after she had regained her breath.

He shook his head.

"I'm going to have to lever you out with something. Pull up these boards and lift the cross-beam away from you."

"And you're not carrying a crowbar by any chance?" she looked hopefully at him with a half-hearted smile.

He shook his head, "No."

Her bottom lip trembled and she looked away from him.

"What will we do?"

"I'll have to find something to use," he replied.

"But there's *nothing* here."

"There might be in the barn."

Her head swung back to him.

"You're going to *leave* me?"

"Only for a few minutes."

"Leave me *here*? All by myself?"

"Sweets, we don't have any *choice*! I have to find something to get you out of there!"

She raised her hands to her face, wiping the hair and rain away.

And tears?

The rain eased slightly and the wind blew through the house, chilling them both.

"Okay," she said with a deep sigh as she looked back to him. "You're right. We don't have any choice, do we?"

"No," John agreed.

She sighed again.

"Then make it quick," she replied in a quiet voice.

John nodded. "I will. I'll be back as soon as I find something to help get you out."

He smiled, but he knew it was fake.

He turned from her quickly, trying to hide the fear in his eyes.

She can't stay wedged under there.

I HAVE to get her out somehow!

But how?

He walked past her and out the front door as thunder rolled through the valley.

"Hurry, honey!" she called after him.

He walked out onto the decking, stared out into the night and across at the barn.

It was his only hope.

There's got to be something in there I can use, he thought to himself.

There has to be.

What if there isn't?

He hoped to God that there was.

Sixty-four

Every step he took brought him closer to the barn and further away from Sherrie.

He didn't want to dwell on what she must be thinking. He didn't want to think about the horror she must be experiencing being left stuck in a condemned house all alone on a night like this.

He looked up into the dark sky and watched as lightning flashed overhead.

Will this ever end?

He studied the barn as he walked closer towards it. At first he thought it was new, certainly constructed more recently than the farmhouses. But as he got closer and the lightning allowed him to study it, he realised the barn was probably just as old as the farmhouses. It was just kept in better condition. It looked as if it had been painted just recently, the red paint shiny and reflective in the rain, and there was no sign of the dilapidation that was present in the farmhouses.

Who keeps a barn all spic-and-span while they let their house rot away?

Thunder clashed around him.

He kept an ear out for Sherrie, just in case she was calling for him. But in the rain and with the thunder, he knew he had very little chance of hearing her now.

He wrapped his arms around his chest. He was shivering even more now and his breath fogged in the air around him as he walked. His chest and arm wounds were itching under his shirt, but the pain in his cock was just a dull ache.

He wanted to think about Helen and what Fox must have done to her in that small room.

All that BLOOD!

But he couldn't. His mind wouldn't let him.

He wiped his hands on his jeans again.

Can't think about that now...

Sherrie was in trouble and he had to fix that problem first.

He just hoped there was something in the barn that was strong enough to use as a lever.

If not...?

I don't know.

What will you do?

I don't know!

He stopped out the front of the barn. Standing in the rain, he concentrated on his hearing and listened for what seemed like an eternity.

All he could hear was the never-ending pelt of the rain on the ground around him and on the barn roof. It was accompanied by thunder as it rolled on by.

The barn had two large sliding doors, painted in red with a white sash running diagonally across both doors.

He stepped closer and reached out for the handle.

Then he changed his mind.

Be careful.

He had to be, for Sherrie's sake.

Wiping the rain from his eyes and running a hand through his hair, he turned and walked across the front of the barn and down one of its long sides.

He knew what he was looking for, and he found it about halfway down.

Walking as quietly as he could, trying hard to keep his footsteps from sloshing in the wet grass, John sidled up to the barn's window.

The sill was at shoulder height, so he made sure he stood to the side of the pane before carefully looking inside.

He wanted to make sure he wasn't about to be surprised by anything – or anyone.

He knew he'd have to wait for some lightning to see what was inside the barn, but a few seconds wait wasn't going to hurt.

He peered through the window.

But he didn't have to wait for the lightning.

He could see inside already.

He spotted the large bales of hay first. Dozens of them, lined up along the far wall of the barn, some stacked three high. He looked for any farm equipment, but he could see none. In the far corner was a workbench. Nailed to the wall above the bench was a variety of tools. Different sorts, different shapes and sizes. Almost a dozen. From saws to hammers, sanders and screwdrivers.

Yes!

John was sure he could find something to help get Sherrie out from under the floor.

He couldn't tell what they all were from this distance and in this light, but he was sure he could make do.

Pretty impressive tool collection, he thought.

And then he remembered Fox.

That's probably what he uses on them...

And all of a sudden John felt sick and weak all over again.

I can't do this.

I can't beat Fox.

You have to try.

How can I beat someone like that?

First thing's first. Get Sherrie out!

Yes! I have to do that first.

Concentrate on Sherrie.

YES! I'm coming, my love!

His eyes darted to the other side of the barn, across to where the two sliding doors were. There was no sign of anyone inside.

Good.

And then his eyes spotted it.

He saw the reason he could see so clearly into the barn without the aid of the lightning.

A burning candle sat on one of the hay bales.

A candle?

It burned a soft light in the night, licking at the air.

The rain fell heavier. Thunder and lightning clashed almost at once.

He had no choice. He had to get those tools and get Sherrie out of here.

Maybe I can't fight Fox at his own game, he thought as he dashed back through the drenched grass to the front of the barn. *I just need to save myself and Sherrie. I have to think about her now.*

And about us.

His breath steamed from his mouth as he reached out to the barn door and slid it open.

It squealed along its rusty old track as the lightning struck overhead.

Just get the tools, get Sherrie and get the fuck out of here!

He stepped into the barn, closed the door behind him and dashed straight over to the old wooden workbench.

Thunder shuddered the earth. Rain battered the roof.

Yes! he thought. *So many to choose from!*

Hang on, my love. Here I come!

He reached up for the nearest one.

"I knew you'd come," Zoe said from behind him

Sixty-five

He turned to face her.

She was standing near one of the hay bales, wearing the bondage outfit she had worn at the church.

The black leather straps circled her breasts and stretched down her stomach. He could see the diamond shining in her belly button. His eyes dropped lower. The straps between her legs were missing.

He could see all of her again, including her pink, shaved lips.

Zoe...

He followed her long thin legs to the ground. She was wearing no shoes.

"I knew if I waited for you, you'd come to me," she continued.

Her hair was no longer in braids; it was wet and untied. It framed her face and fell from her shoulders in a chaotic mess, resting on the tops of her breasts. There was a dark bruise on her forehead and a jagged cut on her left cheek. Helen's half-heart pendant was still hanging around her neck. She looked soaked through.

John opened his mouth to speak, but Zoe took a step forward and held out her hand.

"You don't have to say anything, Johnny," her voice dropped in pitch. "You're here now. That's all that matters."

She smiled at him.

John's heart sank.

Oh, Zoe...

"You're back with me," she stepped closer to him.

John moved back against the workbench.

"I'm not here for you, Zoe," he said slowly. "I'm here to get some of these tools, and that's all."

Zoe tilted her head to one side, a puzzled look crossed her face. "Tools?"

John's mind spun quickly.

"Yes," he said. "I need them."

"What for?"

"It doesn't concern you."

"*Everything* concerns me," Zoe said as she stepped closer.

"Just let me take some of these and then I'll go."

"I don't want you to go, Johnny."

"I have to. And I *will*."

"That's not part of the game," she replied.

The wind howled around the barn. The rain pounded the roof.

John kept his eyes on Zoe while his hands fumbled behind him on the workbench, feeling for anything he could use as a weapon.

"There is *not* a game, Zoe..." he told her.

"Life's a game, Johnny."

"Not mine."

"You're wrong about that," she smiled as she stepped closer again.

She was standing in the middle of the barn now. The flickering candle made her body glow and shimmer in its light. Shadows ran up and down her torso, making it seem alive with energy.

Lightning flashed through the barn window and was followed by the loud growl of thunder just seconds later.

"You still want me, don't you?" she asked as she placed her hands on her hips.

He said nothing.

Zoe smiled. Slowly, she squatted down without taking her eyes off him. He watched her as her legs spread wide, opening herself to him.

Oh God...

"You want more of this, don't you?" her voice was a sexy growl.

John said nothing.

She smiled at him and brought her hand over to her pussy, spreading the lips wide and showing him her soft velvety interior.

"You want more of *me...*"

He watched her as the pain burned through the bandages of his cock.

She slipped two fingers inside and slid her fingers back and forth.

Lightning flashed.

He watched on numbly, his hands no longer searching for a weapon.

"We *can't* do this," John finally said.

Her head tilted.

"This isn't right," he continued. "We *can't.*"

"Yes we can," she smiled at him.

"*No!*"

A frown crossed her face and she paused for a second to look at him. Then she smiled and stood up straight.

"I know," she nodded as she stepped even closer. "I understand. I know what this is all about."

John just watched her.

She crossed her arms over her breasts and pushed her right hip out to the side.

"Where's your girlfriend?" she asked, looking around him.

"She's *not* my girlfriend."

Zoe smiled. "Okay then, your lover."

"She's *not* that either!"

She smirked, and moved her hands to her back. "Oh, yes she is!"

"You don't know what you're talking about."

"Believe me, Johnny, I know *exactly* what I'm talking about."

She pulled the revolver out from behind her back. "And I have one bullet left that says I'm right!"

John's eyes darted to the gun in her hands. He braced himself to run.

"I wouldn't do that if I were you," she said, aiming the barrel at him. "I tend to get a little nervous when I've got my finger on the trigger. I wouldn't want to hurt you, believe me. I want to keep you intact, if possible."

He froze in his spot.

Shit, what the fuck do I do now?

"I find Mr. Revolver has a wonderful skill for making people tell the truth, Johnny," she said as she took another step towards him.

The candle was behind her now, off to her right. The flame threw flickering dancing shadows across her face. John couldn't read her expressions anymore; it was too dark to be sure.

"So let's play a little game of Johnny Tells The Truth, huh?"

He sighed deeply and nodded, hanging his head and looking to the floor.

Thunder rolled.

"It'll be a change for you, won't it?"

He looked up into her eyes.

"Not used to telling the truth, are you, Johnny?"

Play it cool...

"I...I don't know what you mean..."

Zoe shook her head. "No, no, we're not going to play it that way. It's not going to work, Johnny. I know more about you than you can imagine. So don't even *try* to hide anything from me."

She took one final step.

They were face to face now.

He could smell her, feel her breath and her heat.

The revolver was pointed at his face.

"After all," she smirked. "I can hardly miss you at this range."

He was silent for a few seconds.

"Okay," he whispered finally.

"Good," Zoe said as she swung around next to him and lifted herself up to sit on the workbench.

Her arm brushed his and left a wet patch on his skin.

Is she wet from the rain? Or is that oil spread all over her?

She rested the gun and her hands in her lap, just below the shining diamond in her belly button. She pulled her legs tightly together, cutting off his view of her pussy.

"You play the game properly and no one will get hurt," she continued.

John turned to face her.

So beautiful.

So crazy...

"So, I'll ask again," she smiled at him. "Where's your girl-friend?"

"Sherrie's at the farmhouse."

Zoe tilted her head and frowned.

"Which one?"

"The closest one. The one Fox owns."

"Why is she there?"

"I wanted her to be safe. I didn't want her coming over here, just in case anything went wrong."

"You left here in *that place*?"

He nodded. "It was for protection too. If Fox was here and I didn't come out, she knew what would've happened. I told her that if I'm not back to her in ten minutes, to start walking back to Hepburn Lakes and call for help."

Zoe smiled and shook her head.

She picked up the revolver and pointed it at his temple.

"Bong! I'm sorry, we have a wrong answer," she mimicked a TV voice-over man. "Care to try again, Mr. Murdock? Your time is fast running out."

"It's the *truth!*"

He looked deep into her eyes, but he knew she could tell he was lying.

"Try again," she replied. "*Quickly...*"

John sighed. "We were looking for Fox. We checked out the first farmhouse but there was no one there. We went to the second and while I was looking around, she fell through the floorboards and she's lodged there now. Stuck. I can't get her out. I came over here to see if there was anything I could use to get her out."

Zoe smiled and placed the gun back in her lap.

It's so close. I could grab it before she has a chance to move.

Too risky!

I have to do something.

It's all too risky!

Life's too risky for you, John. Everything's too damn risky!

"It's much easier when you tell the truth, Johnny. I thought you would've known that by now."

He just stared at her. Lightning flashed through the window.

"There's no way Sherrie would've just let you leave her in that shack. That's not like her. She would've been by your side no matter what, if she could. I know that much."

"How can you? How can you know all this? How?" he asked.

She looked away from him, across the barn to the hay bales on the other side.

"Johnny, where do I start?" she sighed. "There's so much I need to tell you."

He waited.

"I tried to tell you back at the church, I really did. I wanted you to know, but there was never a good time." She stared across at the candle flame. The shadows and light danced across her whole body. The diamond in her belly button flickered the reflection. "I *did* try to tell you at the church, Johnny. But you wouldn't stop and listen."

Thunder broiled above them.

"I was going to tell you when I got back from getting us the food this morning. I had it all planned," she smiled to herself, her eyes far away in her thoughts. "I was going to untie you and we'd sit at the table, like a real couple, and have breakfast together. Just like a *real* couple, for the first time. Just you and me, Johnny. After all this time, just you and me."

The rain eased on the roof. Suddenly the barn became very quiet. The silence between them stretched.

Zoe sighed again.

"But when I came back to you, I saw the knots, Johnny. You'd untied them somehow, I don't know how. But you'd re-tied them all wrong. When you're into the scene like I am, you notice the little things. The tiniest little details are the most important. I could tell you'd untied the ropes around your legs and also the leash on your cock ring. I could tell..."

Damn...

She knew!

"And then I just lost it. All my plans were shattered. You told me you would stay there on the bed, you told me you wouldn't move. You *promised me!* But you lied. You *lied* to me!" her eyes were still focussed on the flame. "I never thought you would lie to *me*, Johnny. Not after all we'd been through together."

A new wave of rain began pelting on the barn roof, and lightning flashed in the night.

"Zoe..." he whispered as he leaned towards her.

She closed her eyes, "Don't!"

Her hands clasped around the revolver.

Easy...easy...

Don't do anything stupid!

He leaned back against the workbench.

"And then *she* turned up. Out of nowhere she just walked into the church," Zoe shook her head and opened her eyes again.

Thunder shook the barn. The candle flame spluttered for a second or two.

"She was never meant to be a part of this," she continued. "I only wanted what was mine, Johnny. I only wanted to be loved."

John sighed and shook his head.

"Zoe," he whispered again.

She didn't stop him this time.

"I don't know what to say," he continued. "You know how I feel about you. I told you that already. But you can't capture love. You can't force your way into my heart. You couldn't keep me tied like that forever, you know."

She nodded and closed her eyes. Her bottom lip quivered. "I know," she whispered.

He eyed the revolver.

Grab it!

No, take it calm and easy. I'm winning here now. I'm winning!

"Now, I know we've all got problems and I know you've had a shitty life so far, but I meant everything I said about helping you get away from all that. I want to help you make a better life for yourself and get on your own feet and have the life you deserve to have."

She smiled. Tears escaped from the corners of her eyes, running down her face.

"Thank you," she whispered.

"We've all got problems we have to fix. And, at the moment, we both have the same problem. That's *why* I'm here. *That's* why we trekked this far through all the rain and all the mud and shit. We came this far so I could finish something for both of us."

She opened her eyes, turned and stared into his.

"I'm here to *kill* Fox, Zoe," he whispered to her. "And I don't care what it takes. We'll do it. And we'll do it together. We both deserve at least that. But I want you there with me when I do it. I want you to see him die in front of you. I want you to have your revenge for all those things he did to you!"

Zoe's expression changed. Her forehead creased. The scar in her left eyebrow shortened.

"But don't you get it yet, Johnny?" she said.

The rain increased.

"Ricky Fox doesn't exist!"

Sixty-six

The earth spun around him. The sound of rain and wind and thunder was loud in his ears.

He stared straight at her, but he was looking through her.

"That's what I wanted to tell you," she said to him. "Ricky Fox doesn't exist."

John's stomach turned over. He felt sick and weak and had to hold onto the side of the workbench. He felt as if he were going to topple.

Thunder shook the barn.

What?

What is she telling me?

No Ricky Fox.

No Fox.

"But….you said…" was all he could manage.

Zoe looked at him with sadness in her eyes. "I'm *sooo* sorry, Johnny." She reached out and touched his hair. "I made him up. He doesn't exist. It was just a story to get you to believe in me."

John felt hot and sweaty, like he was boiling up with fever. His chest was heavy; he couldn't breathe properly. He was being suffocated and there was nothing he could do about it.

The rain eased to a patter on the barn roof.

No! But…?

She's lying. She has to be!

She's lying now!

She doesn't want my help.

She's lying to get me to go away.

She MUST be!

He stared to the floor. Stray pieces of hay were caught in cobwebs under the workbench.

"But *Helen*…and all the blood…"

"That was *me*, Johnny. All me. I did all that."

John's mind drifted. He couldn't take it all in.

This isn't happening.

It can't be!

Why is she doing this to me?

She's LYING!

Why is she lying to me now?

"At first I just wanted what was mine," she was talking in a low quiet voice. John had to concentrate hard to listen to her. He had to keep his thoughts from running wild.

"I just wanted to take back what was mine. I just wanted to be *loved.* Is that too much to ask? I was going to tell Helen all about your little arrangement with Sherrie. That was *all* I was going to do, Johnny. I promise you. But it got out of control. *Waaay* out of control. "

John nodded, "It sure did."

Zoe turned from him and stared across the barn.

Lightning flashed outside.

Everything was silent.

No rain and no wind.

They sat for a long time.

"Fox *doesn't* exist…" he whispered.

"No," she replied. "It was all just a story to get you out here."

"But your history, your whole life…"

"Fabricated," she said in a small voice. "All lies, Johnny."

Thunder rolled in the distance.

"Just like yours," she continued.

He looked at her, but didn't say anything.

The silence in the barn was almost unnatural.

"I had to lie to make you believe in me," she continued after a while. "I had to get you out here. I needed you to trust me and to follow me out here. I was going to make sure you paid for what you'd done in the past. I wanted to ruin you. I wanted to make you pay *sooo* bad. That was the idea. I made it all up to get you out here. But then it went all wrong."

"Helen's dead?" he closed his eyes, waiting for the answer in the silence.

"Yes, Johnny," Zoe replied. "I didn't lie to you about that."

John hung his head, the earth feeling like it was slipping away from him.

"And…*you* killed her?"

"Yes," she replied. "Out there in the farmhouse. There's a bedroom in the back and –"

"I know, I know," he interrupted her. "I saw it."

"Oh," she sounded sad.

The wind gusted once more, howling in the night.

"It wasn't meant to happen that way," she continued.

John's mind was gearing up again, working through the events of the weekend as he remembered them, trying to piece it all together, step by step.

"And the calls from Fox? His men following you?"

"All lies," she muttered.

"You driving across the country to escape him? The fight you had with him?"

"Lies," she nodded. "It's *all* fake, Johnny. The whole thing."

The rain began to fall again.

John looked deeply into the candle flame across the barn.

Oh, Helen. Why? Why!

"Oh God," he shook his head.

"I thought it would be over so quickly," she continued. "I just had to tell Helen what you were doing. That would solve it all. But it got bigger, Johnny. Out of control. The whole thing just spun out of control and the longer it went on the more lies I told and the deeper I got. I wanted to tell you. I wanted to let you know! Believe me, I did!"

John ran a hand through his wet hair. Lightning flashed through the window.

"Helen wouldn't believe me," she continued. "Amazing, huh? I tried to tell her. But she wouldn't listen. She wouldn't believe any of my story. And, boy, she put up a fight. She fought for you, Johnny. Be proud of that fact. She fought for you *sooo* hard. And then I guess I just went a little too far."

John turned to her as thunder echoed through the valley.

The rain fell harder.

This can't be happening. My God, I have to get out of here.

I have to get Sherrie and we have to go! Leave now!
Shit! Sherrie! I have to get to her.
How long has it been?
I have to get to her before Zoe does.
She'll be going crazy.
Like the rest of us...
"I didn't want it to end up like this, Johnny. I really didn't." She turned to look at him. "It just got out of hand. The scenes got bigger and bolder. I couldn't stop myself. I set out to destroy you, but I couldn't. I wanted what was mine. But it was *sooo* good to be with you."

She paused before continuing.

"And I think I fell in love with you."

He stared back at her. Their eyes locked. He didn't know what to say.

"I just wanted you to love me too."

He sighed, spoke slowly. "But Zoe, I..."

She nodded, "I know, I know..."

Silence fell between them.

"I love Sherrie," he whispered. "I'm sorry Zoe, but I love Sherrie."

She nodded.

"I know," she raised the revolver. "And so do I."

His eyes darted to the gun pointing at his head.

"Game's over!" she said as she pulled the trigger.

Sixty-seven

He dived at her, tackling her and flinging her back against the workbench.

The gun fired close to his right ear as they fell backwards, the bullet shooting into the roof of the barn. His ear stung from the noise, a loud ringing taking over from the rain and thunder.

John reached out and struggled to pull the revolver from Zoe's grip. He could hear the hammer falling over and over as she pulled the trigger.

The gun was empty.

No use to me now.

He slammed her hand against the workbench and the gun jarred free, slipping across the bench and falling to the floor with a clatter.

He spread himself across her, trying to pin her to the bench. She struggled underneath him, clawing at his back and hair.

He reached up above the workbench for the tools, trying to grab a hammer that hung there. She grabbed at his left arm. He reached higher and then he felt her teeth bite into his wound.

The pain sliced up his arm and into his mind. He buckled forward, crashing down on to her. He heard the back of her skull hit the workbench hard. She froze for a moment, as if stunned, and then continued fighting him.

"She's mine," she yelled at him. "You leave her alone! She's *mine!*"

He reached out across the workbench with his left hand.

He noticed the quickly spreading bloodstain on his torn shirt. She'd opened his wound with her bite.

Bitch!

Fucking bitch!

He grabbed what he could find as firmly as possible. Metal or steel, cold and heavy.

He raised it above her.

"No!" she gasped. "Don't! Please?"

He stopped and looked at her; stared into her eyes.

Is that fear?

Or another lie?

"Please don't, Johnny," she pleaded and tried to smile. "You know I really *do* love you."

The gash on her left cheek looked deep.

Probably got it when she drove into Sherrie's car.

Serves her right.

I want to make it deeper…

The bruise on her forehead was darkening too.

"We can work something out," she continued. "We have to, for all of us."

John continued studying her.

What's the truth and what's a lie?

I don't know anymore.

It's all so confusing…

"Please, Johnny." Pain crossed her face as she talked. "You're *hurting* me."

He climbed off her, pushed her away in disgust, but still held his weapon high, ready to strike.

"I *do* love you, Johnny," she smiled as she sat up slightly on her elbows. "And I *know* how much you love Sherrie. Well, I do too. Maybe this is the best for *all* of us. Maybe we can *all* live together. We'd make a great threesome."

John sighed deeply and shook his head. He took a step away from her, lowering the weapon as he did so.

"You're not well, Zoe," he said to her as thunder rolled over them. "You need help. You're *sick…*"

"All the help I need is here," she replied. "You and Sherrie. Let's go get her and we can all go home together. Think of it, John. The two women you love, in bed with you every night, naked and hot and wet and horny."

She leaned forward, a new gleam in her eye, a smile breaking onto her face.

"It'd be just *sooo* wonderful. We'll do anything you want. *I'll* do anything you want. Fuck me like a dog, cum in my mouth until I gag, cum in my arse until I leak, fuck me until

I bleed…anything. As long as we're together, all of us. It'll be great."

John stepped back further.

"You just don't understand," he said.

Zoe spread her legs wide apart.

"You *want* this," she said. Showing him her wet pussy. "And you can have it all whenever you like. Remember how good we were together? Remember how it felt with my mouth around your cock? You haven't experienced *anything* yet, Johnny. You haven't been *inside* me. Inside my cunt. Imagine how good it would be to stick your hot cock inside me. I want you deep inside. You want to be there too, I *know* it."

Pain pumped through his cock as he felt himself harden.

"This isn't right," he said.

"But it's *good*," she replied.

"You *killed* Helen," he said. "And you *tortured* me! I can't *possibly* be with you."

Zoe rolled her eyes, closed her legs and pushed herself forward to sit on the corner of the workbench. She crossed her arms in front of her breasts.

"Don't get all high-and-mighty with me, Johnny," she said. "Need I remind you that *you're* the one fucking your personal assistant behind your wife's back! *You're* the one not sleeping in the same bed as your wife. *You're* the one who's wanted to fuck me every way you possibly could this weekend. If anything, I did you a *favour* killing Helen! You don't have to lie anymore!"

John tightened his grip on the metal in his hand.

"She called for you, you know," Zoe continued. "I told her the truth, but she wouldn't believe me. And just before she died, just before she let out her final breath, she called your name."

John shook his head, he felt dizzy and sick. Guilt swept over him. The room began to spin.

No! I can't hear this. NO!

He looked to the floor of the barn, he watched the tears well up in his eyes.

"Oh God," he muttered. "Helen…"

"She *really* loved you," Zoe continued in a soft voice. "But you didn't love her."

Nooo, oh no! Oh, fuck, what have I done?

This is all my fucking fault.

All because of me.

"If it helps any," Zoe continued. "I did it quick. She didn't feel much pain. I'm sure of it."

John lifted his head and stared at her. Tears ran down his cheeks, but he didn't care if she saw them – not now.

"How did you do it, *bitch?*" he asked in a strained voice. "How did you kill my wife?"

She pointed at his hand.

"With that."

Lightning struck and thunder roared across the barn.

He looked down at his hand.

And at the fireplace poker.

Its double-pronged tip was covered in dried blood. Some strands of hair were stuck to its side.

"I got her right on the temple, first time," Zoe continued. "It was quick. I assure you."

He dropped the poker. He watched as it fell away from him, almost in slow motion. It clattered to the floor and echoed around the barn.

The rain fell with it.

Zoe took a step towards him.

"I may have done it for me to begin with," she said as she took another step. "But in the end, I did it for *us*. All those years planning, for us. I just can't believe it's almost over. I did it for *all* of us. You and me and Sherrie."

He shook his head.

"We can all be together now. All three of us. We'll all be happy."

"No," John said through clenched teeth. "I won't let you get away with this."

"It's too late, Johnny," she said. "I already have."

"You can't go unpunished…"

"You already *know* I like to be punished. And so do you," she moved closer.

"Where is she?" John asked in a slow calm voice.

Keep a lid on it, pal. Don't lose it.

"You said she was at the farmhouse," she replied with a crooked smile.

"Not *Sherrie!* Where's *Helen?*"

"Well, she's not here," Zoe replied, shrugging her shoulders.

"I know that. *What* the *fuck* have you *done* with her?"

"She's around," she replied stepping closer to him, tilting her head and still smiling at him.

Lightning lit up the barn.

"Tell me, Zoe."

"She's out of harm's way for now. No one will find her. Not yet anyway."

John tensed, "What do you mean?"

"It's simple," she sighed. "She's my security, Johnny. I have to make sure both you and Sherrie will agree to my terms."

"*Terms?*" John's lip curled as he spat out the word. "What makes you think we'll agree to any terms you give us?"

"That's easy," she continued, only a couple of feet from him now. "We *will* all live together, as a threesome. And we *will* all love each other."

"We won't agree to that."

"Yes, you will," she said as she bent down and picked up the fireplace poker. "You have to."

"We won't."

Zoe shook her head, "Johnny, I thought you would've understood by now."

"Look, Zoe," he interrupted. "Your sick little fucked up game is over. You've lost. I'm walking out of here, taking Sherrie with me and I'm going to find Helen's body and then we'll go straight to the police."

"I wouldn't dooo thaaat," she replied in a little girl's voice as she stood back up with the poker in hand.

"I'm *going* to do it, and I'm going to do it *now!* You don't control me, Zoe, not anymore."

He marched past her, heading for the door.

"Yes I do!" she called after him.

He kept walking.

You need some of the tools for Sherrie!

I can't risk it. I can't stop now. I'll find another way to get her out.

How?

I'll get her out somehow. I just can't stay here! Not now!

"She's at the church," Zoe said from behind him.

John stopped in his tracks and turned to face her.

She was licking the tip of the poker, licking off the dried blood and hair that was stuck there.

Helen's blood and hair!

"She's at the *church?*" John repeated.

"Well, sort of," Zoe continued as she licked. "Nearby anyway."

John turned to leave, "You're one sick *fuck*, you know that?"

"Aren't we all?"

He placed his hand on the barn door.

"Don't go to the police, Johnny!" she called after him.

He rested his forehead on the cold wooden door and closed his eyes. He just wanted everything to go away.

"And give me one good reason not to," he replied.

"Game one is over," she called back in a sing-song voice. "But game two is only just beginning!"

"Huh?" he turned to face her.

"Life's full of choices, Johnny," she smiled at him and rested the poker across her left shoulder. "And so is this game. You can play it my way, or yours. But believe me, my way is much easier. Want to hear the rules?"

He nodded slowly, a heavy feeling of uneasiness settled on him as the thunder shuddered around the barn.

Things were about to get a whole lot worse.

He knew it.

"My way is easy," she continued. "You and me and Sherrie go home together and fuck until we're exhausted for the rest of our lives. Easy."

"Go on..." he said.

"To help you decide that my way is the best, I've got some security up my sleeve."

She fingered the half-heart gold pendant still hanging around her neck.

"Helen's somewhere near the church, that's true. But there's nothing to link her to me."

"Apart from my testimony…and Sherrie's."

Zoe smiled, "Good boy, you're thinking finally!"

She looked pleased with him.

"But the trouble is," she continued, "you and Sherrie have been having an affair. A *loooong* hot steamy affair. Your very own secret little fuck-fest. Helen was in the way. Suddenly she goes missing from work. Then, so do you. And then, so does Sherrie. All *very* murky, don't you think? Gossip will already be rife at American Eagle Electronics. The cards you leave for Sherrie are still at her home. She kept them all in a little vase on the top of the dresser in her bedroom. She'd look at them every night when she was alone, you know that? Reading the little love notes you'd write on the back for her. Knowing that one day she'd be yours. Now, you're both together but your wife is missing… You go home and call the police and say I killed her? Come on, they're not going to believe all that."

"We've got enough proof."

"You might *think* you have," she continued as lightning flashed across her face. "But when the cops find her body, they'll find *your* cum inside her mouth and pussy. They'll find *your* pubic hair deep inside her, and they'll find a glass covered with *your* fingerprints by the body. I made sure there was no trace of me anywhere."

John's breathing became shallow. His mind was spinning once more. "What?" He couldn't think straight. There was too much information and not enough time to process it. "*How*? Why would you *do* this?"

"Why? Because I love you and want you, Johnny! And always have. The how was easy. I didn't just shave you and give you head for the fun of it! I needed your pubic hair and cum. So I took it! And the glass you used when you untied yourself is with her now too. Even this fireplace poker has your fingerprints on it!"

"But it has *your* fingerprints as well…"

"I know. But I also know where I've touched. I'll wipe my prints when I leave it by the body, just like I did when I left the glass."

"You fucking murdering *bitch*," he said between gritted teeth.

"They'll add this to the stories of you acting weirdly at the hospital. Witnesses will say they saw you at the shopping mall with a strange woman. The stories will just pile up next to the evidence, Johnny. What do you think they're going to decide? All dirty fingers will point to bad boy Johnny and his little slut Sherrie."

"You've had all this *planned?*" he whispered as thunder crashed around them.

She nodded, "Yes. Well, this scenario and a few others. It all depended on how you reacted, Johnny, and how far to the edge I could push you. I've had a variety of options that I've been planning for a long, long time."

"You're sick, Zoe. I mean, *really* fucking sick! You need help."

"No, not me," she said as she stepped towards him. "But it looks like you do! Now, you can decide to have a happy life with me and Sherrie, or you can take your chances and try to convince the cops you didn't bring your wife all the way up here to beat her to death and then fuck her corpse. Your choice."

"I'll *never* choose *you*," he replied.

Zoe's face quivered. A shadow fell over it.

"And neither will Sherrie when she hears what you've done."

Silence.

"I just want us all to be together, Johnny," she replied.

"It's never going to happen, okay? You *understand?* Can you get that through your evil little mind? *NEVER!*"

"That's up to you, Johnny," she said in a small voice as her eyes fell to the ground. "Everything you're looking for is here and back at the church. Everything. You have no idea how close you were to your wife in the past few days. So *very* close."

The rain fell heavily on the roof.

"And I have everything I need," she continued. "All the evidence to tie it all to you. It's all back at the church, Johnny. The rest of your life is back at the church. Freedom or captivity, it's up to you to choose. It's all back at the church."

Zoe turned from him and walked away towards the hay bales at the back of the barn.

Thunder rolled across the wet, cold night.

"It's your game now," she said over her shoulder. "Your turn to choose."

Sixty-eight

John ran blindly.

He couldn't think of anything other than getting back to Sherrie and getting out of this madness.

Gotta run. Gotta go. Go gogogogo!

He had turned around and opened the barn door slowly as Zoe walked away from him. He fully expected her to try and stop him. He was braced for an attack of some sort, for her to change the rules again.

But she hadn't.

He'd stepped out into the cold night; his breath fogged and the rain pelted down on him. He felt colder than ever before, even colder than the night he spent chained to the X-frame at the church.

But he didn't care. He had to run.

Sherrie.

He had to get back to her and set her free.

They had to leave, to get away from all this.

And soon...

We have a lot of work to do.

Lightning lit up the sky as he ran towards the farmhouse. His feet squelched in the wet grass, splashing through puddles and sliding in mud. He stumbled at one stage, his left foot sliding to the side. He fell forward, his body stretched out, arms reaching for something to grab, and landed heavily on the grass. He slid through a puddle for a couple of feet, dirt and water splashing into his eyes and mouth.

Slowly, almost exhaustedly, he climbed back up and kept on running. The wind blew its chill through his chest and legs. His wet clothes felt like a coating of ice.

Blood continued trickling down his arm.

Fear crawled inside him as he ran closer. Thoughts ran through his mind faster than he could catch them.

Helen, oh my God, Helen. How could she? How could Zoe do that to you? Oh my God, she's mad, fucking crazy! And now she's after Sherrie and me! No, nonononono!

He reached the farmhouse.

Finally!

Running up the steps, he came to a halt on the deck.

Thunder joined the ringing in his ears from the gunshot back at the barn.

He turned and looked back into the night. The barn stood large and imposing in the semi-darkness.

No sign of Zoe.

That can't be right.

It's too easy.

Why would she just walk away?

"It's your game now," she had said. "Your turn to choose."

It's all so fucking crazy!

He leaned against one of the pine trunks propping up the verandah, trying to get his breathing under control.

Keep calm, don't let Sherrie see you like this. You can't panic her!

The trunk moved slightly under his weight and the verandah shook in protest.

Don't think about that now. Get Sherrie out of there before this whole shack falls in on itself!

Carefully, he reached out for the doorframe and took a step inside.

His eyes slowly adjusted to the extra darkness.

"Sherrie?"

No answer.

"Sherrie?" he said again, louder.

The wind howled in the night.

Still no answer.

No! Please, no!

Lightning double-flashed above them.

He saw Sherrie's body, lying on her side, her head thrown back.

NO! Please no! Oh shit, don't let it be. Please...

He knelt by her as he reached her side.

"Sherrie?" he said in a small voice, his eyes beginning to fill with tears. "*Please*? Sherrie?"

He shook her shoulder.

She jumped with fright, letting out a high-pitched cry.

John fell backwards, his heart pumping triple-time.

"Shit," she turned to face him. "Don't *do* that! You scared me half to death!"

John rested on his elbows, allowing his breathing to get back under control. His heart felt as if it was going to break out of his chest.

Yes! Yes yes yes. Thank you, yes. She's still alive!

"I thought you were…" he began but stopped quickly.

"Frozen to death?" she finished for him.

Not quite, he thought to himself.

"I *could've* been," she continued. "You took so long! What the hell kept you?"

"It's a long story," John muttered, looking out past the metal sheets that were the far wall. His eyes focussed back towards the barn.

What's she doing now?

"It always a long story with you, John," Sherrie replied.

Silence fell between them as the rain continued its heavy beat, pooling in the puddles around them.

"Did you find anything?" she asked finally.

"Huh?" he replied, turning back to face her and clearing his thoughts.

"You know," she pointed to the floorboards around her. "A crowbar or something. Anything to get me out?"

John stared at her.

What do I tell her?

The truth?

How can I?

I don't even know the whole story. There are pieces still missing. Where can I begin?

"No," he heard himself say. "The barn was empty."

"*Shit!*" she muttered. "What are we going to *do*?"

The terror in her voice was rising. He could hear it.

"Keep calm," he said as he crawled to her.

"Keep *calm?*" she replied. "*You're* not the one sitting stuck under these floorboards. *You're* not the one sitting in a fucking pool of water! *You're* also not the one who was left here in the middle of the fucking night while your lover goes off to find something to get you out with. You're not the one who had to sit and wait in the darkness, thinking about Zoe and this Fox guy and wondering if they'll get me first!"

Thunder rolled down the valley.

Sherrie sighed.

"You were gone so long, honey," she said.

"I'm sorry," he replied, bending down and kissing her on the cheek. "I searched for anything I could use, but there wasn't anything. I had to check thoroughly."

She nodded, "I know. I guess time just seemed to drag. It was like you were gone forever. I called for you a few times, but I guess you couldn't hear me."

He shook his head, "No, I couldn't."

"I must've fallen asleep or slipped into shock or something," she continued. "I didn't mean to scare you when you came back."

"That's okay," he smiled. "I didn't mean to scare you either."

Wind howled through the house. The verandah creaked loudly.

This place sounds like it could collapse at any second!

"We'll work out something to get you free," he said.

"Well, thinking caps on, bucko. Let's think fast!"

"Can I try pulling you out again?" he asked.

She nodded, "You can, but I don't think anything's changed. Of course, I could've lost some weight while I was sitting here. It's not like I had a three course meal or anything to pass the time while you were gone."

"Ha ha," John replied. "Very amusing."

"Think it'll work this time?" her eyes pleaded for a yes.

"Worth a try," was all he could say in reply.

"*Anything's* worth a try right now," she agreed.

She lifted her arms high. He reached around her and waited for her to wrap her arms around his neck.

"Here goes," he said as he steadied and then pulled upwards.

Sherrie lifted, further this time. He was sure of it.

"John?" she said in a small voice as he pulled harder. "It
hurts."

He gritted his teeth and pulled one last time.

Sherrie let out a growing moan.

Shit. Damn it. Fuck.

He eased her back to the ground.

"Jesus," Sherrie said, reaching down and feeling her
side. "I think I may have broken something."

"Well, you're the nurse."

She smiled at him through the pain. "Never a nurse,
John. Just a humble personal assistant."

"And a damn sexy one," he smiled at her.

She let out a short laugh, "Oh yeah, I'd be the girl-in-a-
hole pin up for September, that's for sure!"

"Couldn't think of one finer," he replied.

Zoe...

What are you doing now?

He stood and looked back out into the night, across the
field to the barn.

"It's your game now," she'd said. "Your turn to choose."

Then why don't I believe her?

Why do I feel she's still in control?

"...me out?"

He turned back to face her.

"Huh?"

"I said, there's nothing from around here you can use to
get me out?"

John shook his head. "I don't think so."

"It's just with all this wood and stuff just lying around, I
thought you could use some of it."

"There's nothing strong enough or long enough." He
turned around, looking at the house once more.

Lightning flashed around them.

"I need something long and sturdy to lever the cross-
beam off you."

The rain fell harder in the night.

The noise echoed loudly around them as it fell on the metal sheets on the verandah.

The verandah creaked.

The verandah...

Those two old pine trunks aren't going to support that verandah forever.

And then it hit him.

The trunks!

Strong and long and sturdy and hard...it just might work!

Jesus, it has to!

"Stay here," he said to her.

"Ha ha! *Very* funny, Mr. Comedian," Sherrie replied.

He turned and walked out the door.

"Where are you going?" she called after him.

"Not far."

"Don't leave me *again!*"

"I'm not," he replied as he walked over to the closest trunk. It was cut just to the right length and ran from the decking up to the corner of the verandah. It was wedged into the corner of the verandah, but didn't seem to be nailed or held there in any way. Only the weight of the verandah's roof was holding it in place.

"Just cover your head and your ears. This could be loud and messy."

"I hope you know what you're doing!" she called.

So do I, he thought as he reached out to the trunk and pulled on it.

It moved slowly at first.

He pulled again, with more force.

And then it came towards him.

He pulled harder.

Thunder rolled down towards them.

The trunk came away in his hands and the verandah lurched forward with a loud high-pitched squeal of twisting metal.

The second trunk in the other corner stayed firm for a few seconds before it slipped to the side, giving the verandah no support at all.

The front of the house shook as the verandah tore from its rusted old attachments and nose-dived into the decking. Falling in on itself, the verandah sent metal and wood and rain flying in all directions. It twisted in a spiral, squealing as if in pain.

When the commotion ended, the far end of the front of the house was completely blocked off with the debris. But the area near the doorway was free of rubble.

Yes!

"It's my game now," John said to himself as he balanced the long trunk in his hands. He turned to look at the barn. "My turn to choose."

My rules. My game.

Time for the attack.

<u>Sixty-nine</u>

"**Y**ou ready?" he asked her.

"Is this going to work?" she sounded worried.

"It should," he replied. "Trust me, I'm the engineer, right?"

"Okay," she nodded. "If you say so!"

"Just remember to pull yourself up as soon as you can."

She nodded in the darkness, "Ready when you are."

John stepped behind her and took up his position.

It hadn't taken him long to prepare it all.

He just hoped it would work.

The pine trunks from the verandah looked strong enough, but he worried that if they'd been standing outside as posts for too long, weathered and drying out, they might just snap in two like twigs once some pressure was placed on them.

Not going to happen, he told himself. *It can't! Please, just let this work for us.*

The first trunk was wedged down beside Sherrie.

There wasn't much space to use, but with Sherrie moving to one side and guiding him, he managed to place the end of the trunk as far under the floorboards as possible. He just hoped it was pushed far enough under to lift the cross-beam. The trunk stuck out of the hole at an angle, rising to John's shoulder in height.

The other trunk he placed on the floorboards behind Sherrie, using it as a brace for his wooden lever.

This has to work...

"Ready?" he asked again.

"Like you wouldn't believe," Sherrie replied.

"I'll take it nice and slow. Let me know how you're coming along and whether you can get out."

He watched the back of her head as she nodded.

"Here goes!"

He placed his feet on the trunk that was the brace, stopping it from moving or sliding away. He grabbed hold of his makeshift lever and pulled down on it, slowly at first.

After a few seconds, the floorboards moaned and moved slightly.

John's eyes darted from the floorboards to the lever and across to Sherrie.

She had both arms by her sides, pulling herself upwards, shaking side to side as if she were trying to work her way out like a cork in a champagne bottle.

The trunk was bending already as John pulled down on it more.

Keep it steady.

The floorboards moved slowly higher.

Yes, just a bit more!

The wind blew through the night and all around them.

John pulled down harder, his arms straining as the load increased.

The boards creaked and rose higher.

"It's working," Sherrie said as she pulled herself further. "I can feel the crossbeam lifting!"

The rain fell harder.

John needed to wipe the rain or sweat from his eyes, but he didn't have the time. The lever moved closer to the ground. He pulled it to his side, turned around and leaned on it now, pushing it further down, putting all his weight against it.

It inched closer to the ground.

Closer...closer...

The trunk rubbed against the claw marks on his chest. He eyed the bloodstain on his shirt and hoped Zoe's bite hadn't done too much damage to his stitches. But now wasn't the time to worry about that.

I'll get to Zoe next...

The floorboards lifted more.

A grating sound filled the air.

Thunder struck at the same moment, drowning the noise.

John pushed down harder.

And with a crack, the lever gave way.

Shit!

He heard Sherrie cry out!

No!

The log slammed into the floor with John on top of it. It gouged into his side, kicking the breath from his lungs and sending pain along his damaged arm and shoulder and through his body. His head hit the floor hard. Stars scattered through his vision.

He lay there in the silence.

No! Damn it, no! NO! That was our only hope!

He closed his eyes tight. His hands balled into fists.

The rain continued to fall.

What are we going to do now? There's nothing else left to try. She's beaten us. She's won!

"Are you okay, John?"

It was Sherrie. She was whispering to him.

By his side.

He opened his eyes and turned to look above him.

She was staring down at him, a look of concern on her face.

He stared back.

"You okay?" she said again.

"Yeah," he mumbled. "You're..."

"Yep," she nodded and smiled at him. "I'm out."

He rolled off the log and sat up to look at the floor.

The trunk hadn't snapped at all.

The crossbeam had.

From where he sat, he could make out the hole in the floor where Sherrie had been. It was bigger now, a large pile of floorboards strewn all around, and sitting in the middle of the pile, like a broken jagged knife, was the snapped crossbeam.

Yes! It worked!

John brushed himself off as Sherrie held out her hand to him.

He smiled, took her hand, and stood up. He turned to face her and kissed her lightly on the lips.

"How are you?" he asked.

"I'll live," she smiled back.

"That's good to know."

"I'm just glad to be out of that hole."

"I'm glad you are too."

They hugged in the entranceway for a short while as the lightning lit up the night.

"Thank you," she whispered in his ear.

He looked into her green eyes.

"I wasn't about to leave you here, you know."

She smiled as she bent over, wiping the moss and splinters from her legs. "I know, I just wanted to say thanks. It was horrible down there. Wet and yucky and really disgusting."

He nodded. "I love you, you know that. I'd do anything for you."

She snuggled into his shoulder. "I know," she replied. "That's why I love you so much."

They stood silent as the thunder rolled on by.

"But we *have* to see this through to the end, don't we?" she asked.

"Yes," he replied. "We do."

"But if Fox isn't here, where is he?"

Jesus, where do I start?

What can I tell her?

"The answers are back at the church."

She turned to look at him.

"The *church?*"

He nodded.

"How can you be so sure?" she looked confused.

John sighed.

"I just know, that's all."

"How?"

Damn, I have to tell her.

I have to!

But not here.

Not now.

There's plenty of time for that.

"I found some things," he replied. "In that back room… and in the barn. Helen's back near the church somewhere."

"We came all this way for *nothing?*" she asked.

"No," he shook his head. "By coming here we learnt the truth. Finally."

She stared at him and he smiled at her.

He turned to be by her side and placed his arm around her.

She noticed the blood on the arm of his shirt.

"You're injured," she looked concerned. "Are you okay?"

He nodded, "Must've just opened the wound slightly when I fell to the floor."

"You want me to check it for you?"

He shook his head. He didn't want to know what damage Zoe's bite had done. Not yet, anyway.

"Come on, my love. We've got unfinished business to take care of."

They walked out the front door and around the twisted remains of the verandah.

Lightning glowed in the night sky as they walked out into the rain.

"Will Fox be at the church?" she asked as they walked down the muddy driveway.

"Fox is the least of our troubles now," he replied.

<u>Seventy</u>

The pines stretched out in front of them.

"Couldn't we take the road?" Sherrie called from behind him.

"No," he replied. He was walking faster, head down, pushing through the rain. "Too exposed. It's dangerous. This way is safer."

"How do you know we'll even find the church this way?" she continued. "We're not even retracing the route that got us here!"

Because this is the way Zoe came, he thought to himself. *It has to be!*

He'd decided that while they had been hiding in the forest, taking a diagonal route and walking by the river on the other side of the road, Zoe had been making a direct line to the barn on this side of the road.

That's how she got here so fast and was waiting for us.

"John, *please,*" Sherrie called from behind him. "Slow down!"

No time, I can't.

Lightning jagged above them.

"You're walking too *fast!*" she called. "*Please!*"

He stopped in his tracks and turned to face her.

She walked towards him looking tired and worn-out. Her long hair was plastered across her forehead and on her shoulders. She was walking with a limp and holding her side. A painful expression flashed across her face every time she took a step with her right foot.

Poor Sherrie.

She just doesn't understand...

Doesn't she have a right to?

Yes, she does.

Zoe said she loved Sherrie too.

She said she was doing all this for her.

There were still pieces missing. And John wanted to fill in some of the gaps. The more he knew, the better his chance of beating Zoe at her own game.

Time to play the game like she does. Time to know everything before I strike.

The rain fell heavily around them, punching into the ground and their bodies.

He waited until she had caught up to him.

She smiled, "Thanks. You were walking too fast."

He couldn't wait any longer. He needed to know now. No matter what.

"You knew who Zoe was," he said to her. "You *know* her, right?"

Her smile vanished as thunder echoed around them.

"Yes," she looked to the ground. "I know her."

"How?"

"It's a long story, John," she began, her face turning dark.

"We've got time."

"I don't really want to talk about it now."

"Honey, I think we *need* to."

She sighed. "I don't know where to start."

He turned and put his arm around her once more. "Come on," he said. "Let's talk while we head back."

She nodded and smiled up at him.

More pieces...more pieces of the puzzle...

They continued walking through the forest, sludging through the wet undergrowth and being careful not to slip.

The wind blew through the pines, but not nearly as hard as it did in the valley. They weren't as cold now. It was almost as if the forest kept the worst of the wind and night from them, sheltering them as they walked.

Thunder rolled above. John noticed the thunder was moving away, taking longer to break after each bolt of lightning.

Maybe this storm will soon be over.

Maybe...

"I'm listening..." he prompted her.

She sighed deeply.

"Anything you tell me might be able to help us *stop* Zoe. You know her better than I do. Anything you can tell me could help. *Please?*"

"Okay," she began after a few more seconds of silence. "Here it goes! I've known Zoe for a few years. Probably about five in fact. Before I met you, we used to live together. Actually, even when I met you, she was still living with me. But eventually we grew apart. It wasn't the same as it used to be. She moved out after we had a big fight. We used to be good friends, but then something happened and it just changed how we were with each other. We couldn't live together anymore. So, she packed herself up and left. I haven't seen her for at least a year."

She fell silent.

John didn't say anything.

"I got such a shock at the church," she continued as they walked further through the forest. "I mean, I had *no* idea whose Jeep was out the front. She never owned a car when I knew her. But when I talked with you on the phone I could tell you were scared and in danger. And when you didn't show up at the hotel, I feared that maybe something had gone wrong and you were *really* in trouble. So I parked the car out of sight at the end of the driveway and walked the rest of the way.

"It was so quiet when I got there. I couldn't hear anything. I first thought maybe the place was deserted and I'd missed you somehow back at the hotel. But after a few seconds, I could hear a voice from inside the church. I walked around to the side and looked in the window. I could see Zoe standing there near the kitchen. I didn't see you then. I couldn't see the bed from where I was. But I saw her."

Lightning flashed.

"I didn't know what she was doing there. My mind couldn't connect it all together in those few split seconds. So I just barged into the church and asked Zoe what the fuck was going on. Then I saw you down on the bed all tied up and in a dreadful state. And then I *knew.*"

They walked in silence for quite a while.

The pieces were beginning to fit together.

"She loves you, you know," John said.

"I know," she nodded. "And I loved her...for a while."

"You were living together as lovers?"

Sherrie nodded.

John was too tired and too exhausted to be surprised. Part of him suspected anyhow. After what Zoe had told him at the barn, what else could he think?

"It was a one bedroom apartment, John. We were a couple for a while."

"And you never thought to tell me this?"

"I wanted to. But I didn't know how you'd react. I would've told you one day, John. Honestly, I would've. But I saw it as a little side-step that I took, just to experiment and to see what it was like. It didn't work out, so I didn't think it mattered."

"What broke you both up?" he asked.

Thunder rumbled in the distance.

"You did," she replied.

He closed his eyes and let out a sigh.

I did...

Of course...

Then he turned to face her.

"That's what all this is about, you know..."

She nodded, "I know. From the moment I saw you tied to that bed in the church, I knew. She swore she'd hurt the next person I fell in love with. She told me she would. But it was part of our huge final argument and I just thought it was an empty threat. I had *no idea* she would take it this far."

John nodded.

"This is all *our* fault."

"You can't think that way," he replied.

"But it's *true!*"

They walked on together. He squeezed her hand.

"Was she always that extreme?" he asked. "In bed, I mean."

"Yeah," Sherrie replied. "She was a rough fuck, that's for sure. She was always into tying me up and spanking and stuff. For a while I enjoyed it, but then it just got too dangerous. Her games always got out of hand. She was always pushing to the edge."

John nodded.

"And further…" she whispered.

"She wants us all to live together, as a threesome."

Sherrie sighed and ran her fingers through her wet hair.

"I can't believe this is happening," she muttered. "When did she tell you this? At the church when she had you tied up?"

Here goes…

"At the barn."

"*What?*"

"She was at the barn, waiting for us. That was when she told me why she was doing it all."

"You said *no one* was at the barn!"

"I know."

"*Why?*"

"Because I thought it was for the best."

She shook her head and let go of his hand, "Really?"

"Yeah," he muttered.

"You *lied* to me, John," she said in a firm voice.

"I know," he replied. "I'm sorry, but I *did* think it was for the best. While you were still stuck down there in that hole, I didn't think telling you what Zoe said in the barn was going to help the situation."

She nodded.

They walked through the rain.

Silence.

"I *don't* believe it!" Sherrie continued after a short distance. "That's why you were so long?"

"Yes."

"I can't believe you stayed there and actually *talked* to her!"

"I didn't have much choice, she still had the gun."

"*Jesus!*"

They walked on in silence.

"She said she'd made Fox up."

"She *made him up?*" she turned to look at him, surprise in her eyes.

John nodded. "He doesn't exist. It was all a story to get me out here."

Sherrie walked on in silence, shaking her head. "*No...*" she finally said.

"She's the one who abducted Helen. She told her about you and me having an affair. But Helen didn't believe her, she said it wasn't true. So Zoe killed her instead."

"Oh, John. I'm so *sorry.*"

John walked on, his head down in the rain.

"Now, Helen's back at the church somewhere and there's evidence to prove I'm the one who killed her. She's set me up perfectly, sweets. And she's going to use our relationship as extra proof."

"*Shit!* I can't believe this is happening..."

"Neither can I, but it's true. That's why we have to get back to the church before she does. We have to find Helen and we have to stop Zoe!"

"I understand," she said in a soft voice.

"It'll be dangerous."

"I know."

"She's *totally* insane," he continued.

"I know that *now.*"

"And I understand if you want to continue walking on past the church and back to Hepburn Lakes."

Sherrie stopped and turned to face him, her bottom lip quivered. "Oh, honey, I want to be with *you!* I can't leave you to fight this battle yourself."

He smiled at her as his heart beat hard.

"You can walk away if you want to," he replied, reaching out and touching a soaked curl on her forehead.

She leant forward and kissed him on the cheek. "No way. Anyway, looks like this is *my* battle as well."

He looked deep into her gorgeous green eyes. He knew she meant it and he loved her even more.

"Okay," John nodded. "As long as you're sure."

She nodded. "I'm here for you. I want to see this through with you. I want to be *yours* forever."

"You can leave at any time. I'll understand."

"I won't be leaving, *ever*."

John leaned forward and kissed her hard on the mouth. He felt her salty wet skin and live hot tongue. He wanted her so badly.

Right now.

Make the whole world disappear.

If only it were that easy!

He pulled away from her.

"I'm yours too, you know that," he said.

She nodded.

The rain continued to fall.

They turned and walked through the forest.

If only I hadn't gone to the hospital that first time, he thought to himself.

If only Helen and I could've worked things out.

If only...

"Too late for that now, buddy," Richard called from his mind.

You!

"You're so far up shit creek, pal, you can't see the sun for all the turds."

I don't need this right now!

"So your little fuck-mate turns out not only to be horny and kinky, but she's also been fucking your *other* little fuck-mate too!"

Shut up.

"It's a small world, my friend. A small world."

I don't need you right now!

"Looks like everyone's screwing everyone!"

I can handle this. I can do this myself!

"I wonder if Zoe fucked Helen too, just before she killed her."

Get out of my head!

"Or maybe *after*..."

Get the fuck out of my head!

Lightning struck around them.

Sherrie was the first to see it.

She stopped in her tracks.

"Look!" she turned to him as she pointed.

John saw it too.

In the middle of the forest, in a tiny clearing just to their left, sat a small wooden caravan. It was badly weathered, and looked to have been abandoned a long time ago.

Both its tires were flat and it was propped up on one side by a pile of weed-covered old bricks. The brown paint was peeling from the wooden slats on its sides and the tin chimney was infected with rust.

The arched iron roof was tarnished and bent, but it looked whole from where they stood. The rain bounced on it and slid to the sides, falling to the large puddles on the ground.

The door to the caravan was wide open and the interior was dark.

Was Helen here? he wondered.

But there was no sign of anyone.

It wouldn't hold many people anyway, he thought. *Just one or two at the most.*

John squeezed Sherrie's hand and smiled.

I can't leave here without checking...

They turned and started walking towards it.

Anyway, he thought. *This maybe just what we need!*

A place to rest.

A sanctuary from the cold winds and wet driving rain.

A shelter from the dark night.

And a place to plot their final moves...

Seventy-one

They sat in the cold dark silence. The rain fell heavily on the iron roof.

The caravan had very little room on the inside and its musty disused smell was overpowering. A small wooden bunk with a tatty linen mattress was attached to one wall, and a small stool sat nearby on an old moth-eaten and dirty rug. In the far corner was a metal basin, eaten away with rust, that probably once served as a hand-bath. A thin curtain hung from the far wall, tied at the bottom and draping over a window that had been sealed shut years ago by a half-dozen nailed boards.

I shouldn't've got my hopes up, John thought as he looked around once more. *Helen wasn't going to be hidden here. That was way too easy. Not Zoe's style. I should've known that...*

He shivered.

Even though they had closed the old wooden door and were out of the driving wind and the cold rains, he just wasn't able to get warm again. He felt cold and numb, and he hoped it was because of the weather and nothing more. He still hadn't checked his arm wound.

He sat on the edge of the rickety bunk while Sherrie sat across from him on the small wooden stool. She was rubbing her arms and staring at the floor.

"You okay?" he asked.

"No," she muttered in reply.

"Me either," he whispered.

Thunder rolled around them.

"I thought the storm was going," Sherrie continued.

John nodded, "I thought so too. Maybe this is the second wave?"

"Just what we need..."

"It's the least of our problems, honey."

"I know."

"We have to stop Zoe soon."

"I know."

"But I'm not sure how."

They looked at each other as lightning flickered through the cracks in the thin wooden walls.

The rain fell and the silence between them was long.

"Use me," Sherrie said finally.

"Huh?"

Sherrie's eyes were bright with the idea. "She's doing this to get back at *me*. She's hurt because I left her for *you* and she wants to hurt you so it hurts *me*. If *I'm* the one in the frontline, if *I'm* the one in danger, she won't do anything."

John tilted his head, "Sherrie, she's *sick*. I mean, really *crazy!* She could do *anything* to *anyone!* How can you be sure she won't hurt you?"

"I just know it."

John fingered the wound down his left arm, running his hand across the zigzagging stitches, feeling them in the dark. "I don't know, it sounds too risky. I don't want you getting hurt."

"Do you have any better ideas?"

"Not at the moment, no," he agreed. "All I know is we have to find Helen and get out of here."

Sherrie looked at him across the darkness.

"You mean take her *with* us?" There was worry in Sherrie's voice.

John shrugged his shoulders, "Yes. I think so. I mean, maybe. I don't really know at this stage."

"How are we going to explain a *dead body* to the police?"

"*Helen's* body, you mean. I don't know. We'll work it out later…"

"No, I don't think we'll work it out later. If you take Helen's body with us or they find us with it and we tell them what's happened, do you *really* think they're going to believe us? If we do that, it still works out for Zoe! You can't beat her that way."

Thunder echoed as the rain eased slightly.

John nodded after a few minutes of thinking. "You're right. Even if we do, we still play into her hands."

"Exactly!"

"I can't get rid of some of the trace evidence she's used against me. If we take Helen with us we'll just be handing Zoe what she wants."

"So what do we do?"

"We've got no choice," John replied. "We have to make her see reason and admit to what she's done."

"Will that be *possible?*"

"I have no idea," he said. "Maybe if *you* talk to her. Maybe you can make her agree to tell the cops everything and turn herself in for some psychiatric help."

"But you said she's crazy!"

"I know."

"Do you think that will work?" Sherrie asked.

"I have no other plan…"

"When do you think we'll see Zoe again?"

"She'll be at the church," John replied.

"Are you sure?"

He nodded, "It's all part of the game. She'll be there waiting for us to see how we react. She'll be watching us. That's all part of the thrill for her."

"This is all so fucking *crazy!*" Sherrie balled up her hands into fists and hit at her thighs in anger.

John nodded in the night as lightning flashed outside.

"How's your head and ribs?" he asked her.

She smiled a lop-sided smile. "I'll live. What about you?"

"I can't feel much. I'm too cold. I think that's a good thing."

"Probably."

They fell silent for a time, listening to the rain above them.

"You should've told me about her," John continued. "And what you two used to do."

"It's *not* something I'm terribly proud of, John," Sherrie replied after a deep sigh. "I'm trying to forget it myself. I'm hardly going to tell the man I love that I had a lesbian relationship just before we met."

"Still, if you had told me –"

"It would've made *no* difference to what Zoe was going to do to you. It wouldn't've made you any more prepared and it wouldn't've helped you in any way."

The rain eased more, lightly falling on the roof.

The silence between them was long and hard.

"I'm cold," Sherrie whispered.

John stood from the bunk and moved to her side. He took her in his arms and rubbed her back and sides, trying to get the circulation flowing in her body.

"I wonder what time it is," she said.

"No idea," John replied. "Zoe took my watch when we first got here, after she handcuffed me to the Jeep."

Sherrie shook her head and sighed.

John pecked her on the cheek.

"Don't worry about it now," he replied. "We'll have plenty of time to talk about what happened once we're out of this situation. Don't worry about what's past now."

"If we *get* out of this situation…"

"We will."

He continued to rub her shoulders.

"I don't know if this is helping," he whispered in her ear.

"Just having you close to me *is* helping though," she replied.

She turned to face him.

He could smell her and feel her warm breath.

He kissed her hard on her cold, wet lips. They parted and let him through. Their tongues danced wantonly, seeking and finding each other. Their breath steaming from their mouths.

He ran his hand through Sherrie's hair, brushing it from her face and pulling it away from her neck and shoulders.

Sherrie's hands glided up and down his back. Her breathing quickened and the warmth returned to her lips and face.

They hugged each other tight as thunder growled around them.

"John," she whispered as they kissed. "I love you."

"I love you too," he replied.

This is all that matters.

This is all I want.

"Jooooohhhhhnnnnnyyyyy!"

At first he thought it was all in his mind, so he pushed it to one side.

But then he heard it again.

"Jooooohhhhhnnnnnyyyyy!"

Out in the night.

And close by.

Sherrie froze.

They were both still, faces only inches apart, listening into the night.

"*Jooooohhhhhnnnnnyyyyy!*"

"It's her," he whispered.

"I know," Sherrie nodded. "She's close."

The rain sprinkled lightly across the roof of the caravan, just enough to make it hard to pinpoint where Zoe was calling from.

"Jooooohhhhhnnnnnyyyyy! Cooooome toooo meeeee, Joooohhhhhnnnnnyyyy!"

Fear charged up John's spine.

"What do we do?" Sherrie asked.

He didn't answer.

"Do we stay here?"

John shook his head, "No. She *must* know we're here, that's why she's calling."

"You mean she's been *following* us?"

"Probably."

"Why?"

"It's all part of her *fucking* game," he replied.

"Pushing us to the edge?"

"Yeah, more of her edge play."

"Why, John?"

"To see how we react, maybe?" he shook his head. "I don't know, honey. I just don't know anymore. She's so fucking *crazy!*"

"*Jooooohhhhhnnnnnyyyyy!*"

"What do we do?" Sherrie asked.

"I don't think we have any choice. We have to go outside."

She nodded.

"I love you," he whispered as he kissed her hard and fast.

"I love you too. And always will," Sherrie replied.

"We'll get through this," he replied, staring into her beautiful green eyes. "You and me, we'll survive this."

"I know."

"We won't let her win. She *won't* beat us this time."

She nodded.

He grabbed both her hands and squeezed them.

"You ready?" he asked.

She nodded.

"Okay," he ran his hand through her hair once more. "Let's do it."

They turned to the door.

"Jooooohhhhhhnnnnnnyyyyy!"

John reached out to the handle, turned it and slowly opened the door.

Lightning flashed, blinding them with its light as the door swung wide.

John stepped in front of Sherrie, moving her to stand right behind him, and peered out into the night.

The rain was falling as a mist, light and soft.

"Stay here," he whispered to Sherrie as he stepped down from the caravan.

His feet sloshed heavily on the earth as he took a step forward into the night.

"Jooooohhhhhhnnnnnnyyyyy!"

Her voice again. It seemed to echo from all around them. He tried to pinpoint it but couldn't as thunder rolled across the sky.

He stepped deeper into the night.

Show yourself, bitch...

The mist hung in the air, making it hard to see beyond a few feet. The night was cold, but the wind had dropped. The mist settled on him as he walked. All was still except John, who took another step further away from the caravan.

"John," Sherrie called quietly.

"Stay there," he said over his shoulder. "At any sign of trouble, shut the door and barricade yourself inside. Okay?"

"Okay," she called back.

He stepped forward again.
Careful.
Take it nice and slow.
Wait for her to call again.
Work out the direction.
And then nail the bitch.
With what?
It doesn't matter.
What will you use?
My own two hands if I have to.
Lightning flashed above and illuminated the pines in front of him.

He looked up to the sky in time to see the second flash of lightning.

When he returned his eyes to the pines, she was standing in front of him, leaning against one of the trunks.

She had a smile on her face, and her arms were across her breasts.

Zoe...

Her hair was plastered down her face and body. The rain made her skin shine and her diamond sparkle. She was wearing the leather strap bondage outfit and she was still barefoot.

She was only a few feet away from him.

"Hi, my lover," she said.

John's heart began to pound hard, his breathing increased and he stopped dead in his tracks.

"I knew you'd come to me," she continued. "You can't deny what we had together. You can't go back with Sherrie, not after you've tasted me. And I *know* you like what you tasted."

John stared at her.

"Is this all part of the game?" he said through clenched teeth.

Zoe's face fell.

Thunder drummed loud and deep.

"Is it?" he asked again.

She shook her head, "No, Johnny. It isn't. I miss you and I want you back. That's why I'm here. I want us to be together forever. I made a mistake and I'm sorry, but I want to be with you. Can you forgive me?"

"*Forgive* you?" John couldn't believe what he was hearing. "Are you *serious?*"

"Please...?"

"You tortured me for days and you *killed* Helen! Do you remember that? You *killed* my wife!"

"You didn't love her anyway," she replied.

John's mouth opened to reply, but he couldn't think straight. He didn't know what to say to her. He shook his head and just stared.

"John?" Sherrie called to him.

Zoe's eyes darted over his shoulder towards the caravan.

"Stay where you are!" John called back to her.

"Does she *fuck* as good as I do?" Zoe asked, staring back at him. "Does she?"

John didn't answer.

"Does she give you what you want, fulfil your dreams like I do, Johnny? Does she make you cum so hard it hurts? Does she bend over in all the positions you like? Does she drink every last drop of your cum? Does she?"

No reply.

"I'll take that as a no, then," she continued. "And you're right. I know, I've been with her too, remember? She can't satisfy you like I do. I know that already. But you're giving me up for *her?*"

"I *never* loved you," he replied. "So I can't give you up."

"You're turning me down again..." she said to herself. "After everything, you're still saying no."

"I *love* Sherrie," he said. "I *never* loved you."

Sadness swept across her as lightning broke the night.

"I swore this would never happen, Johnny," she said in a sad, soft voice. "I swore no man would ever break my heart again."

"I'm sorry, Zoe. But I still want to help you. I think you need help."

"I swore you'd never break my heart twice. But you have."

John stared at her, his mouth wide.

"*Twice?*"

"How could I be so *stupid?*"

Thunder rolled and the rain returned in a wave, hard and heavy, beating into the ground and trees around them.

They stood in silence.

One last chance...

"Zoe, come with us and we'll get you some help," John held out a hand to her. "If you tell the police everything, they'll understand and use it in your favour. With a few years of the best doctors and psychiatric help, you'll get better. I promise."

"I don't need your promises, Johnny," she replied, rubbing her shoulders. "I don't need you at all anymore. I should've known nothing would've changed."

"Let me help you," he reached out further to her.

"No!"

John took a step towards her, "Please..."

"NO!" Zoe screamed and took a step backwards.

John let his arm drop away and fall to his side.

"Stop hurting John to get revenge on me!" Sherrie called from behind him.

He turned to see her walking towards them.

No! Get back!

Zoe looked puzzled, "What are you talking about?"

"You know *exactly* what I'm talking about," Sherrie was by John's side now. "I'm through with you, Zoe! I told you months ago. So, just leave John and me alone! Leave us and take your sick evil games elsewhere. I don't love you anymore! *Get it?*"

Zoe smirked, "This has got *nothing* to do with you, Sherrie. This is all between John and me!"

"Huh?"

"I'm not here for revenge on you!" she continued, her smirk widening and stretching the jagged cut on her left cheek. "I left *you,* remember? This is between John and me."

"But I don't even *know* you!" John replied.

"Really?" Zoe placed a hand on her hip. "Think *really* hard, John. Be truthful to yourself and think *really* hard. Go back through the years and find me. You will. And *remember* what you did to me. I'm there, you just have to find me."

"Zoe, I don't know what you're *talking* about!"

"Don't start believing your own lies, Johnny. That's when you've become *really* sick, when you can't even remember what's the truth and what's lies anymore. Are you that *far gone?* Have you deluded everyone, including *yourself?*"

The rain fell heavier.

There was silence between them all.

Lightning slashed at the sky.

John looked between Zoe and Sherrie.

They were both staring at him.

"Pal, it's time the truth came out," Richard said loudly in his head. "It's time to sweep away all those lies..."

Seventy-two

"**Y**ou're *so* blind," Zoe continued. "You can't even see it anymore. You can't remember, because you've blotted it all out. Covered it all up…"

"I don't know what you're talking about," John replied, but he had an uneasy feeling about the direction the whole conversation was taking.

Thunder rolled.

"What's she talking about, John?" Sherrie asked.

"I have no idea," he replied.

"I think you do," Zoe continued. "But I don't know if you want your lover-girl here to know it all."

Sherrie put her arm around John. "I stand by him, Zoe, no matter what! *Nothing* you can say can change how I feel. Nothing you can do either."

Zoe laughed, "Sherrie, you're so loyal. So blinded by everything you feel for him. So noble. And so fucking *boring*…"

John stepped forward, shielding Sherrie.

"You *won't* talk to her like that," he replied, staring straight at Zoe.

"*Yes*, Johnny. *No*, Johnny," Zoe mocked him. "Whatever you want, Johnny."

The rain fell in a steady torrent around them. The night was cold. Their breath fogged and hung in the air.

Rivulets of rain streamed from Zoe. Down her hair and over her breasts and erect nipples, snaking their way down along her tight stomach and around her belly button diamond. Down to the valley between her legs. And deeper.

"Think back, Johnny," she continued. "Think right back to your past and the events you've buried in it."

This is crazy.

She's crazy!

We're playing to her rules again.

Yes, we are!

She said this was my game.
MY rules!
We're not playing by hers any longer...
John grabbed Sherrie's hand.
"Come on," he said. "We don't have to listen to this bullshit. We're leaving."
He turned and marched away from Zoe, heading back towards the caravan.
Sherrie followed.
"Think about Patricia Bourke!" Zoe called to them.
Who?
"Who's Patricia Bourke?" Sherrie asked as they neared the caravan.
"I don't know," John replied.
Lightning crisscrossed the sky.
Patricia Bourke...I know that name...
From where?
"Remember 'Pattie the Fattie'! Remember what happened to her!" Zoe called again.
John stopped in his tracks and turned around.
My God! 'Pattie the Fattie'? From college?
He let go of Sherrie's hand.
"*John?*"
And stepped back towards Zoe.
"You *know* 'Pattie the Fattie'?" John called to Zoe through the rain.
Zoe shook her head.
"I *am* 'Pattie the Fattie'," she replied.
John's world shook with the thunder.
What?
No!
But she was...ugly. She was disgusting.
Zoe's different. She's crazy but she's different.
She's LYING!
She has to be. She can't be Patricia Bourke.
It's not possible.
She CAN'T be!
It's just NOT POSSIBLE!
As if reading his mind, Zoe stepped towards him.

"I'm Patricia Bourke, Johnny. And I'm taking my revenge."

He stepped back away from her.

No, no, nono. She's lying. She has to be!

"She's not lying, pal," Richard said in his head.

Fuck off, how would you know?

"It's what I've been trying to tell you, pal." Richard continued. "Don't let the lies you've created over the years blind you to what really happened."

Fuck you!

"Open yourself to the truth for the first time…" he whispered in his head.

Fuck off, go away! I don't need your fucking voice in my head now.

"John?" Sherrie was by his side.

He turned to face her. He didn't know what to say. He stared at her, confusion in his eyes.

"She's lying," John said to her.

"I don't care," she replied. "I just want *you*."

"She's *lying*," he said again.

"Let's go," she took his hand.

He shook his head.

No!

I won't run from this.

I can't.

My game.

MY RULES!

John let go of Sherrie's hand.

"What did you do to Helen?" he called to her, trying to change the subject.

Zoe tilted her head and smiled, "You don't want to know that, Johnny."

"Yes," he nodded and stepped closer to her. "Yes, I do. I want to know *now*. You'll tell me how you did all this. You'll tell *us* how you planned and acted out your little sick fucking game that you dragged us into. And you'll tell us *now!*"

"My, we are *forceful* when we've got our back up against the wall," Zoe replied. "I like it!"

"Tell us!"

"Of course, I always preferred it with my *front* up against the wall..."

"TELL US!"

Zoe sighed.

The rain fell heavier as lightning flashed.

"Too much truth is obviously a health hazard for you, Johnny."

He stepped closer to Zoe. They were only a few feet apart again. "Tell me," he said through clenched teeth, the rain running over them.

"You *don't* want Sherrie to hear this..." she warned.

"She'll hear it all, I don't care! Now start talking or I'll fucking beat it out of you."

Zoe smirked, "Even I know you haven't got it in you, Johnny. You're too weak, too easily led and manoeuvred. You couldn't hit me or beat me if you tried. You're not the kind of person who can stop events or change them. You never have been, have you?"

John looked to the puddles on the ground around him.

His hands unclenched, his head spun.

She was right.

"Please, Zoe," he said in a soft voice. "Tell me it all. I *need* to know."

Thunder rolled.

Zoe leaned up against the closest trunk in the forest.

"Okay," she said. "You have to know anyway, I guess. Revenge is no fun unless the victim knows. And it's clear to me now that you don't know. I can't believe you've lied so much even you believe your own lies. But this is all because of how you treated me and Maureen O'Reilly. I don't know how much you remember, I don't know if you even *knew* it at the time, but you hurt me so badly, and so deeply. You *violated* me. You and Laura Austin."

Laura? What does she have to do with this?

"Do you remember a post-game party Donny DuBois threw at the house he was renting just off campus?"

"Which one? There were several."

"The one I was at. Maureen was with me."

He nodded, "Yeah, I do. But I didn't speak to you that whole night."

Zoe's eyes fell to the ground and her face broke.

"You *really* don't remember, then," she replied. "That makes it even worse."

"I met Helen that night," he replied.

She looked at him.

"I didn't know that," she said.

"Just after I left, I met Helen. Her car had broken down," he continued.

She shook her head, "It's a small world."

"Secrets, John?" Sherrie said, by his side again. There was an edge to her voice now. "More lies and secrets?"

He didn't know what to say.

Rain drove hard into them and the forest.

"And do you remember my mother's funeral?" she continued.

"Your *mother?*"

"Yes," Zoe's voice was quiet now. He could hardly hear it above the rain. "You attended the funeral, and then walked out halfway through it with Laura Austin. You made a spectacle out of yourself to go out and *fuck* Laura Austin."

Laura?

It was Zoe's mother's *funeral?*

Zoe was looking deep into his eyes.

"You *can't* remember?" she said. "I don't know why I'm surprised by that."

"Lies upon lies," Richard whispered.

This is crazy!

She's doing it again!

My game.

MY FUCKIN' RULES!

"Tell me about Helen," he yelled loudly in the night.

Zoe jumped at the force of his words.

"I want to know and you'll tell me. *NOW!*"

She sighed. "You hurt me so much, Johnny."

"Tell me..."

"I lived my life, lost weight, changed my name, changed everything about me so that I could never be reminded of who I was. 'Pattie the Fattie' no longer existed. She was the first one I killed. My new life was a good life, Johnny, and I'd forgotten about you totally."

"This has nothing to do −"

Zoe held out a hand to stop him.

"Yes," she nodded. "It *does*. Listen and I'll explain."John fell silent as thunder rolled in on the night.

"I changed everything about me. I changed my whole life to prove people like you wrong. And I did it! I was successful. I promised myself never to be hurt like that again. Never to be hurt in the same way Johnny Murdock hurt me. I got my belly button pierced and I put a diamond there to prove I was truly beautiful and to remind me of what you had done to me. And I got on with my life. It took me years, Johnny, but I did it all the same. I swore a man would never hurt me again. I sought out the love of another woman instead; a soul mate, a true and real person I could spend the rest of my life with. Someone who would never hurt me like you did.

"I met Sherrie and we were happy. *Sooo* happy for so long. She was perfect in every way. Kind and loving and she wanted to be with me. Just *me!* But guess what? Who knew it would happen like this? *You* came along, Johnny. *YOU!* You came back into my life like a whirlwind and snatched away the only person I truly loved."

"Oh God," Sherrie muttered from his shoulder.

"You'd hurt me again, Johnny. Just like you did in college. And the saddest thing is that you probably had no idea about how much you hurt me on each occasion. Once I can live with, Johnny, but twice is taking it too far. You had to suffer. You *had* to pay."

Lightning flashed and thunder followed.

"Is it getting any clearer now, Johnny?" she asked him. "Do you remember now how much you hurt me? Want me to continue?"

He shook his head.

His mind was spinning.

He couldn't remember any of it.

She's lying, she must be!

"Can you understand the *pain*, Johnny? No? Don't worry, you will. You'll know soon enough..."

The rain sounded louder in John's ears. So did his heartbeat. His breathing increased and he felt hot all over. Boiling up, he stared unblinkingly at Zoe.

"Sherrie and I had a huge fight the night she told me she had fallen in love with someone else – with *a man!* But not just *any* man – *you!* I told her it wasn't that easy. I told her I'd make her suffer. She couldn't just end it like that. But she did. So I knew what I had to do.

"It wasn't difficult to find you or your wife. I knew Sherrie had accepted your offer to be your *Personal Assistant,*" she spat the words out with disgust. "It was just a matter of waiting and biding my time. I followed you home one night. Saw where you lived. The rest was easy...

"Helen let me in without even a second thought. I said I was an old friend of yours, just blown into town – pretty much the same story I told you – and Helen accepted it without any suspicions. Or maybe she thought I was an old flame of yours and just wanted to check me out. You people are all so *gullible!* She was sleepy and off guard and it was easy to attack her and knock her out. I tied her up and gagged her well, and put her in her wardrobe in the main bedroom. You were *sooo* close to her, Johnny, all night, and you didn't even know it."

"You *fucking sick demented bitch,*" he said.

"Oh, it gets better," she replied. "Helen woke up Saturday morning. But I let her know that if she said anything, made even one little noise, that I would slit your throat. I even showed her the knife that I would do it with. Sliced it through her right ear to prove to her it was real sharp. She co-operated from that moment. Of course, I drugged her for most of the time – so she couldn't do too much. She was unconscious for hours."

"Zoe, you're sick. You need help," Sherrie said.

Zoe shook her head, "Not me, girlfriend. It's your lover you need to worry about!"

"Go on," John said in a deep voice.

I have to hear this out. I need to know it all.

"It was early. I had enough time to drive the Jeep to the hospital before you got up. I'd hidden it down the next street before you arrived home on Friday night. Anyway, I took the Jeep to the hospital and used the knife to cut myself and smear the blood on the headrest."

She pointed to the healing wound on the top of her hip. "Remember this?"

"You said you got that –"

She nodded, "I know, I know. I said I got it when Fox called. Well, big surprise here, Johnny! I *lied!* I used the blood to smear on the headrest so I could prove to you Helen had been abducted. I caught a taxi and came home then, had a shower and had just enough time to check Helen was still drugged and get your breakfast ready before you woke."

She giggled, "Sherrie's time working at the hospital came in handy. For a while, she was studying to become a nurse. Did you know that, Johnny? Not only did I learn about all kinds of drugs, but she showed me how to give injections and also how to treat wounds. Which was pretty lucky, Johnny, for your arm, I mean. How're your stitches holding up?"

"Get on with it," John replied.

She sighed, "Might as well. You need to know all this, I guess, so it hurts you more. So you know the kind of pain I've been through since the day I met you."

Lightning flashed around them, making Zoe's wet body shine.

"We had a great day on Saturday, Johnny," she continued. "I remember how great I felt with you while we were shopping. It was like we were finally a real couple, together at last. I enjoyed every minute of it. Finally, just you and me. Together.

"Our little side-trip to the K-mart was just to make you realise something had happened to Helen. To build my story in your mind and to make you accept it as fact. Anyway, we had a great day. It was *so* good that I forgot what time it was. Totally forgot. And the day just slipped away!

"Then when I got home from the hospital before you, Helen was awake and had almost managed to escape. She'd untied half the ropes and was trying to call the police when I got there. I didn't have much time; I had no idea how long you would be. I ran up the hallway and flung myself at her and we struggled. But I managed to knock her out with one of your lamps. I hit her hard, Johnny. I panicked and I didn't know whether I'd killed her or not. I really had no idea at that stage. I got her hidden again just in time. Just before you got home."

Helen, I was so close to you. So close...

I'm so sorry I couldn't save you...

"It was so risky letting you into the bedroom that morning, Johnny," she smiled at him. "You went to the wardrobe and got some clothes, remember?"

He nodded slowly as he remembered.

"You were right next to her, Johnny. She was in the next section of the wardrobe, hidden in with her clothes, but you didn't look. If she'd made any noise, my game was over! I love to live on the edge, Johnny. It's the *thrill* that counts – and you took me all the way."

"You killed her then?" John asked.

Zoe shook her head, "No, no, she was fine. Fractured skull, maybe. But fine. I brought you here to the church and tied you up, telling you I was going to get Fox. What I really did was drive back to your house and get Helen. I still had the blue alien key ring with the spare front door key on it. You never took it off me, Johnny. I brought her up to the shack at Redlingford. I didn't want you to work out what was happening too soon. We spent Sunday night talking about you and what you were doing behind her back. But she never believed me."

Zoe stared into the distance and shook her head, "She *never* believed you would cheat on her. Hard to believe, considering all the problems you two were having."

Silence fell with the rain.

Sherrie squeezed John's hand.

"By Monday morning," Zoe continued. "I'd had enough. She wouldn't admit it. Even after I had twisted and burned her nipples with the fire poker. Even when I slowly inserted it into her pussy. It's amazing to watch flesh liquefy, Johnny.

But she still wouldn't believe you had cheated on her. That's dedication, I guess. Or blind love. Or stupidity. Her head was still bleeding. I got a bit carried away with the spade from the fireplace too. Hit her a few too many times. So, I guess there wasn't much strength left in her. She just started to fade away, mumbling incoherently and not making much sense. She wouldn't take orders and she couldn't stand by herself. Plus, the smell of burning flesh was too much in that little room in the shack."

Zoe sighed. "It's a shame. She was a nice lady. I would've liked to have tasted her before she went. But there wasn't enough time. I tried to make it as painless as possible, Johnny. Believe me, I did. There was so much blood by then and I knew her wounds were hurting. So I made it easy for her. One strike with the poker and then I strangled what life was left from her to make sure she was really dead. She didn't even fight it."

John's legs went from under him. He splashed into the wet undergrowth, kneeling in the puddles, his mind and world spinning out of control.

Thunder echoing all around him.

Helen…my God, Helen!

"I don't know if I really ever planned to kill her," Zoe continued, almost to herself now. "I was going to let her go and watch as she left you and destroyed your life. But she didn't believe me, so she wasn't going to do what I wanted her to do. And then she was dead. Totally dead. And I'd been to the edge again. Right to the edge this time. The furthest I've ever been."

Silence fell with the rain.

John stared at the wet muddy ground.

After a while, she continued. "Luckily, I had another plan up my sleeve. I needed stuff to make her death point to you. So I got your cum and pubic hair and some skin from your arm wound and I planted it on her body after I moved it closer to the church. There's enough to lead straight back to you and your girlfriend."

John could feel Sherrie's arm on his back, trying to comfort him.

"*Why?*" he heard her ask. "*Why* do this to him?"

Zoe's face fell.

"It all made sense at the time," she replied. "John would be arrested for murdering Helen and he'd be thrown in jail. You would've come back to me then, Sherrie. And we could've been together forever."

Silence settled over them once more.

John let out a deep sob.

"That was the plan anyway," Zoe continued. "But it all went wrong. And things changed between us all. Johnny, we were so good together. I just don't know what I want now."

Zoe turned to plead with Sherrie, "But I never wanted *you* to find out, Sherrie. That wasn't in the plan. I didn't want you coming up and finding us at the church. I *never* wanted to hurt you. But now you know everything anyway!"

"Yes," Sherrie replied. "I do."

"And you'll *never* take me back now…"

"Exactly."

John looked up from the ground to stare at Zoe.

She dropped her eyes to his.

"So we see it out until the end, Johnny," she said. "There's nothing more for us. This game goes all the way to the edge."

John watched as she took a step backwards.

Lightning flashed long enough for her diamond to reflect the light.

And the troubled look on her face.

"All the way," she repeated as she turned to leave. "To the edge…and beyond."

Seventy-three

They ran through the night.

"John!" Sherrie called. "Slow down! You're going *too fast!*"

He had no choice. He had to get there before Zoe.

He had to play the game to his rules.

The rain fell heavily around them. The ground was slippery and dangerous. But it didn't matter. John knew what he had to do.

His body's numbness had gone. He was hot and sweating now. Each of his wounds ached and itched, his sweat aggravating the open sores.

Keep going...

Gotta get there first!

Keep going!

Lightning flashed, illuminating their way.

And as they ran, John thought about what Zoe had said. Patricia Bourke.

Could she really be "Pattie the Fattie"?

He couldn't believe it. Although he quickly realised he couldn't really remember what Patricia looked like. All his mind would conjure up was an image of an ugly teenage girl with rolls of fat around her stomach and big sweaty, clingy hands. When he tried to picture her face, or Maureen O'Reilly's, he realised he couldn't.

She's changed so much...

"And so have you, pal," said Richard in his head.

John wanted to close his eyes and wish him away, but beating Zoe back to the church was more important.

"You *still* don't remember what happened, do you?" Richard continued. "All those years of lies have settled on your brain. You need to dig through it all."

Go away! I've told you before, get out of my head.

"If you dig through all those lies, my friend, you'll find the real reason behind all this."

Huh?

"Think back to the party. Try and remember…"

Thunder rolled behind him in the night.

John ran harder as he cast his mind back.

I told you I was going to the party Donny DuBois was holding and that you should come along.

You said, "Jam it," and kept typing.

"Wrong pal, first mistake. I was trying to finish a biology assignment. I told you I would meet you there later."

Really?

And as John thought about it, he remembered.

You're right. That is how it happened!

The party was boring. And so were the people. They just wanted to get on Donny's good side. The guys were mostly from the team and most of the female flesh was better left on the rack.

Patricia and Maureen O'Reilly were there too, hoping to get lucky. Their sad make-up and rolls of fat made them only good for teasing and laughing at.

"Do you remember now? They were a bit drunk," Richard continued.

Patricia and Maureen? Never! They never touched the stuff.

"I know. But someone had spiked the punch. Remember? It was in that big punchbowl in the lounge room."

Oh, I didn't know it was spiked.

"And you'd had a couple too, pal. Remember?"

John scanned his memory but he didn't remember having any drinks. The party was so bad he'd kept completely sober. At least he thought he did.

He remembered standing in a corner for most of the night, checking out from afar Christie Baker's breasts.

John smiled.

Ahhh, Christie! A girl with class, tits and ass.

Those amazing tits that defied gravity.

A true natural wonder of the world.

John remembered deciding to go home after an hour or two. There was no action at the party other than the sly glimpses of Christie Baker's breasts.

He remembered slipping out of the main lounge room and skilfully dodging the hot and clammy hands of "Pattie the Fattie" and Maureen. He was wiping his hands and heading down to the front door when it opened and Helen walked in.

"Whoa there!" Richard interrupted his thoughts. "Back up a bit."

Why?

"You've skipped everything!"

No, I haven't. It's all there. The party was dull. I left. It's that simple.

"No, not so simple," Richard replied. "You just don't remember properly."

There's nothing to remember!

"Yes, there's plenty, my friend."

John shook his head as he ran through the rain. He thought about looking back for Sherrie. But he didn't.

No time...

"Why were you wiping your hands?" Richard continued.

Huh?

"According to *your* version of events, you slipped from the lounge room, dodging Patricia and Maureen. You said you were wiping your hands as you left."

So?

"Why?"

I don't know. It doesn't matter!

"But it *does*, pal. It matters so much!"

John's mind spun, trying to work out why this was so important. But Richard had started him thinking.

Why was I wiping my hands?

"You had punch on them. They were all sticky from the punch!"

Okay, John thought as he ran. *If you say so. It still doesn't matter, though. I must've spilt some on me.*

"Jesus Christ!" Richard yelled. "How *blind* are you, pal? Think *back*! Think back to the lounge room!"

There's nothing to think back to!

"Yes, there is!"

I was walking through the lounge to leave. There was no one around. Most of the guys had picked a girl or two and they were off in the rooms somewhere screwing each other's brains out.

"Good pal, keep going!"

But that's it!

Richard sighed. "Were you in the lounge alone?"

John nodded. *Yeah, I think so.*

"Where were Patricia and Maureen?"

Oh, they were there too.

"Exactly!"

They were in the lounge, in one corner, talking to each other.

Lightning flashed.

And suddenly John remembered...

Shit, there is more!

They cornered him before he could reach the door to the hall. They were both drunk on the punch and they both wanted him.

"Hi Johnny," Patricia had said. "Having fun?"

"No," he replied. "Can you move, Pattie? I want to leave."

"Don't leave so early," Maureen said. "The night is still young. There's plenty of time to have fun yet."

"I'm going home," he pushed past them, but Pattie grabbed him by the shoulder.

He turned to look at her. She was smaller than him...

The same height as Zoe!

...and she looked up into his eyes.

"Johnny, *don't go*. We could *all* have fun together. Just you and me and Maureen."

John's mouth had curled. "No thank you, I'd rather fuck a corpse than you two fat turds. I'm not *that* drunk!"

His words hit home and caused the desired reaction. Pattie's eyes fell to the floor and Maureen put her hands to her face.

"Let's face it girls," he'd continued. "No one's going to be opening up your pussies for a very long time. They'd have to be blind or blind drunk to stick it into your fat mouldy cunts."

Shit, John thought as he ran. *I'd forgotten all this!*

"Forgotten, pal?" Richard replied. "I don't think so. Maybe *removed* is a better word for it."

Maureen hadn't been able to stand the insults. She ran off deeper into the house, her hands to her face, crying loudly.

John turned to go.

But Pattie the Fattie had grabbed both his shoulders as he walked, tipping him off balance and slamming him into the lounge room wall. Her body was on his, her lips reaching for his. Her disgusting breath filled his face and her sweaty hands were all over him. He struggled for a few seconds and grabbed her hands, pulling her from him and spinning her around, pushing her back against the wall.

"*Yes!*" she had moaned.

John shook his head, "Never! Not with me, you fat ugly piece of shit."

"*Please*, Johnny," she said. "I want it to be you in me for my first time."

"No way!"

"I dream about you. I want you so bad. Please! Stick your huge cock in me. Make me bleed."

Shit!

And then John remembered it all.

Everything…

He slid to a stop by the side of the nearest pine and doubled over.

His breathing was hard, his head pounded, and he felt like he was going to be sick.

"You remember now?" Richard asked him.

John nodded.

Oh my God! Yes! How could I forget that?

"Because you wanted to. You *needed* to."

And that's why Zoe is the way she is?

"Partly…"

Jesus, no…

"Fuck me, Johnny," Pattie the Fattie had said.

She was drunk.

And he was a little too.

But that was no excuse.

No excuse at all…

He remembered it all.

He pushed her away from him, throwing her aside without another thought.

He walked to the centre of the lounge room, suddenly feeling claustrophobic and needing some space away from Pattie. He reached for a glass and poured himself another drink of the punch sitting on the table. He could hear Pattie crying behind him, but he wouldn't turn around. He wouldn't give her the satisfaction.

And then the far door opened. Donny DuBois and Marty Klavan stumbled into the room, laughing with each other.

"Did *you* do that?" Donny yelled to John in a slurred voice. He pointed over his shoulder. "Maureen's in the next room crying her eyes out and puking her guts out."

Marty laughed next to him, "It's *sooo* fuckin' funny. You should come out here and watch, Murdock!"

Donny slid to a stop in the middle of the room and pointed at the collapsed figure of Pattie, huddled in one corner.

"Fuck, man," he said, still pointing. "You've mind fucked *both* of them?"

John took another drink of the punch. He didn't want to talk. He wanted to get out of there. Suddenly the party had turned from boring to sickening.

"She wants you to fuck her?" Marty asked, bumping into Donny's shoulder.

John just stared at Pattie as she cried on the floor.

"*No one* would fuck her," Donny replied. "She's too dog ugly and way too fat."

"Yeah, I know," Marty said. "Unless you could fuck her and *hurt* her."

John saw the gleam in Donny's eyes. There were no second thoughts, he could tell.

Donny staggered towards Pattie.

"Yeah," he half-muttered. "Make it *hurt*."

John put down his glass and turned to leave. But his eyes met Pattie's.

He could see the fear in them.

He stopped in his tracks and just stood there.

Then Donny was by Pattie's side. Marty was there too. They both reached down, pulling her up. Donny grabbed a handful of her hair and lifted her roughly to her feet. "Don't, *please*..." she whispered through tears.

"Shut up, *bitch*," Donny spat back at her. "One sound from you and you're *fuckin' dead*, you understand?"

She nodded slowly, tears running down her cheeks.

"Don't hurt me," she whispered.

Donny laughed. Marty sniggered.

John just watched on.

"Please..." she said again.

Donny turned angry then. He swung her around and slammed the front of her body hard against the wall. Her head cannoned off the wall and she let out a muffled cry.

He grabbed her hips and pulled them towards him. Pattie mumbled something, but John couldn't hear it over Marty's laughter.

Donny lifted her dress up and over her ass.

And Marty pulled down her oversized plain panties.

They could all see her fat white arse and, between her legs, her hairy pussy.

John felt sick. He turned and poured himself another cup of punch using the silver ladle.

"I want it to be with *Johnny* for my first time," she yelled.

Donny pulled the handful of her hair back hard again, then let go of it. She yelled in pain as her forehead hit the wall hard.

"Don't worry, bitch, you'll *never* forget your first time," Donny said to her through clenched teeth.

She dropped her head and stretched her legs further apart. Almost as if she finally realised she was beaten. As if they'd broken her spirit.

Donny had placed his left hand on her fat arse cheek and spread it to one side.

He turned to look at Marty. They both smiled at each other, a sick and twisted smile.

John did nothing. He felt frozen, unable to control the situation.

Marty turned around and surveyed the lounge, his eyes finally coming to rest on the punch bowl.

He leaned over and whispered in Donny's ear. Donny turned and looked at John.

And at the ladle still in his hand.

Donny's smile grew wider and he reached out to the food table with his right hand.

"Give it to me, Murdock," he said.

The silver ladle.

John stared down at it in his hands.

He didn't move, didn't take his eyes from it. He knew what was coming. Before he could react, Marty was by his side.

"Quit stalling, asshole," he said as he ripped the ladle from his hands. The punch spilled from the ladle all over John's right hand as Marty took it away from him.

By the time John looked up, Donny had the ladle and was bringing it towards Pattie.

Donny let go of Pattie's arse just long enough to rub his hands together. Some punch had spilled on his hands too.

His hands were sticky now, just like John's.

But Donny didn't care.

He knelt down by Pattie's arse and positioned the long silver handle of the ladle, resting it on the lips of her pussy.

"Ready?" he had asked.

"*Please, don't hurt me,*" Pattie whispered.

But he did.

He pushed in hard and fast.

The ladle resisted at first, but then slid easily inside.

He pushed it in hard and deep.

Very deep.

And Pattie screamed.

As she screamed, she turned to face John. She looked him right in the eyes. He could now remember the hate and sadness in them, mixed with fear and revulsion.

"Johnny!" she cried. "*Help me!*"

And John had closed his eyes, turned around, and headed for the door as quickly as possible.

He had to get out of there. That was all he could think of doing.

Pattie's screams followed him out of the lounge and into the hall as he left her alone with Donny and Marty.

"Remember now?" Richard asked in his head.

John knelt by the pine, his back against the trunk. He wrapped his arms around his body and closed his eyes to the rain.

I can't believe that happened!

"It did," Richard continued. "And you blocked it out."

I was drunk. So were they.

"It doesn't matter."

I blocked it out because it was so terrible.

"But Zoe didn't. She remembered. She remembered the suffering and the pain and the humiliation. You left her there, pal. You left her in the lounge room, on her knees, the ladle so far inside her she had to get help removing it."

Oh God!

"You just walked out of the room and down the hall."

And then I met Helen.

"Yes," Richard said. "You wiped your hands clean and walked straight out to meet Helen."

It was the happiest night of my life.

"Only once you removed the events that made it the worst night of your life. You thought you were above those other guys, better than them, and finding Helen that night proved it. At least, in your mind…"

No wonder Zoe's so crazy! Something like that would change anyone…

"And all she was trying to do was be noticed by you."

I realise that now. But I was younger then. Much younger. How was I to know?

"She'd forgiven you for what you did at the funeral. She was willing to try again."

Huh?

"Come on, pal. Let's open up all the way. Let's get all the skeletons out of your closet…"

"Are you *okay*?"

John opened his eyes. Sherrie was standing over him, a worried look on her face.

"No," he muttered as lightning flashed and the rain poured down. "No, I'm not okay."

<u>Seventy-four</u>

Side by side they walked through the rain.

Thunder rolled and echoed deep into the night.

"You want to talk about it?" Sherrie asked as they walked.

He shook his head, "Not yet."

"Okay," she replied. "But I'm here for you when you want to talk."

"I know," he replied as he turned and kissed her forehead. He smiled at her.

She's so good to me. So loving and loyal. I just hope this time I can be as loving and loyal too.

The rain fell heavily.

Sherrie's hair was a mess and John could see the wound she'd received when Zoe had driven into her car. It was high on the side of her head, and it looked deep. But it wasn't bleeding anymore.

That's the main thing.

"Just don't run off like that again," she continued.

"I won't."

"It *scared* me. And you left me all alone."

"I know. I promise, it won't happen again."

She hugged him.

"I love you," she said.

How can you?

"I love you too," he replied. He hoped he sounded as if he meant it.

The rain continued to fall.

They walked on in the night.

"You ready?" asked Richard in the silence.

Yeah. We might as well...

"Okay, you start the story."

John sighed. He knew what had to follow.

I had no idea the funeral was for Patricia's mother.

"Yes, you did," Richard replied. "You've just decided to forget it."

And it was before the party Donny DuBois held?

"Yes, quite a while before."

For some reason you and I and some of our other friends attended the funeral.

"Uh-huh, not *us* – just *you*. And you had one *particular* reason, pal."

Laura?

"Laura. Yes, well done, my friend. You're starting to think through this already! Laura was there because her mother was a close friend of the family. *You* were there to see her. 'It won't look so suspicious if we both go,' you'd said to me. Like *that* was going to stop you! I told you to jam it. I wasn't going!"

Everyone tried to sit as close to the exit as possible, aiming for the back pews, and far from prying eyes.

"Wrong! You sat down the front. As near to Laura as possible."

Really? I don't remember that...

"That doesn't surprise me, pal."

During the service, I turned and looked along the row and I saw Laura Austin staring back at me.

"Close, but no cigar, my friend. Don't you remember? She was sitting *next* to you! You'd purposefully headed down the front to sit with her. Can't you remember even that?"

No. I mean, well, maybe. It's all so confusing.

"Lies will do that to you..."

I didn't know who she was at the time, didn't even know her name, but I wanted to know her. Very badly.

Richard chuckled. "Boy, you old romantic you! What have you been doing? Reading those one-buck romance novels? You'd known her for about two months then. It was a Monday morning and because you had an out of state football game on the weekend, you hadn't spent any time with her since Friday. You two were fucking like it was going out of style at that stage, and two days apart must've been like a drought of epic proportions for both of you. Think, Johnny, *try* to find the truth."

Are you sure? I can't've made all this up.

"Really? But you're so *good* at it! Lies are your forte. You should know that by now. Think of all the lies you told Helen to keep your relationship with Sherrie a secret."

Laura was sitting about fifteen feet away.

"She was sitting *next* to you with her hand on your thigh...and then higher."

But outside, when we met, we introduced ourselves.

"Pal, you've just confused stories, that's all. You've merged two different events into one. You already knew her when you decided to sneak out of the funeral. The mind can do that sometimes. It compresses things. You just like to help it by sprinkling a few lies here and there too. It *makes* a better story if you compress it all into one!"

We did have sex in the toilet though.

"Oh, yes, you did that. But it wasn't your first time with her. It was one of your last."

Thunder rolled by and he remembered all.

She *was* sitting next to him. He was fondling her groin and she was rubbing her hand across his cock. They both got hot very quickly.

They both needed more.

She was wearing that cheeky grin he loved and he smiled back at her.

They both knew what they wanted.

John looked around to make sure no one was watching.

He looked back into her eyes and bent forward, whispering his plan into her ear.

She giggled loudly.

Heads turned towards her and she blushed and slumped down in her seat. But as she settled back down, the heads turned away and back to the priest, who was giving his sermon.

John continued to watch her, smiling at her...loving her.

"Don't worry," he remembered whispering to her now. "I'll make it all up to you."

She smiled again.

He remembered he was hard and pulsing, his cock pushing to break through his pants. The room was hot and he felt claustrophobic.

Waiting a few minutes more, he timed it just right.

The priest's back was turned when he stood up.

Faces began to turn and a murmur ran through the whole room. People were watching him, but he didn't care.

He made his way along his row, excusing himself time and time again, as his legs knocked the knees of other mourners.

Finally, he made it to the end of the row. He straightened himself up, kept his eyes on the floor in front of him and walked up the aisle and out of the room.

"Back up, pal, think *again!*" Richard said in a deep voice. "Someone grabbed your arm, remember?"

John thought about it for a second. He didn't remember that at all.

"Patricia grabbed you as you were walking down your row. She was sitting in the row in front. She turned around and grabbed you, remember?"

John was about to shake his head.

But then he *did* remember.

Shit, yeah. I do! I was almost at the end of the row when my arm was grabbed. I turned around and Pattie the Fattie was staring up at me. She had tears in her eyes.

"Do you remember what she said to you?"

Lightning flashed around the forest.

He could see her now. The image was clear. He watched her lips move.

"Don't go, Johnny," she had asked. "*Please?*"

He looked down at her. Took her hands in his and smiled consolingly.

Jesus Christ! He remembered it all now.

He bent down to her, leaned over to her ear.

And he whispered into it.

"You can sit here crying your fat little eyes out, for all I care. I've got something better to do."

My God, how could I be so heartless?

John's eyes filled with tears.

"A bit too late to show remorse, pal," Richard said in a sad voice. "The time for that was years ago. You can't take back the words that forged Zoe into who she is today."

He remembered standing back up and leaving the row, smiling as he did so.

He remembered the total silence in the room as he walked up the aisle. There was just one loud solitary weep.

It came from Patricia.

Everyone's eyes were upon him and he wondered if anyone had any idea what he had said to her. He didn't know if they did and, at the time, he didn't care.

He walked from the room.

And then, a couple of minutes later, so did Laura.

"Clearer now, is it, pal?" Richard said.

John hung his head.

I can't believe I did that.

"You did."

I can't believe I'd forgotten it either.

"I think you know exactly why you blocked it out."

Because I was an asshole.

"More than that, my friend. You blocked it out because it doesn't fit the nice, suave, successful guy you think you are now. It just doesn't fit. You're as shocked as anyone would be to find out you did those things. And the worst part of it is that Patricia let you get away with it. She didn't tell anyone, she didn't call the police when she was raped with the punch ladle. She didn't tell anyone. She moved on with her life and tried to make it better."

Until...

"*Exactly!* Until you come back into it to steal Sherrie from her. She loved you once, pal, and you broke her heart. Then you broke it a second time."

John nodded.

I know.

"She's not so crazy now, is she?"

Probably not. She's just fighting for what's hers. It makes more sense now.

"The truth always does, my friend."

I should apologise.

"I think the time for that has long gone. For you and Zoe...and Helen."

I should say something to Zoe.

"She still loves you in a strange, twisted way. I think she finally was content when she had you tied to the X-frame at the church. Finally you were hers and she could do what she liked to you. To apologise now only shows you pity her."

Not a good idea.

"No, I don't think so."

I want to do something…so she knows I've changed.

"Pal, the game's too far gone. You can't control this now. All you can hope for is that you win."

He nodded.

I have to win. For Helen and Sherrie.

"And for you. But you can only beat her by playing your rules."

I know.

"You have to be the one who calls the shots from now on."

I'm trying.

"Try harder."

I will. Thanks, Richard.

"Good luck, pal. You're going to need it."

And with a clap of thunder, Richard was gone from John's mind.

Just like that.

As suddenly as he had been taken from them all in the car accident that killed him four years earlier.

Just like that…

I miss you pal, John thought.

But there was no answer. Richard was gone.

Just silence.

Poor Zoe.

It's all my fault.

I know that now.

But I've got to win.

I have to.

"You okay?" Sherrie asked as they walked through the night.

He nodded.

"You're very quiet."

"I'm wrestling with ghosts from the past."

"Oh…"

"And the present."

"Sometimes it's good to talk these things through with somebody," she continued.

"I know."

"A good friend or someone even closer."

He nodded. "I just did."

She looked confused by his comment, but he smiled and kissed her once more.

"Come on," he hugged her. "The quicker we get to the church, the quicker this will be over for all of us."

Lightning flashed and lit their way through the forest.

Game's end was near.

<u>Seventy-five</u>

The rain was heavy when they arrived back at the church.

For once, John welcomed the noise of the rain. It covered their footsteps and voices as they approached.

"Where do you think she is?" Sherrie whispered by his ear.

"Helen or Zoe?"

"Helen," she replied.

"I have no idea. We'll just have to check everywhere."

Slowly, they edged towards the church. The night was dark and the pines were hiding them at the edge of the clearing. John could see a glow from the church windows, but he had no idea if Zoe was inside.

"You stay here," he said over his shoulder to Sherrie.

"No way!" she grabbed his hand. "I go where you go."

"I want you to be safe!"

"I won't be safe unless I'm with you."

John sighed, his breath fogging in front of him.

"Okay, but at the first sign of trouble, head for the forest again, alright?"

Sherrie nodded.

He held her hand tighter; squeezed it.

"Here we go," he said as they stepped out from the trees and headed towards the church.

Lightning flashed around them, but he couldn't worry about that now. He had to check the church to see if Zoe or Helen were in there.

I have to know.

And it's time I started playing the game my way.

They were almost to the church wall. And then they were blinded.

At first John thought it was another flash of lightning, but it lasted too long. It didn't go away. He put his hands up to his eyes and squinted at the light.

The lights.
The security lights!
Fuck!
Something else forgotten!
He sprinted for the side of the church, pulling Sherrie with him.

She yelped with surprise as they charged for the wall and slammed into it.

John pulled her down low. He was breathing hard, the rain dripping down his face and onto his chest.

"Security lights," he said between breaths. "I forgot about them."

Sherrie looked up at the side of the church.

"Well, she knows we're here now!"

"If she's here."

Sherrie nodded, "Yeah. But I'm kinda guessing she's around here somewhere."

John agreed.

She must be.

"Stay low," he said after a few more seconds. He turned himself around to face the church and slowly stood.

He peered into the window.

He couldn't see much because of the warped stained glass, but there was enough light from inside for him to be pretty sure that the church was empty.

No Zoe.

No Helen.

Damn.

He slid back down against the wall.

"Anything?" Sherrie asked.

He shook his head.

She sighed deeply. "Well, on the positive side, maybe she doesn't know we're here, or maybe we've beaten her back. So, what do we do now?"

Thunder rolled across the sky.

The security lights automatically shut off, leaving them once again in darkness.

The rain pelted down loudly on the roof of the church and splashed hard into the puddles surrounding them.

"I don't know," John replied. "Zoe said Helen was back at the church. Or near it."

"Near?"

"Yeah."

"Is there any other place around here that you know of?"

John shook his head. "No," he replied, looking into the darkness.

Think...

Think about what you saw out here Saturday night. Where else could the body be? Where else could Helen and Zoe be?

He re-traced his steps Saturday night.

And then it hit him.

So simple!

He should've thought of it earlier.

"Quick," he grabbed her hand as he stood up.

"What?"

"I know where to try!"

"Where?"

"The machinery shed!"

"Huh?"

He pulled her along the side of the church, splashing through the puddles as they ran. Nearing the back wall, the security lights flooded the area once more.

They reached the corner of the church and John pointed across to the shed standing behind the church.

"The machinery shed! She must be in there!"

He turned to face Sherrie. There was hope in her eyes.

The rain fell about them as he took her in his arms and kissed her hard. Her lips were wet and salty, but warm too.

"I love you," she whispered as they parted.

"I love you too," he replied as he smiled. "Come on, let's do it!"

They ran across the open area between the back of the church and the machinery shed.

The rain fell hard, slanting across and thudding into them like flies.

The security lights at the back of the church flooded the area with light.

But John didn't care. He'd almost won.

Nothing's going to stop me now.

I've beaten her. Beaten her at her own sick, fucked up game!

They slid to a halt outside the double doors and window of the shed.

John cupped his hands and looked inside.

He couldn't make anything out. It was too dark and too hard to see. His breath quickly began steaming up the window.

"See anything?" Sherrie asked.

"No, too dark."

The rain fell heavier.

"Here, help me with these," John said as he threw back the metal latch on the double doors.

Sherrie pulled open one door as John opened the other.

They stood in front of the shed with both doors open.

So dark in there...

Lightning flashed about them, a double fork of light.

It illuminated inside the shed.

Noooooooooo! John's mind screamed.

But there was no doubt about it.

The shed was empty.

Seventy-six

He leaned against the door of the shed and closed his eyes tight.

Thunder rolled across the sky.

I can't let her win again! he thought.

She said Helen was near the church. Near the church...

"Honey, you okay?" Sherrie was by his side.

He nodded, but kept his eyes closed.

"There's nothing here," she said.

He nodded again.

Near the church...

But where?

She said near the church.

Where else? WHERE?

And then his stomach flipped over.

Oh Jesus fucking Christ!

The graveyard!

It all made sense to him. He remembered the freshly dug mounds he had seen on Saturday night.

She's done this before, he thought. *She's killed before! And that's where Helen will be.*

In the graveyard.

Oh God! Oh God!

He opened his eyes as lightning flashed again. It was one last chance to check the shed, but he knew it was empty.

Sherrie was kneeling down, looking at the ground, her hand stretched out towards the puddles.

"There's drag marks here," she said to him. "And they're not very old."

"Huh?" He tried to concentrate on what she was saying, "What do you mean?"

"Someone's dragged something, or someone, out of here just recently and left two drag marks in the ground. Look!"

John bent down next to Sherrie. There was enough il-lumination from the security lights for him to make out two long trails left in the ground. They were gouged deeply into the mud and the rain was pooling in them. They started from somewhere in the shed, crossed some tyre tracks and led off towards the side of the church.

And towards the graveyard!

Maybe Helen hasn't been buried in the graveyard yet.

Maybe Zoe's doing that now!

Oh God!

Shit!

I have to stop her!

I have to stop it all!

John stood and grabbed Sherrie's hand.

"Quickly," he said over the thunder. "I know where she is!"

They turned and ran back through the mud and puddles to the side of the church. He didn't have any trouble spot-ting the paved path heading off into the bushes. Almost by instinct he knew where it would be.

And he was right.

The rain fell heavy and hard as they ran down the wet, slippery path.

As they did so, they left the floodlights and the church behind them. The night swallowed them again in its claus-trophobic blanket of dark.

"John," Sherrie called from behind him. "Slow *down!*"

But he didn't have the time. He couldn't. He had to get to the graveyard.

Have to save Helen...

She's dead!

But I still have to save her!

The cold night air seemed clammy now, closing in and pushing down on them with the rain.

It was dark, but he knew what was up ahead.

Come on, come on...

Quickly!

A new set of lights illuminated from in front of him.

Yes!

He squinted for a moment as he ran onto the tennis court, but he didn't stop.

He knew where he was headed.

He turned, his feet sliding on the wet clay of the court, and sprinted towards the gap in the trees and the path to the graveyard.

"John!" Sherrie called from behind him.

Not now. I have to get there!

"John! *Stop!*"

No! I can't! Not now!

"John, Helen's *here!*"

Huh? What?

John skidded to a halt just a few short feet away from the path to the graveyard.

He turned around slowly.

Sherrie was standing to the side of the tennis court, leaning on one of the tennis net poles. She was breathing hard, her chest heaving, and her eyes were looking away from him. Her finger was pointing across the court.

To the gazebo.

And the X-frame.

John followed her gaze.

No, oh no, Jesus, please no…

And through the rain he could see her.

Helen was tied to the X-frame in the gazebo.

Or what was left of her…

Lightning flashed above them. John could see her naked, battered and twisted body, the black and blue bruises, and the dried blood.

Nooooo!

This can't be happening!

Nooooo!

He ran towards her, sprinting across the court and up the steps into the gazebo.

Sherrie called out to him, but he didn't hear her over the thunder and the rain.

He didn't look back.

All he could see was Helen's beaten body.

All he could hear was the pitiful cry in his throat.

He stopped in front of her.

"Oh, *Helen*," he whispered as he reached out and touched her cold, bloodied face.

She was tied to the X-frame in exactly the same position he had been on Monday night. Her bruised arms hung above her, stretched across the top of the X, and her cut and burned legs were tied at the bottom. John could see the damage done to her breasts by the fire poker; dark, ugly burn marks where Helen's nipples used to be. They made the skin look as if it had melted on her body before drying into a putrefying black mass.

He could only imagine the pain she must've gone through.

Helen's head looked different, out of shape; a large piece of skull near her forehead was compressed in an unnatural way. Her hair was matted and full of dried blood, and in some places missing completely, having been pulled out at the root.

Her face was turned to the side, looking away from him. Her eyes were shut and her mouth was open in what looked like a half-scream. John thought he saw tears rolling from her eyes, but he realised it was just the rain, rolling from her body.

Zoe must have dragged her from the shed.

He stepped closer, reaching out to touch her.

Oh, Helen, I'm so sorry.

But he couldn't do it.

He lowered his head in shame.

I can't even touch you. Not now.

His eyes looked lower.

Between Helen's legs.

And he saw the silver ladle sticking out from Helen's vagina.

No! No, Zoe…you didn't!

Fuck!

No! No, how could you?

Oh fuck! No!

Lightning struck, reflecting off the silver handle.

He fell to his knees.

Nooooooooo!

The rain fell heavier, bouncing from the gazebo roof in a deafening cacophony of sound. Thunder rolled in.

You won't do this, he thought as he reached out for the ladle. *You can't do this to her! It's not her fault!*

He grabbed hold of the cold handle with shaking hands. It was sticky – just like it was all those years ago.

I won't have you treat her like this!

Slowly, he began pulling it from her body.

It came down slowly, streaked with blood and mucus and melted skin and darker specks of something.

John wiped the tears from his eyes.

Lightning struck as he continued to pull.

This is all my fault! But I wasn't to know. I didn't know then that all this would happen! How could I fucking *know?*

You deserved better, Hèlen, so much better.

I'm so sorry. I'm the reason you're here!

And there's nothing I can do about it now.

Thunder rolled.

And Sherrie screamed.

The thunder got louder.

Even louder.

The ladle slipped out of Helen and through his hands, falling to the floor with a clatter.

There, it's done…

The thunder continued.

John sighed deeply, turned around and looked out to the tennis court.

Sherrie was yelling at him, frantically waving her hands in the air.

He couldn't hear her.

"What?" he called.

The rain was too heavy on the roof.

The thunder too loud.

But then he realised it wasn't thunder.

It was a motor he could hear.

Revving.

Getting louder.

He turned to his left just in time to see the tractor speeding towards him.

With Zoe at the wheel.

Seventy-seven

John had little time to react. He felt frozen as he watched the red tractor charge straight at him, bearing down on him with seconds to spare. The sounds of the tractor's motor filled his ears and shook the gazebo as it sped closer. The front loading scoop was positioned high enough for its teeth to spear right through John's chest if it made contact with him. The teeth were large and sharp; mud, grass and tree branches were stuck between some of them.

John turned to Sherrie. She was waving at him still, pleading with him to jump.

He looked back to the tractor. Zoe was smiling at him.

He turned and reached for Helen, fumbled with the straps holding her legs to the X-frame.

Gotta get her out of here.

Gotta!

His fingers wouldn't work. They couldn't undo the straps.

Come on, John, concentrate. You can do this!

His forehead furrowed. Sweat rolled. He concentrated hard.

The rain and thunder and motor noise were deafening. The gazebo was shaking.

Come on!

Concentrate!

He could feel the enormous size of the tractor looming behind him.

"No time, John," he heard Sherrie's voice in his ear. He looked up at her, but she was already pulling him backwards.

He grabbed at her. Tried to stop her.

But it was no use.

She pulled and they tumbled.

They fell down the steps together, stumbling backwards and hitting the ground hard, sliding through the clay and the water. John's back jarred as he hit the ground, a pain sliced through his hip and his head bounced on the wet clay.

The rain poured into his face as the tractor roared past him, smashing into the gazebo with force and speed. The teeth from the front scoop bit through the sides of the gazebo like paper, tearing at the timber and sending fragments flying. The tractor rolled forward, its wheels stopping as they reached the floor of the gazebo.

The motor revved.

For a moment, all was still. Nothing moved.

The motor revved again and the scoop came crashing down on the floor, breaking through the wood and shaking the whole structure.

The gazebo held for a second or two more.

But then it folded under the weight of the tractor. It buckled and fell in on itself. The tractor rode up on the crushed floor and charged through two of the poles holding the roof in place. The roof teetered and then fell backwards, taking the other two poles that held the X-frame and Helen's body with it, crumbling back into the old wooden seats behind the gazebo.

John watched as Helen's body flipped backwards with the X-frame. He saw her face once more, for only a split-second, before she was gone from his sight, lost under the twisted metal roof that fell on top of her.

The tractor continued its slow course of destruction. It used the crushed roof as a ramp, driving up and over it. The metal screamed through the night as it was crushed under the weight of the tractor.

Helen!

The gazebo crushed lower, splitting and spreading. Timber and metal popped and bent, gave way to the greater force.

Noooooooo!

John wiped the rain from his eyes and backed away across the court on all fours.

"Come on." Sherrie was pulling his arm. "We *have* to get away from here!"

The tractor stopped its forward movement.

John watched its wheels churn on what was left of the gazebo.

Helen! No!

He shook his head.

After everything, I couldn't even save you this one last time.

Damn it! I couldn't do it!

He didn't want to know what the tractor had done to her. But he could imagine.

And from underneath a pile of rubble to the side of the gazebo, John spotted her right arm sticking out into the night.

Oh my God...

He could see her forearm and her hand, sticking out between two pieces of metal. Her palm was reaching up to the sky.

Almost reaching for me...

Thunder rolled and rain pelted down.

The tractor's motor moaned and then coughed.

John's eyes darted back to Zoe.

She was looking over her shoulder, staring at him.

She smiled.

And threw the tractor into reverse.

"Run, John!" Sherrie called.

"Stay here!" he said over his shoulder.

"What?"

"Stay here, don't move!"

He got to his feet as the tractor's tyres reversed on the rubble below it.

Now or never!

He sprinted for the tractor.

"Are you crazy?" Sherrie called after him.

The tractor continued reversing over the crushed gazebo, gaining speed now.

Zoe's eyes were concentrating on driving as she made sure her path was clear behind her.

Lightning filled the night.

The tractor drove back down the partly-demolished steps and bounced heavily onto the tennis court, sending mud and water and clay splashing backwards.

Zoe turned from looking over her shoulder.

But it was too late.

He was already there.

Thunder rolled as John jumped onto the tractor. He climbed upwards, reaching for her.

He slipped on the greasy step. Fell suddenly. But managed to hang on to the sidebar with his left hand.

Zoe looked surprised.

"Johnny, *no!*" she said as she reached out with one hand.

John regained his footing, used the step for leverage and stretched higher.

The tractor continued rolling slowly backwards.

He grabbed her throat with his right hand and squeezed hard. He could feel the tight cords in her neck swelling. He could feel her voice trying to escape.

He squeezed harder.

She tried to fend him off, but she couldn't get a tight enough grip. Her face started to change colour. He could see she was in pain.

"This has gone far *enough!*" he spat at her through clenched teeth.

She took her other hand from the wheel and sat forward in the seat, trying to claw at his eyes.

He swung his hand backwards with every ounce of energy he had left, taking her with it.

Gravity and momentum were on his side.

He threw her from the driver's seat.

She flew through the air and landed in a large pool of water on the court. She skidded for a few feet, her body gouging through the clay, the breath knocked from her.

He jumped from the tractor and landed nearby.

Before she had a chance to move, he was on her.

Pinning her down under him, he noticed she was wearing jeans now, and her old sneakers. She was wearing her black top too; the one with all the animals and the words *Natural Selection* printed underneath. Her wet and clay-covered hair was held back in a ponytail.

"You've gone too far, Zoe. There's no saving you *now.*"

"You got here too early, Johnny," she replied, smiling up at him as she tried to regain her breath through the rain. "The security lights signalled your arrival. Sloppy of you to forget about them, Johnny. I hadn't finished digging your grave though. You would've been quite at home next to your wife."

"Shut up!" he yelled at her.

"Yeah, that's it, Johnny. Be a man. Be a man finally. For the first *fucking* time. You tell me how it's going to be. Pin me down and yell at me! Yeah, Johnny, *do it*. It's a real *fucking* turn on!"

Zoe tried to struggle from his grip.

John held her down harder. His hands on her arms, his body on her chest, one leg across her hips.

"*Wanna fuck?*" she asked him. "Right here? Right now?"

He stared into her dark evil eyes.

I thought you were so beautiful and so innocent once...

"Don't get too excited, Johnny," she continued as lightning flashed. "Don't want your girlfriend to know you're thinking of fucking me again. Anyway, is your shredded cock up to it?"

"Shut *the fuck* up!" he shouted.

I have to think...

She continued to writhe under him.

"Killing Helen wasn't going to fix the past, Zoe," he said to her. "One death can't fix what happened to you."

Zoe laughed in the rain. "One death? Oh, Johnny, do you think you're only worth one? You're the cause of many! Don't you get it yet? *So many*, you have no idea!"

He looked at her, puzzled.

Thunder growled around them. The rain hit hard.

"I don't understand," he said in a low voice.

A smile spread across her face. "Think, Johnny. You don't really believe I *own* all this, do you? The church and the Jeep and the tractor and everything? Do you? Are you *that* stupid? People used to *live* here, Johnny. People used to live at Redlingford! I know this church hasn't been used often in the past few years, but I can guarantee the graveyard has been quite busy recently."

John's mouth opened. He tried to speak. Nothing would come out.

What?

Events clicked into place, his mind spun.

No!

"You're responsible for it all, Johnny. *Every* death. *Every* hurt. *Every* pain."

Noooooooo!

"All. Your. Fault."

He shook his head. He tried to say something but nothing would come.

This isn't real. It can't be!

He looked up across the court. He needed Sherrie.

More than ever.

She wasn't there.

Huh?

Panic sliced through him.

His eyes danced frantically, looking into the bushes for Sherrie. He moved his body across Zoe so he could view more of the court, his eyes searching the night for Sherrie.

"Oh yeah, baby," Zoe spat. "Move lower. I like your body on mine. Fuck me hard."

He ignored her.

He looked for Sherrie.

She wasn't there.

No!

She was by the pole! She was!

But where is she now?

And then the pain spl'it him in two.

It charged up his cock and balls, through his stomach and into his brain.

He rolled from Zoe, clutching at his groin, landing in a large puddle of rain and clay.

Shit, damn it!

He'd let his guard down, just for a second, and she'd struck.

"Nothing beats a man quicker than a good old knee to the balls," Zoe said. "You should know that, Johnny. It's *always* been part of the game."

She smiled at him as she picked herself up from the ground.

"You've *ruined* my clothes," she said as she wiped the clay and water from her jeans and shirt. She checked her ponytail, making sure it was still all in one piece.

He stared up at her. The rain fell hard against his face. The thunder shook the ground below him.

I just want to close my eyes, he thought. *And make it all go away...*

But he knew it wasn't possible.

With his right arm, he dragged himself away from Zoe. Pain was digging into his hip.

"You won't get far," Zoe watched him struggling. "I won't let you. Just remember, Johnny, you're *mine!*"

He kept sliding away from her, through the water and clay and rain.

"And I'll end this game *my* way!"

She reached into the back of her jeans and pulled out the revolver.

His eyes darted to it.

She pointed it at him.

"Don't worry," she smiled at him. "It's newly loaded. I had plenty of time to change clothes and reload while I was waiting for you two to get back here."

His back hit the tennis net pole and sent new pain through him. He stopped crawling, exhausted.

There's no use.

He reached out his hands to shield his face as lightning struck.

This is it!

"You had your chances, Johnny!" she said as her finger started to squeeze the trigger.

She smiled at him.

Yes, I did...I had my chances...

Then she turned away from him, pointing the gun to her left.

He followed her aim.

She was pointing at the tractor.

It was speeding towards her now, the engine revving.

Sherrie was at the wheel.

NO!

John climbed up and sprinted towards Zoe.

NOOOOOOO!

She pulled the trigger.

Once.

Twice.

Before she could fire a third time, John cannoned into her, knocking her from her feet.

He heard a cry and looked up at the tractor for a split second as he and Zoe flew through the air.

Sherrie was falling from the tractor's side, a splash of blood shining in the security lights.

Sherrie! No! Jesus, no! Not you too!

John and Zoe tumbled in the wet and the clay, rolling over and over again.

Pain charged along his shoulder and through his hip.

The gun jarred from Zoe's grip. It clattered and sloshed nearby.

John held on to her tightly, rolling with her, determined not to let her go.

They slid to a stop near the demolished gazebo. Side by side, they lay in the water, clay and mud.

"You *fucking* psycho *bitch!*" John yelled in her face.

The rain fell around them, striking like bullets.

"How *dare* you!" Zoe spat back, slapping a palm across his face. There was real hatred in her eyes. "Who was the one who took a young girl and *warped* her? Who was it who delighted in publicly embarrassing her every chance he got? Who was it who stood by and watched as two guys raped her and shoved a *fucking silver ladle* up her cunt? *Huh?* Who turned away from me when I pleaded, when I *begged,* for help? Who's the *fucking psycho,* Johnny? *Who?* You tell me!"

He shook his head.

"Who's the *fucking psycho*?" she screamed. "Who *ruined* my fucking miserable life?"

John reached out and rubbed some of the clay from her forehead. He ran his finger across the scar in her eyebrow. He traced the outline of the scar on her cheek.

He didn't know what to say.

He had no energy left to try...

And she didn't give him the chance.

She smiled at him and then dug her fingernails down through the wound in his left arm. She pushed hard, her fingernails scraping through his shirt and digging in deep. The pain sliced through him and he could feel the stitches popping one by one as she dragged her fingers down through the wound. Almost immediately, blood began to soak his shirt once more.

His scream split the night and his head felt light and his stomach churned.

He lost control of his arm and she escaped from his grip.

Before he knew it, she had staggered away from him.

"You don't win that easily," she said. "You can't win by charm anymore, Johnny."

John looked up at her. She was smiling down at him.

He looked past her, trying to see Sherrie. But he couldn't find her anywhere.

The tractor was in the way. Still moving.

Slowly rolling straight towards them.

He looked back to the steering wheel, thinking maybe Sherrie was back on the tractor, but the driver's cabin was empty.

The tractor rolled closer. Its front scoop sitting low now, parallel to the ground. Its teeth pointing directly at them.

He sat up quickly.

Pain bit at his hip.

His hand moved to his back pocket.

And he remembered...

Yes!

He smiled.

Of course!

My game.

My rules.

And one last chance...

Quickly, John got to his feet, picking himself out of the wet clay. He was holding his arm, trying to stop the blood flow.

He took a step towards her.

She put her hands on her hips and stood there, different emotions flooding across her face.

Work quickly!

The noise of the tractor's motor was getting louder as it rolled towards them.

"Zoe, *please*," he said in a calm voice.

Her head tilted.

He held out his hands to her.

She didn't move.

"I'm sorry," he said.

Zoe's face fell. Her bottom lip quivered and her forehead creased.

She looked away from him, to the ground.

"Really?" she asked.

"Yes, I am."

"You know, that's all I ever really wanted, Johnny."

This is it!

He leaped forward and punched her square in the face.

He felt her nose crack under his fist and the blood began to gush immediately.

She crumpled in front of him, hitting the ground heavily. Her back slammed into the water and clay, her head bounced hard.

John looked up at the tractor.

Almost here!

His hands fumbled in his back pocket.

Come on, come on! Quickly!

He pulled out the handcuffs and slapped one around her wrist. The teeth clattered and locked tight.

She was on the ground, shaking her head. Her other hand was trying to stop the flow of blood pouring from her nose.

Dazed and confused, she didn't fight back.

Using the cuffs, he dragged her a few feet across the court. She slid through the puddles and the clay.

He attached the other cuff to the nearest tennis net pole.

The teeth clattered and locked into place.

She was cuffed to the pole.

The tractor edged closer.

She was right in its path.

He bent down to her ear. "The game stops here," he whispered.

She looked at him, blood streaming from her nose, a look of fear on her face. It all dawned on her then.

"No!" she yelled as the sat up and pulled on the handcuffs.

Lightning flashed.

John saw a glint of gold around Zoe's neck.

He reached down her shirt and grabbed the half-heart gold pendant. With one swift movement, he pulled it from her neck.

She screamed at the top of her voice. She turned around and placed one foot on the pole for leverage and pulled harder at the cuffs, but they wouldn't let go.

She pulled at them, her free hand tearing at the skin on her cuffed wrist, trying desperately to escape, fighting to get her wrist to slip from the cuff's grip.

But it was no use.

The tractor was almost upon them now. The teeth on the scoop looked sharp, wet and hungry.

John turned his back and walked away.

The game stops here.

He headed up the court, where he could now see Sherrie.

She was sitting to one side of the court, leaning against one of the perimeter trees. Her left hand was holding the wound in her right shoulder. It was bleeding badly, John could see.

He smiled at her.

She smiled back.

"No!" Zoe screamed into the night. "Help me, *please!*"

John resisted the urge to turn around and watch. He kept his eyes on Sherrie.

And Sherrie kept her eyes fastened on his.

The tractor continued behind him.

The motor slowly turning in the night.

Can't be long now.

"I did it for us!" Zoe yelled. "For *both* of *us!*"

John walked on, not looking back.

"I love *yooooouuuuu!*"

There was the sound of metal on metal, a long grinding metallic crunch. And then a sickening squelch that was drowned out by one single short scream.

Then there was silence for a few seconds, followed by the sound of crushing wood and metal echoing in the air.

By the time John reached Sherrie and bent down to look at her wound, only the low chug of the tractor motor and the occasional rumble of thunder broke the silence.

"You okay?" he whispered to her.

She nodded.

Sherrie's shoulder wound wasn't too bad. The bullet had passed right through. There was just a lot of blood soaking into her wet shirt.

He took off his shirt and split it in two, wrapping one half around Sherrie's shoulder and the other half around his arm to stop the bleeding where the stitches had burst open.

His wound looked deep and ugly. But he didn't care.

In the rain, he bent forward and kissed Sherrie.

They sat there for quite a while.

Holding each other.

When they were ready, they stood up and turned back to the gazebo.

The tractor had rolled over the tennis pole and had come to rest embedded in the wreckage of the gazebo. Its motor still turned, but the piles of broken timber and metal from the gazebo had stopped it from continuing any further. Its wheels churned over and over in the clay.

The tennis net pole was bent to one side, completely flattened by the tractor, and the cuff was still attached. The chain had broken and the other cuff couldn't be seen. There was a massive amount of blood pooling in the clay puddles around the pole, and a solitary sneaker off to one side.

John could see the deep red drag marks that stretched from the pole to under the tractor. Somewhere at the front of the tractor was Zoe's body.

John sighed.

The game was at an end.

They stepped closer to the carnage.

"Stay here," John said.

Sherrie shook her head, "No, I won't."

He turned and stared into her eyes. He kissed her lips.

"*Please*, honey. I'll only be a minute."

She looked deep into his eyes as if searching for something. After a few seconds she nodded. "Okay."

John turned from her and walked slowly across the court to the tractor.

The motor continued to run.

He thought about turning it off, but changed his mind. Let it run out of fuel in its own time.

Let it die too.

Wearily, he walked past the front of the tractor. He didn't want to look, but he knew he had to. He had to make sure.

He couldn't see much through all the broken timber and twisted metal. The front scoop was embedded deep into the wrecked remains of the gazebo.

But he could see her ponytail.

It was laying just to the right of the tractor on a pile of metal and timber. The rain was soaking through it, rinsing the blood away. Her roots were there too, and a part of her scalp was hooked onto a sharp piece of split metal.

Blood ran down the front of the tractor's scoop and its grill was splattered with blood and other dark wet debris too. It dripped down and was pooling on the broken wood caught underneath it.

He'd seen enough.

Game over, Zoe.

Turning from her final resting-place, he crawled across the slippery wet metal and planks and made his way over to where Helen's hand reached out from the rubble.

He knelt by her hand and tried to think of something to say.

But words wouldn't help now.

Thunder rolled around him and the rain began to ease slightly.

He reached out with the half-heart pendant in his hand and dropped it into hers. He tried to close her cold fingers around the pendant, but they were stiff and wouldn't bend.

He noticed her index finger was missing. The wound was a jagged mess and there were marks around the skin. It looked as if it had been bitten off.

Oh Jesus...

"Goodbye, Helen," he whispered.

He turned away and hurriedly clambered from the wreckage that was once the gazebo. *A place where I couldn't even save myself.*

Or Helen...

His feet sloshed down onto the clay of the court once more and he walked back past the tractor.

Lightning flashed and a reflection in the clay caught his eye.

He stopped, turned and bent down to it.

Sitting in a small puddle was Zoe's belly button ring and diamond.

A small piece of bloodied stomach flesh was still attached to it.

Must have come out when we fought...

He reached out to pick it up.

Stopped.

Then changed his mind.

He stood once more and smiled at Sherrie.

She smiled weakly back.

John stepped forward, crushing the diamond under his foot, pushing it deeper and deeper into the wet clay.

It all ends here.

He walked back to Sherrie as thunder rolled in the distance.

The rain had eased more, coming down now as a fine mist.

He put his arm around her and hugged her tight.

"Come on," he said. "Let's get out of here."

She looked up at him with a worried expression on her face.

He smiled, bent forward and kissed her.

"Don't worry," he said. "It's all over now."

They walked from the tennis court with their arms around each other. The silence around them was almost unnatural. With no rain and no thunder, it was as if the whole world had suddenly stopped.

And in that silence, John heard the jangle of his key ring on his right hip.

They stopped on the path while they still had the lights shining around them.

He reached down and unhooked the key ring from his belt. He smiled at her as she watched him. He pried the keys apart and took one from the ring. Then he hooked the key ring onto his left hip.

He reached around her with his left arm and hugged her once more, ignoring the pain in his arm.

"I love you," he said.

"I love you too," she replied as she rested her head on his shoulder.

It hurt his shoulder wound to have her lean on him like that, but he didn't care.

Not any more.

In his right hand he held the red key.

The red key to freedom.

John smiled into the night as the security lights from the tennis court turned themselves off, throwing the area back into darkness. Only the chugging of the tractor engine was left.

He gripped the red key between his fingers and then flicked it into the forest.

Freedom.

Finally, they were free...

Steve Gerlach is one of Australia's few thriller writers. Born and bred in Australia, Gerlach's fast-paced, cut-to-the-bone style is a refreshing voice in the dry, barren Australian literary scene.

Steve's background includes many varied roles. He has worked as an editor for a book publisher; as the editor-in-chief of an Australian motorcycle magazine; editor and publisher of an international crime magazine, Probable Cause; a researcher and columnist for a major Australian daily newspaper; a Technical Publications Officer in the security industry; marketing executive for an international telecommunications software company; a writer for Australian Defence training and software producers; and currently works as a freelance writer.

He was also the Historical Advisor on the Australian film, Let's Get Skase.

Steve Gerlach lives in Melbourne, where he is currently working on a new novel or two.

The next Steve Gerlach release
by Probable Cause Publishing

LAKE MOUNTAIN

Coming late 2016

37.3500°S, 144.1500°E